Postcard
from London

THE HUNGARIAN LIST

Postcard
from London

AND
OTHER
STORIES

IVÁN MÁNDY

TRANSLATED BY
JOHN BATKI

LONDON NEW YORK CALCUTTA

SERIES EDITOR *Ottilie Mulzet*

Seagull Books, 2021

Original Hungarian stories © Judit Mándy, 2021

First published in English by Seagull Books, 2021

English translation © John Batki, 2021

This compilation © Seagull Books, 2021

ISBN 978 0 8574 2 886 8

British Library Cataloguing-in-Publication Data

A catalogue record for this book is available from the British Library.

Typeset by Seagull Books, Calcutta, India

Printed and bound by Versa Press, East Peoria, IL, USA

CONTENTS

A VISIT WITH FATHER (1972)

He was perched on the bathtub's edge. As if he were sitting on a bed—where any moment he might lie down. He touched a towel, then the sleeve of a bathrobe. He took out his razor, only to put it away immediately.

He turned off the light, and now sat in the dark. It was better this way. This way he had a better chance to think matters over . . .

What did he have to think over?

He would visit Father, take him the apples and the lemons. And maybe a few handkerchiefs. He was always asking for apples these days, as the best for one's health. The lemons were needed for lemonade. Just like an athlete in training camp. As soon as he gets his hands on the lemons, he rushes off, looking for Schlemmer. Father was convinced only Schlemmer could make a real lemonade. Schlemmer alone was the only one worth his salt in that whole bunch. The rest of the staff should be summarily fired. 'They call themselves nurses, kiddo!? Where on earth did they find such louts!'

A pound of apples and a pound of lemons in brown paper bags on the kitchen table. Ready. Everything all set to go. Including the overcoat and scarf on the hook.

But I've got to talk to the Professor, I've got to see him. But what if there's someone in his office . . . Family, visitors, a friend, one of his writer or artist friends . . . Under any circumstances I've got to talk to him. He mustn't let Father out just yet. He must understand that . . .

Understand what?

That I don't want Father back here again? That I don't want him to come back? That I want to be alone, free to sit here and stare into space. Free to bring someone up here, perhaps, from time to time. Or not bring anyone.

Father mustn't come back here. Mother is another story. When she gets back from the hospital, she'll take to her bed like a good girl. Yes, I'll stick her in bed, and take something in for her every once in a while. Of course, I'll have to talk to her, too, but at least that isn't so . . . At least she doesn't mess up my manuscripts, she doesn't lecture me about my development as a writer.

I've got to talk to the Professor.

He turned on the light. Tugged at the towels hanging from the rack, as if the Professor in his white coat were hiding behind there. Or sitting right here on the edge of the tub, leaning forward.

'Your father is better! Who would have dared to hope for such improvement.'

And he would try to smile and nod in agreement. Thinking meanwhile that this must be another one of Father's nasty pranks. After seeming to be ready to give up, ready to throw in the towel, now this, all of a sudden!

A worn hospital gown on the Professor, who is so gaunt and kind of misshapen. One shoulder sloping, out of whack. They say there's something wrong with his lungs. Sipping his coffee from a delicate little porcelain cup. Forever drinking espresso, as if dipping his cup into some invisible river of coffee. By the side of his desk, the metal bed, always made. Maybe he'll drop into it straight from his desk. Right in the middle of coffee and conversation.

'Mr Zsámboky, guess who was my teacher! The only man I've ever learnt anything from! Not your neurologists and psychiatrists! I'll tell you who it was: Dostoyevsky! Yes, the only one who . . .'

And then nothing but Dostoyevsky. Fine, fine, but what should we do about Father showing such nice improvement?

'And what about you, Mr Zsámboky? What are you working on these days?'

'A novella, I guess.'

You guess? You damned idiot, you know very well it's not a novella, but something longer . . . Something you've got to buckle down to, requiring peace and quiet. Such as being able to lie in bed for a while after waking up in the morning.

That morning he'd woken to a crash. Or a dull thud, rather. Then silence. Peaceful morning sunlight filtering through the blinds. All was quiet next door, in the other room. The door was closed. Yes, he'd closed the door for the night. You never knew when Father would go to sleep. After hours of pacing, smoking a cigar and leafing through old English illustrated magazines. Although lately he'd be mostly lying in bed, but without turning off the light.

Opening the door he saw no one, at first. The morning silence, the furniture's silence. Blankets tossed all over the sofa, socks flung far apart. A towel impossibly crumpled into a ball. Father had apparently lugged in a washbasin to perform his toilette on the sofa.

A toppled chair by the window. And up on the sill of the wide open window stood Father, his spindly legs bent, shivering. Like an exotic plant in that limpid morning light. Freshly shaved and hair combed smooth, there in his pyjamas on the windowsill. Slowly swinging his arms, as one about to take the plunge. Brisk morning air streaming through the window. The trees of the park reaching up so high. Any moment Father might leap over onto one of those branches. And crouch there, in his pyjamas.

János made a move, as if intending to reach for a vase.

'Please go back to your room,' said Father from up there. 'I wanted to do this while you were . . .'

János made his way to his father's other side, bumping into the radiator on the way. 'You were just waiting for me to come in, the only reason you've created this whole scene.'

'Oh, Mister Know-it-all.'

'Come down from there!'

'Impossible.' Father shook his head, crestfallen. 'They're coming for me today.'

'Dr Bonyhadi's coming, and nobody else.'

'And nobody else? You say, nobody else?' He coiled himself, like a goalkeeper bracing for a shot. 'Don't kid yourself. Bonyhádi's already written a report about the bugs and this whole thing. He has to do that, it's a case of infection. You think he's coming alone? You're greatly mistaken. And so are they if they think I'm going to wait for them.'

'Father!'

'What.' He straightened up somewhat, and peered at János. 'Look at all those imbeciles prowling about on the street!'

'Will you please come down from there?!'

'Stop yelling! You think that'll solve anything? I won't let them take me away.'

'No one's going to take you away.'

János was marking time behind his father's back. His hand made a move, but reached only empty air.

Father kept sneezing up there, catching a cold. 'Well, kiddo, this time you really ...!'

'I really what?'

This whole thing felt like some hoax. As if Father had tricked him to come in, so that from up there ... His voice trembled as he asked once more:

'I really what?'

He was suddenly exhausted. He would have liked to sit down.

'Go ahead, kid, go back to sleep! It's all right, go back to bed.'

Recalling all this was so infuriating. And downright humiliating.

Zsámboky grabbed a towel and slammed it into the bathtub. The soap dish slipped and cakes of soap went skidding down the smooth white slope.

He left the bathroom and entered the living room. That smell was still there. The odour of old shirts. Of socks, and handkerchiefs crumpled into balls.

Father had used the radiator as a foothold to climb up on the windowsill. So why did he need a chair? He could have reached the radiator without one. Why had he dragged the chair over?

How long did this scene go on? Later there were several others in the room. There was Dr Bonyhádi, looking around rather hesitantly. As if he needed to pluck Father from somewhere up on the wall.

'Gyula, I thought I'd find you in bed!'

'Why should I be in bed?' Father shrugged. 'I haven't been able to get any sleep lately.'

The pharmacist, from next door, stared mesmerized.

'My dear Gyula!'

'What's this my dear Gyula?!' Father was blinking irritably. Unexpectedly, he yawned. Started to rub his lower back. 'Oh, should have done it earlier . . . too many people in the street now.'

Bonyhádi and the pharmacist lifted Father off the windowsill. He winked at János. 'You look exhausted, kid. Pooped out, huh?'

Zsámboky walked over to the sofa. Warily he pulled back the blanket and reached under the pillow. There might be a message there.

Before the windowsill episode, Father had been in the habit of hiding all sorts of little notes under the blanket and pillow. 'No one is to blame for my death, least of all my son János. I know I've been a nuisance.'

What did he mean by this?

And what was this 'my son János' business? He'd never used that ceremonious tone before. Always hated that sort of thing.

He would slip little notes under the pillow, and old razor blades. Once he even tried to saw away at his wrist.

János happened to be on his way to the bathroom at the time.

'That's not a very good idea,' he said, without stopping.

He found tobacco shreds under the pillow. A few shreds of tobacco and nothing else. He sat down on the sofa, and could almost hear that voice again. What's the matter kid, can't take it any more?

Father was spooning chicken soup when the ambulance came. Made by the pharmacist's wife and brought in on a silver tray.

'Just put it there,' Father waved to her. He sat at the table in his dark-blue suit, Bonyhádi and the pharmacist by his side.

'I should've travelled more. Travel always agreed with me.' He looked up from his soup. 'That hotel in Zürich . . . The rain was falling and I just watched it from the hotel window.'

The pharmacist opened the door for the ambulance crew. By then János was totally numb. Then the next thing he was sitting in the ambulance with his father. The old man seemed shrunken in that threadbare brown overcoat. He sat in silence now, and kept tugging at the fingers of his glove. His eyes were sort of glazed, like a wound glazing over. His mouth gaped without a sound and his chin trembled.

János watched that trembling, slack jaw all the way to the hospital.

But Father pulled himself together once more. When he stood on the flagstone of the corridor, facing the man in the white coat.

'Gyula Zsámboky, journalist, at your service!'

He looked around, as if expecting the others to show up. Old colleagues from editorial offices, cronies he used to chat with in coffeehouses and on the street.

Then he hunched his shoulders and his jaw began to tremble again. As he stepped a little closer to the nurse, he was so stooped again. 'Pardon me, but I think there's been a mistake . . . I shouldn't have been brought in here . . . This is a matter for the police because of the bugs and the infection.'

'No, there's been no mistake.' The attendant placed his hand on Father's shoulder.

Father looked back once more at János, a strange sort of respect in his eyes.

'You've really done it this time.'

What did he mean by that?

Zsámboky opened the window. Fresh air! Fresh air! Ever since he'd placed Father in there, he has been airing the room religiously.

The truth is, nothing had been accomplished. For a while Father lay in that gloomy hospital ward in a daze, as if knocked out. János sat by the bed. When Father looked up, it was that glazed look again. From time to time he raised himself for a despondent wave of the hand.

His overcoat hung on a window knob. His few belongings lay folded over the metal bedstead. One of his shoes had some kind of goo—creamed spinach?—petrified on it.

Then one visiting day a beaming nurse greeted János. 'Have a seat! Your daddy will be here right away!'

He sat on a bench by the rough-hewn trestle table. Next to him, a slack-jawed man in a hospital outfit. A woman wearing a polka-dotted kerchief held out a cup for the man. He drooped his head lower and stared at the cup. Here came Father now. Draped over the attendant as if he'd found a long-lost friend. The nurse handed him over to János, who sat him down on the bench. Father was silent. An apprehensive smile appeared on his face before he spoke.

'You still haven't got a decent ribbon?'

'Ribbon?'

'Typewriter ribbon. No one can read your stuff, your typing's illegible. Do you still have your typewriter? Nah, even if you didn't, you wouldn't tell me.'

He was practically lamenting.

'Try to raise a little dough, will you?'

János touched his shoulder. 'It's all right, Father.' With that, he left him on the bench. As he looked back from the door of the visiting room, Father called out after him:

'Make sure you buy a decent ribbon!'

Zsámboky was in the kitchen. Two brown paper bags on the table. Dour, hospital paper bags. A pound of apples, a pound of lemons.

Then there was the time Father received him out in the garden! That's right, it was a formal reception. He sat on a bench, surrounded by a semi-circle of patients in hospital gowns. A stocky individual with a white moustache turned to János. 'Your father's quite a man! The things he's done!'

'Such as?'

'Oh, like when he financed *Burgtheater*!'

'*Burgtheater*?!'

'That was some film! A real work of art!'

János stood still, eyeing his father on that bench.

'Take that stuff inside, kiddo! Then I'd like you to meet the gentlemen.'

He trotted indoors with the packages and placed them on the nightstand. He gazed at the empty bed. The pillow, and that dark-brown hospital blanket. Ready to swallow you up. In any case, Father had at least managed to get up. He left this bed and went out in the garden.

Burgtheater!

But Father, we saw that together at the Phőnix! Fifty-fillér tickets. Yes, I remember we sat in the fourth or fifth row.

And you claim that you financed it! What did you finance? Tell me, what did you ever finance?

Zsámboky stood in the kitchen, angrily squeezing the paper bags. He suddenly froze. Someone was watching him. Someone standing in the corridor in front of the kitchen window. He saw the shadow of an overcoat, a hat.

The pharmacist waved at him.

János waved back. Then somehow he was unable to move from the kitchen table. That's how Father would show up in front of the kitchen window. Stop for a moment and peek in.

After all, he's been back already, here, in the building. He did not ring this doorbell. He also avoided the pharmacist's place. But he dropped in at the Mógers', whereas in the old days he barely said hello to them.

'We had a very nice little chat,' said old man Móger. 'My wife gave your father a jar of compote.'

So, a jar of compote from the Mógers. At the Hegedűs', he asked for a hat. What did he need a hat for? In any case, he's been back, here in this building.

'We heard your father's feeling better . . .'

I've got to go see the Professor. Maybe I'll take him one of my old books. Inscribe something in it . . . Nah, he would think I only did that because . . . Maybe when that damn collection of stories is published at last!

He galloped down the stairs, carrying the two paper bags.

Once he had to drag Father back from down here. Toward dawn he had woken up suddenly. Father was not in the adjacent room. He had not heard any noise, yet he knew that Father was not there. Blankets and pillows lay tossed all over the place. And no Father. He threw on some clothes and stepped out into the murky grey staircase. He found the old man on the third-floor landing, cowering close to the wall. Black overcoat, hat and scarf. And such terror in his eyes. János stopped a few steps above him.

'What are you doing here?'

'I'm going away, kid. I've got to go.'

'Why are you standing around then?'

'I thought maybe . . .'

'What did you think?'

János paused. The man delivering newspapers went past them. There was no one else in the staircase. When the delivery man was gone, János stepped closer to his father. 'You thought I'd come for you anyway. You think I don't know?'

Father, if that was possible, hugged the wall even closer. Then, unexpectedly, he bolted. His ungainly shoes kept skidding all over, as if he were trying to dodge from himself. He scurried downstairs, with hands in his pockets.

János caught him on the second floor. He grabbed the old man's shoulder. 'That's enough now!'

Father clutched the banister with both hands. The smell of that overcoat overwhelmed János. His hand couldn't find Father's shoulder under that coat.

The delivery man reappeared. Father let go of the banister. They trudged upstairs as if returning from a walk.

Afterwards, Father made tea for himself. But he kept his hat and coat on as he sat on the kitchen stool sipping his tea.

Father, you sure pulled some neat tricks! You always had something up your sleeve!

Zsámboky was now seated on the bus. He took a lemon out of the bag. Turning it in his hand, he eyed it as if he'd meant to slice it up on the spot.

Sometimes you simply disappeared. At other times you would drop in to see me. Oh, just to say farewell, in the middle of the night. You would stand there in the doorway. And I'd get up, and the whole rigmarole would start all over again. 'I must go away . . . these bugs, around my eyes . . . do me a favour, take a look at them, at least do that for me!'

Yes, I did. I inspected your face every night. Your forehead, the shadows around your sunken eyes. The whole routine, the whole inane routine. Father, I've had it up to here!

The bus speeded past trees. Here was the park.

Zsámboky got off.

Maybe I'll drop in at the Barbara. I could use an espresso. A good strong one.

How long had he been coming to this cafe? When did he first stumble in here? To this tiny little table in the gallery upstairs. Where he would spread out his scraps of paper when he could no longer stand it at home. He would stare off into space for a while, then maybe start writing. Anyway, the place was a great spot to sit around in.

There he stood under the unlit neon sign of the Barbara. By the grey row of plate-glass windows. Would he find Father in there, sipping coffee and chatting with the waitresses?

He entered, and looked around warily. Downstairs, a balding, bespectacled man sat by a large plate-glass window, contemplating a pile of lottery stubs. Some tables away, a woman wearing a cowboy hat clutched an empty Coke bottle.

The girls waved from behind the pastry counter, as if they were tossing balls at him. At the end of the room was the counter with the espresso machine. All around the walls, mahogany wainscoting.

He went upstairs. Next to the last table by the window. He put down the bags and looked around. For the time being he was the only customer. The girls would be around in a minute. Giggling, bowing and swaying, with their trays.

Once upon a time there may have been a children's theatre up here. Performances of *Little Lord Fauntleroy*, things like that. The adjoining chamber must have been the changing-room. Heaps of coats, scarves, hats. And after the performance, an abundant tea would be served. The performers were saluted. And they'd visit at each other's tables.

'Not working today?'

A waitress with a blonde bun was swaying in front of him, a mischievous smile on her face.

'I just thought I'd drop in for a minute.'

The waitress brought his coffee, then stopped by his side, her tray lowered.

'Is your father still in the hospital?'

'Yes.'

He sipped his espresso slowly, deliberately. Then he suddenly blurted it out.

'Did I ever tell you we used to live in a hotel? Back in the old days.'

'In a hotel?'

'A nasty little dump, near the train station.'

And he was off. Back at the hotel. Hotel Adria. Father, sitting on the edge of the bed in his tattered dressing gown, smoking a cigar and playing the violin. The scores lay scattered over the bed. But he didn't pay much attention to those scores. In fact, he didn't even really play the violin. He preferred to pluck at the strings with two fingers. He was humming, 'What a pretty itsy-bitsy pair of shoes, ladies' shoes, ladies' shoes . . .' when the boy stepped in front of him.

'Father, I'm not going back to school tomorrow.'

Meanwhile he drew lines on his trousers with his fingernail. Those stupid, loose knickerbockers, always hanging lower on one knee. He eyed the bedspread and the scattered sheet music. He had not been to school for weeks and weeks. No, it was no longer a matter of just cutting a few classes. This could not be fixed up that easily.

A foggy winter morning. The class stands up to salute Professor Pázmán as he enters. They stand at attention facing the teacher. The student on day-duty makes his report: 'Sir! Present in class, thirty-six students. Three absent: Barasics, Mark, Zsámboky. Nothing else to report.'

'I'm not going back to school.'

'So you're not going.' Father didn't even look up.

'I mean . . . ever again.'

Father looked at him now. A smile of sorts hovered in the corners of his eyes. His cigar ash dropped onto a musical score.

'You know, Father, I'm writing . . . You saw that story about the guy falling asleep on a park bench.' He leant over the bed. 'You said it was like Maupassant . . .'

'Yes, something like that.'

'So I'm going to write stories.'

Father raised the bow. He lightly tapped the boy's shoulder with it. 'Yes, yes, you're going to write stories!'

Zsámboky looked up at the girl with the tray. 'He thought it was a natural thing to do! I'd drop out of school, drop everything, and from then on it would be just me and that school notebook, you know, where I wrote my first scribblings.'

A customer was coming up the stairs. Then several heads hovered into view. They wavered hesitantly by the banister. Some withdrew and disappeared.

'And your mother?' The girl twirled her tray. 'What did she have to say?'

'Mother . . .'

Shoved so unexpectedly into that hotel room, she'd stood in front of Father, her forehead deathly pale. 'And what is to become of your son? Have you given it any thought, Gyula, what is to become of your son?!' Father was sitting on top of that old, brown trunk. His trunk from college. Reading something. As if he had not even heard Mother, who kept shouting. 'Are you even aware that he's not attending school?! He hasn't been to a class in months!'

'See, Mother was no longer living with us by then.'

'So your parents were separated.' The waitress nodded.

'It happened in the summer. Mother and I were coming home from Lake Balaton.'

Mother and son sat by the window in the train compartment. Evening was falling. The dull glimmer of the lake was left behind. The shadows of thin trees. The slope of the embankment. 'Are we coming back next year, Mother?' She put her arm around his shoulder and did not reply.

There they stood at the station. 'So, kid, did you get a suntan?' Father leant closer to him.

'Take a look at him,' Mother said.

'It's a bit too dark to see.' He drew János closer. 'Me, I never tan.'

Suitcases and packages surrounded them. And the tumult of the station. Dim lights in the colonnade. The whole scene was so soporific. And yet Father's voice could be heard quite distinctly. 'János is coming home with me, and as for you, Ilonka . . .'

Mother did not come home with us to Gyár Street. Father packed Mother into a cab and sent her to her aunt's. Did she cry? Did she scream? I only recall that Father stuffed her into a cab.

'Years later, they got back together again.'

'Years later?' The waitress tapped her tray.

'After the war, Father showed up at our place. By then I'd been living with Mother for years, long past the hotel era—in fact, the hotels themselves were gone. One afternoon, Mother was heating up some food in the kitchen. The window was open to the courtyard gallery. And all of a sudden there stood Father! As if he'd been standing there all the while, with that rakishly tilted hat of his. 'Well, Ilonka?' Mother was speechless, all she could do was gape at him. And Father leant in through the window. 'I'll be staying here for a while. No need to make a big deal out of it. Only be a few days.' Meanwhile he was swinging a little package. 'How nice, you brought us sweets, Gyula!'

'Oh no, just my shaving kit and a few things.'

Zsámboky had to smile. 'Mother thought it was sweet pastry . . . In spite of all that happened, she somehow still expected things like that.'

He looked up. The waitress was gone.

Brown paper bags on the chair. Two humble guests who had to share a seat.

He took the bags and stood up. On the way out, he slipped the money into an apron pocket.

'See you!'

'So long, Jánoska!'

Another bus ride. Then a garden, a corridor, a room. Maybe the nurse would greet him with: 'Here to see your dad? Oh, that papa of yours!'

Oh yes, Father was out on the town. Dropping in on folks, looking up friends. Naturally he wouldn't skip the Deepwater. The waiters have sighted him there more than once. 'Your papa was here! Looking great . . . Back home already?' And somehow his reply would sound weird and formal: 'No, he's not allowed to come home just yet. Those obsessional fixations may recur any time.'

Those obsessional fixations! He kept repeating that. The waiters and the coat-room lady said nothing. They knew I should have brought him home. That I should have brought him home long ago.

To stand behind my back again, as I type. Nibbling on a piece of cheese, reading over my shoulder. 'This is dreadful, how can you write such awful stuff about your friend?!' 'What friend?' 'You know very well the one I mean! You used to visit him and his wife all the time, their door was always open to you, and now . . . ! You can't do this . . . abuse their hospitality like this!' 'Hospitality!' 'You know very well it's not right!' 'That's enough, Father! That's enough!'

Zsámboky looked out the window of the bus.

An actor occupied the bed next to Father's. Two suicide attempts so far. But Father was going to get him back on his feet now. Of course he'd start by taking away the man's cigars.

Tell me, Father, do you clean everybody out?

Starting with me. The way you'd harvest the income from my books and stories! You did a thorough job, I've got to admit. Somehow you always managed to get wind of a paycheck that was due. And there you were, standing at the cashier's, leaning on the counter. Or you'd waylay me in the corridor. Catch me in the doorway on my way out.

Then one day you did not receive a penny. That's right, Father, not one red cent. Although you laid the usual rap on me. That if it hadn't been for you, Mother would have stuck me in a post-office job. (Probably true.) That you were the one who placed my first writings for me, who had to fight those pitched battles with editors. (True enough.) But I still refused to give you anything then, or later. This was a crushing blow. It was the first nasty uppercut you had to take.

On the other hand, you really did a job on Mother. You sold off her clothes, her books. Yes, those special limited editions that you said you despised so much. What could we do? Mother had a weakness for them. Whenever a new set was issued, she'd subscribe immediately. Then you would swoop down. To make it worse, you patronized her. 'Ilonka, how can you stand having those things around!'

And the things you did to Olga Lux!

János almost stood up from his seat in the bus. He had an urge to pace back and forth.

Good God, Olga Lux was waiting for us at home! That's right, when you took me home from the train station. In other words, right after you stuffed Mother into that cab. A thin, sad-eyed woman. The daughter of a jeweller. In those days, you told me many an uplifting tale about jewellers. Something about how they were the pioneers, the original goldminers. One thing is sure, the Lux family followed you around in a pack. The plump, indignant figure of Sándor Lux . . . 'You think we don't know what you're after?! No man in his right mind would go for such a musty old maid! She's not the woman for you, take it from me, I'm her brother!'

So you married Olga. I was supposed to call her Tini . . . 'Tini will take care of you, she'll walk you to school.' Tini took care of me. She stayed with me even after you donned a grey sports cap and took off on a world tour. And with whom? With one of your lady loves, Father. At least, that's what little Bőhm said, you know, your old buddy from the newspaper. 'Your father went off with one of his lady loves.' About a month ago I bumped into little Bőhm, he hadn't heard yet that you were in the hospital. He said he would visit you. He'd known the girl you took off with. A waitress at the Cafe Abbazia. But you didn't forget about me. No, I can't say you neglected me. You sent me paper cut-out soldiers: dragoons, uhlans, cuirassiers, white-helmeted British colonials, feather-capped Italians. The Luxes paid us furtive visits at the Gyár Street flat. They'd sit in the gloomy room and hold family councils. Tini wept. Tini always wept.

The bus passed an empty field, then an enormous tarpaulin-covered building.

We took a lot of walks, Tini and I. She took me to see her sisters, Teri and Margit. Teri lived in a villa, there were stone steps we had to climb. We could not stay for long because of her migraines. She had to take afternoon naps. Teri was a blonde. Tall and blonde. She didn't even look like the rest of the Luxes. At Margit's, we could stay as long as we liked. Some days we even slept there. In that tattered, dark flat somewhere behind the Boulevard. Her husband, Simi, a former stockbroker, had such a frightened smile. Her daughter, Dutzi, played dominoes and ate a lot of com-pote. We had huge pillow fights at bedtime.

Tini also took me to her parents'. They sat under a lampshade pulled down low. They regarded us and sighed. Sándor, in shirt-sleeves and dangling suspenders, would occasionally pop in from next door. Just a quick peek. Then he would slam the door and dis-appear. 'You may bring the child any time,' Tini's father said, 'but I don't want to see Gyula's face in this house again.' He had a white beard and his hand shook. But I knew he had once been a gold-miner and a trapper, racing in dog sleds over the snow.

Which was the hotel where you threw Tini out? It must have been the Hotel Adria . . . 'Always whining and making faces, can't you give us a little smile just once . . . ' No, Tini didn't have much to smile about. There we sat on the stairs, on the third-floor landing at the Hotel Adria. She stared at the threadbare carpet and fiddled with the fringe. You want to know what she talked about? The Grand Hotel! The Grand Hotel on Margit Island, where you took her for your honeymoon. You really outdid yourself on that impressive honeymoon, didn't you, Father? We better not go into whose money it was. 'Those palm trees in the lobby . . . We sat by the window and watched the rain soak the trees, the shrubs, the gravel paths. Your father said, let's just watch the rain.' Yes indeed, Father, you loved to watch the rain.

Tini suddenly looked me in the eye, there on the steps. Her face so ravaged and aged. 'Talk to your father . . . ask him to let me in, why can't he let me in?' I put my arm on her shoulder. 'I'll give it a try, Tini.' Except you weren't very easy to talk to, Father. 'I'm doomed to live surrounded by sourpusses!' That's what you kept shouting. 'I've got to put up with these musty, glum faces, but I've had enough!'

How long did Tini sit huddled there on the steps? You tossed her coat and a few other things after her. So she wouldn't go away empty-handed. But she didn't want to go away at all. I don't know how you managed to pry her away from those steps.

But it wasn't over that easily. Tini kept coming back. Crawling back, as you put it. She stood in the street, opposite our window, and called out: 'Jancsi! Jancsi!' I had to go down to her. I had to take walks with her on the street and in the park. She would ask me about school and, of course, about you. Do you know that at times I still dream about her? She stands on the street and looks up at our window. I still hear her voice. That desperate, piercing voice. 'Jancsi! Jancsi!'

Sometimes she came upstairs. You never paid much attention to her. You sat on the edge of the bed and played the violin. Score sheets scattered around you. At times Tini ran into Mother, who was also in the habit of visiting. That didn't seem to bother you too much, either. 'Let them devour each other!' But they did not devour each other. Instead, they seemed to become friends. Tini once asked mother: 'Did he leech off of your family, too?' Mother kept shrugging. And you egged her on. 'Go on, go on Ilonka, unburden yourself!' Meanwhile you didn't put down your violin, not for a moment. Later, other women would visit. They would launch into explanations, screams or sobs, but you just kept playing your violin.

Zsámboky got off the bus.

He was standing next to a vendor's stall. Shoelaces and coat hangers hung suspended, mirrors, pocket notebooks, and handbags lay on the counter.

There were stalls all around. And small houses with gardens. In the distance, a grey barracks-like building. Old World War One–style barracks.

I must have a talk with the Professor. I've got to see him.

He set out toward the grey building.

He greeted the gatekeeper. Then he was in a yard, among the pavilions. A few more steps, and he stopped.

Father!

There was Father, seated in front of one building. He sat on the trunk of a toppled tree, reading. He wore his dark-blue suit, a folded handkerchief in the breast pocket. His spectacle case lay on the tree trunk by his side, along with a few cigars wrapped in brown paper. One hand was absent-mindedly smoothing down his hair. He turned the page. Then he leafed back, to re-read something. He barely glanced up:

'What's up, kiddo?'

A VISIT WITH MOTHER (1972)

He took down the dark-blue dress from the top shelf. Dark blue, with a white lace collar. The collar's edge was slightly yellowed, as if it had been stained with nicotine. Under the dress, he found a green sweater and a checked skirt. To the side, a stack of handkerchiefs. A Holy Bible. How did the Bible end up on this clothes shelf? He'd never seen Mother reading it. The icon of the Holy Virgin was still there on her nightstand, but this Bible . . . Dried flowers in cigarette tins. A blue box, with a gilded inscription: Memphis. A spill of brownish sachet powder near the sweater and skirt. János brushed it back with a finger, and flung his mother's dress over his shoulder. He shot a parting glance at the Memphis box and the Bible as he turned away from the closet. He gently laid the dress on the sofa. Plain but still somehow quite dignified. Yes, this was the one he would take for her.

A small suitcase lay open by the sofa. Her clothes would go into that. But first they must be folded neatly. Should he have asked Mrs Kovács . . .

Nonsense. This much I'm still capable of doing myself, folding her dress!

He went back to the closet. He pulled out a pair of stockings from that tangled heap. He held them up in the air. One stocking had a run. Mother would never have worn something like that. But now she'd have to. This one time, perhaps, she'd put up with it. They had suggested black stockings, or at least something dark.

He sat on the sofa, next to the clothes, the stockings still dangling from his fingers. It almost felt as if Mother were lying there on the sofa, and he were explaining to her: Look, Mother, this is your only pair of dark stockings, and just because of one little run . . . He twisted the stocking around his wrist and sat like that for a while. He half expected to hear her voice: 'Won't you please make me a glass of lemonade . . . A nice little glass of lemonade, János! Oh, you know how to make the best lemonade!'

I make the best lemonade.

He practically tore the stocking off his wrist and threw it into the suitcase. He touched the shoulder of the dress. But he still did not fold it, as if he'd felt a sudden onset of pity. Just let it lie there a little longer.

That waiver! I still have to write that waiver or disclaimer, or whatever. I think I better type it.

The typewriter was in the next room. That high-topped, towering old typewriter by the window. (Even this was only a rental. I never seem to get enough money together to buy a decent type-writer.) Sitting at the machine, one could see the park below. He could stare for hours at the people walking through the park.

A hefty dark-haired girl was raking the gravel walk at a rather somnolent pace. Her face was not much to look at, but what a body! He peered sidelong into the next room.

Listen, Mother, what if I brought her up here . . . We would cuddle a bit, and who knows, maybe later . . . I don't expect you to be crazy about her, but then you never were crazy about any of my women. With the possible exception of Panni Sárosi.

He leant forward slightly, waiting for that voice from the direction of the sofa. He sat like that for a while.

He placed a sheet into the typewriter and began to type.

The undersigned states that he waives any claims. That's right, Mom, don't be angry now, but I waive any claims to those hospital things of yours. The things you wore in there. I'm not bringing home any of that. I'm not claiming anything.

Signature, date.

Well, that's done. Your hospital clothes will stay in there. The coat, the sweater, a few shirts. And this dark blue dress is going in.

He pocketed the waiver. Again he stood by the sofa. 'All right, Mother, it's time to go over, let's take a stroll.' He made a small adjustment to the shoulder of the dress. 'It's not far to the hospital. The hopspittle, as you used to call it.'

The hospital was indeed close. Perilously close.

Earlier, this had given him quite a few uneasy moments. Mother could materialize any time. Through the walls, through a crack in the door. And there she would stand, in the middle of the room, smiling her mischievous girlish smile. 'I think I'll just drink a nice cup of tea. I'll have my tea here. In there you simply can't get a decent cup of tea. Oh, is someone here? Do you have a guest?'

János folded the collar of the dress. It felt like bending someone forward by the nape of the neck.

'Mother, how did you do it? Just tell me this one thing. Whenever I had a visitor, you simply gobbled her up. Even though you had the decency to retire to your own room. You went to bed, and lay low, behind your books and medications. The door was closed between us. But all I had to do was go out for just one second, and by the time I came back . . .'

By the time he came back from the bathroom or the kitchen, the girl would be gone from his bed. One moment she would be there, lying under the blanket, and the next she was gone. Leaving a rumpled pillow and a blanket flung aside.

The door to the bedroom was slightly ajar, casting a thin strip of light. And that soft voice in there. 'Please don't mind me, dearie, I know you didn't come here for my sake . . . but as long as you're here, could you fluff up my pillow . . .'

'And she would fluff up your pillow for you, Mother. And help you turn on your other side, for good measure. But that would come later, you know, when she would still drop by, but no longer really for my sake.'

He lifted the dress, laid it across his arms and began to circle the room. Meanwhile, he intoned in a lulling voice:

'Why, sometimes the girl would answer the door to let me in, and just stare as if I were some stranger. She'd barely say hello before flitting back to your bedside. Usually she'd manage to visit when I was not at home. Somehow she had a knack for scoping out those times.'

He sat down in a chair. The dress sagged a little in his arms.

'In the end, of course, she would stop coming. Mother, you wore her out with your endless tales about our family. Our exclusive family. Oh, this was not an easy family to be accepted in! But who would want to be accepted into our family?! For God's sake, why did you have to keep harping about the family?!'

He leapt up and slammed the dress into the suitcase. Then he just stared at it.

'Who was that girl who washed your hair? Yes, that's right, she gave you a shampoo and a rinse. I opened the bathroom door when she happened to be taking a break. There she sat on the edge of the tub, smoking a cigarette. Your head was hanging over the wash-basin, wreathed in lather. A towel around your neck. In the first place, how did she manage to drag you out to the bathroom? What did you talk about, on the way from the bed to the bath? One thing for sure, there she was now, sitting on the edge of the tub, smoking. She waved me off so nonchalantly. Shoo, out you go!'

He bent down and started to straighten and fold the dress.

'Well, all right, Momma.'

He jogged down the stairway with the suitcase, blinking warily at the doors he passed. All he needed was someone sticking out an inquisitive head. Where to, Mr Zsámboky?

Whew, I made it, he thought when he got downstairs. A close shave. But I'm sure I forgot something. What have I left out? He felt like opening the suitcase right there, on the spot.

'No, son,' he heard from somewhere, 'you never forget a thing.'

'How can you be so sure, Mother? What if I'd left a stocking at home? And I'm taking only half of a pair?' Suddenly he was back on the subject of the family again. 'Tell me, didn't we have enough postal workers in our family? Yet you still wanted to stick me in the post office, don't you deny it now. A secure job, and all that.'

Dazed and bewildered, he stared off into space.

'But why did you have to tell Itza Balla that I nearly died of acute colitis at the tender age of two? Why on earth did you have to brief her about my colitis? And what else did you brief her about? One thing I know for a fact: you brought up the mild tea. That I drank only herbal teas, because my system could not tolerate strong tea. Tell me, Mother, what did you hope to accomplish by that?'

He stood in front of the hospital. A pale green edifice with an enormous grey flight of steps. A fountain next to the gate.

The gatekeeper nodded toward Zsámboky with distant benevolence. Ought to sit down in that booth and have a chat with the old man. About the outbreak of the First War, or the counterfeit currency scandals of the Twenties. But now it was too late. Too late also to banter with the lady behind the cafeteria counter. And toss back a cup of java standing up, surrounded by white-smocked doctors and patients in pyjamas. That doctor with the bent back, did he treat Mother a long time ago? The cafeteria lady had green eyes. She used to think I was in television and for a while was after me to get her on a quiz show.

The staircase led up to the hospital wards. He used to take this route upstairs whenever the lift was busy. But this time he turned and went downstairs. Endless narrow stairway. Distant clatter of dishes. Kitchen noises. So the kitchen must also be down here in the basement somewhere. And the laundry. Where they boil those yellowed bedsheets and hospital gowns. Then the main staircase abruptly ended and a metal stairway began. Grey prison stairs. One hand clutching the banister, he cautiously slid his foot forward. He did not have the least bit of confidence in that feeble, dangling foot. The other hand spasmodically clutched the suitcase.

Mother was waiting somewhere down there. Her head might pop out of some door in the basement and peer about. The next thing you know, she's out in the corridor, wearing that unbelievably loose hospital gown. I am bound to run into her in the corridor. Or down at the bottom of the stairs. She'll be sitting on the last step, her foot tucked under her, smoothing out her gown over her knee.

A gaunt, grey-haired woman awaited him in the storage room. She asked for his waiver.

'So you're not taking the clothes home?'

'No . . . I'm not.'

The woman, paper in hand, gave him a questioning look, as if she expected him to change his mind. Then, in a slightly offended tone: 'Come take a look at them.'

'Take a look?'

'At the clothes. You have to identify them, make sure they're all here.'

'Identify them? . . .'

A dimly lit corridor, with metal doors, one of which was opened by the woman. An abysmal dark chamber. János flattened himself against the wall and stayed like that until the light came on.

Endless rows of coats hanging from metal rods. Men's and women's coats. Trousers and skirts. The green blur of a cardigan in the distance. As if someone had just taken it off. Baskets and boxes under piles of clothes. What was hiding crammed inside them?

Suddenly the light went out. As if a gigantic black overcoat had been thrown over the place.

'Power failure,' the woman said.

János practically froze. Power failure! Now I'm stuck in this storeroom forever.

The woman clicked on a small torch.

'Follow me!'

They made their way through the racks of clothes. From time to time, the woman illuminated a coat, as if conducting some sort of security check. Was she going to ask one of them to step forward?

The light flashed on buttons—buttons, belts and buckles. Ladies' shoes on top of a chest.

The torch-beam picked out a coat, slithered over the lapels and crept inside the lining.

'Her reversible!' János said, stopping in front of the mocha-brown spring and autumn coat.

'What was that?'

'Oh, nothing . . . It's just that you can turn it inside out, and then it's like having another coat . . . That's why Mother liked it so much. She always said it was like having two coats in one.' He stopped, and touched the sleeve with his free hand. 'This is what she wore when they took her away.'

That was what they had put on her. The ambulance crew lifted her out of bed, and then threw this coat over her shoulders. They'd known the ambulance was on the way, and yet it all happened so unexpectedly. Her things had to be thrown together in a hurry, tossed into a small bag. Mother sat on the edge of her bed. 'My Diana . . . my jar of smelling salts . . .' The ambulance men lifted her up, and she grasped their shoulders. Like some strange root, she hung from their necks. In the meantime, the lift had been sent up. The whole floor was astir. Neighbours wandered in and out of the flat. They seated Mother on a kitchen stool and placed her in the lift like that. By then she had her coat on, as she sat on the kitchen stool, in the lift. For days afterward, that kitchen stool remained downstairs in the vestibule.

Under the coat, various articles lay folded on top of a crate. A hand flung apart the sweater, the skirt, the blouses. He had to inspect them one by one. 'All in order?'

'Yes.'

She placed an inventory slip in front of him. He signed. The light came on. He contemplated that coat in the dim gloaming.

'So it had a belt!'

'Everything is as we found it.'

'I mean I'd forgotten about the belt ... that it had one ...'

'Shall we go now?'

Out in the corridor, the woman cast a glance at the suitcase. 'I think you want the third door on the left.' And she was gone.

Zsámboky did not enter right away. He fished out some banknotes from his wallet, tens and twenties. He had the suitcase propped between his legs. He counted three twenties and two tens. Then crumpled one of the twenties back into the wallet. That was still quite generous! Forty would be enough. He stood there for a while longer with the suitcase between his legs. His hands patting his pockets. Did I put my wallet back? Did I put it away? If I ever get out of here, I'll have another coffee.

He again had a momentary vision of Mother sinking out of sight, perched on that kitchen stool.

He entered the room. The man in the white lab coat rose by the side of a table. It had a steeply slanting top, like a huge drawing board. A sheet of paper was tacked on it, some kind of chart. Tin gurneys surrounded the table. On each gurney, a bundle, covered with a sheet.

'Well sir!' The man in the white coat looked expectantly at János. As if he'd been waiting for him among all these little boats. Like some coach whose crew no longer competed.

'It's my mother . . . Mrs Zsámboky . . .'

'Oh yes, your dear mother!' (As if he had meant to add: 'Your dear mother and I were getting to be good friends!')

János contemplated the lumps under the sheets. The pointed shoulders, the contours of an arm, as they lay there, on their sides.

The man in the white coat stepped forward from behind the table.

'You should have seen this place between Christmas and New Year's! You know how many were sent down?' He surveyed the trays. 'We have a full house here.'

He took the suitcase from János, and placed it on the table. 'Let's see, what have we here.'

I'm in for it now, János thought. I'm sure I forgot something.

The man in the white coat clicked open the suitcase without a glance at its contents. He stroked his face, then massaged it with both hands. As if he wanted to remould it. 'You, sir, must act quickly.'

'Beg your pardon?'

'The quicker the better. From here, you'll be going to the undertakers, right? You must notify them about your dear mother.'

'Notify them, yes.'

'Then they might come and take her away today . . . so I'll have some breathing space.' Pause. 'Don't mean to rush you, but surely you understand my situation.'

'Of course.' János turned toward those lumps again. (Maybe I won't have to look at her, please don't make me look at her.)

The attendant reached into the suitcase. 'I'll be lucky if I have time to bolt down a sandwich! If I'm lucky!' He took out the dark-blue dress with the white collar and gave it a light shake. That dress was so withered, practically transparent. And that stain on the collar. He will toss it back, for sure.

The morgue attendant lifted a silver necklace. He waved it in the air, just like the stockings. At the sight of the handkerchief, he vented an exasperated smile.

'My dear sir, she won't be needing this . . .'

And he flipped the handkerchief at János, who barely managed to catch it.

'Naturally you're concerned about your dear mother, but still . . .'

The dress and a few other belongings were laid out on the table. The suitcase was empty. János stepped over and shut it. The lock snapped open. He pressed it down again.

'Ah, an old piece,' nodded the attendant. 'A family heirloom, no doubt.' He stared off into space. Then abruptly: 'Don't you want to take a look?'

János stood there among the tin gurneys. Bearing those little bundles. He stood there, unable to move.

'Surely you'll want to take a last look?'

Gentle reproach resonated in that voice. And an intimate familiarity. As if he had taken many a long walk with Mother. During the walks, they talked about her son. About János, who would soon be coming to visit her.

He stepped over to one of the gurneys and pulled back the sheet.

All at once, Mother was in front of János. Translucent pallor, lying on her side. Crouched sideways, one knee drawn up. Her forehead even more prominent now. This made her face somehow girlish. A curious little girl, pressing her forehead against the plate glass of a shop window. One hand clutching her shoulder in a chilly gesture. Greying hair stuck to her forehead.

'Of course, we'll comb out her hair.'

That dry, greying hair . . . And her skin, too, so dry. She'd asked me to rub a little moisturizing cream on, massage it in . . . (All those jars! Half-empty, or only a smidgeon left on the bottom. The trace left by a fingertip in the cream.) But the moisturizing rub would have to wait now. And so would the reading. Even though Mother had set out the book on her nightstand. She waited for me to sit down and start reading. 'Well, then, at least tell me a story . . . about your comings and goings.'

My comings and goings . . .

He stepped closer to Mother.

The attendant drew back, as if not wanting to intrude. He pointedly studied the chart, and looked up only at my voice.

'She wanted me to graduate.'

'Graduate?'

'Yes, graduate from high school. She wouldn't put up with my dropping out and that sort of thing . . . I mustn't abandon my studies, that's how she put it. No, that was simply inconceivable! That her son . . .'

He stopped. He stood in front of the tin gurney, and contemplated that face.

WHAT WAS LEFT (1972)

He skimmed through a letter, looked at a photo. Pushed back a drawer. Then pulled it out again, and started to rummage.

Open drawers, scattered letters, old diaries and photos surrounded him.

Zsámboky leafed through the grey pocket notebook. Wavy lines. Pages and pages of nothing but wavy lines. Then a few names scrawled in tottering, overlapping capitals. Ambrus, Bán. That was in First Grade, Room 1-B, Maria Theresa Elementary School. A drawing of a soldier, rifle at shoulder arms. A sentry box. Again the wavy lines. Then a page in Mother's slanting cursive.

Zsámboky sat down at the table. As if that was the only place where he could read this.

Wednesday, 15 Oct. 1924. In the evening, O's fist, G's hands around my throat.

In the evening . . . Mother considered that detail significant. Significant enough to write it down in a notebook filled with wavy lines and all sorts of scrawls.

He put down the notebook. Then grabbed it to read again. *Wednesday, 15 Oct. 1924. In the evening, O's fist, G's hands around my throat.*

O is Olga, Father's second wife. She had such a lugubrious air. But she must have had her pluckier moments. As for G—well, that's Father, Gyula.

Otherwise there was nothing surprising in the entry. He still had a vivid memory of that scene in the Gyár Street flat. It was not long after the separation. That is, after Father dumped Mother and took up with Olga.

Zsámboky stood up and walked around the table.

I must have been six, no, not even that. But you, Father, spoke to me as one man to another. As someone you could bring along to your favourite cafe. 'Your mother will turn you into a total idiot. Your mother has no interests, even the theatre puts her to sleep. But Tini will take you to all sorts of places. Tini . . . oh by the way, that's what you should call Olga.'

I was sick at the time. My bed was in the living room by the window. On Gyár Street, we had several rooms. Dining room, bedroom, Father's study. Father, you and your study! Used mostly for bull-sessions with your friends. When I was sick, I had the living room to myself. The bed was placed by the window, giving me a view of the street. That, too, was your idea, Father. Let the kid see a bit of life, a little action.

It was quiet now, the numbing afternoon lull. (Never again did I have afternoons like those on Gyár Street.) The window gave on a small side street. There was a pharmacy on the other side. Almost within reach, as close as Aller's *Illustrated Home Journal* on my bed. Near enough to touch. But my headache was so bad that I didn't feel like lifting a hand. I had a strange sensation that Aller's characters were standing around downstairs in the lobby. Csengő and Bengő, those two loveable rapscallions. Mr Hobogász, Papa Pimpók and sons.

Papa Pimpók . . .

Father, remember when we used to called you Papa Pimpók? I think it was me who stuck you with that moniker. And you would grin pleasantly, Papa Pimpók, until one day you threw the clothes brush at me. You were brushing your winter coat in the hall, and I started with that Papa Pimpók stuff. Without a word, you threw the brush at me. That was the end of Papa Pimpók.

But on that afternoon I could almost see him standing by the lift in our staircase lobby. And those Keystone cops from Chaplin films too, complete with rubber truncheons. The ones who were always chasing Chaplin and stumbling over each other. There they sat on the windowsill, tapping their truncheons against their knees.

A newspaper lay tossed on the table in my room. Someone picked it up and browsed through it. Suddenly there was Mother, smiling at me. How did she get in here, without ringing the doorbell or knocking? Wearing a hat and unbuttoned overcoat, she sat by my bed and held my hand. She asked me questions that I could not understand. I just stared at her as she sat there, then stood up and walked over to the window. She traced a forefinger over the windowsill, looking for something.

Then she placed a bar of chocolate on my blanket. That's when the two of them came in, Father and Tini. Mother didn't turn to face them. She kept her eyes on me, even when Father picked up the chocolate. 'Where'd you get this? Take it back where it came from!'

Zsámboky circled the room, as if fleeing the memory of that afternoon. No, he didn't want to see how they stuffed that bar of chocolate back into Mother's handbag, how they grabbed her and marched her to the door.

The two of them, Father and Tini, dragged her to the door. Tini's little fist landed in Mother's face, and Father's hands clutched her throat, choking her. He jumped out of bed, wanted to run over to her, but someone picked him up. It wasn't Father and it wasn't Tini. Maybe it was the girl from next door who had rushed in, hearing the shouts. Mother vanished from the doorway, and the others stood at his bedside. 'Go away!' he screamed, gasping and breaking into sobs. 'Go away!' Tini nodded. 'All this is Ilonka's doing.' She was going to add something, but Father snapped at her. 'Why don't you go make some lemonade for the kid! You can't even make a decent glass of lemonade!' 'Jancsi, see how he talks to me?' 'Oh stop yammering!'

A little later, it was Father who brought the lemonade. 'Here you go, kiddo!' He also brought an empty cigar box that I could sniff. For a deep whiff of cigar scent.

Father, you bought those cigars by the case. The brands you smoked! Trabuco, Portorico. Regalia Media. You were still a big shot then. You still had that lot, right? Yes, you acquired a building lot.

Zsámboky slowly shook his head in amazement.

Father had acquired a lot, a building site for the new National Theatre. Whose idea was it originally? Father, who did you scam? No doubt, you must have scammed someone. And maybe more than one party.

Zsámboky could see a group of gentlemen in dark suits and starched collars, the victims of Father's scam. How did he do it? What was his knack? Jaws clenching a torpedo-shaped cigar, he would forge his way into City Hall or the Ministry building. There was no stopping him, once he zeroed in on his victim and went to work . . . Meetings would be cancelled and appointments missed, because the journalist Gyula Zsámboky was holding forth inside the office of a certain personage he had targeted. Who knows, it might have been the Lord Mayor himself. Of course, the secretary would have been buttered up well in advance.

Gyula Zsámboky, journalist.

Whatever happened, that's how he introduced himself. That's how he girded himself for battle, whether it was loans for the building site and the construction, or, later, for piddling amounts. Did he ever actually work for a newspaper? A real paper with editors and offices to report to?

Zsámboky looked around in the room. As if he could drag Father forth from the depths of the room, and have the truth out of him at last.

Forget it, what difference would it make now.

But let's linger for a moment on the entrepreneur. Yes, Father, just what kind of entrepreneur were you? I know precious little about that phase of your life except for the few times you took me out to the building site. There were surveyors taking measurements and sticking stakes into the ground. Later, there were no more surveyors and the stakes disappeared. I had the whole lot to myself, to race around in my Indian outfit with the feathers.

One winter, you opened a new skating rink.

Chinese lanterns glowed all over the place, everyone in fancy-dress costumes. You were an Eskimo, at the head of the snake, an endless snake formed by people holding on to each other, winding over the ice. Torches guttered, women laughed and squealed. Father, who was the lady clutching your arm?

Tini and I stood near the locker room, watching you, the Eskimo, whiz by waving your torch at us.

I tried on the ice skates, but had enough after one or two tentative steps . . . As for Tini, she didn't even try. She just stood there wrapped in her fur coat, watching the snake dance.

What an impossible little kid I must have been! When Father asked me to join the snake, an unnameable terror took hold of me. I never learnt how to skate. Nope, I never did.

Wavy lines, undulating lines . . .

Again he was looking at that small notebook. Those wavy lines drawn by a First-Grader's hand. Pages and pages of wavy lines. Then, scrawled in tottering capitals: Artilleryman. Infantryman. Marine. Jail-keeper. Bán. Ambrus.

My two classmates, Bán and Ambrus, recur frequently. Maybe I enlisted them as jail-keepers. But why did I need jail-keepers? Artilleryman and infantryman I can understand, but why the jail-keeper?

Father, you were in jail one time!

It was after the building-site era, but before the great crash. At any rate, you had lost the lot by then. The construction of the new National Theatre had to be placed on hold.

It was well after you had dumped Mother, but she still came up to visit the Gyár Street flat, accompanied by Aunt Vali. You had fobbed Mother off on the aunt with the balcony-sized bosom. Presiding officer of several ladies' clubs. The Lux family, seated around the big dining-room table, stood up to greet her. Tini went to make tea. By then she no longer snarled at Mother but greeted her like an old friend.

Father, you should have seen the fuss made by the jeweller's family over Aunt Vali as the chairwoman of so many worthy charities took her seat in their midst.

'So what's this I hear about Gyula?'

'Nothing very savoury!' Dr Sándor Lux paced the room, possibly the only one in the company not overawed by Aunt Vali. I think he hated you the most there, Father. For trying to clean out Olga and the entire Lux family.

Old man Lux was mumbling into his quivering beard, something about foreign capital.

'Gyula cooked up a scheme to attract foreign investors.'

Sándor's thumbs kept snapping his suspenders.

'Why not? An infusion of fresh blood never hurts!'

Is that right, Father? You intended to attract foreign investors? An infusion of fresh blood? 'And in the process, he took on an under-secretary of state,' said Sándor, nodding for emphasis. Somehow hearing this made Aunt Vali's head reel. 'An under-secretary of state!'

'Yes, Gyula devoured an under-secretary of state.' Sándor now pointed at Mother. 'He'd already gobbled up Ilonka, made a nice meal of her, and now this poor wretch is next in line.' (He indicated Olga.) 'But none of you will escape him!' (Addressed to the elders of the Lux family.) 'And if you, Madam . . . begging your pardon, Your Ladyship, if you wish to retain your bracelets' (here he jiggled the jangling bracelets on Aunt Vali's forearm), 'then the best thing would be to keep Gyula behind bars as long as possible! Yessir, that's what we're talking about!'

Sándor kept fondling those bracelets. The terrified Lux family looked on, paralysed. Aunt Vali maintained a frosty silence, glancing down at her forearm as if it were a distant tennis court. At last she grasped Sándor's hand.

'Nonetheless, we must get Gyula out of there at any cost.'

'Is that what Your Ladyship proposes to do?'

'And then there's this,' said old man Lux, who pulled out a newspaper from somewhere under his beard, and carefully spread it out on the table. 'There's an article about Gyula in here.'

'So now the press is taking an interest in Gyula?' Aunt Vali's massive embonpoint jutted over the paper. 'Plans for an international circus . . . negotiations with Ben Blumenthal. Is that right, Gyula was negotiating with Ben Blumenthal?'

' "Ben" Zsámboky!' Sándor guffawed. 'That's what the papers call him. ' "Ben" Zsámboky's circus.'

'Gyula's the victim of bad press,' said Mother.

Tini broke into sobs. Mother kept repeating that Gyula was a victim of bad press. Mother Lux said not a word. Mother Lux had not said anything during the entire proceedings. She measured Aunt Vali with sidelong, slightly hostile glances. Then got up unexpectedly, went over to Mother and caressed her face.

'Ilonka, you have such lovely complexion!'

Sándor yelled at her.

'Why don't you leave Ilonka out of this?!'

Mother Lux retreated to her seat by her husband's side.

I forget how the council of war ended.

The upshot of it was that the Lux family departed together with Aunt Vali. At any rate, Sándor latched on to her.

'That Sándor is such a ladies' man!' Tini sighed.

Oh yes indeed, Sándor's creative shenanigans with the ladies had even been immortalized in a popular cabaret song.

Father, there you sat in the slammer, surrounded by jail-keepers. You made yourself quite at home, had your record player and books brought in. Tini was indefatigable in replenishing your supply of cigars. I somehow can't visualize Mother ever visiting there. Once she sent you a package of pastries. You didn't even bother to open it. 'Ilonka and her creampuffs!'

They made us wait for you in the corridor. First we had to walk through galleries and small rooms where wardens sat at desks and stamped papers. They didn't even look up, just stamped our papers. Then came a corridor . . . A dim, rather nasty corridor. There were others standing next to us, but I could not make out their faces. I don't recall where you came from, but all of a sudden there you stood in front of me in your dove-grey sweater. The warden behind you. 'Gyurkovics is all right!' you said, waving in his direction. You told Tini not to cry, and caressed my head. 'So, kiddo, have you been to any football games? I think you and me we'll go see the Austria–Hungary game together. Unless I am greatly mistaken, they'll be getting tired of me here real soon.' Again, you repri-manded Tini. Then, after another reprimand for Tini, you turned on your heel and left, as if you'd found the whole scene tremen-dously boring.

Gyuri Fenyő refused to greet me on the street. Heading straight at us on Nagymező Street, he passed us with averted eyes. Tini and I were on our way to a bakery she'd heard about. She knew where all the specialty shops were: for belts, clasps, buttons . . . She rummaged in little boxes until she found what she was looking for. Then she would bargain. Oh she was an expert at bargaining! The shopkeeper stood his ground, put up a good fight. Then he slumped over the counter. 'I give up! Why don't you just take anything you want . . . the whole shop, for free!' But he ended up escorting us to the door, and even threw in a fancy button for me.

Gyuri Fenyő averted his eyes, catching sight of us on the street.

'You can thank your father for that,' Tini said.

I stared at Gyuri's back. Why was he playing games? I was sure he would turn around and next minute we'd again be discussing football and everything else. But he did not.

Gyuri lived next door; he used to come over to our flat to play football. That's right, football. We would play right in the living room, with Father and his pals. Having palavered, and smoked their cigars in his study, suddenly they'd all pile into the living room.

'How 'bout a little exercise!'

Father led his team in like a coach. Out rolled the ball from its place in the corner.

Jackets thrown down, they formed a circle and passed the ball. Nice little touch passes. After that they practiced heading the ball.

Tini protested, appalled.

'This is not a football field!'

She couldn't stand the sight of Father's friends. 'Lazy good-for-nothings! All they do is leech off your father!'

With Father in the slammer, these friends made themselves scarce. Just like Gyuri Fenyő.

Zsámboky again started to pace the room. He reached into a drawer.

And what folder is this? 'János Zsámboky, 4-B'.

A folder with a blue ribbon. Below the name, inscribed in Father's familiar, scratchy handwriting: Poems.

So this is where he kept his poems. In my Fourth-Grade folder. Once he asked me to make a selection. 'But someone else should also look it over. I think there's enough here for quite a decent little volume. Why don't you let your friend Lányi read them. Yes, per-haps it would be best if Lányi handled the whole thing.'

Because he's an expert on these things, right, Father? Because he has some expertise in poetry, is that it? As for me, I can hustle up the money and find a publisher. ('Listen, kiddo, this isn't your kind of thing! Nah! You can describe fairly accurately what you see, but as for poetry . . . !') Yes, you had plenty to say on this head. About my being a hard worker and a good typist. ('Kiddo, half the battle was won when you learned to type. Although I must say you balked at typing up my poems . . .')

'That's right, balked.'

Maybe some day I'll show this bundle to Lányi, but it won't be for a while. As for publication . . . Although that's what you always had in mind. The publication of your volume . . . your own book of poems.

He put the folder on the table and pulled the blue ribbon tighter.

Still, you did have two chapbooks published, Father. You know I've never even seen the first one. Where did you manage to hide it? The second one, that's a different story. Gold letters on a black cover. Gyula Zsámboky: Poems. That must have been at least fifty years ago. How was it received in your literary cafes? At the Abbázia? At the Kovács? Up in the galleries at the Cafe New York? Did you send Mother a copy? Did Mother receive a copy of Poems by Gyula Zsámboky? By then you had passed her off to

Aunt Vali. Did she by any chance read your poems aloud to Aunt Vali? And what about Tini? What kind of face did she make when she beheld your volume? When you presented her with the printer's bill? I would have liked to see the face she pulled then.

Another tug at the blue ribbon.

A letter fell out of the folder. Not really a letter, just a few lines without any address, from a certain Agnes. *Darling, did you ever notice how much stifled desire goes into whispering?* Hm, stifled desire . . . *You hear that soft, gentle sound and fever tingles throughout your body. It's like a tender caress. Darling, can you hear me whisper? Please refrain from caressing me now, I can't let your knowing fingers fondle me now.*

Father, those knowing fingers of yours!

Zsámboky fluttered his fingers in the air, contemplating them with a bemused expression.

Knowing fingers. Could be the title of a heart-to-heart feature column in some family periodical. So there are letters, too, hidden away in here. Typewritten sheets, handwritten memos, pages torn from a notebook. And poems of course, material for your upcoming volume.

A photograph.

A boy wearing a school cap, his collar turned up. Four silver stripes on the cap, for the first four years of high school. The next year, a single gold braid would be sewn on, but that was to be the last . . .

That year I didn't receive a midterm report card. *Due to his prolonged illness we are unable to grade him.* Something to that effect. How did those absences begin? What was that first morning like, when I stayed home in our hotel room? Because by then we were living in a hotel. A rather crummy hotel, in fact. None of those entrepreneurial ventures had panned out. Tini's money was gone. Tini herself was gone. Tell me Father, how did the Lux family react when you sent her packing? I must say, it was nice work: first you passed Mother off on Aunt Vali, then you sent Tini back to the Luxes.

In any case, it was just the two of us in the hotel room. You would bring so many picture magazines! The illustrated weeklies. I perused them on quiet winter mornings. I had seen Lily Damita in the films, but she was something else on these pages.

Darvas was the first one . . . Lili Darvas, back in the Gyár Street flat, one afternoon as I sat on the sofa's edge. We were preparing to go out somewhere. My skinny legs resting in Tini's lap. She was tugging at a new pair of socks, trying to pull them over my feet. It was tough going, the socks practically stuck to my feet. On top of it, the insidious material irritated my skin and gave me a nasty itch. I was dying to tear those socks off. But suddenly I was no longer aware of them. That photo in *Theatre Life* caught my eye—Father must have tossed the magazine on the sofa. I stared at an actress who stood in front of a door, head tilted back, arms akimbo. Her face reflected absolute terror: something was about to happen to her, any second. Tini reprimanded me. 'Stop wiggling your toes!' I didn't even hear her. I had eyes only for that actress. Father passed in front of the sofa. 'Aha, Lili Darvas!' As Tini's yanking grew more and more violent, the sock kept slipping out of her hand. I gaped at Lili Darvas in a daze, oblivious to the world. They were coming to get her. What would they do to her? What were they going to do to her?

Lili Darvas was the first one.

And then came the weekly illustrated magazines. Father's magazines with all those actresses. Each one of them had that alarmed, defenceless look.

Professor Pázmán, jacket thrown over his shoulders, stepped out of the teachers' lounge. He marched down the corridor and entered the homeroom of 5-B. The class stood up in unison to greet him, the boy on day-duty gave his report. 'Absent: Gráf, Mészáros, Szeverényi and Zsámboky.' Professor Pázmán, known among his students by the name of 'Gamó', looked up over his glasses. 'Márton! I want you to go and visit Zsámboky tomorrow.'

Next day, Márton showed up at our hotel. He lingered in the dim corridor in front of our door, hesitating to come in. I gestured impatiently. Get a move on! At last he stirred. 'Gamó sent me.' He adjusted his schoolbag under his arm. 'What's up with you?'

There were four silver stripes on my school cap. Then one gold stripe was added on. And nothing after that.

That school cap with its gold braid . . . I had it for quite a while, wore it long after I quit school. Like the times I escorted Eva Szóbel to her dancing lessons.

He rummaged through a drawer, as if looking for that old school cap. Maybe it was on the top shelf in the closet, among Father's old hats.

I remember removing the badge with the coat of arms and putting it in a box. But which box?

He opened the closet. His hand slid along the top shelf. The empty top shelf.

There is nothing here, except dust. Father left only one hat behind. It had been crushed to death, the sweatband totally blackened. And even that, I gave away. Or else it was left at the hospital.

What was our high-school coat of arms like? The Imre Madách High School coat of arms?

Again that folder . . . His fingers tapped on the bundle.

Don't be mad at me, Father! Perhaps I will show it to Lányi some day, but not right now . . .

This business letterhead! Whose letterhead was this? Did you scribble poems on the back? No, there are no poems here.

Thiergärtner and Stöhr, Inc. Central Heating and Hygienic Equipment Installed. Aha, a letter . . . addressed to the Radical Party. That's right, Father, you were a member of that party. The Radical Party.

Enclosed you will find our estimate regarding the total cost, including material and labour, for repairs on the heating system at 31 Podmaniczky Street. Looking forward to receiving your esteemed order, we remain respectfully yours. 26 October 1946.

What were you, some kind of heating inspector?

The circulating hot-water heating system sustained damages due to freezing. Our inspection indicates defects . . .

And so on, in itemized detail filling four pages. Did you request this estimate? And what happened to the heating system? Was central heating restored? Or were the Radicals left out in the cold?

But they treated you rather shabbily, Father. They should have found a more suitable position for you. After all, back in the autumn of 1918, you had been present on that ferry along with Count Károlyi and Oscar Jászi crossing the River Tisza toward the French command post at Szeged. You, the young journalist, stood side by side with Károlyi and Jászi. They were firing at the ferry from the shore, bullets whistled in the air.

'That's right, kiddo, those bullets had a nasty zing. Károlyi didn't even bat an eye but Jászi kept flinching. I gave his arm a squeeze and he smiled at me.'

Zsámboky scratched his chin.

Anyway, the Radicals should have found a better job for him.

And here is another letter.

We ran into his nibs at the Omnia coffee house, and right away he stipulates that we mustn't bring up astrology, Buddhism or Holland. I hit the ceiling. How does he presume to dictate to me what topics to discuss just because he . . . And when was he ever a journalist? That's what I'd like to know, my dear Desi, when was Nándor Arki ever a journalist?

Nándor Arki. The character who stipulated in advance: not a word about astrology, Buddhism or Holland. But you, Father, I trust you really let him have it, right there, at the Omnia.

Old buddy!

That's what it said at the top of a sheet. Old buddy! And nothing else. Only the salutation and then not a word.

Who could have been this old buddy stranded here, saluted forever? One of those old-time cafe fixtures? Rustled up from his lair in some coffee house? Somewhere in the provinces? No longer even able to leave his bed . . . From time to time the door opens, someone looks in and closes the door again. Father had meant to buckle down and write a serious letter, perhaps he really had something to say to this old buddy who raised his head for an instant, to pause a moment before dropping away into impenetrable obscurity.

Did Father ever serve in the army?

No way! Whatever put that idea in my head? There was simply no way Father could ever have been a soldier. Why, he was the one who saved me from being drafted. He stashed me away in a hospital. That was during the war. He lugged a pile of medical certificates to represent me before the draft board. Oh, he gave them the whole spiel! 'Here is my son's contribution to the homeland!' Father standing at something like attention in front of the draft board. (To show that even a mere civilian knows military manners! Mere civilian, what am I saying. One of those old-time frontline reporters, a First World War–battlefield veteran, Franz Molnár himself, confronting General Konrad Hötzendorfer!) Father placed a book on the table. Silence reigned in the room. The officers sat stiffly, staring at the book in front of them on their beloved bare table. *The Girls of Aliga. A Novel for Young Girls*, by

János Zsámboky. Did any of them even touch that book? Turn a few pages? Or did they just gape at Father, who stood there with his head tilted to one side, still at something like attention. At any rate, Father left the place in one piece. He even managed to solicit an article from one of the colonels. You, sir, must write a story for us! We are expecting a piece from you! It was, however, a sergeant who eventually sank my file out of sight. How did Father butter up that sergeant? One thing for sure, he didn't have any money. By then, he hadn't had any money for a long time.

Zsámboky dug into the contents of the folder. He arranged the sheets. The essay . . . There is an essay somewhere in here about General Görgey. Arthur Görgey, one of Father's favourite hobbies. He haunted libraries and scribbled notes on slips of paper. 'I'm going to write this! I've got to do it! I don't care if it gets printed. That sort of thing doesn't interest me. I'll let you enjoy the laurels. But still . . . the truth has finally got to be told about Görgey. The only real man among a bunch of attitudinizing loudmouths.'

A library card. Reading-room request slips. District Tax Office. What did they want from you, Father? Or was it Mother they were after? Yes, maybe this was for Mother. Garnishment order. But you're involved in it, Father. She had to take out the loan because of you. Or perhaps you took it out in her name—after all, she was the one who still held a modest job. But what happened with General Görgey? People were counting on you to deliver that essay. Your friends, and others as well. Someone was even planning to translate it.

At any rate, you hung Arthur Görgey's picture on the wall. The only real man in this country.

And what about Kossuth?

Who was that old fool who accompanied you home from the cafe, weeping and blubbering? 'But my dear Gyula,' he moaned, 'at least recognize Kossuth's role in exile . . . ' 'Oh, come off it!'

(For some reason this really got the old man's goat.) 'What do you mean, oh come off it?! Just think, in the eyes of the world, Hungary came to be linked with the name of Kossuth!' But Father merely waved off this notion, making the old man crumple on the table.

Poems slipped from the folder. Yellowed sheets, torn edges. He shoved them back in with rapid, rather nervous movements. Two lines still managed to stand out in front of his eyes:

In this land among us you strode
Like some Englishman among savages abroad.

A creak in the hall.

Zsámboky peered out. He did not turn on the hall light. Outside the glass pane of the front door, the grille of the lift loomed like a man in a black overcoat. Patiently waiting, as if he had all the time in the world.

Gyuri Fenyő did not say hello to me on the street.

Zsámboky stood in the hall, hands clasped behind his back. Again he could see Gyuri Fenyő turning his head away on Nagymező Street.

What was Father's last afternoon in the Gyár Street flat like? Did he sprawl on the sofa? Stretch out and relax for one last time? One thing is certain, he was alone. His friends had evaporated long before that. And Olga was in hospital. Something went wrong with her lungs, she ended up in a sanatorium. I was sent to stay with Mother. Aunt Vali consented to Mother's having me over for a few days. *While things were ironed out.*

So Father was left by himself. He lit a cigar and paced the empty rooms: across the dining room into the bedroom. Stared out the window at Gyár Street. Lingered in the hall, listening to the sounds from the staircase. Waiting for something. A visit from his foreign investors, perhaps. Why not? Investors dropping in, sitting down in the study and launching into major negotiations.

'Mr Zsámboky! We're going to secure that building site for you, because you are obviously the right person to get something accomplished in this city.' The foreign investors would all line up, headed by the great Ben Blumenthal himself. Side by side in the study: Ben Blumenthal and 'Ben' Zsámboky.

But no one came to see Father.

So he strolled out on the balcony over the courtyard, smoking a cigar. Down on the second floor was Verő's Dance School. In the summer, the windows opened and girls wearing colourful outfits sat on the windowsill. But it was wintertime now. The windows were shut tight, and not a soul seemed to be around. There was no sign of life up on the fourth floor, either. One day Father, while shaving, expostulated with Olga: 'If I'd only hooked up with Magda Tauszig, instead of you . . . There's a girl with some life to her. Do you have any idea what that is? Life?!'

Nothing but closed doors throughout the building. Two pairs of eyes watched Father from behind the windowpane of one flat. Old man Fenyő said to his son Gyuri: 'What's he doing out there?'

I've got to kick Gyuri Fenyő's butt!

But where would I find him now? Or for that matter anyone else from Gyár Street?

Zsámboky lumbered back into the living room.

A pocket diary from 1926. A small black diary. On the first page, in pencil: Mrs Ilonka Zsámboky.

Mother was staying at Aunt Vali's at the time. Only one room in the flat was heated, Aunt Vali's. Mother was cooped up in a little cell of a room . . . But they were hardly ever at home. Constantly attending soirées, balls, lectures. Aunt Vali was always dragging Mother off to readings. And me, too, at times. All those ladies' clubs! Aunt Vali the presiding officer. Usually there was an honour guard of boy scouts around the podium. They turned up at Aunt

Vali's flat, too. Those boy scouts with their cowboy hats were always hanging around at her place. They camped out there. Wherever Aunt Vali went, there would be boy scouts, you could count on that.

22 Jan. Endre's lecture at the Gellért.

Endre? Who was this Endre?

Oh yes, it was Father who dug him up somewhere. 'He latched on to me at the Liberal Arts student-aid office. Did you know I founded that place back in 1917? Anyway, that's where I met him, a down-and-out loser. His ambition was to be a journalist. He had to bide his time until the conservatives seized power, then he wangled his way aboard the establishment daily. Very much your mother's type!'

So Endre gave a talk. Perhaps Aunt Vali helped to organize the event in the lecture hall of the Hotel Gellért.

I, too, must have been there!

Endre offering a toast, standing tall near a column. Mother, Aunt Vali and I sitting at a table in front.

Where else did you take me, Mother? Of course, there was no way of avoiding Aunt Vali's readings. Aunt Vali, arms loaded with bracelets, trailing her evening gown up on the podium. Reciting poems of her own composition. Alabaster-bosomed ladies pining . . . and knights sworn to the banner of the Holy Virgin. Her husband, Uncle Gábor, refused to attend these events. He had inoculated me against smallpox. Mother said I didn't cry at all, because Uncle Gábor had such a light touch . . . Mother also said that Aunt Vali was unfaithful to Gábor, but she had her reasons.

Her reasons . . .

Mother's face so girlish and enigmatic as she said this.

Her high forehead and eyeglasses. Grey hair sticking to her temples. Looking not really like hair, more like some kind of pressed flower. Strangely, this made her face even more girlish, even more vulnerable. Her face, when she came home after cataract surgery. Somehow she could not resign herself to being confined to bed, to not being allowed to walk about. (Eventually she did get resigned to it.) Periodically, she would vanish from her bed. She had a knack for disappearing—as if she had been planning the prank long in advance. She would send me out for a glass of water or something. When I returned, there was only the empty bed, the crumpled sheet and tell-tale dangling blanket. I'd have to go look for her. But not right away. I'd sit down on the edge of the bed and muse. She's gone . . . Mother upped and went away. Vanished into thin air. And then I'd set off on the hunt. Opened closet doors, in case Mother was squatting in there among the clothes. Then check the bathroom, and the toilet. The first thing I would see was her hand. Those thin fingers groping in the air. That blind face. Mother in her nightshirt, turning in circles. Revolving slowly, round and round, surrounded by doors and furniture.

Once I had to retrieve her from the outside. I yanked her back from the balcony. Flattened against the wall, in a nightshirt, dark glasses, head bandaged. The kerchief sliding down over the back of her neck. Fingers pushing away from the wall, as if she wanted to flutter off over the courtyard. And still her face strangely that of a young girl.

Now why on earth did I ever want to be a gendarme?

Zsámboky wearing his stretched old sweater stood observing his face in the mirror. That malignant-looking yellowish brown spot. Little by little, it was taking over his whole forehead.

That's right, I wanted to be a gendarme. The hunter. Crouched in a steaming swamp, ready to strike. Galloping, hugging my horse's neck. Bitter, seething with fury, the desperate fury of pursuit. The gendarme has no wife, no children. Not even a sweetheart. He has nothing except the chase.

'A cop keeps following me.'

That's what Father said when I escorted him down to the scale at the corner chemist. He was supposed to weigh himself every week. He started losing weight at an alarming rate in those days. He began to have obsessional symptoms. Bugs crawling over his face and eyes, things like that. He had trouble sleeping, and the weight loss was appalling. 'Make sure you check his weight regularly,' said Dr Bonyhádi.

So I checked his weight. Every week, I took him downstairs and stood him on that scale. Except it wasn't all that easy. Each time, Father seemed to get cold feet at the last minute. At times, he tried to bolt. As soon as we stepped outside the front door, he would fake to the right, suddenly reverse and take off in the other direction, his long winter coat flapping behind. But I stayed right on his heels.

'Procedures! What good are these procedures?' he whimpered, as I dragged him back home.

6 Feb. Little Jancsi was here, we went to the music hall.

We went to the music hall a lot, Mother and I. We saw the Japanese magician. The two sisters who tossed balls at each other. Once we saw a seal that knew how to count.

I visited Mother on Sundays. Sometimes we just stayed chatting in that cramped room of hers. In the evening, she made me say goodbye to Aunt Vali.

Wrapped in shawls, Aunt Vali sat in the light of the bridge lamp. 'And what hotel are you living in now? The Adria? Never heard of it. Is that woman still with you? Of course she is. That Olga. Or Tini. Is that what you call her, Tini?'

Aunt Vali pulled me very close. She stared into my face. That's when I said, clearly articulating each word:

'Jewellers have it best!'

There was a momentary silence. Then Aunt Vali burst into a kind of harsh laughter. She was practically quaking. 'Oh, but of course, Tini's father! Tini's father, the jeweller!'

Mother grabbed me and rushed me out of the room. But that cackling laughter could still be heard.

'Jewellers have it best!'

Zsámboky tossed the diary into a corner.

I gotta hand it to you, Father, you coached me beautifully. 'Jewellers have it best!' I don't resent your marrying Tini, and taking all her money, but your making me say that to Aunt Vali . . . Whatever got into you, Father? What was the big idea? That I, like some diminutive knight, a Lilliputian hero, should confront her and . . . Let's leave Tini out of this! She knew nothing about it. It was you who walked with me that day, all the way to Mother's front door. Smoking your cigar, you smiled and nodded at me. 'A jeweller must be as smart as a fox. He works with his brains. Aunt Vali doesn't have the foggiest notion of this. You ought to tell her, kiddo. You know, just drop a casual remark when you're saying goodbye.'

Father, the brim of his canvas hat turned up, merrily smoking on that street corner. But no more Cuban cigars or Portoricos, much less Regalia Medias. These were thin little Fájintos, Cigarillos . . . they fell apart the moment you lit them. His jacket was quietly fraying. Loose threads dangled from his trouser cuffs that had deeply embedded mud stains.

But again and again Father went forth to do battle.

Those special supplements of his! Children's and comic supplements. Several newspapers were eager to carry them . . . both in the capital and in the provinces.

Tini sat between the sink and the table in our hotel room. Her eyes narrowed to slits. She whimpered. 'I spent my last pennies on him! I scraped together my few remaining pennies!'

You know, Father, at times I still see Tini like that, scraping together her pennies. You didn't pay much attention to her, perhaps you didn't even hear her endless snivelling. Sometimes you yelled at her. 'You're asking for it! Want me to throw something at you? Stop bringing me down! You're such a limp wet rag! And just now when I need every ounce of my energy. Do you know who I ran into today?' But the name failed to impress Tini. She merely picked up the empty bottle and went down to the corner shop to buy spirits for the alcohol burner. And whenever the two of us were left alone, she practically implored me. 'Stay in school, Jancsi! So that you'll have a job, a decent job!' Just like Mother . . . yes, it was just like hearing Mother.

Olga Lux . . . I was supposed to call her Tini.

Once she was ready to call the cops on Father. She was going to have the cops take him away.

'It's all over, my dear!' she screeched. 'We're through, mister!' Then she collapsed in the hallway, right in front of the door.

Now where was that door and that hallway?

One thing for sure, it was not Gyár Street. Those Gyár Street days were long past by then! It wasn't a hotel, either. It was some housing project, where Father managed to hustle up a room. I think he knew the caretaker or something. Tini had just come home from hospital. She'd been to hospital a lot lately. And she arrived that evening—God only knows why!—to look for her antique china at our place. Her family heirloom china.

Well, there wasn't much china to be found in that flat. There was no bed, and no table either. We had two chairs, loaned to us by the caretaker.

Father was perched on the armrest of one of the chairs. He wore his winter coat and my knit stocking cap, long tassel dangling. He raised the violin to his chin.

We were not expecting Tini. We were not expecting anyone, least of all Tini.

Father wearing my stocking cap, violin in hand, perched on the armrest of the chair. 'All right, kiddo, I'm going to perform my musical clown act for you.'

The knock on the door came as he was raising the bow.

'Now who the hell could that be?' He yawned, as if tired of the whole thing already.

I was the one who opened the door for Tini. Father did not budge from his perch. He pulled the cap all the way down to his chin.

'You seem to be in a good mood today!' Tini said, pacing the empty flat, still in her overcoat. 'How come you're in such a good mood?'

Father, still perched on the chair, the cap pulled down to his chin like a mask. Tini still circling. She raised the lid of the large brown trunk, Father's college trunk. It was our only piece of furniture beside the chairs. As for the bed, our arrangements were quite casual. An old grey rug thrown in a corner with a few towels for pillows and Father's winter coat for a blanket.

Tini was rummaging through the trunk. She'd practically climbed into it.

'So you sold them?!' Her sharp, angry face emerged from the trunk. 'You went and sold my china?!'

'Enough already!' Father yanked up the cap to uncover his face.

But Tini's screams got wilder and wilder. 'You cleaned me out completely! You leeched off my family!'

Father slid off the chair. In cap and coat, he walked over to Tini and grabbed her arm.

Tini screamed as he flung her into a corner. She lay motionless for a while. At last, her fingers started to scrabble on the floor like someone groping for broken eyeglasses—although she did not wear glasses.

'It's all over, my dear!' she screeched, getting to her feet. 'This time you really did it! You'll get what's coming to you, just you wait!'

She turned to face me for a moment. Perhaps she wanted me to go with her. But her eyes were so full of revulsion.

She tugged at her scarf once, and set out to go. But she collapsed in the hallway before she got to the door.

She had her hat on. She lay there, her coat flung open, scarf loose, hat squashed.

I think I was the one who dragged her back in. Because you, Father, did not deign to step outside after hearing that crash. You didn't even stick your nose out of the door. So I had to drag Tini in somehow, grabbing her by the shoulders. You were standing by the window.

'Watch how you hold her!'

'Why, how should I hold her?' My reply came from somewhere behind Tini's neck.

You watched me standing there holding Tini till I was practically blue in the face. Then you shrugged. 'Just put her down anywhere.'

I peeled off her overcoat and laid her down on the rug. I don't think you heard her muttering when she came to: 'A den of thieves!'

That night you went out somewhere. You made sure not to stay home.

Zsámboky knelt on the chair as he tugged at the ribbon tied around the folder.

One sheet stuck out. A flyer for a Christmas book sale. On the margin, in Father's clear, legible hand: *Lányi should make his selections from my old volumes at the libraries of the Academy and the*

National Museum! And, at the bottom of the sheet: *I chose Lányi only on account of his editorial ability.*

His editorial ability . . .

All right, Father, you gave Lányi his due. But did you ever take the trouble to look at his poems, just once . . . No, Lányi's poems didn't interest you the least bit. You didn't think much of anyone in our group, save for Fabulya. Only Fabulya . . . perhaps because his poems were full of falling snow, and you liked that sort of thing.

Zsámboky wandered from room to room. Next he found himself in the bathroom, holding a photograph. Where did it come from? A moustachioed man wearing a bowler hat in an arbour, walking stick resting against his knee. On the table, a bottle of wine and a wineglass. But it doesn't look like he's been drinking. One thing you can be sure of: no one else is allowed to sit at this table. No drinking buddies, not even his wife. This arbour is his and his alone. It is grandfather. The 'other' grandfather. That's what he called his mother's father: the 'other' grandfather. Perhaps because he never knew him. The 'other' grandfather died years before Zsámboky was born.

'Consider yourself lucky,' said Father. 'You didn't have to put up with him. You should've seen the faces he made when I asked him for his daughter's hand!'

(I can just see the scene, Father. It's not too difficult to imagine.)

This grandfather, like Grandfather Zsámboky, also worked for the post office, but on a totally different level. He was a postmaster with a passion for holding inspections. Always investigating some case. That's how the two met. The 'other' grandfather was touring the provinces and descended on Grandpa Zsámboky's little village post office. He was aching to put some miserable wretch behind bars.

'He tore out all the drawers!'

That's Mother speaking. According to her, Grandfather would throw a tantrum if he didn't find at once what he was looking for. He would yank out every drawer and toss the contents behind his back. Meanwhile his mother and wife and daughter all danced attendance on him.

There was one other thing. That little old whip.

That's right, whenever Mother did something wrong, out came the little whip. She had to bend over the chair, and it began ... Not only while she was a child, but even later on. Yes, that's what I think she said: even later on. At times she tried to escape, desperately racing from room to room. No use, of course. Someone was always there to catch her. Then he would shove a chair or stool in front of her, and she would get what she had coming. Plus an extra helping, for trying to run away. Afterwards, she was expected to thank him for the punishment.

Zsámboky leant against the edge of the bathtub, contemplating that moustachioed man with the round bowler hat. Sitting alone in his bower. A bottle of wine and a single wineglass on the table.

More lines, wavy lines ...

He was again in the bedroom browsing through the small notebook. The grey pocket diary riddled with those tangled, wavy lines. Mother's entries and his doodles.

Recipes, so many recipes! Hussar's kisses: 280 grams flour, 140 grams sugar, 140 grams butter. Walnut rolls. Elvika's brioche. To 2 litres of flour add yeast, 20–30 grams, in lukewarm milk ...

My Dear Uncle Pongrác,

For the past few days I've been staying at Vali's.

Right in the middle of all those recipes, suddenly these two lines.

My Dear Uncle Pongrác.

Mother, where was your Uncle Pongrác by then? I think in the Benedictine order. Anyhow he was a monk of some sort. One thing for sure, he had left the world behind. He hardly ever visited his family.

What could you have hoped to achieve by writing those lines? Pongrác never laid hands or eyes on this notebook.

Whatever the case may be, this is a call for help. Oh, Pongrác, come and take me away, the sooner the better!

Why? What was it like at Aunt Vali's? She in her large chambers, and you in that cramped little hole in the wall. Did she preach a lot? Lecture you on account of Father? 'How could you ever marry him? And let him kick you out like that? And now you intend to stay here forever . . . Ilonka, my dear, is that what you have in mind?'

Zsámboky turned the pages.

Recipes, laundry lists and more wavy lines. But perhaps there are a few other entries hidden in here somewhere. I'd like to know what went on in that flat when Mother and Aunt Vali were home alone after an evening out.

The flat was right above a cinema. You could always hear the distant rumble of the piano accompaniment.

Overcoats, robes and dressing gowns of various colours hung on the clothes-rack in the dim hall. Aunt Vali had a tremendous number of peignoirs. But most of the time she was wrapped in a white terry-cloth robe. White terry-cloth robe and scarves. That's what she wore sitting in front of the correspondence piled on her desk, answering her invitations, or as she stood stirring her coffee in the kitchen.

Zsámboky browsed through those faded, barely legible lines in the hope of an entry perhaps intended for Father. But no, there was nothing. Then, printed in gigantic letters:

Why couldn't you have come sooner?!

Followed by blank pages.

He leafed back.

Why couldn't you have come sooner?!

But Mother, who was it who should have come sooner? Who, tell me, who? Was it Endre, who gave that lecture at the Gellért? But the man was a dunce. He could almost see Father, nodding in agreement. 'That didn't faze your mother the least little bit. She fell for characters like that. And army officers! But what can you do, kiddo. Poor thing, she always had a weak spot for uniforms.'

Mother, tell me it wasn't an army officer or someone like that! Tell me it wasn't Endre . . .

Zsámboky really hated this Endre character who one night at the Hotel Gellért . . . What a pompous simpleton! Well, it's all the same now. But why couldn't it have been a decent, bearable sort of person, say, a teacher or a doctor? Of course, the profession didn't really matter. Mother, I hope you didn't fall for that sort of thing.

He chuckled quietly.

But you, Mother, always fell for them! You could hardly wait to fall for someone. First of all, there was Father. Even after he kicked you out.

Kicked you out . . .

Sorry, but there's no nicer way of putting it. The way Father put you in that cab and sent you packing to Aunt Vali! No woman in your place would have spoken to him after that. That's right. No woman would have, except for you. And you even let him visit you after that, at Aunt Vali's. Was he going to ask for your hand again? 'Oh, Ilonka, let's start all over!' No, I don't think it was like that. Anyway, he came up to see you at Aunt Vali's. (The two of you let him in.) You did not tell him to keep away. (So he sat down by your side, held your hand and started on one of his spiels. 'Oh,

Ilonka, I wouldn't leave you in a lurch like this! I'm having a little villa built for you, that's where you're going to live. A place where Jancsi can visit you on weekends. I was thinking that Hűvösvölgy would be most suitable. Pasaret is an alternative but that neighbourhood is getting to be so nouveau . . . full of upstarts. It's not for us!' Mother, you listened with open mouth, mesmerized—and that's no exaggeration. It must have really impressed you, the way Father deliberated over the site. The way he dismissed Pasaret. He came to visit more than once, bringing progress reports. 'The construction is underway, pretty soon you'll be able to move in, Ilonka. I want you to set the table in the garden when I bring the boy for his first visit. Ah, you simply can't imagine what it'll be like, having tea alfresco!')

Could you simply imagine that, Mother? Did you really try to imagine that? To the point of visualizing 'Ben' Zsámboky, entrepreneur extraordinaire, personally supervising the construction. 'Ilonka, I have to see to every detail personally!'

And yet . . . whatever made you decide to do it? To go out there once, and take a look for yourself? Forgive me, but I don't believe it was you who came up with the idea. It must have been Aunt Vali. 'Let's go Ili, let's take a look!' That's right, Aunt Vali called you Ili. Little Ili! So Aunt Vali and Little Ili went out to Huvosvolgy. And what did they find? Did they find a house under construction? A half-finished villa? With only the roof missing? Far from it! An empty lot, overgrown with weeds. A goatherd and a grazing goat. You went up to the goatherd to inquire: 'Do you by any chance . . . ?' But he merely shook his head. And you stumbled on, still looking for your villa. Still the little girl refusing to believe she'd been once again made a fool of. Did you start sniffling? Did you break into sobs? Be as it may, you persisted, wandering through the shrubs that grew in wild profusion there. Aunt Vali in your wake, wrapped in scarves and shawls. 'But it's obvious there's nothing to be found here! Nothing! Can't you see?'

Mother, there was nothing for you there.

Just a meadow overgrown with weeds. A goatherd and his goat.

Zsámboky held an old sepia-tint photograph. An ID photo. A man with a pointy moustache and clear, cheerful eyes, wearing a buttoned-up fur coat. A half-fare railroad pass for Dr Gábor Berendi, Budapest, 1908.

'Poor Gábor left us too soon!'

'Come on, Ilonka! Gábor simply took his leave when he had enough of Aunt Vali. You know, kiddo, Uncle Gábor used to visit us quite often in the Gyár Street days. Never with Aunt Vali, though. Always alone. We'd sit by the funnel-shaped speaker of the old victrola you had to crank up by hand. Guess what his favourite record was? *Steinhardt on the Telephone*. He kept playing that one over and over. Steinhardt was a riot, one of the best cabaret comedians ever. Uncle Gábor sipped tea and listened to records. *Steinhardt on the Telephone* . . . that was his favourite.'

Mother chimed in. 'And I remember taking so many walks with Uncle Gábor when I was in high school . . . He would be waiting in front when school let out. The other girls were real jealous of me, because Uncle Gábor was such a handsome man. "Where to, maiden? How about a stroll in City Park? Or shall we have a Dobos torte at Gerbeaud's?" That's what he called me, "maiden". "Uh-oh, I can see something's wrong. Tell me maiden, what's weighing on your soul." He always noticed right away if something was amiss. We'd walk down Kossuth Lajos Street, and Váci Street, then out on the Corso. The girls all turned green with envy. Sári Bendekovics was always after me, she was dying to be introduced to Uncle Gábor. I think Sári was head over heels in love with him.'

Uncle Gábor and Mother taking a walk in the Inner City. Uncle Gábor greeting an acquaintance. They stop to chat for a moment, and Uncle Gábor introduces his niece. They stroll on, checking out the shop windows. Mother grasps Uncle Gábor's arm and points at a hat. 'What do you say, maiden, shall we try it on?'

Two feet slid in front of Zsámboky. A pair of splayed female feet on the floor.

That was Tini, lying in the hall in front of the door. Bending over her, the boy sneaked a sidelong glance toward the room. Perhaps Father will come out, after all . . . Tini's hat squashed, her hair messed up. What's that in her hand? She's still desperately clutching her handbag. The boy grasped her shoulder, trying to lift her. As if they were playing wheelbarrow races, with Tini as the wheelbarrow. Trying to turn, whoops, she slipped from his grip. He somehow managed to pick her up off the floor, and haul her into the room. How he did it was a mystery.

Father stood by the window, watching the boy stagger in, reeling, with Tini in tow. Once he spun around, there was no stopping. One of Tini's shoes flew off; her stockings hung loose.

Father stood by the window. No, he wasn't going to budge. He stared at the boy and kept repeating, 'What a dummy! How can anyone be this dumb?'

Then Tini and the boy stood in the blue-tiled vestibule of her building on Népszinház Street. Tini rang for the lift while rummaging in her purse for change.

The janitor's wife, a chubby woman with a shawl wrapped around her waist, arrived from the direction of the courtyard. Her eyes lit up when she saw Tini, as if to say, 'So you're back, Miss? Decided you've had enough at last?' But when they got in the lift, all she said was, 'You've lost weight, Miss Olga.' She eyed the boy with sidelong glances, as if little Jancsi had something to do with the abduction of Olga Lux from her home on Népszinház Street. She accompanied them down the corridor, and rang the doorbell for them. As if Tini hadn't enough strength left to press the button.

Tini's mother opened the door. It appeared she intended to talk only to the janitor's wife, and merely motioned for Tini to come in.

'There's just one thing I ask,' said Tini's father, seated at the head of the large mahogany table, his hands clasped as if in prayer. 'Talk about anything, except Gyula . . . I don't want to hear one more word about Gyula! I want to forget that name, Gyula Zsámboky!'

Of course, Gyula Zsámboky was the sole topic of conversation.

Even Sándor emerged from a back room. 'Ah, Gyula and his Sunday supplements! Pray tell me about Gyula's supplements! Where can I find them? In which newspaper? I would sure like to subscribe to that paper!'

And yet those supplements did get published.

Zsámboky stared at a drawer. As if he expected to find those ancient newspapers there. Really, where could they be? Where did Father hide those papers? *Chocolate Cake.* That's what the supplement was called. The cover featured a boy wearing a sailor suit, eating chocolate cake. It was carried by Hungarian-language newspapers in Yugoslavia and Czechoslovakia. The venture got off to a good start. It just did not last very long.

No, Father, somehow your Sunday supplements failed to jell. First the printers let you down, then it was your associates. Then Tini's money ran out. You squeezed every last penny of her savings out of her. You ran around looking for subsidies. City Hall gave you an occasional pittance. One of the councilmen wrote children's verse. Or was it a police officer? The superintendent of police?

As for those subsidies . . .

We trotted over to the Cafe Simplon, the Simplichek, as you called it. Ah, those lavish breakfasts! Complete with coffee, butter, jam . . .

We did not take Tini to the cafes. No, not to the Simplon, nor to any other.

'One look at her and my appetite is gone!' Father said, grinning at me from the other side of the table. 'Anyway, our luck's bound to change now. Soon we'll be moving out to Margit Island, kiddo. Well, yes, I know, that's where I took Olga ... honeymooning, what idiocy! But this time it's going to be different. We'll just have to leave Olga out of the picture. Anyway, I'll be editing a little paper on Margit Island. I'm working on a deal with the restaurant and hotel managers. These are cosmopolitan minds, they can understand the potential in something like this. "Mr Zsámboky, you've got the right editorial concept ... You're a man of ideas!" It'll be a weekly paper, just a few pages, the format perhaps like a menu. Folded casually and elegantly, lying right next to the place settings, there for the patrons' convenience. Hotel guests will find it in their rooms on the desk or the night-stand ... Yes, I'm going to write about Margit Island ... its past ... the construction of the Grand Hotel, and the small hotel, all of this of course illustrated by the best artists, I'll even bring Walter Trier from the Ubu in Berlin, I'll offer him a contract ... Kiddo, I think we should move to the small hotel, what do you say? It has the right kind of tone ...'

The Grand Hotel and the small hotel ...

But we remained at the Hotel Adria, in that dank side street near the train station.

As for the paper, that classy paper with its limited circulation, there was no mention of it ever again.

... *ipse senator oves supposuise fuit. Sed pudor in stipula ... stipula* or *stipulam* ... Father always checked my Latin lesson. 'Let's hear that passage by heart! And if you'd be so kind and translate ...' And I would begin to recite, teetering on my chair between the sink and the table in that hotel room.

Ipse senator oves ... The senators themselves tended the sheep. In the old days, when the Romans hadn't yet gone soft.

I must have been fairly good at Latin. After all, I knew those senators by heart.

Well then? What happened?

Did someone make a rude comment? Did a classmate say something nasty to me? Or a teacher, in front of the whole class? Did Professor Pázmán send me home for some reason? Did he rub my nose in the fact that I lived in a hotel? No, it must have been some classmate who did that.

Or was it something else? But what?

... the senators tended the sheep themselves; there was a time when they cast aside all luxuries and tended the sheep ... *ipse senator oves* ...

12 March. Jancsika is sick.

What was wrong with me?

There is no entry on the next two pages, so it couldn't have been very important.

16 March. Chickenpox. Jancsika is taking it so well.

Was I really, Mother?

18 March. Again visited J. at the army barracks.

Where did you visit me, Mother? What barracks?!

The J. is always me: Jancsi, Jancsika. And I seem to recall the chickenpox. But those barracks! What barracks were those ... ?

Zsámboky sat cross-legged on the carpet. His hands kept turning that small black diary, Mother's diary for 1926.

We camped out in a succession of hotel rooms, Father and I.

Park Hotel, the Savoy, the Archduke Joseph, Hotel Adria. Bars of soap in soap-holders. Green, yellow, pink ovoid bars of soap. Towels on the rack by the sink. Blankets thrown over the bedspread, ever so casually. Hotel staff are experts at tossing a blanket ever so casually. The low soporific hum outside in the corridors. White curtains drawn tight. Mirrors in unexpected places.

That was at the Park and the Savoy.

At the Archduke Joseph, the bars of soap were missing.

And at the Adria, the worn brown blanket had cigarette burns, and fresh towels were seen only every other week. Bedbugs dropped from the ceiling like dive bombers.

The Park, the Savoy, the Archduke Joseph and the Adria . . .

And somewhere in-between, the barracks!

Oh yes, when they sent us packing from the Savoy, Father took our show to the Colonel's place. The Colonel's wife's place, to be precise.

Zsámboky stretched out on the carpet and studied the pattern of motifs.

The Colonel's wife happened to be an old flame of Father's. Gizu . . . Gizu something. 'Greatest gal I've ever run into, kiddo. Naturally, I ditched her.'

Yes, Father carried on a correspondence with this Gizu, they had quite a correspondence going.

The barracks . . .

He huddled with knees to chin in a trench on the parade ground. An endless flat expanse, the ground frozen solid. If he raised his head, he could see the obstacle course, and beyond that, the stables. But he hunkered down in that trench. His head felt heavy and there was a nasty buzz in his ears. A little while before, a girl had hopped over the trench, she even called out, 'C'mon, Jancsi! I'm waiting!' Then there was silence. He tried to get going, but it felt like forging his way through a tunnel. After a few steps, he plopped down again and held his head. Who knows how long he had been sitting like that, when he heard the music. The clear soft tone of a violin. He tried to raise his head.

Father was playing his violin in the middle of that vast empty expanse. Perched on the armrest of a chair, he wore a winter coat and a tasselled stocking cap. He lowered the violin and waved the bow toward the boy. Then he played on.

A tall brunette stood by the chair. She listened to the music, her head tilted to one side, chin tucked into the folds of her scarf.

Magda Tauszig!

Meaning, everything would be all right from now on. Magda Tauszig was here and Father was playing his violin. Soon he would clamber down from that chair, wave the bow, and they'd be off to Gyár Street. Just the three of them, returning to the flat on Gyár Street.

Zsámboky rose to his knees on the carpet.

Someone must have pulled me out of that trench, wrapped me up and taken me inside. But where? Whose room? What was that room at the Colonel's like? And anyway, how come the Colonel let Father and Tini and me just march in? How could he put up with that? Of course, his wife . . .

Gizu! Gizu Dunsics was her name!

Tini and Father hovered around my bed. Tini stayed awake several nights. The chickenpox brought a nasty itch but I was not allowed to touch it. 'Don't scratch, Jancsika! It'll mark you . . . for life.' Who said that? Mother, of course. When she placed chocolate bars and oranges on my blanket, Tini's nose started to twitch. 'Don't make a scene now!' said Father. 'No histrionics!' He was equally terse with Mother. 'Just leave the stuff you brought, and scram!'

But Mother refused to scram. Some days, she stayed late into the evening.

One time, all of them sat in the room next to mine: Father, Mother, Tini, the Colonel and his wife. Conversing in low tones, so as not to disturb the patient. The door was closed but some light filtered through the cracks. It was dark in the room, but I could plainly see Aunt Vali standing in the doorway to the hall. She seemed hesitant, like someone lost trying to decide which way to go. Should she join the others next door, or move toward my bed? She set out toward me, clad in that grim greyish-brown gown bedecked with enormous funereal buttons. As she came closer, I could see she was headless. She had no head. When she stood in the doorway I had not noticed this fact, but as she slowly moved closer and closer . . . Those buttons from top to bottom on her repulsive gown, and her head nowhere to be seen, all of a sudden here she was standing by my bed.

My eyes riveted on those buttons, I leapt up to shake her shoulder. I must have screamed, for Father and the others all rushed in. Only then did the buttons disappear.

At times, the Colonel's wife stopped by my bed and gave me a tentative smile. She seemed a bit intimidated by me . . . Just how long was this boy intending to remain in bed?

The girl I had seen hopping over the trench reappeared, too. She brought me books, and read them to me, sitting at my bedside. *In the garden, the bailiff shot himself in the head.* And she showed me the illustration. The bearded, balding bailiff stretched out in the garden.

Sometimes she ran past my window and lightly tapped the pane.

She wasn't the Colonel's daughter. But she lived there in the barracks. Upstairs, in the Captain's flat.

Zsámboky visualized the bookcase in her small room. The girl took down books and threw them on the rug three at a time. 'I've got all of Jules Verne! Have you read *Around the World in Eighty Days? Journey to the Centre of the Earth?*'

The Captain himself appeared. He stepped over the books lying on the floor, picked one up, and started to browse. And he stood there, reading.

The girl sprang to the piano stool.

Correction! The piano was at the Colonel's. In the same room as my sickbed. From time to time, Father would drag Gizu Dunsics to the piano. That's right, he'd practically have to drag her.

'Chopin! Give us a little Chopin!' Father's eyes swept around the room. 'No one can play Chopin like Gizu!'

And Gizu performed on the piano.

The rest of the household sat and listened. The Colonel, too, must have been there. Surely he would have wanted to hear his wife play. But what if he actually hated her playing? And anyway, wasn't he getting sick and tired of communal life with Father?

Gizu played the piano.

Suddenly, Father stood up, stepped over to the piano and started to sing. A Polish revolutionary song. 'Ostrolenka's bloody star'... Gizu banged away at the piano and Father, turning red in the face, sang.

No, Father did not sing. Certainly not that kind of song. At the hotel, he might have sung occasional snatches of music-hall songs. Walking on the street, at times he hummed melodies.

So where on earth did I dream up this Ostrolenka bit? And why do I keep seeing Father standing by the piano? With fiery face, palm of one hand pressed against his temple, as if he himself were a wounded revolutionary hero. Ostrolenka's bloody star, indeed ...

Sometimes the girl, too, sat down at the piano. The Captain's daughter. She played the piano lots of times while I still had the chickenpox.

She also brought me cartridge cases. Empty cartridge cases. We had started to collect those before I got sick.

There were targets scattered all over the firing range. We would show up and scour the field.

One time, we caught a glimpse of Dr Sándor Lux out there. His overcoat unbuttoned, he was striding down the firing range, among the targets. He must have been looking for Olga. I think he wanted to talk to Olga, but in the end he did not come in.

One evening it was just the two of them out there: Father and Olga. The moonlight flooded the empty range. They walked arm in arm among the targets, stopping from time to time, and Father would point at the moon. I had never seen them strolling so peacefully. As a rule, shadows of dark arguments trailed them. I had seen Tini lash into Father only to receive a couple of prompt slaps in the face. But now they really seemed made for each other. Father bent down and caressed Tini's face. Then they walked on. They didn't notice me.

I was waiting for that girl. We had arranged to meet there, but she stood me up.

She and I spent much time loitering together. We watched the recruits wrestling, shirtsleeves rolled up, caps on their heads.

The recruits had two brass buttons on their caps.

The officers wore tall black shakos.

'But they're not all alike on the inside!' she explained. 'Some are lined with white silk, others lilac . . . daddy's is green, light green.'

The piano was covered with a purple shroud. That's what I stared at, lying in bed.

How long was I confined to bed? How long did this whole affair last?

Zsámboky again sat cross-legged, arms around his knees.

And what was that girl's name? She ran past my window one last time and waved to me. A lanky boy with glasses and a student cap was running after her. They raced around right in front of the window.

At last the bed was made and covered, just like the piano. Mother stood in the room.

'So Ilonka dear, the child's going back with you now?' The Colonel's wife eyed me with that timid smile again.

'Oh yes,' Mother nodded. 'Aunt Vali said it would be all right if he spent Easter with me.'

We stayed for Easter Mass at the barracks.

The organ boomed and a sea of helmets surrounded the chapel. Helmets and flags.

'God bless, Ilonka dear!' From somewhere in the sea of helmets, the Colonel's wife raised her hand in farewell. 'Goodbye, Jancsi! Stay healthy now!'

There you stood, Father, near the Colonel's wife. You had dumped Tini somewhere, and there you stood, waving your hand among the crowd of officers and their wives.

'Going to stay with Mom for a while, kiddo?'

Zsámboky picked up the folder again. Let's take another peek at those letters! There should be some from Gizu Dunsics.

A flattened cigarette package. Symphonias. But Father smoked mostly cigars. Perhaps this was meant for someone else. Someone to whom he gave not just two or three loose cigarettes, but a whole pack. He must have handed it over with such a grand flourish! And there's something scrawled on it. A message or something. *Gyula, my crazy little darling! I love you so much!*

What's this, Father? Did you take her to the cinema? Get on a tram with her, and ride to the end of the line and back? You always loved that sort of thing. Travel, oh yes, travel! You took the bread-girl at the Cafe Abbazia on a jaunt over half the continent. But for this new flame, all you could afford was a pack of cigarettes, and a ride on the bus or the tram. *Gyula, my crazy little darling!*

Magda Richter.

Zsámboky put down the folder.

That was the name of the girl in the barracks! Magda Richter, Captain Richter's daughter. Gizu would say, 'That Richter girl is here for you again!'

She liked to drop in. Race downstairs and drop in at the Colonel's flat. The fact that I was being given a bath did not bother her. I received a thorough scrubbing in a huge tin washbasin. They set the washbasin in the middle of the kitchen, and plopped me down in it. But why in the kitchen? Wasn't there a bathroom? Or could it be they didn't want me to . . . Could it be they didn't want me using their bathroom?! So Tini plopped me in the wash-tub. Father appeared briefly, to smoke his cigar, browse through the paper, wave at me. Then he was gone. And suddenly there was Magda, standing in the doorway. Tini was in the process of vigorously scrubbing my neck. 'Wash behind his ears! Make sure you wash behind his ears!' Tini did not send her away. (Far be it from her to dare order anyone about in those barracks!) I splashed water at Magda, and drenched Tini too. The whole kitchen was flooded. Gizu finally put an end to it. 'Haven't you had enough?' Magda squeezed the sponge in my face and ran off.

I didn't see her at the chapel. When Mother and I said our goodbyes, Magda wasn't there. Plenty of officers, wives, boys with school caps and girls wearing sailor blouses, white stockings and black patent-leather shoes . . . but no Magda. I wanted to run upstairs to their flat, but there was no time.

But Magda Richter had to be there in the chapel. She wouldn't have missed Easter service. She just didn't want to see me again. Did we have a fight? Something must have happened . . .

Officers' shakos, turned upside down. The insides lined in red, green and lilac satin. Captain Richter's was light green. We bent close to gaze at his shako in the hall. 'Put it on!' Magda whispered. 'Why don't you put it on? Are you afraid to do it?'

The greatcoat and the sword hung on the coat rack. The upended shako, gloves tucked inside, sat in front of the mirror. I touched the visor. Then it felt as if the hall had turned upside down. I could still hear Magda's laughter, then a door slamming. My face remained suspended there in the mirror. My two fingers held the visor while I stared at myself. I was simply unable to move. Someone grabbed my shoulder. 'It's not enough that you hang out here every day . . .'

He could still hear that voice. 'You hang out here every day . . .'

The Englishman!

And again *Englishman among savages!*

Solitary soul's orphaned dream, Memory,

Denizen of a vanished village,

I am bound for the d'Este court . . .

Material for that volume of poems.

An invitation card for the Hanukah evening programme at the Buda Jewish Home for the Aged and Orphans. It gives us great pleasure to invite you . . . But what is this Hanukah? And what kind of Hanukah evening programme? Benefit for the aged and orphans . . .

János stood in a room, tugging at his scarf, staring out the window at the pouring rain. He could hear Father's voice from somewhere in the depths of the room.

'Listen to me, kiddo! Just listen to me for a change.'

The iron railing of the balcony shone black in the rain. An eiderdown comforter stirred in the window across the courtyard.

'First you go to Katona József Street, then you drop off a package in Zugló.'

The light was on in the room. Father stood in hat and coat, getting ready to go out. The blanket had slid off the unmade bed. On the tabletop, a drawing board, littered with breadcrumbs and bacon rind.

'Try to keep the addresses straight.' Father handed him the small packages. 'Now go! For God's sake, son, are you awake?'

János mumbled something and slipped the packages into a pocket.

Out on the street, he heard the roar of an aeroplane flying very low. Torn tram rails, cobblestones in heaps, tiny glittering slivers of glass. On the pavement lay a chess piece. The black queen.

He entered a room where the shattered blinds hung loose. A balding man sat in a chair, a huge red carbuncle on his neck. A woman was affixing a Band-Aid on it. 'Why must I always see this thing on your neck? It's way past being just a pimple! Would you like a cup of tea?' she said, turning to János.

János placed the bundle of documents on the table, and went on his way.

Lajos Kossuth was seated at a kitchen table. János stood in the kitchen, fumbling with the strings around a folder. Lajos Kossuth sat in front of him, in an armchair. White beard, braided pelisse. Yellowed hand resting on the lap-rug. Meanwhile the string refused to be undone.

'May I help?' a woman asked.

János was almost certain he was at the wrong address.

'Who sent you?' came the question from the armchair.

'Father, the things you ask!' The woman reached over János' shoulder and undid the string. Now it hung from his finger. János swung it back and forth.

The rain blurred the buildings. János went on his way, staring at the soaking wet string on his finger. From time to time, he flapped his wrist as if he had a yo-yo. Where else was he supposed to go? Who else did he have to see? What was that address? He dipped his finger, then abruptly jerked it up again. The string was gone.

A candle flickered below the marble memorial plaque. A shy, awkward flame cowering in the draughty vestibule.

He stood in the entranceway of the building on Gyár Street, gazing up at the memorial plaque.

Erected in Memory
of those taken to their death from this building
between 7 and 17 Jan. 1945:

Ervin Bokros	*Béla Löbl*
Béla Frank	*Vera Nádas*
Magda Friedmann	*Zoltán Nádas*
István Hajdú	*Mrs István Hajdú*
Géza Lengyel	*Géza Lengyel, Jr*

A crate was being nailed down in the courtyard. The sound of hammering resounded throughout the building.

He heard steps in the lobby. Someone stopped behind János.

'Did you know any of them?'

He did not reply. He kept re-reading the list of names.

'Did you know any of these people?'

After that, silence. He was left alone with the plaque. With those names arranged in two columns. The building's tenants.

And now it's the Radical Party again!

'Budapest, 4 October 1945

To the Honourable Members of the Central Election Committee, Budapest:

We hereby appoint Messrs. Artur Stein and Gyula Zsámboky to represent the interests of our Party.

With democratic respect, the Hungarian Radical Party.'

Illegible signature.

So, the Radical Party appointed you ... to represent the Party's interests.

In 1918, you had stood in the pouring rain under the balcony of the Hotel Astoria. Count Károlyi was making a speech. Later you wanted to go up and talk to him, but a marine blocked your way. An armed marine guard accosted you in the corridor. What did you say to him? Did you just wave your hand and turn to go?

Yet you as a young journalist were there on that ferry. They were firing at the ferry from the opposite shore, but the journalist Gyula Zsámboky stood his ground by the side of Count Károlyi and Professor Oscar Jászi.

And now you had Artur Stein.

I hope you showed moderation when you hit on Mr Artur Stein, and refrained from borrowing his jacket, shirt and tie . . . to represent the Party in a suitable outfit. ('You know, my dear Artur, in this country, the first impression is all that matters!')

Yes, Father, you certainly knew how to make a first impression!

That white scarf of yours! Where did you acquire it? I never got to wear anything like that. As for you—you hadn't purchased a thing in at least thirty years. So, where did it come from? You wore it even in the hospital. You had a wonderful way of winding it around your neck, such casual elegance. Anyway, I brought it home from the hospital. I tossed it in the hall closet. Why there, of all places? I must have wanted it out of my hands in a hurry. I wanted to be free of all of those things of yours I brought back from the hospital.

But I repossessed your dark-blue winter coat—you know, the one you wore so proudly. I brought it back from the hospital and wear it to this day.

You didn't have too many things at the hospital. I left your suit there, and your grey sweater. And your shoes too. I hope you're not angry with me. They got soaked and caked with creamed spinach during your hospital stay.

The items I carried in there on *that last occasion* were few. A single pair of pyjamas. I had the janitor's wife iron them. During that last period, you had her do all your ironing and you even sat in their flat, watching TV. She folded an embroidered handkerchief and slipped it into the breast pocket. I hope the mortuary assistant left it there. He didn't take me in to see you lying there. And I didn't ask him to.

I've been meaning to ask you . . . Father, how come you gave up so suddenly?

We were sipping espresso in the hospital cafeteria. 'Well, kiddo, we should stop in at the Museum of Fine Arts next week. Tell me, don't you ever go to a museum?' Nothing to it, I thought, here we go, the two of us strolling through the museums now.

Then suddenly you took to your bed. That hospital bed was one cavernous hole, ideal for swallowing a person. 'Lemons!' you howled from that dark hole. You kept asking for lemonade, always for lemonade. But those last few lemons I brought were never made into lemonade for you.

Father, what if I had been the first one to go? The first one to check out of here. Not by getting married—you would have followed me. You would have followed me anywhere. There was only one way out.

It would have been fun to see how you handle it.

First, you would have collected the last few payments owed for my writings. Then, maybe organize a memorial reading. *My poor son, such a promising start.* A modest audience, an awfully modest little crowd. As for a repeat performance, forget about that! A new edition of my works? Nothing doing! And abroad? Royalties from abroad? Fat chance. Better not count on any. So what would be left then? What, indeed.

Anyway, you were the one to go first.

Do you know that Olga Lux hasn't the slightest inkling of what happened?

The last time we saw her was on that corridor. You and I were seated on a long wooden bench. You weren't up to going out in the garden. 'We'll be just fine sitting right here, kiddo!' You practically shrank into that hospital robe. Not that you were the least bit demoralized. You were reminiscing about a cabaret singer who was your roommate back in college. Suddenly you switched to the subject of advertisements—the ideas, the imagination that went into those ads! Take that silver-haired old gentleman for instance, he won your eternal admiration. The one sipping brandy in a capacious armchair. It is evening, the moon shines through the open window. He sits dozing in that armchair, all comfy. The newspaper has slipped from his hand to the floor. 'You know, whenever I feel especially lousy, I just think of my old friend in the brandy ad.'

That's when Olga Lux appeared in the corridor, in the company of several doctors and nurses. She wore a nurse's cap. Her eyelids drooped like she hadn't looked up in a long time. And she was so fat, morosely fat, as if she'd put on all that weight out of sheer depression.

You barely paused in your narrative to greet her.

'Hello there!'

'Hello, Gyula!' And she moved on with her little group.

So she had become a nurse. At last she'd found a secure situation. Wasn't that what she always wanted? I don't think she ever married again. She'd lost her appetite for that.

Perhaps one day she'll drop in for a visit. She'll somehow track down my address and ring the doorbell. 'Hello, Jancsika! Is your father at home?'

She'll look around in the kitchen. Next thing, she'll be in a nightgown, making coffee.

She might even move in with me . . . Why not? My stepmother. *Call her Tini. She'll take care of you.*

That's when Zsámboky came across the letter. Two pages, in pencil on white paper.

My Dear Gizkó!

Well now, so it's Gizkó! What a chummy tone. After all, this friendship went all the way back to childhood. What did she call you? Gyuszi? My little Gyuszi? Still, she deserved better than a pencilled note. But this was probably intended to be a first draft. To be rewritten in its entirety. Details like that always mattered to you.

'You can't just whip up a letter like that! You kids nowadays haven't the foggiest notion of what a letter is.'

. . . I sit alone at a table like someone taking shelter from the storm. People are walking and talking around me, the sounds of an alien world where nothing is intimate and cosy and warm.

Could we stop for a moment?

The table you mention is probably this very table. It was Mother who gave you shelter from the storm, after she'd found that miserable little job and was able to rent a flat at last. I had been living with her for some years. And you—well, you had outstayed your welcome everywhere else. I must say, Mother wasn't too eager to take you in, she didn't exactly jump at the idea. But you didn't care. You needed a place to stay and here you stayed.

I am fully alive only in my memories, the idyll of childhood floods over me whenever I think of You, and these memories will never lose their roots or flowers . . . The others around me . . . it's best not to talk about them! Wherever I turn, I meet deaf ears, although once they seemed to possess heart and soul.

True, Father, we didn't talk much during those last years. And when we did talk, there was not much joy in it. You put down my stories, and I ignored your poems.

You and I are able to open the floodgates and commune, banishing all those intervening decades, just as if we were sitting here face to face.

You certainly opened up your floodgates!

Shadows hover around me, they come and go, and talk to me at times, but only from a distance. They live in some other life of their own, the mother and her son. I am not complaining, I can't complain, after all, occasionally they even invite me to the dinner table.

The dinner table!

As for talking to me . . . My son seems to have forgotten those years spent with me, where was his mother then? She would condescend to show up on Sundays. But why stir up the past? What else could I expect from Ilonka—all she ever cared about was success (that is, what she, poor thing, imagines to be success) and now, believe me, Gizkó, when she sees her son's name in print, it's as if she'd never come bursting into that hotel room. 'Gyula, what's to become of your son? I hope you're aware that he stopped attending school? That he doesn't plan to graduate?' That's all she kept moaning about, that I should talk to Jancsi about his schooling. Which was not such an easy matter, for the last thing Jancsi wanted to discuss was going to school. Whenever his mother came, he simply disappeared. The kid had a fantastic sixth sense, somehow he could scent approaching danger, and he took off, for the park or the street. I can still see the scene when Ilonka showed up accompanied by her Aunt Vali. They had decided to take the boy away from me because I was not providing him with the right environment, they threatened to place him in some kind of institution, they claimed they had the means to do it,

Zsámboky stood up, letter in hand.

perhaps some kind of reform or correctional school—at any rate, that sort of place

What kind of place? What kind of institution?!

He read it again and again.

reform or correctional school

No, Father, that can't be right. Mother would never have done that! You know very well Mother would never have done that! All right, she wasn't overjoyed when I left school, but . . .

The telephone started to ring: an angry, annoying ruckus.

Zsámboky made a move toward the small table.

He stood by the telephone without picking up the receiver. The phone rang resentfully, then abruptly gave up.

He turned back to face the room.

Emptied drawers, scattered letters, notebooks, diaries. The folder on the table.

He slipped the letter among the poems and other papers, and attempted to tie the ribbon around the folder.

All right, so maybe Aunt Vali came up with some such notion, in case I didn't take my exams, in case I failed to comply . . . Maybe she suggested something like that to Mother, perhaps she bullied her, but Mother would never have sent me to reform school or anything like that . . . To an institution. A correctional institution.

The ribbon came undone, and the papers slid out.

He did not attempt to bundle them up again. He merely contemplated the heap on the table-top.

Father, you made this up! You made this all up!

THE SWEET SMELL OF SUCCESS (1972)

He stopped in the doorway. As he was leaving, hat and coat on, he stopped to look back at the flat. Those two rooms opening into each other.

He went over to a chair and grasped its back. Next he pulled the blinds down a bit, and straightened the tablecloth. He looked out of the window at the snow-covered park. He walked past the sofa. Paused for a moment. The stillness and silence of the rooms. He liked this silence. He liked to linger like this in the empty flat.

In the lavatory, he pulled the flush chain. In the bathroom, he inspected the cakes of soap. He sat on the edge of the bathtub. Took off his hat. Were he a smoker, this is when he would light up a cigar. If he smoked. Father smoked cigars. Some pretty crummy brands: Fájintos, Cigarillos. Near the end he smoked cigarettes, but he seemed ashamed of them. Mother smoked cigarettes until she gave them up. She learned to give up many things.

And me? Never smoked in my life.

He strolled back and forth in the hallway, as if out on an esplanade. He stopped in front of the mirror.

Come to think of it, have I ever done anything in my life?

He turned on all the lights. In both rooms, and in the bathroom and kitchen. He fiddled with a lemon on the kitchen table. A hard, tough old lemon.

Time to go.

He turned off the lights. Darkness invaded the flat. He lingered by the bedroom window, looking out at the park.

Time to meet your public.

The slip of paper in his pocket. The invitation from the cultural centre. A panel discussion on a film, a certain film. As it turned out, the leading actress had another commitment and the director was abroad. 'I hope you'll be able come!' He could envision the girl from the centre, pleading. 'Please don't let us down.'

He turned around, and addressed the dining room.

'A panel discussion about my film.' He paused. 'Father, I told you I wrote a film script.'

He waited another moment or two in front of the dining-room door. He was ready to go at last. He locked up the flat. But he paused once more, outside the glass pane of the front door. He peered back into the dark hall. Just like a visitor about to ring the bell. Then he pocketed the key and galloped downstairs.

The flat was left to itself. That brown dining table littered with empty ashtrays. Around it, the chairs. In the other room, an emaciated sofa. Next to it, the armchair. A dark imprint on the worn upholstered back. The outlines of a head. In fact, just like someone leaning back to enjoy the dark and the quiet.

After he got off the bus, he walked past gardens. Tiny little backyards all snowed in. In one of them, a washbasin half-buried in snow. Blinds and curtains drawn everywhere.

A glum, grey building on the corner. As if it had been dragged out of storage for the occasion. Long, deserted corridors behind dim glass partitions. Two boys in sneakers running down the stairs. When they spotted Zsámboky, they scurried back up and disappeared on the second floor.

'Won't you come in?' The slim, dark-haired girl opened the glass door. One of her shoulders drooped, as if pushed. She smiled a rather hesitant smile.

The two of them stood in the corridor. From upstairs came thuds, as if people were jumping off footstools. A piano struck up.

'That's the ballet class,' said the girl.

A small office, with bookshelves. In the corner, a table with coffeemaker and cups. She took out a bottle and glasses from one of the cabinets.

'A drop of cognac, you're probably chilled. I always get chilled to the bone.'

Then, while the coffee was brewing:

'Wouldn't you like a poster? To take home?'

'What kind of poster?'

'For the panel discussion.' She tossed a rolled up sheet on the table. 'We won't have much of a crowd.'

'Klári Ritter!' Zsámboky pointed at one of the names. 'Didn't you tell me she had another engagement?'

'When the poster was printed we didn't know that. Or that your director was going to be away.'

'My director!' Zsámboky guffawed.

The girl peered out into the corridor.

'We'll wait a linger longer.'

They had another cognac. Zsámboky eyed a page from a notebook on the desktop. He began reading it in an undertone.

'Julie was quite surprised that the city gentlemen supported her and did not let her go . . .'

'I'm supposed to translate that into German .' Again the girl peered out into the corridor.

' . . . like a plucked crow, to fly away if she could.' He looked up from the sheet at the girl. 'Should we wait longer?'

2

They were there, both of them. Mother lying on the sofa, under a grey-green blanket. Father, wearing a high-crown hat, sitting in the armchair by the door. His long white hands in his lap. Massaging his fingers with slow deliberation.

'You might as well take off your hat.' Mother's voice came from under the blanket.

'I won't, because of my hair.'

'Your hair? Why, what kind of hairdo are you sporting now?'

Father did not bother to reply. He surveyed the room. 'Running around, he's always running around.'

'János gets many invitations. Readings, talks . . . He was even asked to go abroad.'

'He was not invited abroad.' Father gestured. 'He'd like to be, but he hasn't been.'

'What about that group in Vienna?'

'Well, that was some kind of relief action. Knitted vests and scarves and that sort of thing.'

'What are you talking about?' Mother raised herself a bit.

'Well, if not exactly scarves, at any rate . . .' Father stood up, as if he were about to depart on a journey. 'Books, let's say, it was books they sent him, all kinds of works on philosophy. Philosophy books in German.'

'Why shouldn't they?'

Father was still standing by the chair. 'Well, for one thing, he never bothered to learn German. Or any foreign language, for that matter. And when have you seen him reading a book on philosophy?' He set out slowly, along the chair, staying close to the furniture. 'How many times have I begged him to read Bölsche at least!'

'Well, at least he made something of his life!'

Father turned back toward her. 'Yes, tell me about it!'

Mother fell silent. She huddled under the blanket and said nothing.

Father stood with a far-off look. As if gazing back at her from some distant region. He shrugged and moved on. Suddenly he stopped.

'And what about this, Ilonka?'

Mother's head emerged from under the blanket. 'About what?'

'This TV!' Father was circling around the TV set. 'Any way you shake it, this here is a television set. A TV.'

Mother, wrapped in her blanket, sat up. 'And why not?'

'But he never wanted to have this thing.' He extended his arm toward the set. 'He never even thought of owning one.'

'How do you know that?'

'He was perfectly happy with that little radio you bought for him. But television . . . TV . . .' He looked out at the park. He held the edge of the curtain. 'This must have been that woman's idea.'

'What woman?'

'That schoolteacher he's been seeing lately.'

'The girl before that was a teacher, too.'

'No, that girl worked in a cafe.'

'It wasn't anything very serious.'

'It was plenty serious. But she left him. She ditched our Jancsi.'

'She did not!'

Father moved away from the window. He entered the bedroom. 'At any rate, they chucked out your little radio. And they chucked out that big old bed.'

'My son was never interested in those little floozies.'

'Only little floozies ever interested him. Waitresses, nurses, tram conductors.'

'Tram conductors!'

'Well, at least the easy chair's still here.' Father grasped the old, cracked armrest. He lowered himself into the chair. 'Fortunately, we still have this.'

3

The girl cast an anxious glance back at Zsámboky. 'Well, we might as well go and take a look.'

Zsámboky felt as if he had been standing behind her like this for ages. That's how familiar the fine dark down on the nape of her neck seemed to him. It would take only a small movement of his hand to glide there.

They were in the corridor again. Standing very close, almost touching. The piano had stopped playing by now. The street was dark outside behind the large glass door.

'And this time we made sure the posters got sent out well in advance.' She was whispering, as if afraid she might wake someone.

A lit-up buffet counter loomed in the depths of the corridor. A stocky, grey-haired man eating a salami sandwich waved at the girl. 'What's happening, Magda? Has Rakonczai arrived?'

'Not yet.'

The man with the sandwich turned away.

'Who's this Rakonczai?' Zsámboky asked the girl.

She was staring at a pillar. Her shoulder trembled.

Was she crying? Perhaps it would be best to leave. Just turn around and split. But he stayed, standing by her side. Then unexpectedly he found himself blurting out:

'Tell me, do you always fall asleep on the bus?'

'Pardon me?'

'That's what you said in there, that you always fall asleep on the bus. You never know how you got here.'

She was still regarding him with the same frozen expression, the face of a stranger. Very softly, almost syllable by syllable, she said:

'We had to cancel Anikó Láncos' performance too. What can I do? There's simply no interest, people just don't come.'

'And the hall?'

'What hall?'

'Well, where this . . . event was going to be . . .' He fell silent.

They were standing among grey-black pillars, as if in some waiting room, surrounded by silence. Kids wearing gym outfits appeared on the stairs, then scattered like so many matchsticks.

'The ballet class,' Zsámboky said.

The girl nodded.

Zsámboky moved a little closer to her. 'You also said that your shoe once got stuck in the asphalt. It was so hot your shoe got stuck.' Since she still didn't say anything, he added: 'You arrived barefoot, your shoes in your hands.'

The girl flashed him an alarmed smile. 'Let's go. Maybe someone showed up, after all.'

They moved on.

'Once a little old lady fell asleep in the rest room,' she remarked on the way. 'We found her the next morning.'

'So people do come here every once in a while.'

'Well, mostly to be someplace warm. And oh yes, when Béla Szente was here.'

'Béla Szente?'

'The pop singer. Don't you know him? He could barely get in here. His car was mobbed. I had to call the police.'

'Well, not tonight.'

Flags in a corner. Rolled-up flags. Dusty windowpanes, blackened walls.

'Well, then . . .' The girl paused in front of a door.

Zsámboky ventured a vague smile.

She turned a doorknob. It did not give.

'Seems to be locked. Should I look for the key?'

'Nah, what for?'

She was still holding the doorknob.

'Would you like to see our cinema?'

4

'Nowadays he makes very good money.' Father stood by the TV again.

'Yes, they value his work,' mother said.

'These days they value lots of things. But buying a TV! What's next, a car? That's all we need.'

'Why shouldn't he have a car?'

'He'll turn into an idiot, he's turning into a total idiot.'

'Oh, you're such a sad sack!' Mother's angry, resentful voice. 'Just because you never . . .'

'Oh, what do you know about that!' Father took a step, his hand sliding along the wall. 'For this, I'd read him Andersen's Tales . . .'

'And you spent the tuition money I'd scrimped from my last pennies.'

'For this, I lugged around his scribblings, his STORIES! Nobody wanted them but at last I flogged them . . .'

'You always took whatever money they paid him.'

'Yes, he can thank me for launching him.' He stopped. 'And here's your photo, in a straw hat, seated on a bed of spinach. '

'That's no spinach! It's that garden, the Valkays' garden.'

'Yes, I know, where Gábor Valkay painted your portrait. A no-talent dauber.'

'Oh Gábor had his one-man show . . . and then he kicked you out when you tried to pump him.'

Father's fingers skating over the wall. 'Not one picture remained here, I don't see my etchings. General Görgey's flown the coop. I can see someone didn't like them.'

'Those weren't even etchings! You cut them out of magazines. And you collaged them. You collaged and decoupaged them.'

'Well they beat this spinach bed any time.'

He sat on the sofa's edge.

'He'll end up with stacks of spoons.'

'Gyula, can you tell me what are you talking about?'

'Silver spoons. He'll have lots of them. From one drawer to another, he'll move them from one drawer to another. Silver spoons and knives and forks. He'll dump them on the table and gloat.'

'You don't know what you're talking about!'

'I don't know?!' Short pause. 'He gave me only twenty a week. And by then he was pulling in good money. OK, later he gave me a small raise.'

'That was a mistake!'

'Those days he'd go to the Deepwater, the writers' restaurant . . . To strut among the other pompous asses. And I'd sit in the balcony with my cup of rice pudding.'

'That was charged to his tab.'

'Oh I had a great view from up there, saw what he ordered. He'd always start with consommé. Then the rest of the meal. Followed by a glass of wine and coffee. And then, when I was in hospital . . .'

'Oh, stop it with that hospital!' Mother sat up, the blanket slipping from her shoulder. 'Enough about your hospital!'

'Why? He visited you when you were in.'

'Gyula, stop it!'

'Nonsense!' Father pulled the blanket over Mother's shoulder. 'It's all nonsense!'

They sat in silence by each other's side on the sofa.

5

'He would always drag me to the races!'

They sat in the small projection room. Empty rows of seats under the screen. They roamed from row to row as if looking for some place to sit.

Zsámboky in the first row staring at the screen. Sat down a moment, then stood again. Somewhere behind him the girl slammed one seat after another. Ranting about some guy, for who knows how long now.

'Never a concert or a theatre! Always those motorcycle races that I couldn't stand!'

'As I can well imagine.'

'And anyway I never saw the races. I could never see from all the dust.'

Zsámboky took a left turn. Smack into a new row. Accidentally bumped into the girl. They smiled slightly tired smiles.

'And your film was shown abroad?' she asked.

'Yes, I think so.'

'And the reception?'

'Reception? Did I hear you say reception?'

She sat down. Her face scrunched inward. 'No, I wasn't going to stay with that biker guy.'

Zsámboky too sat down. They sat in silence for a while, waiting for the show to begin.

'I had to eat dust! Those bikes zoomed by, I couldn't see a thing, other than the dust all over, my eyes, my hair, my nose.'

She sprang up, and paced in front of the canvas yelling to Zsámboky.

'First thing in the morning, hop on that bike!'

'Did he race? . . .'

'Hardly! Well before the start we'd scoot through the course to find a place with the best view. According to him! At last we find a hillside. Where we wait until ten, it was at least ten! when there was a faint buzz in the distance and the race'd began. I sat there hanging on to a bush, then every half hour there was a monstrous uproar. Unbelievable dust clouds.'

'As those bikes zoomed by.'

'Exactly. As they zoomed by. Days later I was still shaking off dust.' She stopped and squinted up at the canvas. 'Otherwise he wasn't such a bad guy. And from a certain angle . . .'

Zsámboky, showing interest, leant forward.

The girl sat down in a row with her back to him.

'My girlfriend knows you.'

'Oh really? And who is that?'

The girl did not reply. She dropped her head back and stretched a leg all the way forward.

'Then I dumped him.'

'The biker guy?'

'The biker guy.'

The girl held her pose, head dropped back, leg stretched out.

6

The sound of footsteps. Coughing, throat clearing. The steps stop, right in front of the door.

Father: 'Now he'll ring the bell.'

Mother: 'No he won't. It's Temunovich from the pharmacy. On his way to Mrs Gyergyai.'

Father: 'Ah yes! Although Mrs Gyergyai kicked him out once. Mrs Gyergyai prefers conductors of military bands. It's quite something, a military conductor ... Did you hear that sound? Like someone grinding a steel knife.'

Mother: 'That's Mrs Somogyi's mother.'

Father: 'Ah yes, she always puts a piece of paper on the handrail when she glides by. But she doesn't go out much any more.'

Mother: 'But you know sometimes he'd still ...'

Silence. Then she continues in a funny girlish voice:

'A fact, he never arrived empty-handed. If nothing else, he'd bring a bar of chocolate. He never stayed long because he was very busy but he always brought something.'

'So, what are you saying?' Father gave her a look. 'What are you trying to tell me?'

Mother, in that somewhat dreamy singsong: 'He stopped by every visiting day, although he couldn't stay long.'

'Oh yes, he'd drop by, "What's up, Dad?" And he was gone.'

'You can't really blame him. He had so much to do.'

'So much to do! ...'

Mother paid him no mind. She ignored that bitter chuckle. She just went on saying her say.

'A few times he even brought bananas, when you could hardly get them. Yes, bananas, oranges or chocolate. And he spoke with the doctors . . . the Professor himself.'

'I'd like to know where you are going with this.' Father stood up. He began his walk again.

'I can see you swept this place clean of all pictures, at least you could have left the Görgey.'

'He'd bring me my nightshirt and nightgown, and made sure my small pillow got aired properly. The hospital provided bed linen, except for the small pillowcase . . .'

Father stood by the window. Eyeing the snow and slush on the balcony.

'And how was it with you? Did they provide a small pillowcase?'

'Forgive me, Ilonka, but for some reason I am unable to recall.'

Mother suddenly rose from the sofa and stepped over to Father.

'Did he come in to look at you?'

'Look at me? When?'

They stood side by side. Mother almost nestling against to Father. 'They let him view me.'

'Good for you!' Father stepped away from the window. He advanced deeper into the room.

'When he came down there, into that small chamber in the basement, they let him view me.' She stepped back from the window and followed him. 'At first he did not want to look, but then he did.'

'That'll do, thank you! Don't you find this somewhat in bad taste?'

'My goodness Gyula, you're so refined all of a sudden!' Mother's sarcastic laugh. 'Suddenly you're so finicky!'

Father sat down in a chair, and fiddled with the brim of his hat. Mother stopped next to him.

'He made sure I was dressed properly . . . for the occasion.'

'For the occasion!'

'He brought me my dark-blue dress with the white lace collar, and a pair of black stockings.'

'You don't say! He really did?!'

'He also brought a small white batiste hankie but the attendant made him take it home.'

'That will be enough, thank you!'

'And what did he bring in for you?' She practically leant into Father's face.

With increasing annoyance he fiddled with the brim of the hat. 'This pair of pyjamas, if you really want to know! Because as it happened there was nothing else on hand that was clean. Nothing, not even a shirt! Only these pyjamas! For the occasion!' He choked up. And kept crumpling the hat.

Mother stood by his side. Not for the world would she have moved away.

'But at least they gave you a pair of socks? Gyula, tell me, at least a pair of socks? . . .'

7

Again in that small office.

The girl pushed an envelope toward Zsámboky. He shrugged. 'But I . . .'

'Doesn't matter,' she said. 'You showed up.'

'And since I did show up . . .' He pocketed the envelope.

A form had to be filled out. Name, address, etcetera. Meanwhile the room kept shrinking. Dark splotches spread on the ceiling, soon these would cover all walls.

'Well then . . .' Zsámboky looked at the girl. She'd probably get a reprimand because of the programme. The programme that never happened.

'I'm going too.' The girl took her coat from the rack.

They went out. The girl dropped off the keys at the reception desk. Then, outside on the pavement:

'I've had enough of this place. I'm going to quit . . .'

'You're going to quit?' Zsámboky turned to face the building. Dark rows of windows. A few lit-up rectangles among them.

'You don't think I'd stay here!'

They headed toward the bus stop. The girl put her hands in her pockets.

8

Her thin face and slightly pointy nose nestled behind her coat lapel and scarf. The large red scarf wrapped around her neck.

'They used to wear these back in the old days.' Zsámboky felt the edge of the scarf between his fingers. 'Back in the early Twenties, and even before that.'

'And I've got an offer somewhere, but it isn't certain yet.'

'Hard felt hats . . . they're also making a comeback.'

'I could end up at the film studios.'

'The film studios?' Letting go of the scarf, he eyed the girl with suspicion. As if this one comment had put her in a completely different light.

'As an assistant. A second assistant. I know, I'll have to run around and they'll stick me with everything, from props to the extras, but still . . .'

'And later?' Zsámboky's voice sounded almost irked. 'Where do you expect to be? I know someone who's been a second assistant for thirty years now and still runs around lugging dumb scripts and yelling at the extras. Even after thirty years!'

'I hope it won't take me thirty years.'

They stood in front of the bus. The dark and empty bus. Someone got on only to instantly vanish in the dark. Snow began to fall. Not really snow but a fine and gritty sleet. In a minute, it was all over their faces.

'One thing is sure, I won't remain here. It's either a riot so that I have to call the police, or else, nothing!' She was shouting now. 'I'm not staying here! Do you hear me?'

Zsámboky took her arm and helped her up into the bus.

Unexpectedly a dim light came on. It lit up someone's back and the empty driver's seat.

The girl unwound her scarf. 'And you, where are you heading?'

'How about we go get a cup of coffee.'

They sat in the waiting bus.

9

As he emerged from the lift he bumped into an elderly gentleman. A gaunt old man in a black coat, as if he'd been waiting for him all this time.

'You don't look at all like your father, except for something around the eyes.'

Zsámboky nodded, and sent the lift down.

'It's those letters.' The old man made as if he wanted to descend in the wake of the lift. 'I must have those letters returned to me.'

'What letters?' He had his keys in hand but did not unlock the door. The old man did not seem to expect to be invited in. He appeared to be willing to stand by the door. 'Your father and I carried on a serious correspondence. About Kossuth in exile! Both of us were in agreement that Kossuth in exile grew up to fit the role . . .'

'But my father . . .'

'He is missed very much by all of us. The Monday Group. You know, we used to meet every other Monday at the Cafe Simplon.'

He smiled at the memory. 'Pardon me, I mean the Simplichek! Your father always said: Let's go to the Simplichek! Forward march: to the Simplichek! Yes, your father radiated a certain glee ... a certain cheerfulness ...' He took a step toward the stairs, only to turn back. 'Things are stirring in the publishing world.'

'You don't say.'

'Word got around about my radical new take on Kossuth in exile. There's a possibility of publication.'

'Oh yes, I see.'

'And for that very reason I must have those letters.'

'Well, I'm not sure ...' He kept eyeing the old man, and slowly started to feel numb. He couldn't see himself unlocking the door. But neither did he want the old man to leave. 'I really don't know if Father ...'

'Oh, my old friend Gyula saved everything!'

'You think so?'

'Oh but of course! I'm sure we'll find them in a box or a drawer. With your permission I'd like to help, together we'll find them.'

'Together, of course.' The key slipped into the lock. The old man stood behind him.

'Gyula did not really like Kossuth. He valued him, but did not like him.' He started to scrape his feet on the doormat, practically jogging on it. 'I should have spoken at the ceremony.'

'Spoken?' The look he gave the old man said he'd after all rather shove him down the stairs.

'In the name of our Monday Group. But the state of my health ...' The foot-scrubbing left off. When the door opened, he asked:

'Was he cremated?'

'Yes, cremated.'

He let the old man go first, then entered.

THE ORIGINAL (1974)

Father said:

'All your life you'll be writing about me dragging my blanket around the room.'

He happened to be lying in bed when he said that. Hotel Adria, third floor, Room No. 47. He fiddled with his blanket, patting and slapping to adjust it. He was in fact dragging it around as he rolled over from one side to the other. As if he weren't even really lying in bed, but off on long, endless journeys with that blanket.

Meanwhile he managed to mumble something.

'Is that all you see in me!?'

In other words, just this spectacle. Father lying in bed. And his clothes, on a chair by the bed. The rumpled jacket, the trousers mud-spattered as ever.

Father speaks again, from somewhere. Perhaps from that hotel room, or from a dim corridor. From the depths of a dream.

'Just a minute, kiddo! I always took care to use the clothes brush on my trousers.'

No matter how I approach him, from whatever angle, he always interrupts and contradicts me.

It wasn't always like this. In that first, short novel I wrote, there was none of this animosity or anything of the sort. It was all about the hotel, the Hotel Adria. About Mr Newspaper Editor and his son. Mr Editor without a newspaper to edit. A freelance editor of sorts. Always hustling to place a report here, an article there, and that's not an easy matter. But when he manages to rustle up some funds, he takes his son to the cinema. That's all the son does, waits for his father in that hotel room. One thing alone can make him forget the waiting and silence and hunger, and that is the cinema. Father stands for the world of cinema.

Nothing wrong so far. The boy waiting for that charming, somewhat flaky figure.

'Flaky figure!' Father, shaking his head as he smokes a cigar. 'What are you trying to say? Yes, maybe I did hit up some people and yes, maybe I forgot to repay the loans. But what about the people who pumped me when I was still flush? You know very well how many people mooched off me.'

'Yes, Father, but your flakiness had something to do with that, too.'

He's not even listening. He stands somewhere by the window looking at the street.

'Don't you think the truly flaky types were the ones sitting in the editorial offices? Those pompous blockheads! But I had my own periodicals! I created them out of nothing! Why don't you write about my ventures?'

'They were somewhat shady.'

'All ventures are somewhat shady. I created children's magazines, weekly literary supplements. That's what ate up my money.'

'That money wasn't exactly yours.'

'What's the difference! All I wanted was some decent stuff written for children by real writers, none of that googly-eye stuff! Of course, you fail to see that, you always ignore the essentials!'

The essentials . . . Maybe I hadn't really portrayed him as an actual editor. I refused to cast the old man in some kind of heroic light. Even though strangers collared me on the street more than once.

'Never knew a finer editor than your father! I showed him my poems. After he read the whole sheaf, he told me, "Forget the poetry, my friend. You should write essays." Oh yes, he had a way of sizing up what you had inside you.'

For a brief period in his life he managed real estate. He had a whole block of businesses he never looked at—or so I imagined, knowing how reckless he was.

'Reckless? Your father reckless?'

The man wearing a cap with earflaps, wrapped in scarves, eyed me with shock. We had run into each other at a tram stop, and he recognized me.

'You are Gyula's son! I knew it right away!' (How many times had I bumped into people on the street who greeted me with 'Gyula's son! You must be Gyula's son!') And next thing, we're in an endless conversation about Father.

' . . . how can you say he was reckless? You could always find him at Mr Fein's, the optician's. And don't think he was there only because of the girls, Mr Fein's daughters! He'd give Mr Fein pointers about how to advertise and modernize his business. And not only Mr Fein, but the others as well. He'd come barging into a shop, "Wake up, people! You people are asleep!" That's how he'd always begin. "You people are asleep! While the whole world is passing you by! Are we in Europe?" The man with the ear-flaps paused for a moment to tug at his scarf. 'Maybe your father was a bit rash at times, but he was so full of life!'

Life, action . . . And such an organizer. Gave pointers to the optician. Kept an eye over that whole block of shops. But it all went down the drain. After that he was dead broke.

'You don't understand, kiddo!' Father's really irritated now. 'I was surrounded by people with no imagination! That was my only problem . . . But I had hopes for you, you had a promising start. But then . . . !'

Well, yes. The second round. The second round of the match against Father. That was somewhat rougher.

Mr Editor's halo had become a bit rusty. No more racing around to place newspaper articles. No more dashing off in search of some loan. The hotel era was over. In these later writings, we encounter a lonely elder gentleman. Too broke to stay in hotels, he relies on his son for shelter—the only one he can still count on. And this son happens to be a glum character. He doesn't like to recall the days when his father critiqued his first stories, remarking that there was no need to describe everything in such meticulous detail. Like it or not, it was his father who told him about elliptical depiction.

But now the old man has grown utterly useless. He's holed up in his room, nibbling cheese and shuffling scraps of paper. Scrawled lines of verse and random notes. Notes for some never-to-be-completed essay . . .

'Hold it one moment, kiddo! My essay on General Görgey was just about finished. Yes, the research took ages. As for my piece about Zoltan Ambrus, it was meant to shed light on the Budapest of his day. The city so young and full of talent. Yes, back then it still seemed that something was about to be born here.'

He pauses to catch his breath and resumes.

'And what do you mean I was holed up in a corner? I just wanted to pull myself together, that's all.'

'The old warrior taking a breather.'

'That wasn't very funny. One thing's sure: you didn't give me much time to recuperate. You could hardly wait to dump me in a hospital.'

Round Three. Father's illnesses, the hospital. After a half-hearted suicide attempt, the psychiatric ward.

'What do you mean, half-hearted suicide attempt?' Father lifts his head, fixing me with his penetrating gaze. 'I had intended to leap from the windowsill—no need to dwell on the reasons now—but pedestrians appeared below. Precisely such blockheads as yourself. Should I go splat right in their midst? So I climbed down and was on my way back to bed.'

'You know that wasn't what happened. You most certainly did not climb back down.'

'I saw the fear in your eyes. That's right, kiddo! That frightened and determined look. I knew what was coming. You rushed me off to the hospital in no time flat.'

'I had no choice.'

'Sure, sure. And you conveniently left me behind there. Like some piece of luggage.' (He has other similes: an old overcoat, a threadbare scarf . . .)

He keeps harping on this. That there was nothing wrong with him, I just forgot about him in that hospital.

And the things I write about him. That even in the hospital he mooched off others. Borrowed another patient's suit to go out for a stroll. (Yes, he still had a voyage or two in him. He did not give up that easily.)

'And is that all you can say?!'

He is standing in the hospital garden. Flailing his arms in outrage.

'You forget how hard I worked on Geza Aldor's family! I convinced them not to abandon Geza, not to leave him *in there*, get it, kiddo?! To take him back home, to not give up on him.'

He falls silent and just stares at me. I know what comes next. That I, on the other hand, gave up on him.

And what can I answer?

'It's too bad, Father, but that's how it went down. It can't be changed now, even if you won't ever accept it.'

And he will never accept it.

In my dreams, he still comes and goes, expostulates, protests. He lives his own life. Somehow, he gets wind of everything. Some old, netherworldly newspaperman must have told him that I got married after he died. In the corridor of dreams, he accosts me with a gentle reproach. 'You didn't even introduce me to your bride, kiddo . . .' And he still stubbornly insists that I arrange for him to return home. 'I'm fed up with prowling around.'

Any way you look at it, everything came from him. These streets and squares, doorways and courtyards, cafes, films, football fields and editorial-office corridors. Waiters and journalists congregated around him. Peddlers of razor blades, agents, gadabouts and gawkers. And women! All those women!

He dragged and tugged at a blanket as he rolled over in bed. And I wrote it all down. Was that how it really was? It makes no difference. That's how I remember it.

THE PEBBLE (1989)

How did it find me? Who slipped it into my hand? A coffee-brown pebble, shedding a few grains of sand. The instant I laid eyes on it, everything, everyone, faded away. I stared at it in my cupped palm. The Arabian. Came from the desert. Endless stretch of sand. Watched caravans go by. Saw so many things. Cities laid low ages ago. Hovels and palaces buried over time. Perhaps there was a girl who picked it up once, just to hold it in her hand and gaze at it. Yes, a girl, an old man and a man with a black beard. It passed from hand to hand. They spoke to it. It said nothing but understood everything. Forever on the move, a glimmer you could rely on. And not a trace of ostentation. Its slim shape and delicate lines. Reminded you of a fish. A petrified fish. But no! There was nothing quite like it in the whole world.

At home I placed it on the edge of a bookshelf, and turned to face the uproar. Father, Mother and Aunt Vali. Aunt Vali built like a block of flats. From time to time, she liked to *drop in* on us.

'Well, well! Look what he picked up this time!'

'Where did you find that thing?'

'Where indeed?! The street or the playground.'

'Take it down from there!'

'What is it, anyway?'

'Didn't you hear, take it down at once!'

The air was thick with insults. Real abuse! But none of this got to the pebble. What did they matter! When it had numbered princes among its friends. Princes who placed it on silken cushions. And bowed low and murmured prayers on certain days. They prayed and they sipped coffee. On *certain* days.

So I took the pebble to the staircase. Installed it most ceremoniously on a window ledge. I bowed my head and my fingertips gave it a light caress. A moment of contemplation. Then I inched backward. For a side view, sort of. And a final peek from the top of the stairs. I could come back any time and take it down. Hold it in my hand.

What if I ran all the way down to the ground floor? Would I still find it in place, waiting for me?

I started down the stairs, but kept looking over my shoulder. At the first turn, I raced back up. I wasn't going to leave that pebble alone in this dank old staircase!

So I took it down to the park.

Just the two of us on a bench, side by side. Watching the swings fly.

Girls soared toward me. And just as abruptly, they disappeared. Vanished into thin air. I heard their laughter in the distance.

I squinted at my Arabian. It was plainly bored. Terrifically bored. This place was such a drag. A dusty little park, nothing but ordinary pebbles.

But where could I take my pebble? What was there to see?

There was the Danube. Those piles and piles of pebbles by the Danube.

Pebble hills and pebble mountains.

Puddle-pebbles sunk in puddles.

Throwaway pebbles.

But what would any of this mean to a desert pebble? Nothing. Less than nothing.

I'll have to think of something. Tomorrow ... or the day after. Just be patient, pebble.

Waves of patience and wisdom emanated from the pebble. The wisdom of desert pebbles.

Darkness was falling when I headed home.

I paused in the staircase to press the pebble to my face. I dragged it along my cheek as slowly as possible.

'Is that you?'

It was Emmi, a few steps up. Emmi, the girl from the fourth floor, laughing noiselessly.

'What are you doing?'

I couldn't say a word.

Emmi moved closer. She took my hand, meaning to peel away my fingers one by one.

'What are you hiding? Show me!'

I still couldn't speak.

And she, with a wicked little laugh:

'A pebble!'

'No, it isn't!

'Oh yes it is!' She paused for a moment. 'You were kissing a pebble!'

'What are you talking about?!'

'You heard me!'

She let go of my hand. Still eying me, she repeated:

'You were kissing a pebble!'

She ran past me down the stairs. She paused on the landing to look back, then she was gone.

I pressed against the wall. Quickly and unobtrusively, I pocketed the Arabian. I never wanted to see it again. As if we had never met.

I unglued myself from the wall. Headed upstairs. I pulled out my Arabian and gave it another caress.

Accusing stares awaited me at the dinner table.

Father glanced at us and remarked casually:

'Did you two have a nice a walk? Maybe took in a film?'

Not very funny. In fact, downright below the belt. Especially as my Arabian now sat by a dinner plate. A white dinner plate, on the white tablecloth.

Mother heaved an unearthly sigh:

'Oh, my little Jancsi . . .'

Aunt Vali hoisted herself halfway up from her chair. Her double chin quaking, menacing.

'What's this "Oh, my little Jancsi" business? The child should be . . .'

A single gesture of Father's hand silenced the two women. He continued in a nasty, cutting voice:

'Pray, tell, will your friend be joining us for dinner?' (Turning toward the women.) 'Why not? It's quite all right. I'd just like to know what does he usually have for dinner? What's his favourite dish?'

He leant over the table.

'Of course, the question remains, will he find our company suitable. For such a . . . distinguished guest. That remains to be seen.'

Dinner company! An assembly of pebbles at dinner table. Pebbles with all kinds of holes and passages. Heads tilted, hollow eye sockets, twisted mouths, tiny, yet somehow terrifying teeth.

By now Father was practically cantilevered across the table.

'I'm sorry I didn't invite the right crowd for you. And now, may I ask you to . . . get out of my sight! And take this fine young man with you!'

Suddenly the room was a shambles. Chairs tumbled and plates crashed, as Father snatched off the tablecloth.

'Get lost!'

By then the two of us were in the other room.

I sat on the edge of the bed, the Arabian by my side. I did not bother to turn on the light.

A pale streak of light filtered through the crack under the door. And shouts. Recurrent sobs. Father's voice again:

'. . . I'm just as fed up with the two of you!'

Then silence.

Even the streak of light was gone.

I drew the Arabian closer.

'You've got to understand, Father isn't always like that . . . He takes me to the cinema a lot, we go to the Tivoli and the Turán . . . Films and football games. We have a team we follow, the Thirty-Threes. Not a very strong team, always on the point of being eliminated in the playoffs. I know, this doesn't mean much to you. The Thirty-Threes . . . playoffs . . . But never mind. I just wanted to say that . . .'

I was stuck. It felt as if I would never speak again.

I faced the pebble again. No, I couldn't claim it was *mine*. No, I'd never, ever . . . It was unthinkable.

But that brownish glimmer in the dark! Made you feel you were in the desert. The desert at night.

After torrid days, the nights are cold here. You really have to bundle up in your blankets.

Then the wind begins to blow. A sharp, ice-cold desert wind.

A GRAND OLD CAFE (1974)

'I'll be right back, kiddo . . .'

Father stood up. Using two fingers, he lightly propelled himself away from the edge of the table top. On the way out, he nodded at the waiter. He stopped at one of the tables to bend down and peer into someone's newspaper. He greeted a chubby customer. Waved in the direction of a wrinkled, oversized vest. The girl selling cigars accompanied him with her tray as far as the revolving door. She must have said something, for Father smiled and nodded. Ever so casually, he plucked up a cigar and disappeared.

He's off to see someone, the boy thought. Drop in somewhere. Check out some place.

The ruins of breakfast lay on the table. The full-course breakfast. Empty glasses on a tray, eggshells in the egg cup. Leftover bits of butter and jam.

The cigar girl passed by the table. She smiled at the boy. Sort of like at a package the father had left behind.

From the other tables they turned to stare at him. A greying matron gave him a rather disapproving glance. (No school today, sonny?) The old, hunchbacked newspaper vendor swept past.

'Would you like something to read?' The waiter looked down at the boy from somewhere on high. 'A sports section, with the football write-ups? Or a theatre magazine with pictures of actresses? Not very interesting stuff. Wait, I've got something for you.'

The leather-bound little book looked like it might have contained the wine list. A wine list that not every guest gets to see.

'Our Visitor's Book.' With a nonchalant gesture, the waiter flipped the cover open. 'Oh, a few lines, or just an autograph. You know, the people who've been here. You'll find some of the names familiar . . . Anyway, it's worth a look!'

Vilma Bánky.

That was the first name. Vilma Bánky! She's been here? Here, in this cafe? She'd walked down between this row of tables here. The waiters lined up for her. Waiters and customers. Then she sat down . . . perhaps at this very table. The waiter bowed and handed her this book. She was back home, visiting from America. By then her films were showing in all the cinemas. So she came home for a visit, and dropped in at this cafe. Next to her, another name. Rod La Rocque. Her husband. For she hadn't come alone, she'd brought her husband with her. Vilma Bánky and Rod La Rocque marched into this cafe, arm in arm.

Emil Jannings.

In one of his films, he played a doorman who'd been dismissed for some reason and now roamed the streets.

Names, names and names. Some were impossible to decipher. But Franz Lehár's was clearly legible. The date underneath. The day he was here. Father had known him back in the days when Lehár was the conductor of a military band.

The boy looked up.

He was surrounded by empty chairs. A newspaper tossed on a table. A jacket on the back of a chair. A rumpled jacket, sleeves dangling.

The boy stood up and went over to it. A blackened cigarette holder in a breast pocket. He took it out and put it back. Tram tickets dropped out of the pocket, and all sorts of paper slips.

He wanted to explore the cafe.

He went past the billiard table. White and green balls rolled slowly into a pocket. Slowly and without a sound.

He returned to the Visitors' Book, put it under his arm, and sat down at another table.

He looked for Vilma Bánky's name without success. Yet it had been right there at the top of the first page. The very first name. Now it was replaced by all these illegible scrawls. As if in the meantime someone had defaced the book.

Franz Molnár.

This was the name, clearly legible, on one of the pages. Of course, Franz Molnár. Good old Molnár! Father knew him, too. In the old days, they'd worked on the same newspaper. Back then, Molnár wrote little feuilletons, humorous snippets about kids.

'No one else could write about kids like that!'

Father, as if holding forth at some distant table. 'He should've stayed with that kind of material. Those plays he wrote . . . pot-boilers!'

The boy sat down in a back booth.

But what about the others? The customers. Perhaps they were up in the galleries. Or took shelter in the card room. Yes, the cafe's clientele might have decided to lie low in there.

He went upstairs. Small tables with chairs folded up. The carpet rolled up, as if waiting for the cleaners.

He slipped into a small side booth.

This is where the Editor used to sit. That awe-inspiring, austere Editor.

Snow-white hair, glasses, a huge pile of manuscripts in front of him. Nobody dared to approach. Only when he waved someone over.

'He never called out,' said Father. 'He merely waved. But when he waved, you knew it, even if you had your back to him. Even if you sat in the opposite corner of the cafe with your back to him. No matter who you were, you stood up and marched over to the

Editor's table. And the whole cafe would watch you on your way to that table.'

Now the boy sat at that table. There was a good view of the ground floor from up here. You could see the area fronting the boulevard, and the other part, facing a long, narrow side street. You could see the solitary phone booths. The vast dining room sunk into the dark depths. A grand staircase led down to the dining room.

He leant forward and looked down into the deep. Raising a finger, he waved toward one of the tables. A shadow rose from that table and set out toward the gallery. Now the boy waved toward the various parts of the cafe. First in the direction of the boulevard, then toward the side street.

He felt that his table was surrounded. By writers young and old, world-famous professionals and unknown tyros.

He fled toward the lavatory.

He pulled a curtain aside and plunged into total darkness. His hand crept along the wall, groping for the switch. There was a futile click, but no light.

White spots loomed in the dark. The sink, the urinal, the wall tiles. Two booths with doors, like two jail cells.

Who could be huddled in there? It seemed as if someone was standing in front of the urinal as well. Night editors, cruising the streets like old tramcars. After work, they'd head straight for this cafe. They'd order ham and eggs. And while they waited for their orders, they'd clamber up here, half-asleep, with a cigar dangling from their mouth. He thought he heard the groans and wheezing of travelling salesmen.

And midnight vagabonds, who spouted such waterfalls! Or else the barest of trickles. So that the man would just stand there, staring at the wall.

The boy entered a booth and slid the bolt shut. He did not sit down. He stood and watched the greyish-blue light up above. There was a strange kind of light swirling up there. Light? Or was it smoke?

He was back at the lavatory sink.

Father would wash his hands without even looking. But there were others who went through a whole ritual, practically a bath. And yet others who didn't even turn on the tap but merely stared at their faces in the mirror.

A den of peace and quiet.

Except at times someone would start to cough. Hoarse and choking hacks that brought up old deposits of phlegm, archaeological layers. Then others would start to cough, until the whole place was one big rattling uproar.

He continued exploring the galleries.

Another curtained booth. Tablecloths and napkins in a heap. They had collected the wrinkled, stained tablecloths to be carted away. All those stains! Brown spots left by sauces … red wine, black coffee. Smudged cigar ashes.

There might even be a customer lying wrapped up in that bundle. An arrogant slob who had contributed more than his share of stains. Who had spilt sauces on the tablecloth.

They'd tied up the saucy fellow in a bundle. A bundle of dirty laundry.

In the central part of the gallery, a mass of tables and chairs pushed together. As if the furniture had been shoved here in the wake of some catastrophe. Here they stood now, offended, left behind. Diminutive green-baize tables. Perhaps from the card room. And those slender, high-back chairs came from a club of some kind.

There was a club here once. The cinema-owners' club.

A photograph, showing a moustached man with a stiff collar smoking a cigar. But somehow so full of worries. Probably the owner of some cinema. Those owners who never watch any of the films. They just dart through the lobby with their hat on. This one didn't have a hat. Perhaps he'd lost his cinema. He lit up one last cigar, and after that . . .

But perhaps this was a card room. The players sat at the green baize-covered tables. Some had been here for a whole week. Originally meant to just pop in for a moment, then stayed here, stuck. At first he would still run downstairs to phone. 'I'll be home in an hour, maybe an hour and a half.' He ran down to phone a few more times, then became oblivious to everything.

The boy went down the stairway from the galleries. He tilted his head to the side and clasped his hands behind his back. As if he were part of a group. The rest of the company had left him lagging behind.

In the kitchen, gigantic kettles. Deep and dark bays with cooking ranges. Knives and ladles on tabletops. A cookbook and a white apron. Maybe it was taken off only a moment ago. Someone had made a remark to the chef. Some kind of complaint about the food. He said not a word in reply. Simply took off his hat, his apron, and walked out. But he did not go by himself. The other cooks, sous chefs and scullions all accompanied him. Only the kettles stayed behind.

The tables were laid in the dining room. White tablecloths, plates, silverware. A white-crested napkin plopped on the plate. Condiments in various jars. Salt shakers, pepper mills, ashtrays, toothpicks.

The restaurant was waiting for customers. It lay, as if covered with a grey net, nearly lost in that thick, impenetrable gloom beneath the marble stairway. Red carpeting on the stairway, red carpeting in the restaurant. But all of it lost in the grey twilight.

The boy strolled past rows of tables. He glanced up at the galleries. He thought he saw someone draped over the balcony handrail, as if waving in boredom toward the lower depths.

The dark cube of the aquarium. The lights turned off long ago, but the water still remained. Stale, turbid water. The rigid, watchful glare of a fish. Rigid glare in that netherworldly liquid.

He sat down at a table. On the edge of the seat, as if afraid of being taken to task. He moved over to another table, where he sat more comfortably. He waited a bit. Then he clinked a knife against the edge of the plate.

'Waiter!'

His voice rang out in the dining room. Then there was silence.

He stood up, as if to move to another table.

He stood at the foot of the stairway, surveying the empty cafe. The phone booths, the card room.

Suddenly the stairs lit up, like a resplendent bridge.

The boy stepped back, and held on to a table's edge.

Up at the head of the stairs, wearing a silver turban, came Vilma Bánky herself! Her head tilted back, she smiled as she advanced downstairs. By her side her husband, Rod La Rocque. Wearing a tail coat, Rod La Rocque raised his hand in languid greeting. The corpulent Emil Jannings hurried ahead, as if he did not care to meet them. But bespectacled Harold Lloyd moved up from behind to link arms with Vilma Bánky, and came down the stairs arm in arm with her.

Franz Lehár appeared in tails and white gloves. Lehár, whom Father had known in the days when he conducted military bands. Franz Molnár wore a monocle and thrust his hands into his pockets. He stood slightly to the side, by the banister. Perhaps he wanted to make way for the white-haired man with the spectacles who carried a briefcase under one arm.

The Editor! Authors were milling around him. Writers whom he had waved over to his side, and writers who would have liked to be waved over to his side. Writers whose names were known overseas, and writers whose names were unknown even in this cafe.

Newspapermen raced down the stairs. Awesome, two-fisted journalists who had entry everywhere, for whom no doors were closed. And scribblers of two-line items, and others who did not even get two lines. Gofers who were sent for beer and cigars. Hacks of the yellow press, slimy little blackmailers.

A balding master of ceremonies ambled by at a leisurely pace, so sunk into himself that he seemed to be totally alone. Actors and actresses around him. Street vendors. A seller of pocket notebooks was swept up right next to Vilma Bánky. A flea-market stall-keeper was explaining something to Emil Jannings.

Waiters appeared. Maître d's and newspaper hawkers, old waiters and busboys. A maître d' with a clipped moustache raced up and down the stairs as if he personally intended to seat everybody.

The boy stood at the foot of the stairs. He watched the lit-up stairway, the guests of the cafe thronging down the stairs. More and more new faces kept turning up.

A bucket rolled down the stairs. A morose, rusty old bucket. It shoved the guests aside in its furious headlong tumble.

The boy leapt to catch it, but no use . . .

The lights went out. The guests vanished.

Two ladders stood on the uppermost step. Two white-wash-spattered, lanky ladders. Behind them, the cafe tables covered with drop-cloths, the chairs shoved into a heap, the curtains drawn and pulled. The ladders loomed over the dark flight of stairs. Stood there, gaping down into the depths.

A FEW WORDS ABOUT AN UNCLE (1993)

In memoriam: György Rónay

A chubby man in a grey overcoat appears in the corridor. Merrily whistling. Suddenly he stops for a moment. He knits his brow.

'Well, well, look who's here!'

In front of the door stands a small, skinny boy, in a shabby coat.

'Good evening, Uncle Béla.'

The man pulls out his keys. His eyes are on the child. In his palm a bunch of keys, like a dead bird.

'So, what brings you here?'

'Dad sent me,' comes the reply in a very low voice, from behind his back.

The hall is handsome and brightly lit. The red runner on the floor like a long tongue sticking out.

The uncle takes off his coat and hangs it in the closet.

'What's new with your father?'

'Nothing. Nothing's new.'

'He's almost fifty. Still just treading water. My esteemed brother. My dear, esteemed ... Of course, when he had money, he lived it up. The racetrack, cards, you name it ... '

The child raises his eyes.

'Uncle Béla ... '

'Yes, son?'

'Did Dad, too, have a regular flat once?'

'Your father owned a house once.' Then, with a wave of the hand. 'But what's the use. Your father never appreciated what he had. He always looked down on me. He found me profoundly contemptible.'

Now Uncle Béla has changed into his grey pyjamas. He stares at the child. That kid, sitting there like a pile of misery. He looks so tired.

By now the uncle is in the kitchen. Is there anything to eat he could scrounge up here? He eats out, in cafes and restaurants, so that . . . Well, maybe something can be dug up.

There's a loaf of bread on the table. That's nourishment enough.

He pulls out a kitchen knife from a drawer. He hugs the loaf to his chest, and saws at it. At last he produces a slice. Spreads butter on it in big chunks.

'Well, this is better than nothing.'

The boy raises his head as Uncle Béla stops in front of him. All he sees at first is the bottom of the plate, getting closer. At last it is in his hands. It feels as if it had somehow been delivered via air mail.

'For me?'

'Of course! Go to it! You might want to take off your cap.'

The boy snatches off the cap with a furtive movement. He swallows large mouthfuls of bread and butter.

Uncle Béla goes through a series of calisthenics in the middle of the room. He slowly squats down, stands up, sticks out his chest, spreads his arms.

The boy wipes the corner of his mouth. He is somewhat less hungry now.

His uncle goes on with his exercises.

'What's up at home?'

'The sole fell off from Dad's shoe. He can't go out.'

'So he'll just have to stay at home.' Then, in a somewhat milder tone:

'Well, let me see. You've already been here earlier this week.'

'Yes.'

'The two of you are always mooching off me. Can't you just, can't you hit up someone else every once in a while? I'm only asking.'

The boy spreads his arms.

'All right. Let's see what we can do. Your father . . . how could a man sink so low . . .'

He opens the closet.

His clothes hang arranged on a long rod, just like in a clothes shop. A black suit, a solid brown one, a light sporty one. Some look a bit more worn than the others. Shoeboxes occupy the floor of the closet.

He takes out a somewhat threadbare suit.

'Here you are.'

The boy slides off the chair.

Uncle Béla now picks out a pair of shoes. A pair of enormous shoes.

'Now we wrap it up, and you're all set.'

He disappears in the direction of the kitchen.

'Now this is what you're going to say at home.' The uncle's voice is coming from the kitchen. ' "Good evening, Dad." Your father will be angry: "Where the hell have you been?" And you say: 'Please take it easy. Uncle Béla is fine, and sends his regards, and he also sent this . . . See?" And cool as a cucumber you place this on the table.'

The boy laughs.

Uncle Béla emerges with an enormous piece of wrapping paper rustling in his hands. He folds the suit with expertise, wraps it and ties the package with string.

'Done and done. Tell me, what do you think of these shoes?'

'Dad's feet aren't that big.'

'So you crumple up a bit of paper, stick it in, and it's ready to wear.'

'That's all it takes, some paper? . . .'

'All right, then I'll wrap it for you. Don't be such a klutz. Watch how I wrap it.'

'I'm watching.'

The uncle wraps while the nephew watches.

Then suddenly the shout:

'And I've had enough of Greta Garbo!'

'Uncle Béla, you don't like Garbo?'

'Of course you're wild about her.'

'Well, not exactly . . .'

'It's all right, you can admit it to me. Everyone's crazy about her. Not me, though.' He pauses. 'Let me clue you in.' His palm is already guiding the boy's shoulder toward the front door. 'Joan Crawford. She's the real thing. Never a poseur, always natural. Do not underestimate her!'

The boy is half-way out of the front door.

'I won't.'

'Believe me, she can act circles around Garbo.'

'Yes Uncle Béla.'

'And if I see you here again, I'll throw you out so fast . . .'

MARLENE DIETRICH (1989)

Three generations met in *Joyless Street*.

Asta Nielsen

Greta Garbo

Marlene Dietrich

Asta Nielsen had few kind words to say about Greta Garbo: 'She does have a cute little mug! But talent?!'

No one had noticed Marlene Dietrich.

For her I forsook Barbara Stanwyck, delicate, cinnamon-complexioned Barbara Stanwyck. And believe me, she had meant the world to me. That gently chiding glance of hers! *You're always at the cinema! I'm glad you like me so much, but you shouldn't neglect your schoolwork . . .*

Well, yes. *Hermann und Dorothea*. I was unable to memorize a single line. One look at Goethe's endless novel in verse was enough to give me the creeps. I hated Hermann, and I hated Dorothea, each of them separately, and the two together.

But the way Barbara Stanwyck looked at me! All right, I'd give *Hermann und Dorothea* a try.

Except the film poster appeared that day. There it was, one bright clear morn, smooth and freshly glued on the billboard.

The Blue Angel.

I was forever hanging around those cylindrical advertising pillars, always on the lookout for new posters, new films. They never failed to take me by surprise. Just dropped from somewhere out of the blue. Right on to that old billboard.

The Blue Angel.

I didn't rush over right away. I approached slowly, stopped once or twice. I wonder why. Could I have been ashamed this was the only thing I cared about?

All of a sudden, there I stood in front of *The Blue Angel.*

Above the title, in giant letters, it said: EMIL JANNINGS. Ah, so this was another Emil Jannings vehicle. Meaning it would be one of those great dramas. The rest of the cast wouldn't be that important, really. All right, so who else was in it? Who made up Jannings' supporting cast?

Under the title, in a rather flimsy typeface:

Marlene Dietrich.

I moved closer. My finger hovered over those letters. Who was this Marlene Dietrich? Where did she come from, all of a sudden? Must be someone new. Or perhaps this wasn't her first film? One thing was certain: *I* had not encountered this name before. And if a name was new to *me*, then . . .

Still, it was a bit strange. A newcomer starring alongside Emil Jannings! Why not Charlotte Susa? She wasn't exactly a star, but still . . .

There were a few other names under Marlene Dietrich's, in even scrawnier letters, if that was possible: Hans Albers, Kurt Gerron, Puffy Huszár, Rosa Valetti.

These days, Hans Albers was playing mostly detectives. Before that, he used to be the bad guy. Two-fisted underworld type with icy eyes. And now he was a cop. As for Kurt Gerron, in this one he was a down-at-the mouth character. A banker on the edge of bankruptcy or something like that. And Puffy! Dear old Puffy Huszár! Those beady eyes in that fat baby- face, always blinking confidently or, if need be, mistrustfully. And Rosa Valetti behind the counter of a seedy bar. That impossibly wrinkled face, ever watchful. Should one of the clientele become too rowdy, she herself would throw him out of the joint.

At the bottom of the poster, in a nervous scrawl: Directed by Josef von Sternberg. I think I've heard about him. He was back from America, back from Hollywood. But what films had he directed over there?

So far so good. But who could this Marlene Dietrich be?

A few more steps, and there she was, right in front of me. On another poster. Bare shoulders, a skimpy little tutu made of tulle. A top hat, tilted at a slightly rakish angle. Leaning over Jannings, bearded, bespectacled Jannings. Her gesture implying she's about to stroke his beard. But not just yet. Perhaps on the next poster.

They flooded the city with posters for *The Blue Angel*. Posters that must have been flying around all night, to cover the walls and billboards by morning.

Marlene sitting on the edge of a table, champagne glass in hand. Nonchalantly dangling her legs. Nonchalantly, but not the least bit aggressively. Most elegantly. *Sorry, I can't help it. These are the gams I've been blessed with. And if you know anyone with legs that even come close to mine . . . Well, I'd really like to see those legs.*

Jannings sat on the other side of the table. With his imploring eyes.

Under that top hat (didn't she ever take it off?), Marlene's face appeared to be rather commonplace. Nothing extraordinary. A face you would hardly even notice on the street.

I turned away to go.

Then I turned back.

That smile of hers! Not exactly friendly. More like cool. Almost scornful. But no, that's going too far. A pitying smile. As if she'd felt sorry for Jannings. As if she'd pitied him. *Just keep sitting there, old man, and admire my legs, as long as you have nothing better to do!*

How long did I stand there contemplating her smile?

I took my leave by saying:

'See you at the movies!'

This meeting, however, had to wait a while. The time it took for *The Blue Angel* to reach the Fortuna Theatre. That godforsaken little cinema tucked away in the courtyard of a block of flats. That's right! Hidden away, there in a corner of that courtyard.

It was a courtyard cinema, the cinema of the tenements. In fact, it was one of the building's tenants, Mrs Beleznai from the fifth floor, who sat in the box office. Another tenant, Buntzi Komlós, worked behind the counter of the refreshments stand. The old grandmother who tended the toilets never smiled. What would she have to smile about?

I raced across the courtyard in the rain.

It was always raining on the cobblestones of that yard.

The cinema itself was steaming with an odour of rain.

Up on the screen I saw my own teacher, Professor Pázmán, appear. Oh yes! Emil Jannings was just like Mr Pázmán. That dank, limp cape and broad-brimmed hat. Storming through the school corridors. Oral exams today! Oh, it would be a veritable bloodbath!

Humiliate them! Humiliate them! That's right! Humiliate those little bastards! Lying low behind their desks, without an inkling of who was going to be the victim of his wrath!

Oh, Herr Professor indeed singles out a victim! And deals with him mercilessly. Afterward, he even adds a little lecture especially for his benefit. Well, well, sonny! How long has it been since you cracked a book? No time for books, eh? But of course, we have no time for such trivia . . . when we are chasing all kinds of loose women! Nothing but tramps! But if I ever catch you at it . . . !

Herr Professor goes sniffing around, ever alert. He finds a student on the street—and he's off on the hunt.

But this time it's something different. There's a cafe and a torch singer.

The young gentlemen have discovered a nightclub. One of those shady dives. A place of ill-repute. Complete with a singer. *The Blue Angel.* The *chanteuse* Lola Lola. The students are mad about her. But let's face it: not only the students. Respectable citizens. Fathers with families.

Herr Professor gets wind of the place. That hussy must be removed! The club must be shut down!

From his lectern, he surveys a classroom full of shifty faces, averted eyes.

'If I ever catch one of you in there! Or anywhere near that place . . . !'

Jannings and his lectern disappear.

Cut to a smoky little nightclub. At the tables fat, sweaty faces, unbuttoned vests. Foot-stamping, shouts.

'Lola! Where is she! Lola, Lola!'

Her dressing room.

Marlene Dietrich, clad in a silk peignoir, paces the room. She stops from time to time, places her hands on her bare shoulders. Giving them a rest. She looks around, puzzled, as if she did not understand how she came to be here. Her hands glide down to her waist.

They smooth down her hips.

A voice calls her:

'Lola!'

Students pile into the room. Excited, flushed faces. Blazing pimples.

'C'mon, Lola!'

She smiles and waves. The boys disappear.

She sits down in front of her mirror, and examines her face. As if she were just getting acquainted with that face. Suddenly she turns toward me, with a funny little *moue*. What are you staring at, little boy?

I keep staring.

Crumpling the rain-soaked overcoat in my lap, I stare.

With that slightly bored smile, Marlene puts on her top hat. Walks off toward her audience.

Loud applause and cheers.

Suddenly Jannings barges in, angrily gesticulating. But what did I care about him and his students! I have eyes only for Marlene Dietrich as she leans against her piano. And sings in that peculiar, slightly hoarse voice.

Did I fall for her? Could be. What do I care!

Out in the street I felt a bit annoyed.

I barely remembered seeing Jannings! Well, maybe one or two scenes . . . The way he stormed down the school corridor. The way he barged in at *The Blue Angel*, to catch those boys red-handed. Then someone breaking an egg over his head. The cracked egg trickling down his face, his beard . . .

And the rest of the cast?

Hans Albers? Puffy Huszár? Kurt Gerron?

Floating blurs. Hazy, floating blurs.

A voice from somewhere: 'Mark my words! This woman will end up in Hollywood! That's right . . . and you first heard it from me!'

Willy Forst was shot dead. The husband plugged him. Marlene Dietrich's husband. For a while it looked like they were going to get away with it, Marlene Dietrich and Willy Forst. The two of them with their coats on, ready to leave ... the next moment they'd be gone. But the door opens. Enter the husband. He does not say a word. Just eyes the pair of them. Nor do they say anything. They don't even try to defend themselves. They don't even try to escape. No use trying to escape.

Marlene, wearing a grey coat, hugs the wall. The look she gives her husband is almost pitying. Willy Forst smiles a rather wan smile. He spreads his arms—a kid caught in the act. (There was always something of the high-school student about him.) Not a word from the husband. He does not blame anyone. What would be the use?

It seems they will remain forever like that, caught in this room. Caught in this room, in eternal silence.

With a casual gesture, the husband takes out his gun and aims it at Willy Forst.

Marlene still hugs the wall. Her handbag swings inanely on her arm.

Willy Forst is frozen motionless. Suddenly he grabs his chest. He staggers and drops.

The husband lowers his revolver.

Marlene, still by the wall. Her hand moves to her handbag— as if to stop the pendulum of a clock.

What a gesture!

That's what I recall from that silent film.

In those days, after the success of *The Blue Angel*, they dug up a few silent films she'd made earlier.

But it wasn't the real Marlene Dietrich yet in these silents. Not even when she happened to have a starring role. Still, they all had their moments ...

Her old silents were now playing at the Fortuna. At the courtyard cinema, in that old, rundown tenement.

Meanwhile, she had gone to America.

The lords of Paramount invited her to Hollywood, city of motion pictures. Escorted by Josef von Sternberg. At first, the whole trip seemed like a mere excursion. But then . . .

The ocean liner took her to America three times. Twice she returned. But not the third time. By then, Adolf Hitler was in power.

And the co-stars she had across the ocean!

Gary Cooper in *Morocco*. Clive Brook in *Shanghai Express*. She was world famous by then.

Marlene . . . may I say something? Gary Cooper, with that wry sense of humour, was fully your equal, don't you agree? At the very least. And Clive Brook was no slouch, either. The Great Bitter One. No one ever saw him smile.

I could mention a few more names. Off the top of my head.

Herbert Marshall

Cary Grant

Lionel Atwill

James Stewart

Charles Boyer

Not a bad little team. An all-star team, in fact.

But forget about them. Truth is, I could never really pay any attention to them. Next to you, they seemed faded. But why? What was it? What was this radiance? Oh, never mind.

What matters is that once I saw you in a cinema that reeked of rain. The way you put on that top hat. The way you strolled down among those tables. You touched a hand here, a shoulder there. You leant against the piano and sang.

Marlene Dietrich eyes me from somewhere far away.

'Tell me, what do you really know about me?'

AUTOBIOGRAPHY (1989)

Felix and Hollander.

Two names on a white sheet of paper.

The boy stared. Felix and Hollander . . . Who were these two? How did they get here? And anyway, how long had he been sitting here at the table? Staring at the snowfield of that blank sheet of paper?

Someone ran by outside, on the gallery, and tapped on the window. He saw the quivering haystack of a girl's head of hair. Swaying left and right. She knocked again. The boy called out.

Emmi!

But he did not budge. He did not race outside.

Felix and Hollander. If you got this far, you couldn't just dump them. Or could you? Cross them out. Yep, that would be best. Better yet, tear up the sheet.

This blinding white sheet. So hostile and menacing. Impossible to scribble anything on.

Scribble-scrabble!

No! This was not a scribble and not a scrabble. This was something else.

What was going on here? The way he sat here in one place. Not going out to play with Emmi. Not going out on the street. To the park. He could still be up and running in a second.

But he did not budge.

Someone leant over his shoulder.

Felix and Hollander! Two dealers? Business partners perhaps? They were tin soldiers!

How about that, your lordship! Two tin soldiers! When one was enough for Andersen.

Andersen, he says!

One little tin soldier was enough for him.

But Father!

He turned around.

Father was nowhere to be seen, the room empty. Only a squashed cigar stub in the ashtray. Still smoking, as if in mockery.

The furniture seemed to edge backward, distrustful.

No one would ever enter this room again. Not Father, not anyone else. Nobody, nothing existed any more. Only these two. Felix and Hollander. So forlorn on the snowfield of empty paper.

The boy scratched his knee. Next he pressed the pencil against his nose. Traced invisible lines in the air. Lines of all kinds. Then back to knee-scratching.

Suddenly his hand was poised above the paper.

And he began at a manic speed. In a single jangling burst.

Felix and Hollander, two tin soldiers, were old pals. Felix had a battle scar on his forehead, and Hollander . . .

He was stuck.

Tear it up! Cross it out, tear it up!

He did not tear it up. Did not cross it out and did not tear it up.

But he did not continue, either.

He sat in the slowly darkening room.

He was surrounded by pitchers. Pitchers, filled to the brim. Filled to overflowing. Once they might have been faces. Human faces that talked, argued, giggled and whined. Later they made only a remark or two. Terrified whispers. Sighs.

Silence. Here came the silence.

And then, the jovial host took over. Spouting forth his adventures. His recollections. Dipping liberally into his recollections. The rich trove of his memories.

Oh, if you'd known Father! A poet, a real poet! Published very little, but that didn't matter! Never had a real job in his life, yet always managed to scrape together enough money to ...

And here came an avalanche of Father's adventures. Father, founder of magazines. Father the editor. Father the circus director. That was his fondest dream, an international circus. Did I say director?! Come on! That's nothing! Clown! Musical clown! That's right! He himself appearing as musical clown! That was his greatest ambition. To sit on the arm of a chair, holding his violin in the limelight.

Pause.

Then suddenly:

But wait a minute! Let's not get carried away! Did I say poet? Musical clown? Dreamer of dreams?

What about the way he leant over my shoulder? The dreamer of dreams! Leaning over a little kid still in shorts, about to venture into something new ... Sitting down for the first time in his life to face a blank sheet of paper! The way he looked at my scribbles, kind of right through my shoulder, and started in with that sarcastic drawl of his. 'I see! Felix and Hollander! Two tin soldiers. Your lordship is a most original genius! Incredibly original!'

All right, we might as well face it. Andersen did leave his mark on that story. But still! To send one off like that!

His voice faltered.

A glimmer of hope for the assembly of pitchers. A frail little ray of hope. *Perhaps he'll stop now. Look, he's all choked up. Staring off into space. Father and Andersen. Got him all emotional. He's had it. Maybe he'll forget about us.*

But no! First a healthy dose of Father. And now a few drops of Mother. She was the normal half of the family. Typist at an insurance company. Father cleaned her out completely, took her for all she was worth. And he did it with such charm, such élan! Otherwise he barely paid any attention to her.

And the girls! The waitresses at the coffee house! How they would flit around Father with their trays!

The host was waltzing around the table. He gave a pitcher a light tap. A few drops here, a few drops there. He would not neglect anyone.

Those girls at the Cafe Simplon!

At the New York!

At the Japan!

At the Folk Opera!

At the Abbazia!

Pause. A brief, invigorating pause.

The girls at the espresso machine of the Lukács!

At the Darling!

At the Gerbeaud!

At the Artiste!

At the Intime!

He surveyed the entire company. He growled:

But this is my affair! Or am I mistaken?!

The girls on Kálmán Tisza Square!

The high-school girls and their white sailor blouses!

The nannies at Károlyi Gardens!

Lady tram conductors!

That cook from Sas Street! A Junoesque build!

So what if I didn't marry Ida Koch! Why? Should I have married her!?

The pitchers can only cower, intimidated. Terrorized. *What else are we in for? What next?*

The periodicals!

Nyugat. The West. Laying siege to the *Nyugat.* Would give anything to break into print in the magazine edited by Babits! To conquer and triumph. On the way to their offices I hummed marching songs. *'The shady woods of summer call to me, / Those shady woods they fill me up with glee!'* I carried three short stories in my coat pocket. I never took just one. Always three. Always give them a choice.

I also besieged *Napkelet.* The sunrise. Kept bombarding them. Why not? I craved coronation by *Nyugat,* and I craved coronation by *Napkelet.*

A smirking laugh.

Did I say coronation?! Me? Forget about it!

He hummed, angrily. *The shady woods of summer call to me, / Those shady woods they . . .*

He ran out of ammo. But instantly reloaded.

Football and films. There was enough material there . . .

—First of all, let's get one thing straight! As far as I'm concerned it's soccer, and not 'association football'. And I'm a fan. Let that be known! A fan, not an 'afficionado'!

I've had the privilege of seeing Orth play! The greatest Hungarian player! Granted, it was after his injury. He was no longer Orth at his best. He never regained his old form.

And now, time for a little surprise! That's right, my dears! I've got a little surprise saved for you!

Good God, please spare us!

Did you know I once was a sportswriter? Me! That's right, me! Back in 1944, yet! In a devastated city. Rubble piled in the streets, buildings blown sky high. And down in the bomb shelter I dared to ask the question. Was the Ujpest team still the class of the league? Why did the star forward Zsellengér lack motivation?

How many times I'd started to write that piece . . . I buckled down. Put my shoulder to the wheel. No go. A page or two, and I was stuck.

But did I despair? Not on your life! What did the critic Edith Póth once write about me? '*He attacks his material with the stubborn ferocity of a bulldog, and he does not let up . . .*'

' *. . . he brandishes flashy skills that blind you to the flaws he neglects to correct*'. But this latter is not from the pen of Miss Póth.

Layer she wrote a rather nasty novel about me. Well, not exactly about me. I just happened to turn up in it. A minor figure on the sidelines. Doesn't matter. And anyway . . . anyway . . .

He mumbled some more, eyelids drooping. He nodded out.

The maestro is sleepy! Let him sleep! O, may he sleep!

He snapped awake.

—*Quo Vadis* at the Tivoli! That's how it all began. The first film I ever saw. Emil Jannings as Ursus the Strongman. I think he was Ursus. Anyway, he was in it.

May I let you in on a secret?

The pitchers are silently praying.

No! Please don't!

I never really liked Jannings. Too theatrical, if you know what I mean. Fritz Kortner was the real thing! He dwarfed Jannings. Bet you've never heard that name: Kortner! Fritz Kortner!

He tilted forward.

And now almost in a whisper.

My friends! I really don't want to be a nuisance. Far be it from me. I'm not Professor Pázmán. Still . . . Is any of this getting through? . . . How shall I say this . . . Any of what I dished out here. (*Dry laugh.*) Any of my offerings . . .

He drew back.

Can't help it. A tiny demon is egging me on. The demon of curiosity.

Now both palms on the table.

But if I were to ask you, who was Uncle Milkó? Where did I meet him? Where and when? Where did he die? At what hospital? Under what circumstances? That's a clue, you know. I will add, it was the winter of 1944?! Well?

He tosses out another name.

Or Méda Bartos! Where did she teach? Was it Veres Pálné? Or was it some other school?

And Pubi Nadler, where did he play ball? What club did he play for?

Does the name Paulette Mészáros say anything to you?

How about Furu Lohr?

Stefi Jonás?

Oscar Damó?

He shook his head, and smiled.

But enough, enough! This is not a pop quiz. As I've said, I'm not Professor Pázmán. It was an asinine joke. Inane and humiliating.

He kept refilling.

The perfect host knows his duty. His charming duty.

He has poured generous splashes of Father. Father was an inexhaustible source! And Mother, in somewhat more moderate doses. After all, poor dear, she was a more humble personage.

And Aunt Vali! Mother's aunt. The chairperson. The chairperson of all those ladies' clubs. Who recited poems at the Academy of Music, clad in traditional Hungarian formal wear, a sword by her side. The high-school girls nearly exploded trying to suppress their laughter.

So, a few drops of Aunt Vali.

And Olga! Father's second wife. Whom he managed to totally clean out.

Olga and her sisters. The refined Teri and slovenly Margit.

Olga's sisters. Father's brothers. Well, well. Nearly forgot about Father's brothers! Béla and Andor. Béla tried to seduce Mother. Wanted to take her off Father's hands. As for Andor . . . Why deny it! He, too, made a pass at Mother.

One drop of Béla. One drop of Andor. Portioned out. And again a dash of Mother. Who, after all, was maybe not such an innocent little flower. She was always humming snippets of some stupid little ditty. '*Countess Melanie roams dreaming in the park*'!

The host kept refilling. Relentlessly. Inexhaustibly.

He leant over a fat pitcher.

You know I've been thinking about writing a play. A pet project. I really don't want to carry on about it, I'm not a playbill. Still . . . here's the opening, just to set the tone. Perhaps it'll give you some idea. After the start of the performance, a member of the audience rises and saunters up on stage. He looks around as if trying to spot an acquaintance. A friend. A lady friend. He sits down in an armchair. Lights a cigar. Puffs placidly. Suddenly someone steps up to him. No! No one steps up. They all ignore him. And he just sits there having a good time. The curtain's about to come down and he's still in that easy chair. Smoking a cigar.

Well, enough of that!

I might add that I'm not trying for anything earth-shaking in this play, only . . .

I should mention that I'm not entirely unknown abroad.

Abroad!

Mirthless laughter.

That's really nothing to boast about. Let's not fool ourselves. Might as well face the truth. The game is lost. This player can leave the field. He is too old. He shouldn't be on the playing field. Politics . . . political thrills. That's what people want. That's the ticket. Or else cheap entertainment. But you won't get that from me!

Stunned silence.

The fame that eluded him! We are to blame for that, too! We should have translated his works. His works?! His entire oeuvre! *Forget about marriage, kids, travel. Translate, translate! Hunt for a publisher. And pounce on him, like a Doberman. Instead we just kicked back, goofed off. We're in for it now . . . !*

What? Not a word from him? He sits in silence?

He sat in silence. Frozen face. Icy glare. Staring them down.

What do I want from them? Does anything interest them? They're not even listening! They ignore me! Gossipmongers. That's right! Waiting for measly bits of gossip. Intimate details. Trivial news from anywhere. Or maybe not even that. Maybe nothing gets through to them any more. Nothing is understood. At most, a few simple sentences. A word here and there.

He leant toward them. As if articulating a lesson.

Mrs Borbas' flat was flooded.

The Markoses have moved.

Frigyes Nindler bought a car.

Bözsi loves bananas.

Lajos brings up the paper.

Mrs Szenes waits for the bus.

The Bem Embankment.

It's snowing.

Tonsillitis.

Nose drops.

Drip-drop!

He leapt up.

Enough! I'm done! I'm leaving this illustrious gathering. I've already wasted too much time here. I'm leaving you to your own devices. The flat is yours. There! Do what you want! I'll find some other place. A hotel, or whatever.

He walked around the table, without a glance at the pitchers. Not even deigning a single glance.

His hand was on the doorknob.

His expression softened. He smiled.

Now, now! What kind of stupid game is this? Why this dumb sentimentality?

He returned.

He leant over a pitcher with tenderness. As if about to embrace it.

The Dolly Sisters! Mother and I saw them at the Budapest Operetta Theatre. Rózsi Dolly and Joanie Dolly. We sat in a box, and out of the blue I spoke words addressed to the stage . . .

A crack ran down the length of the pitcher. A barely visible hairline crack. The next instant it shattered into tiny fragments . . . Everything spilt out.

He attacked a cookie. A tough old cookie lying on the table.

The cookie resisted, it refused to yield. It fell apart. But that was only a trick. Each piece remained a tough little continent of its own.

Music from a distant room. Radio static. *O little dancer, love of my heart!*

His eyes lit up as he sang out. *O little dancer I'm slain by desire!*

He stopped singing, the light gone from his eyes.

His fingers shifted biscuit crumbs. As if doing a strange puzzle where each move must be pondered carefully.

He used to love sweets. Hazelnut cake had been his favourite. Hazelnut cake and red wine. Just one little glass of wine. One little glass or two.

He staggered around down in the courtyard. In the dim courtyard, among steel-grey garbage cans. A wastebasket in one hand, he lifted garbage-can lids with the other. The lids rose and slammed shut one after another, with grim clangour. Full! All full!

He gave up. He stood in the courtyard among the garbage cans.

He clanged a tin spoon on a tin plate.

I was a Baumgarten Prize winner! Yessir! Winner of the Baumgarten Prize!

All right pops, take it easy!

A CHARACTER OUT OF CHEKHOV (1992)

They held hands, dancing a circle dance in the meadow. They sang and danced. Then the song grew faint and the chain of hands was broken. The hands drew apart. But the boy did not let go of that smooth, soft hand. He clutched it tight. He heard her low, somewhat mocking laughter. 'You want to take it with you?' Yes, maybe he wanted to take it with him.

But the girl's hand disappeared. Everything and everyone disappeared. As if they had never held hands. As if they had never been singing.

Now he lay on a stale-smelling bed. Could be someone had tossed him there. And immediately forgot about him.

But he did not feel like getting up just yet. Maybe they would all reappear. Again form a circle. Clasp hands. And sing that song about the rose once more.

And he was already singing.

'We'll dance around a rose, a rose, and sing a song of roses . . .'

The boy sang.

Now the others would hear him. Wherever they were they would hear him.

Is that so?

They'd hear this tired, feeble voice?

He looked up.

The dingy hotel room was now even dingier, if that was possible. He saw a naked arm dangling from the other bed. Was there more to it? A shoulder maybe, or legs? Or was the arm left

behind to dangle by itself? And when the maid came to tidy up
. . . But no one would come to tidy up. Father never left a tip.
He spilt ashes on the blanket and pillow, and dropped his cigar
stubs on the floor. And he always had Rosie running to the grocer's
for salami and cheese. Except he would forget to pay her. He conveniently forgot to pay for the room, too. And now he'd taken off.
But he left an arm behind. He'd call for it at the desk.

Wonder what time could it be?

Who cares!

It had been settled once and for all one Sunday afternoon.
After seeing *The King of Kings*. He had been lingering outside
the Bodograf Theatre, gazing at the stills. Mihály Várkonyi in
the role of Pontius. Várkonyi, who had been discovered by Cecil B.
Yes! That's right! Cecil B. himself!

Barbara La Marr as Mary Magdalen. She seemed to be gazing
at the boy with profound sympathy. Now my dear, you should go
straight home, and do your Latin and German homework. Tomorrow is Monday, after all. Yes, no denying. And no denying that I'll
never do any Latin or German homework again.

No more school. Not tomorrow and not the day after. Never
again. I've stayed out for weeks already. Father, by the way, always
wrote me an excuse. He never failed to provide an excuse.

'My son, having contracted severe influenza . . .'

When the boy occasionally showed up in front of the teacher's
desk, Professor Pázmán would bow his head, his voice dripping
with ominous sarcasm.

'Ah, greetings, a rare pleasure indeed!'

Next Professor Pázmán would read father's note aloud. Oh,
he'd been anticipating this. Yessir! This was one performance that
never failed. Always a popular favourite. He would not miss it for
the world.

And the class howled with laughter.

' . . . having contracted severe influenza! So, it was influenza! Influenza!'

The boy's had enough of that.

Still, that oppressive feeling in the evenings! Especially Sunday evenings! That tomorrow, maybe, after all . . . But no! We've made our decision. An irrevocable decision.

But maybe that isn't even Father lying in the other bed.

Because one time someone else got out of that bed, as if cast up by a dark wave. It was at night, that's right, in the middle of the night. A balding, pudgy character. Totally wasted and worn out, one hand groping about in the dark. Looking for a chair? For something to clutch at? The voice was thick and pulpy, yet at the same time sort of severe.

'Tell me kid . . . you been with a woman yet?'

The boy sat up. He was unable to answer. Yet another question he was unable to answer. All he could do was stare at that shadowy figure.

He heard Father's voice from the depths of the room.

'Watch it, Tuta! I'm going to kick you out . . .'

'But my dear Gyula, I merely wanted to give the kid a word of advice . . .'

'Let me give you a word of advice: you'll be out on your arse in a second . . .'

'The kid's never going to get laid!'

'Don't you worry about the kid!'

Tuta muttered something, then there was silence. He just faded away.

But the question still hung in the air. Ever been with a woman?

Now a feeble smear of light appeared on the wall, slid to the floor and evaporated.

There was no assurance that the sun would rise. No assurance whatever.

And why on earth did Barbara La Marr cower in that rocky cave? Oh yes, because of her sins! She had to atone for all her sins. But what kind of sins were they? She let down her hair, tore her robes. But why? Why? Perhaps if I cuddled up next to her in there . . . She would tell me all about it. I wouldn't pry . . . but still . . .

He kicked off the blanket.

He sat bolt upright.

And stayed like that on the edge of the bed.

On the table, there was a book with a yellow cover.

Julius Caesar.

De Bello Gallico.

How did that get here? It wasn't here yesterday. Or maybe I just hadn't noticed it? Anyway, did Caesar really write that? How could he find time for that sort of thing? What with one war after another . . . and Caesar always leading his legions. When did he find time to write?

Must have been during a lull between hostilities.

What could it have been like, that lull between hostilities? Short and menacing. It could end any minute.

Still . . . Who smuggled that book in here? Maybe Caesar himself. Caesar the author, leader of armies. Who just happened to drop in at the Hotel Adria.

It must have been while Rosie was tidying the room, shaking the dust rag out the window. Caesar paused behind her back. Maybe he considered patting her behind. He quickly dropped the book on the table, and disappeared.

Now it was time for the boy to disappear, too.

Time for his walk! His wonderful morning walk!

Off to Margit Island. Where else?

For a stroll on those gravel walkways, among trees wreathed in fog.

He would walk past the hotels. The grand hotel and the small hotel. He might even stop in at the reception desk, always so elegant and inviting. Perhaps there would be a room reserved for him. Probably in the small hotel.

But who turned on the tap? And then turned it off at the very last moment? A few more drops, and it would have overflown.

He stared at the water. It was rather turbid. Did someone already wash in it?

He touched the thin line of soap residue on the edge of the sink. Dry. Completely dry. How long had this water been in the sink? Days? He glanced at the mirror. The thin, haggard face provided no answers. His palm, fingers extended, skimmed the water, for the briefest moment. Then his hand emerged, fingers still extended, as if disdaining to take the plunge. Water languidly dripped from his fingers. Why not wash at least up to the elbows. But it was too late for that now. Or was there still time? Bare himself to the waist?

But when did he get dressed? And how?

A cat was insistently caterwauling among the ruined stones of the monastery on the island.

The boy clambered up on the ruins.

Saints hovered in the air about him. Also others, who hadn't made it to sainthood yet. The blessed.

Then he was at the train station.

He entered an empty compartment, for ten minutes. For an hour, at the most. He stared out the window.

Now, transfer to the Vienna Express.

And now on another train, going to Paris.

Berlin, Bremen, London . . .

He loitered around the tracks.

Once more, he was roaming the streets.

A troop of girls was coming his way.

Magda Friedmann, Vera Garami, Susan Bencze and the others. Breasts jiggling under their sailor blouses. Schoolbags clutched to their side, as if they were carrying babies. Always so careful, they never swung their bags. Chattering and giggling. He said hello to them, but no one returned the greeting. Magda Friedmann glanced at him for a moment but did not acknowledge his presence. A high-school dropout. He would never graduate. Probably he would be drafted. And soldiers were off limits. One didn't talk to them.

Once upon a time, in the middle of a walk, Magda had stopped and turned to face him.

'That doctor had such an exhausted, tormented face.'

'What doctor?'

'Doctor Astrov, in *Uncle Vanya*. The one who drinks a lot, but ends up saving a forest from being cut down.'

'What are you talking about?'

Magda seemed to be studying his features, one by one.

'Your eyes have that same misty look. Misty and sad. Like that doctor's.' She paused for a moment. 'Go see *Uncle Vanya* when it's showing again. Or why don't you read it. Do you have the book?'

'No I don't.'

'I'll lend it to you.'

'Thanks, really.'

She touched his hand.

'Your face is sort of like Doctor Astrov's. A character out of Chekhov.'

A character out of Chekhov.

Never in his life would anyone say that to him again.

ON A TRAMCAR (1981)

He and the girl stood on the rear platform.

His hand crept under the cascade of dark hair on the nape of her neck. He gazed at the perfect oval of her face. Her eyes were grey-green that turned a kind of muddy grey when she got mad. Then tiny yellow specks would appear in that muddy grey. And one of her eyes seemed larger than the other. But it made no difference now. Those yellow specks would be appearing any moment. She'd already asked more than once: Where are we going? Where are we getting off, where are we going?

By now she'd had it with asking questions. She slowly turned her head away.

Where were they going? Good God, where indeed? And what were they going to do when they got off? Because eventually they'd have to get off. Were they going to take a walk, as always? He didn't even have enough money for a couple of film tickets. As for *placing a serious order* at a tea-room . . . Two chocolate petit-fours and two glasses of seltzer, Miss! Fat chance.

His hand slipped away from her hair. As if shoved away. Enough already! How long do you expect to linger there, under that mass of hair, on the nape of that neck, in the neighbourhood of that earlobe?

The boy peeked into the interior of the car. The half-empty car. It was all so familiar somehow, the seats so inviting. An older man was reading a newspaper. Now he dropped the paper in his lap, and raised a hand, as if waving toward them. Why don't you two come in?

Indeed, why don't we?

He drew open the door. After you! He let her go ahead. They remained standing near the door for a while. Someone might call out, the conductor or one of the passengers. Get out! What do you want here? Out with you! Out!

But no one said a word.

The boy quietly drew the door shut behind them. Hello, everybody. He hung on to a leather strap. As if he were getting ready for a gymnastic exercise. Pull himself up, and swing over to the next strap and the next.

The girl also clutched a strap. The two of them hung there, side by side.

He took her by the arm. They strolled down the length of the aisle. He led her to a window seat. Then across to the other side. They moved up to the front of the car, and stood next to the driver as if he were an old acquaintance.

The boy's hand again approached the girl's neck. But now there were tiny freckles on this neck. Who was this strawberry blonde?

The girl standing next to him was a strawberry blonde. When did she get on? And when did the other one get off?

They travelled side by side for a space. Then the strawberry blonde got off at a stop.

Someone touched the boy's shoulder. A white-haired man with cheerful eyes, a stocking wrapped around his neck. Or was it possibly a scarf? Could it be a ragged old scarf?

'How's your father?'

'Hello, Uncle Kálmán!'

'Nice of you to recognize me. But your father . . .'

The boy looked out at the trees. Father? Yes, he too had been sitting in the car. But he'd stood up abruptly, touched my shoulder and got off. Someone was waiting for him at that stop. A woman. Maybe it was Mother, maybe it was someone else. You know him, Uncle Kálmán . . .

But by then Uncle Kálmán was gone.

Boys hopped on the tramcar. They ran alongside the car, then they hopped on. They rushed down the length of the car, jostling, laughing, panting. Suddenly he was surrounded.

'What's up? Don't you recognize us?'

'What are you staring at?'

'Cat got your tongue?'

'Hey, he doesn't recognize us!'

He looked at the faces one by one.

Nejfi!

Ugrai!

Váradi!

Barabás!

They all crowded around him. Nejfi, Ugrai, Váradi, Barabás. The kids from the old neighbourhood. Váradi in his white jersey. Then it was only Váradi in front of him, with that pale scar above his eyebrow. Perhaps it wasn't really a scar, only a red stripe. A strange anxiety filled him. Something awful lay in store for this one. He ought to say something. A word of warning. But what?

The smile vanished from Váradi's face, as if he had a foreboding. His eyes imploring now. Leave me alone! Please leave me alone!

'But Váradi, I was only . . .'

But boy in the white jersey was gone. As were the others.

A gentleman wearing a homburg tipped his hat to him. A wrinkled, dark-haired man nodded stiffly. A woman smiled. Friends, acquaintances. For a while, they travelled with the boy. Then the tramcar jolted and ground to a halt. They all got off.

The boy stood out on the rear platform. He reached down and gave a hand to help up Rosie, the governess. And that frog-eyed little girl who was Rosie's charge and who always sat next to her at Károlyi Gardens. He also gave a hand to chubby Vera Rothmann, and to Klári Hegedűs, her hair flying free. There was always someone to help up. All he had to do was let his arm dangle free, and he would feel another person's hand in his.

Now he felt nothing there. His hand hung in empty air.

A girl stood down there, at the stop. Her face unsmiling, and her eyes so alarmed. A yellow star on her coat.

'Magda! Magda Friedman!'

She looked up at him. Her glance seemed to come from so far away. A brief smile hovered on her lips. Then she pulled her coat tighter, and stepped back.

He beckoned toward her.

'Magda . . . come up, get on, Magda!'

She turned her head away.

The tramcar started to move.

The boy made a gesture, as if he meant to jump off. Someone pulled him back. *Have you gone mad?!*

He retreated into a corner. When he looked up, her face was in front of him again. But behind a glass pane now. Magda Friedman looked back at him from the platform of the car in the rear. She raised her hand, as if she wanted to write something on the glass. But then she just stood there lost in the crowd. Overcoats, rucksacks, yellow stars crushed against each other.

I'm going over to her! I have to go over!

He jumped off, so he could hop back on the other car. But he slipped, and rolled down on some kind of embankment.

The tramcar disappeared.

It turned up again later.

By then the buildings had gone up in the air, blown away. The streets were twisted, awry, just like the tramcar rails.

The tramcar itself lay upended in the rubble. It had been corralled, snared and roped. They were in the process of dragging it off somewhere.

The boy's eyes followed it helplessly.

It needed my help! I should have helped and not let it be dragged away.

He stood stock still.

Silence. The silence of extinction. Ruins, ruins and ruins. Stillness itself.

Then the tramcar reappeared.

Where did it come from?

Hardened, grey mud stuck to its sides. No, not really mud. More like sludge. It was grown over with black creepers, as if it had emerged from an oozy mire, from some swamp. Through the broken windows one could see the interior. The leather straps were dangling, ripped and broken. Seats split open. But the signs over the seats somehow intact: Reserved for Disabled Veterans. Reserved for Pregnant Mothers.

And where did this ratty old bag come from? Stuffed with shirts, pyjamas, razor and manuscripts. All sorts of manuscripts. From what bombed-out building had he crawled forth?

In any case, there he stood, amid the scattered cobblestones, and stared at the tramcar.

Closer and closer it approached, exuding a dire hope.

A woman ran toward it, her coat unbuttoned, her scarf flying. And a man with glasses, waving his hand so vehemently. Then a soldier, his coat torn, his arm in a sling. An old man, wrapped in a blanket. A trembling skeleton.

Clutching his bag, the boy, too, started to walk.

A CHAPEL, AFTERNOON (1974)

Sundays you can't go near the lake. Sundays, you simply can't go out. So there's sunbathing in the garden, lollygagging.

'Will you look at that!' János and the landlord standing by the fence, looking at the cavalcade. A thunderous roar, as herds of automobiles and motorcycles crowded the road. The rush started Saturday afternoon. Folks from the capital! Invading this lakeside resort for the weekend. Arriving in cars, motorcycles, trains to inundate the shoreline and trample everything underfoot.

'Yes indeed.' The elderly landlord eyed the road with an indulgent smile. 'You should see what they do to the beach!' János envisioned the beach. Littered with eggshells and sardine cans. The invaders sprawling on blankets and towels. Passing the bottle around. Finished, they heave it in the water. Occasionally a motorbike squeezes in among the naked bodies. The biker swaggering as if he were about to slam full speed into the lake.

Years ago János braved the beach on a Sunday. He'd surveyed the scene somewhat alarmed. Finding a shady spot under a tree, he dropped his bathrobe and headed for the water. 'You really went swimming?' the landlady asked afterward. 'You went in the water on a Sunday?' She chuckled at her husband.

But now János stood alongside his host just like one of the old settlers. One who appreciated what it meant to have this lakeside house.

His wife's voice came from the depths of the garden. 'Could you please bring me a glass of seltzer?'

She was sunbathing on a deck chair by the veranda. Surrounded by books and newspapers. All sorts of small bottles lined up on the ledge.

János trotted to the pantry. After removing a bottle from the refrigerator, he stayed there, squatting. For years I'd been coming here alone. Alone, with another family. The Paczko family . . . they'd discovered this place. It was nice, having breakfast with them on the veranda. Their daughter played badminton with the landlord. She ran the old man ragged. Aniko Paczko. Last year, she sent them a card from someplace in Italy. She wanted to work in films. Not as a director. Maybe as a cutter, or something like that.

His wife took the glass from him. Then handed it back: 'Let's think of something to do today. Because all day in the garden . . .'

The glass in hand, he stood by the deck chair. He couldn't think of anything.

'Why don't you two take a walk up to the old chapel?'

The landlady stood near them; in her faded apron, she somehow looked like a schoolgirl.

'You know that little church, János. I'm sure you've been there with the Paczkos.'

'I'm not sure I remember.'

Again he could see the Paczkos sitting on the veranda, having breakfast. Aniko dribbling honey on a buttered slice of bread. And not only on the bread and butter. Also on her knee.

On the other side of the tracks, up on the hillside. That half-ruined chapel. Near a churchyard at least as old as the chapel. Where no one has been buried in the last fifty years.

'Where are you sending them?' The old man stepped closer, laughing. 'That ramshackle old church and the cemetery?'

'Yes, János, why don't you take Zsuzsi!' said the landlady with an emphatic nod. 'You've been up there with the Paczkos!'

'Yes, that girl of theirs was a fireball.' The old man stopped on the garden path. 'What was her name now?' He scratched his head pensively. 'Wasn't it Aniko? Aniko Paczko?'

'Oh, stop pretending you don't remember her name! As if you'd forgotten!'

János reached for a tree trunk with one hand. He lost his footing on the hillside. He stopped to catch his breath. Then started to climb again, sidling up between slender saplings. Maybe he should always walk like this from now on. Cautiously sliding one foot after another. The meagre little trail winding its way up the hill did not make things any easier. He kept sliding back. Maybe it was better through the trees and bushes. At least there was something to grab onto. He practically dove into the thicket. He tugged at branches as if holding them responsible for this whole struggle.

'What are you doing?' Zsuzsi's hand reached out toward him. 'What are you trying to do?'

He grabbed her hand and somehow fought his way out of the bushes. He continued to reminisce about Aniko Paczko and the old landlord.

'He serenaded her. He stood under her window and serenaded her with his violin.'

'And what did you do?' Zsuzsi asked, without turning around. She was pressing forward as if there were no tomorrow.

'I did not serenade her.' He kept his eyes on Zsuzsi. Look at her go! So familiar with the terrain! She had a way of being at home everywhere. She was already fast friends with the landlord and his wife.

Nasty, gnarly roots. And a much-weathered ladies' handbag. Next to it, a broken comb.

'Why do you have to pick that up?' Zsuzsi looked back at him. There was no anger in her eyes. She was more like a patient nanny.

János deposited the handbag on top of a flat, blackened rock. Very carefully, as if he expected the owner to come looking for it.

At last there were no more trees, as if they had suddenly scattered and run off.

They stood in front of the chapel. Yellowed walls, windows without glass. Even the ground they stood on seemed yellowed.

'Skulls and thighbones,' said János.

'What do you mean?'

'Inside, they heaped up the skulls. After they massacred the village . . .'

'Did the old man tell you that?'

'Not really. But you know, there are some abandoned old churches like this with piles of skulls inside.'

They walked around the chapel. One window had iron bars. Behind that, nothing. Nothing but dead, empty air.

'That's where the priest took refuge.'

'And now, a priest.' Zsuzsi laughed. 'What kind of priest are you talking about?'

Balding clumps of grass around the chapel. Yellowed newspaper sheets. Broken glass. Shattered pieces of glass everywhere among the clumps of grass.

János looked up at the empty window frame.

'Maybe they broke this not that long ago.'

'So what happened to your priest?'

János stepped aside as if he intended to circle the chapel. 'This is where he must have found refuge with his flock. The last handful of followers. Excommunicated by the Church for heretical beliefs.'

'Heretical beliefs!'

'After he'd been driven out everywhere, this was his final stand. He preached his last sermon in this chapel, surrounded by his brethren. There weren't many of them. But they remained loyal to the end. Nobody left the chapel when the final assault came.'

'And then?'

János contemplated the partly collapsed roof. The rusty bars on the window. All sorts of inscriptions on the wall.

Zsuzsi stood close by his side. Then suddenly she wasn't there. She was already behind the chapel on that narrow path winding among the trees and grave mounds. Crooked crosses and lopsided tombstones. Or else bare mounds.

'This one was a pharmacist,' said Zsuzsi, pointing at a marker. The blackened letters were barely legible. 'Mihály Komáromi, Pharmacist, 1810–1892.'

'His pharmacy must have been down in the village.'

'And here's another one.'

'A pharmacists' graveyard.'

'Oh, come on!'

'Why not? This is where they brought the pharmacists. Not just from this village but from all over the place.'

'Here's a teacher! Peter Simai.'

'The pharmacists were probably delighted to have his company.'

A boy came running toward them among the graves. Shoulder-length blond hair. And a beard. That thick, full beard somehow made his face more boyish. With a bright smile, he hopped in front of Zsuzsi.

'Are you coming to the performance?'

As if delivering a message. An invitation to the party. Where the company was already assembled and waiting only for János and Zsuzsi to appear.

A hesitant smile appeared on Zsuzsi's face as she turned to her husband. He spread his arms.

'Well . . .'

The bearded one was already going. They followed.

'It's going to be in the chapel.'

'In the chapel?'

'Oh, not to worry!' Their guide turned around. 'It won't be very long.'

What won't be very long? What kind of performance? In that chapel?! That chapel, of all places!

They followed the leader. Who no longer paid them much attention, leaping from grave to grave.

Was he so positive that we'd follow? What was he thinking?

He flashed an encouraging smile in Zsuzsi's direction. János resented this right away.

Who needs his encouragement? Zsuzsi wasn't all that excited about this whole thing. And me even less. My dear young man, I haven't the faintest idea what kind of event you have concocted here and as a matter of fact I don't really care.

János had to stop. His foot was entangled in some sort of metal loop. Zsuzsi stopped too. Those clear, penetrating eyes gazed at him.

'Will you stop thrashing around for a moment?' Zsuzsi bent down and with two flicks of her wrist freed his foot.

'We should have gone to the cinema.' János kicked the rusty wire aside. 'Should have gone to the cinema instead.'

They emerged from the graveyard.

The small clearing near the hilltop was no longer empty. People were scattered in small groups with a solitary bystander here and there. A middle-aged couple squatted next to a dreary grey-green rucksack. Probably just removed from the man's back. The entire gathering seemed randomly herded together. A girl with a blonde topknot and long skirt. A man with a grey moustache, and others. A beard or two could be seen here and there. A placid farmer's beard above a faded shirt. Another beard that was a rich array of ringlets. The dome of the man's head was balding and rather bedraggled. As if inundated with sleet. Sleet and rain.

'Shall we take a peek?' János waved in the direction of the chapel.

'But they haven't started yet.'

'So what!'

The man had opened up his backpack. Out came the salami, and bread. He sliced it for the woman.

Making themselves quite at home. This made János feel something akin to alarm. That couple making themselves so obviously at home.

'Those Tunnel people!' announced Zsuzsi.

'What Tunnel people?'

'Or at least the leader of the group.' She pointed toward a boy with a reddish beard. 'He's the leader of the Tunnel group. You know, they show up everywhere, sneak in during performances. They remain quiet for a while, and then they create a ruckus!'

'That's their leader?' János brightened up. 'Then I know him. That is, I know his father.'

He felt a sudden surge of relief. As if nothing could go wrong now. As long as he knew the father of the Tunnel boy . . .

'His old man is a director, a television director. He's done a couple of things of mine. He's a nice guy, and I recall his telling me that his son was . . . '

By now he was standing in front of the boy.

'Well, well! Who would have thought!'

But the boy seemed bewildered. As if he'd been addressed in a foreign tongue. 'Your father . . . I know him well . . . ' Strange words, worn out long ago.

János stopped. He simply ran out of words.

The boy did not speak, either. They stared at each other for a while. Then János lumbered back to his wife.

'About time they began . . . ' he mumbled. 'What are they waiting for?'

The man with the rucksack and his wife were still eating in silence. A girl was snapping photos of the chapel. Then she turned around and started to walk downhill.

János stared after her.

'I think they are about to begin,' said Zsuzsi.

'I can hardly wait.'

Two girls stood at the chapel's entrance, as if they were ushers. Flesh-coloured shirts, tattered jeans. Their smiles seemed embarrassed. Embarrassed and shy. Each held a jar and a small dipstick, awaiting the audience.

And the audience stepped up one by one. János followed the man with the grey moustache. His wrist was dabbed with a brush.

'Honey,' nodded Zsuzsi.

'That's right, honey, of course.' And he stared at the golden smudge.

He looked at Zsuzsi's wrist. Then he turned toward a woman, a stranger. As if he meant to check every wrist.

Inside the chapel they stood to the side by themselves.

The bearded ones disappeared. So did the girls by the doorway. The walls were bare. No sign of an altar. No altar and no pews. The congregation must have prayed standing up.

Off to the side, in a dark alcove, the steps leading to the choir seemed to be in surprisingly decent shape. János took a step or two up the stairs.

A bearded head appeared over the gallery railing. After pensively considering the audience for a while, the head withdrew.

No sign of preparations of any kind.

The door was left open a crack. János peeked outside. He gestured to Zsuzsi to follow. But she was busy reading the inscriptions on the wall. She did not even hear János asking her:

'Shall we step outside?'

A grey-haired lady's wrinkled face looked askance at him, as if in disapproval. And the girl with the camera was back again. She came back? All by herself?

People were milling around each other. Hardly a word was spoken. Except for an occasional whisper:

'What's going on?'

'When will it begin?'

Small groups coalesced and fluttered apart as if afraid that someone would disapprove. Then a shocked voice:

'Wafers!'

A pouch of wafers swung overhead on a thin string. The silver-haired older woman stared with a beatific smile. Her lips moved soundlessly. The wafers turned and turned about. 'Medicinal materials' said the blue letters on the side of the pouch.

The Tunnel boy again appeared in the choir. This time he seemed to be looking at János in a familiar way. Perhaps he was willing to engage a conversation now.

'Please form two separate groups! One for women and another for men.'

What was this? What was going on?

By now Zsuzsi was waving at him from the other side of the chapel. A key clicked in a lock. The chapel door was locked.

"Hey!' someone said.

Next to János the man wearing a shirt-jacket shrugged. And Zsuzsi seemed so far away. I should go over to her.

But he did not move. He remained with his group.

One of the hostesses approached the men. The other one, the women. Each held wafers in her hand.

They are going to stick the wafers on our foreheads, János thought. We'll be standing here with wafers sticking to our foreheads.

Instead, the wafers were stuck to the soles of their feet. Feet were lifted as in some peculiar ritual dance. The man with the shirt-jacket kept shrugging his shoulders undecided but the wafer was already stuck to the sole of his sandals. János tried to hide by the wall but without success.

There were three of them up in the choir, watching the distribution of wafers. The Tunnel boy, the mild-mannered farmer and the bedraggled man.

Who knows, maybe the girls would take shaving mugs up there and start shaving those beards.

Now Tunnel boy was alone, Farmer and Bedraggled were gone.

'I'd like your attention, please! Our first number is about to begin.' He smiled a vague smile. 'Free fall.'

He held up a dark green bottle. One could clearly see traces of a label. He raised the bottle high and let it go. With a loud crash, the bottle broke into pieces on the stone pavement. Zsuzsi's face twitched. She disliked sudden noises.

Now her face looked just like on that old school photo. Where she's in her uniform along with the rest of the handball team. The game must have been a disaster; perhaps she'd been injured. Her face had the abandoned look of a dusty, desolate lot on the outskirts.

A moment of silence. Now a crash was heard outside.

Maybe they would keep smashing bottles. Inside and outside.

Meanwhile János had a vision of his room. The dresser, with his shirts neatly stacked. The bar of soap among them. Tabac soap. He was seized by an urge to open that dresser again and breathe in that pleasant, intimate scent.

A small table in the centre of the chapel. With improbably thin legs and covered by a blue- and-white-striped kitchen cloth. On top, two dark grey cylinders made of cardboard.

The women's group parted. An older woman stepped forward. On moccasined feet, she shuffled to the table. She took off her necklace and placed it next to the cylinders. She stood there for a moment or two, then returned to her group.

Who would be next? Zsuzsi? But she doesn't have anything like that on her. And all I have is the keys in my pocket . . . but the keys must stay.

The Tunnel boy picked up the necklace. He weighed the pearls in one hand, then the other. Then, as if setting out on a long journey, he started off in the direction of the old lady. He ambled over to her. And he returned the string of pearls to that wrinkled old neck. Then he seemed to forget about her and was already standing behind the table.

And now the second number!

He picked up a cylinder and showed one end . . .

'Empty.'

. . . and now the other end.

'Empty.'

He did the same with the other cylinder. Empty . . . empty . . . He paused for a moment, and lifted the first one. There was nothing under it. Nor under the other one. He kept this up for a while.

Then suddenly there was a small oil lamp under the cylinder. A touchingly modest little oil lamp.

János looked on, puzzled.

Something else had to happen. They can't let us go like this. They could paint all sorts of motifs on our faces. No, not paint. Tattoo. Flowers, circles, whatever . . . Then two sunflowers could sit down at a table in the cafe. A doppio, says one. A nice, strong doppio. And the waiter would stare in amazement. People at other tables would turn to look.

A broom came flying from the choir. The boy caught it in midair. He started to sweep the floor with florid gestures. The oil lamp blazed up unexpectedly. Next thing the broom was in flames.

'He held it to the flame,' someone whispered. 'It was intentional.'

The boy raced around the chapel with the flaming broom. Then a blackened broomstick, burnt to cinders, flew into a corner. A scary scorched stub of a broom.

The boy now stood among the shards. As if he had just stumbled into this chapel. He looked around seemingly waking from a dream. Perhaps he was searching for a face to pick out from among the others. A companion who would join him for a walk. A walk and a chat. Occasionally stopping and looking around. In the street, in a park, in a garden.

'Let's breathe!' The boy raised a hand. 'Let's breathe together!'

People held their breath for a while. Then a gasp was heard. Followed by hurried, quick breaths. As if they were making an effort.

'Wait up!' said the bearded one. 'Ladies first!'

A deep sigh arose from the women's group.

'Breathe in!' He waved in the direction of the men. 'Suck that air into your lungs. Let it in.'

He waved his arms like a conductor.

'Now the men! And the women! Now the men! . . .'

But the result turned out to be rather shaky. Some simply forgot to breathe. Or breathed at the wrong time. And neither group paid the least attention to the other.

Zsuzsi sent tiny little balls of air toward János. And he returned them. These balls bounced back and forth without a sound.

'Hold it! This isn't going very well!'

The boy motioned for them to stop.

One or two embarrassed, hurried breaths. Clearing of throats. Then silence.

The boy sat with knees to chest in the midst of the broken glass. He was laughing. Or maybe he had the hiccups. He was in no hurry to stand up. He squatted among the shards and shook.

Was he laughing? Or crying?

The chapel door was opened.

But no one started to leave. They stood around the boy with confused expectancy. The older woman leant over him and said something. Perhaps she wanted to convince him to accept her necklace. Or her grass-green moccasins. So that she would leave barefoot without her jewellery.

The boy calmed down. The strange, hiccup-like sounds stopped. He was still hugging his knees, his hands holding his ankles.

The old woman stood up. She looked around as if seeking an intermediary. Someone who could convince the boy. The ceremony should not end like this.

The girl with the camera took a few steps backward. Her eyes measured the light through the windows falling on the boy on the pavement. Someone touched her shoulder. It was the gentle farmer. With a shake of his head he signalled no, no photos. The girl stood around for a while, rather puzzled. Then she turned and left.

The old woman also set out, turning about hesitantly, as if she were still expecting some explanation. Next to her an elderly man wearing glasses kept nodding in a bemused way. The man in the shirt-jacket also left. One after another, they all exited.

János and Zsuzsi stood outside, watching the others depart. Some practically galloped downhill. As if suddenly frightened. Two men propped up the old woman, who kept looking back toward the chapel. She still seemed to be awaiting some sign. But there was no sign whatever forthcoming. And she stumbled on with her companions.

The girl with the camera went off in the direction of the grave-yard.

'Why didn't they allow her to take photographs?' asked Zsuzsi.

'They don't believe in that sort of stuff.'

Unexpectedly, Zsuzsi turned back. She started walking back toward the church.

'I'll take another peek.'

'Why? What do you want to see?'

But Zsuzsi was already at the front door. One hand on the doorknob, she looked inside. János stood behind her. They saw the shattered glass on the pavement and the stump of the broom.

'There's no one in here.' Zsuzsi went inside. 'They vanished.'

'Perhaps up above.' János started to climb the stairs to the choir.

He found no one upstairs. He bent over the railing and waved.

'How could they disappear so fast!?' Zsuzsi sounded disappointed.

'They moved on.' János touched her shoulder. 'Perhaps we should, too . . .'

They lingered for a few moments in the clearing outside.

'They'll find some other ruin and take shelter,' said János.

'Does it always have to be some ruin?'

János was eyeing the train station down in the valley. The arc of the railway tracks and the small houses around the station.

'Someday they will set fire to everything. They'll go on the road and destroy everything they find. Museums, libraries, theatres . . . not even cinemas will be spared.'

'Not even cinemas?'

'No, they'll spare nothing. Perhaps they have no choice . . . '

'The things you say!' Zsuzsi stared at him, dumbfounded. She suddenly turned and ran downhill.

János raised his arm. That golden-brown smudge on his wrist! It was a bit fainter but still quite visible. As if shining from under the skin.

He rotated his wrist and stared at it on the empty clearing in front of the church. Then he too trotted down the hillside among the trees.

WOMEN'S LOCKER ROOM (1974)

Little Mrs Hirmann picked up her tray. 'You're just the man Anikó needed.' She fell silent. She waited for the man at the table to turn toward her.

Cognac glass empty, he sat looking down into the lower part of the cafe. Waitresses circulated among the tables. The young woman with auburn red hair was stationed behind the glass of the pastry counter. While dishing out two portions of Dobos torte, her fingers wafted a barely noticeable wave at the man seated in the upper gallery.

She always does that, thought Mrs Hirmann, that's how she must have met this guy, too.

The customer responded with the slightest flutter of a fingertip. The way you wave to a sister boarding a train. ('If anything happens, just call me.') Still not turning toward Mrs Hirmann, he noted, 'She's such a sweet kid.'

'That she is,' Mrs Hirmann's head bobbed in agreement. She moved over to a neighbouring table where they had asked for the check. Then she was back. 'Anikó needs guidance, a firm hand.' She sighed. 'And you've been to so many places in your life. The girls say you've been to Mexico.'

Still peering down below, the man said, 'No way am I going to let her sit in the window wearing toreador pants.'

'Oh, toreador pants!'

'Hot-pink toreador pants.' He said he just about had a fit when he saw Anikó sitting on the windowsill in her hot-pink toreador pants. A policeman had already yelled at her from the street, even sent up a kid with a message, but Anikó stayed right where she was, nibbling a slice of buttered toast.

Mrs Hirmann swung her tray and chuckled. 'That's her, all right. That's our Anikó.'

The man nodded emphatically: 'I really let her have it.' He wagged his head slowly and ordered a double espresso.

'Well I'll be! . . .' laughed Mrs Hirmann. She shot the man another glance from the stairs. Passing the glass counter, she raised her eyebrows at Anikó. 'I've been getting the lowdown on you.'

Anikó smiled and looked up in the man's direction. 'He tries to be strict with me but he's really sweet.'

'Where'd you find him?' asked the tall brunette by her side.

'Is that his car outside?' the blonde waitress wanted to know.

Anikó shrugged. 'He's not your everyday type, that's for sure.'

Two waitresses flanked Anikó: a thin brunette, and a chunky blonde.

'Looking good,' the manager said, as she walked by. At a staff meeting all had agreed that the sight of the threesome produced a desirable effect. In case a customer's eyes should rest on them.

'I try to be equally nice to every guest,' Mrs Hirmann said, waiting by the espresso machine.

'But it's always girls like Anikó who have all the luck!' The woman working the machine had a tired, glum face.

An array of empty espresso cups covered the counter.

'He'll ditch her, just watch.' Mrs Hirmann shrugged. 'Like Borika was dumped by her doctor. She thought he would marry her, now she'll have to think again.'

'That's because these girls have no idea how to act.' Shishtering steam billowed from the machine.

Up in the gallery, the man rested his chin on his palm. He was trying to recall, how did it happen? Did anyone introduce Anikó to him? How did he meet her? He never bought pastries. He hated sweets.

'Stefi was looking for you,' said the blonde behind the counter.

'Stefi who?' Anikó looked at her.

'You know who! She works the espresso at the Zone.'

The three girls stood side by side behind the glass counter. Anikó took the brunette and the blonde by the hand. 'High time Stefi's husband came home,' she said, smiling.

'Why, where is he?' asked the blonde.

'In Berlin, with the Berczeller orchestra. Been a month now.'

'Ho boy!' said the brunette.

'I don't even dare go to the Zone any more.' Anikó released the girls' hands. She looked at a man standing in front of the counter, but went on talking. 'Last time, she tossed my clothes all over the place.'

'She did?' The brunette shook her head, signalling incomprehension.

'I hear her little sister's a good student.' Mrs Hirmann placed the double espresso on the table.

'Yes, she's curious about everything.' The man picked up the cup, then put it down. She made me write a whole book about my travels. Telling her about it wasn't enough—I had to write it all down for her.'

'You've really been to Mexico?'

The man smiled. He recalled the conversation with Anikó's sister in that narrow little room. 'You actually got to see Josephine Baker and Chevalier?' the girl had asked. 'When I was in Paris, Chevalier happened to be on a tour abroad, but I did manage to see Baker.' Then Anikó's sister mentioned a name that didn't ring a bell. Someone he hadn't heard of, not even on a record. He went to join Anikó in the back of the room and the little sister stopped asking questions. She sat with her back to them, staring out the window. At first he had found this somewhat strange, but you could get used to it. 'I can't send her away from home each time,' said Anikó.

'My husband and I, we'd planned a trip to Vienna,' said Mrs Hirmann. She placed the tray under her arm. 'Then nothing came of it.'

The cafe was nearly empty. The manager in her yellow sweater had already more than once strolled past the tables that were still occupied. As if trying to speed up those few straggling customers.

Mrs Hirmann had to ask. 'Will you be taking her out somewhere after we close?'

The man glanced up at her. 'Sure, we always go out somewhere.' His smile made his face younger. It became a kind, boyish face, and for a moment it seemed possible that he might invite her along, too.

'Of course,' Mrs Hirmann nodded. 'You should take her out.' Now her husband, he wouldn't put up with her coming home even half an hour late. Because she's had customers who'd invited her out, more than once.

Turning her tray, Mrs Hirmann looked down at the man. 'I'm attracted only to men who are serious.'

The next instant a circle of trays surrounded them. Five or six waitresses stood at the table, brandishing their trays like so many bucklers. They giggled, bowing and scraping.

'And how is our dear guest?'

'Haven't seen you in ages!'

'Are you cheating on Anikó with Mrs Hirmann?!'

The man's face was beaming. For a moment he toyed with the notion of ordering a bottle of Cinzano. Then he glanced up at the raven-haired waitress. She always had something catty to say about Anikó. He decided against ordering.

'We were just chatting,' said Mrs Hirmann, tilting her head back. 'That's all we ever do.'

The girls ignored her.

'Last time you had another car,' said one waitress, bending forward.

Before the man had a chance to say anything, one of her colleagues butted in: 'C'mon! It was the same yellow car.'

The waitresses' chorus chimed: 'Oooh, mellow yellow!'

When the manager strolled past, the waitresses scattered. Only Mrs Hirmann remained. She glanced after the manager. 'Not that long ago she too was waiting on tables.' Then she excused herself, to go and add up her checks for the night.

The man was almost the only customer left in the cafe. If the manager strolled past one more time, he'd order something. Although they might have stopped serving for the night. But why? It wasn't even that late.

He was being kissed on the lips.

'Are you cheating on me?!'

Anikó stood in front of him, smiling, her hands behind her back.

'Think I didn't see them flirting with you?' She playfully wagged a forefinger at him. 'You wait right here while I change in the locker room.' And she galloped down the stairs.

The man's eyes followed her. Such a kid, a sweet kid. Who was it who said that some people never grow up? Must have read it somewhere. And if the child in you is dead, you're all done for.

He stared off into space and repeated, 'If the child in you is dead . . .'

Mrs Erszényes, Gizi Berek, Panni Csermák—the women's lockers came in that order. The waitresses and counter girls whose shift was over were already down there. Standing around in front of the lockers, no one seemed to feel like undressing.

Mrs Darvas of the raven locks sat on a stool, dangling her feet. 'Either my husband's waiting outside, or else my boyfriend. They're both worthless.' With the saddest of gestures, she placed a hand on her left breast.

'I hate the way he touches me!' Mrs Bazsó with the blond top-knot held an orange in her hand. She ripped it open, and tossed segments to the girls. 'My husband's a decent sort but he makes me gag the minute he comes near me.'

Mrs Hirmann sat on a chair, tugging the zipper at her back. 'You shouldn't talk like that.'

Mrs Bazsó gave her one look and waved her hand in disgust.

A tall brunette yawned. 'That veterinarian was here again. He keeps inviting me to go swimming. Why the swimming pool, I can't figure.'

'I hope for your sake he doesn't have pipe-stem legs,' said Mrs Bazsó.

'I keep thinking it's all over for me,' said Mrs Darvas, letting go of her breast.

'Stop whining, all of you!' Anikó pranced past the lockers. 'You'll find someone, someone always comes along.' She stopped in mid-gesture, as she was grabbed from behind.

Borika grasped Anikó's waist and in one stroke unzipped her skirt. Slashed her down the middle.

Anikó watched her skirt tumble to the floor, then stepped away from it. 'You've done this before. The time I was standing behind the counter, and only noticed when . . .' She eyed the skirt on the floor and laughed.

'You have a hard ass.' Mrs Darvas regarded Anikó dreamily.

'So do you,' nodded Anikó.

'No, not me.' Mrs Darvas shook her head.

Borika's naughty kid mug leant jeering close to Anikó's face. 'Nobody's is like yours and you know it.'

'Remember Itza?' asked Mrs Bazsó. 'Works at the Mignon now. The bosoms on her! . . .'

'And how are mine?' Anikó stepped in front of her.

Upstairs, the manager sat down at the man's table. 'Everyone envies me. If they only knew the problems I have with all these girls!'

He gave her a sidelong glance. 'Some of them are all right.'

'Mrs Hirmann,' nodded the manager.

'Yes, Mrs Hirmann, for one.' It sounded as if he could go on with the list of decent girls forever.

'So what do you think about her breasts?' asked Borika, moving to Anikó's side.

'What's this, are you her manager now?' said Mrs Bazsó.

Mrs Darvas stared off into space, with a vague smile that made her face suddenly that of a little girl.

'You've got such a sweet little butt.'

She slithered over next to Anikó's butt, looking up at her with tender beseeching eyes, as if not quite certain of her welcome.

Mrs Bazsó said, 'Let's see those bazooms.'

'No, you really shouldn't.' Mrs Hirmann placed her hands by her side on the stool.

Meanwhile Borika, as if obeying a command, pulled down the zipper on Anikó's back.

Anikó dipped her head and her blouse was off. Somewhat hesitant, head still bent, she stood in front of Mrs Bazsó. A vague, triumphant smile began to spread from the corners of her eyes.

'Chin up, chest out,' said Borika.

Anikó lifted her head and stood a little taller.

Borika's finger grazed Anikó's breast and looked at Mrs Bazsó.

Gizi Berek took hold of Anikó's left breast, and Mrs Erszényes took hold of the right breast.

'Can't stand being left out, huh?' said Borika to Mrs Erszényes. 'And who invited you?'

'Let her.' Anikó cast down her eyes. Her shoulder trembled. Someone was caressing and kissing her from below and calling her endearing names. It was just like being plunged into a luxuriant bath.

'Who gave you permission?' Borika put her hand over Mrs Erszényes' hand.

Mrs Erszényes did not let go of Anikó. She was wailing, why couldn't she, if Gizi Berek could, not to mention Mrs Darvas down there! . . .

Mrs Hirmann sat on a stool. Miles away from everyone. 'Stop doing this to her,' she said, her nails clawing the edge of the stool.

'Off to the showers with her!' commanded Mrs Bazsó.

Gizi Berek clung to one breast, Mrs Erszényes clung to the other breast. From below, Mrs Darvas slithered all the way up to Anikó's neck and clung there, motionless.

Anikó's face was one happy grin. She raised her head. Gingerly, as if afraid to shake something loose from her hair.

With an expert move, Mrs Bazso placed her hands on Anikó's breasts.

Mrs Erszényes, thinking they were trying to chase her away, clung all the closer.

Mrs Hirmann slid off her stool and stepped in front of Anikó. 'He's waiting for you. Such a nice man ... such a very nice man.'

Anikó smiled.

Mrs Darvas slithered up and down Anikó's back, nuzzled her hair, whispered in her ear, then sledded down between her legs.

'Me, too,' said a waitress wearing glasses that made her look like a geography teacher. She stepped up to Anikó and took hold of an earlobe.

Mrs Bazsó called out again: 'Off to the showers with her!'

Borika patted Anikó's neck from behind and tipped her head forward. Anikó's downcast eyes swept over her shoulders, breasts and waist, saying farewell to her shoulders, breasts and waist.

Two girls grabbed her arms and marched her off toward the showers.

Mrs Hirmann leapt in front of them. She shouted something, but they pushed her aside. She shook her head, then staggered in the wake of the procession.

'One time I almost let her go,' said the manager.

The man looked at her and raised his cognac glass. He ordered two more cognacs and two double espressos and asked the manager to be his guest. Not for himself, really, but more on Anikó's behalf ...

'I don't even remember what she did that time. Maybe gave a customer an earful. But I sure lit into her.'

The man pulled himself up, visibly stiffened. 'Anikó's not one to talk back. Believe me, she's not at all like that.' His voice grew tender. 'A bit wild, maybe, but only because no one's given her enough attention.' He corrected himself. 'The right kind of attention. Yes, the problem is no one's given her the right kind of attention.'

'I try my best, but this isn't a boarding school.' The manager shook her head and said, 'Believe me, I don't have it easy.'

'None of us has it easy.'

Anikó's head was wrapped in a turban. Around her bottom Mrs Darvas had knotted a towel which she yanked off when Anikó was installed under the shower.

They installed her under the shower.

'Let me control the water,' said the waitress with the glasses. She let lukewarm water dribble over Anikó.

'She needs a good scrub,' said Mrs Bazsó.

They began to strip. Gizi Berek and Mrs Erszényes jumped under the shower.

'I'll handle this,' said Borika and took the bar of soap from Mrs Erszényes' hand.

'No you won't!' Mrs Erszényes grabbed Anikó's breast. A breast as hard as a water-polo ball.

'I'll wash her from behind!'

'I'll do her neck!'

'I've got her shoulders!'

'I've got her breasts!'

They were trampling each other under the shower.

One person alone stood with her clothes on. It was Mrs Hirmann. She stood and watched, bereft of speech. She watched as, splashing and screeching, they swooped down on Anikó, trying to grab her away from each other, Mrs Erszényes attempting to leap from the shower holding one of Anikó's breasts, Borika tripping her, the two tumbling over each other, Anikó's other breast grabbed by Klári with the glasses, who flipped it to Mrs Bazsó, who passed it to Gizi Berek, who . . .

Mrs Hirmann squatted down in front of the shower.

'Anikó,' she called, 'Anikó . . .'

Anikó's face, lit by an ecstatic smile, rose from the torrent.

Upstairs, the man was saying, 'Yes, to bring out the best in someone, with love and patience, that's the most we can hope to accomplish.'

THE NIGHT BEFORE THE JOURNEY (1989)

Riding toward London on horseback, in the rain. Soaked to the skin. Water streaming from my hat down my face. I did not wipe it away. Why bother? And my skinny little nag with white stockings! Enduring the rain with such endless patience. Nid-nodding her head but never looking back at me. Although somehow I still caught a glimpse of her eyes. Those tired, wise eyes. Seemingly grateful. Perhaps because I never goad her, never use harsh words.

Muddy clay everywhere. An evil, dark glistening. Tiny hovels in the distance. Shrunken lights in the windows. Where the charcoal burners live. A whole settlement of charcoal burners, in fact. They are watching. Perhaps not with noses pressed against the windowpanes, but watching, all the same. Rather anxiously. Who knows, I could trot up to a house. Slide off from my horse, and knock on the door. But no! They have nothing to fear on my account! I must get to London, rain or shine. Unless I get mired in this nasty clayey muck.

The horse shook her head. Maybe to reassure me. By now she was feeling quite at home on this turf. And who cared about the rain! Haughtily I unbuttoned the top two buttons of my overcoat. In open defiance of the rain. *We'll see who's the boss!*

Women were passing by. And strange figures wearing caps with earflaps, hands in pockets. Paying no attention to me. Or maybe they were. That low, mocking laughter as they passed! It might have been meant for me and my horse.

Then the horse stopped. Hung her head, refused to budge. I slid my palm along her flank, meaning to give her rump a few reassuring, friendly pats. Might have even mumbled something. Then I just toppled forward and embraced her neck.

The lights in the windows went out.

We stood there soaking, in the mud, in the dark.

I found myself in an abandoned trench.

A long, deep trench. Big enough to promenade in. Instead, I flattened myself against a side wall, forehead first. The wall itself felt like a forehead gone cold. A twig was sticking out of it. The rest of the tree inside that wall of sand. Trapped, unable to break out. The little twig was a signal sent out, a desperate appeal for help. Perhaps people would notice. And try to liberate the tree. Maybe someone would turn up. Some qualified person, who knew a way out. I would think this task was waiting for someone else. I sincerely hope so. A preposterous idea! Never in my life have I done that sort of landscaping work.

Gardening, in a military trench. The very notion! While I'm at it, why not instal a flowerbed? No, that's out of the question.

But still, this tree . . . It can't just stay here, buried in the sand.

My palm inched along the twig. Slowly, carefully. One false move, and it might snap off.

I palpated the soil. I must explore the terrain. What are my prospects here. What indeed! Am I out of my skull? What was I thinking!? I don't even have a lousy shovel! And even if I had one! I wouldn't know which end was which!

The soil crumbling under my palms. I palmed and patted it with both hands. That thin little twig bending so perilously. A grey cloud of dust all over me. Never mind. I couldn't stop now.

The voice, from above, with an official ring to it:

'Where are you from?'

I tried to stand up straight. Couldn't see anything through the grey dust cloud. Who was up there? I shouted into the air above:

'Excuse me? Who is this? What did you say?'

Silence. Then a dry voice:

'Where are you from? What country?'

I collapsed against the wall. I stopped trying to stand up straight. My head felt as if it had been pulverized. And myself, like some creeping vine.

Still, I managed to lift my face.

'Hungary.'

Again, silence. A profound, ponderous silence. Then barely audible, astonished titters. A flurry of whispers, snickering. Some sort of discussion. Hungary mentioned more than once.

But who were those people up there? Officials? Some kind of control commission? All right, we could discuss the matter. Just let me get disentangled first. And if you want to know about Hungary, I can tell you that . . .

An exasperated gesture, groping for something to hang on to. I grabbed empty air and slid back down the wall, sweeping away with me that forlorn, bent little twig.

I was staggering down the length of a desolate street, carrying a pail. In it, wilted flowers, tattered branches and twigs, some muddy soil. Every now and then a flower or two would fall from the pail, perhaps trying to escape. But I picked them up, shoved them right back.

Faces in the windows, behind curtains slightly pulled aside. Stolid stares. But why? Could anyone tell me? Can someone give me a reasonable answer? Could I be all alone here, on this endless road?! This pail is truly a most faithful companion. As for the flowers . . . well, yes, I picked them for myself. They're not for sale. I won't be selling them at the marketplace or on a street corner. No one can take me to task on that account. I'm not violating any ordinance or law.

I looked back.

A trail of dropped flowers behind me.

Fine, fine, it's really not such a big deal. I can pick up after myself. I know my duty. I yelled up at a window:

'Throw me a broom! Can you hear me? I need a broom!'

A steel-grey statue in a desolate square.

A bald man, head bowed, hands linked behind his back. As if meaning to take a step in my direction.

No sign of transfiguration on that bearded face. More like humiliation. No mark on the pedestal, no name or date. No birth and no death. What had he accomplished? How did he earn this gloomy glory? Who could he be?

I moved on.

I continued my journey.

A piece of paper in front of me on the road. A ragged scrap of paper. How long has it been lying there? Did someone toss it there just now? Could be a message for me. Directions. Which way should I go to get to London. I picked it up, blew off the dust. Let's see now.

Dear Sir,

Go find another carpenter! We're through, I've had enough of you. Get off my back, spare me your phone calls, and, most of all, stop bothering my wife!

Respectfully,

(No signature)

In other words, he didn't even bother to scrawl his name there. And what does he mean by 'respectfully'? Is he making fun of me? Some nerve! Go find another carpenter. That's just great. Thanks for the tip. What does he think? That I'm going to London just to find another carpenter?

I rolled the paper into a tiny ball, but did not throw it away. I read it again and again:

. . . stop bothering my wife!

A man's voice in the distance:

'Flóra Ágfalvy called to say there's no screening today.'

The wet glimmer of the early morning sun. Lighting up the grass in the meadow. The bushes, and those strange yellow flowers. Rather common flowers. Do they even have a name? Flowers like that get mowed down along with the meadow grass. But no one's been mowing here. This meadow has gone to seed. Belongs to no one. There are no houses anywhere.

I flung my overcoat over my arm. I strolled into that tall grass. Maybe I'd never emerge from it. Blades of grass bowed in front of me. Only to unexpectedly snap back and hit me in the face.

The skinny head of a horse turning toward me. What an emaciated nag. And surprisingly familiar. Clearly we must have met before. Perhaps she had joined me on the road. Accompanied me for a while. Then she took off. Left me stranded. Maybe I should have spoken to her. Yes, she must have expected something like that. Except I was never very talkative. No I was never what you might call loquacious. Still, she might acknowledge me. Instead of turning away, hanging her head low. Practically disappearing, browsing there in the grass.

Her barely perceptible shudder. What's this? Secret snickering?

Hiding your mug in the grass, and snickering, my friend?

What's so funny? Is it me? The way I stand here with my overcoat on my arm?

Pensively swaying her head now. No, she's not laughing. In fact, her expression is most solemn. A concerned look, one might say. Pondering some problem. Perhaps an extraordinarily demanding mathematical equation. Or better yet, a philosophical problem.

Suddenly she turned my way. Her eyes shining. But of course! She had recognized me all along! The rest was just a joke. She was playing a game with me.

The horse did not move. Just contemplated me. A radiant glow in her eyes. The tremulous glimmering of a lake.

The next moment all this was gone.

Darkness surrounded me. And a kind of insidious silence. I blinked, confused and dazed.

Had they shoved me into a ditch? They threw me out somewhere and shoved me into a roadside ditch.

A dry creaking. The sofa! Of course! My room, and my ageing, grumpy, creaking sofa.

I tried to raise myself on an elbow. I tried again. I kept slipping back.

The blinded window facing me. Those slits in the loosely lowered blinds. And who is that in front of the window? That squat man with the bent back. How did he get in here? What does he want, anyway?

Ah, it's the armchair! But that armchair had never stood by the window. Is that where it wanders at night? Sneaking off under cover of darkness, night after night? What other surprises are in store for me?

I was sitting on the edge of the sofa.

That armchair . . . Ah well. It better confess everything voluntarily. Who sits in it at night? What guests does it entertain?

The head of a German Shepherd on the armchair. Eyes closed, mouth partly open, panting like an exhausted long-distance runner.

Taking one step I crashed into a suitcase.

Suitcases all around me. Open suitcases and travelling bags.

Oh my God! Our trip!

Tomorrow morning, the suitcases would be closed. They were going on a trip. Zsuzsi had already packed everything last evening. She left the suitcases open. Let them breathe until the morning. Those clothes, shirts, sweaters, outfits and the rest, let them have some air. But tomorrow morning . . .

No, not tomorrow morning!

It's this morning! A few more hours, and I'll be gone from this room. From this building. So what am I doing loitering among these suitcases?

But wait, this is still night. The middle of the night.

The door of the bedroom is ajar.

A few hesitant steps, toward Zsuzsi's bed. Ah, that cheerful, even breathing! Sleep! Sleep on!

I drew back.

As if now there were more suitcases in the room than before. Where did they spring up from? What closets? What dark, dusty shelves? Where no one paid them any mind until now. Where they had no more importance than a jar of preserves. But now they've come to the fore.

I'm going to shave. I'll take a bath. I'll lie down again. Maybe I'll catch a little more shut-eye.

I pulled up the blinds, very, very slowly.

That little park down there! Those trees, their leafy boughs, those narrow footpaths with their old benches!

I'd sit for hours at a time on those benches, walk on those paths, linger under those trees.

This was my park. And now I'd close the window on it.

What's going on here? Some kind of farewell? Perhaps there's a chance I might still return! After all I'm not being dragged off to a concentration camp.

Where am I going?

A hand passed over my brow. 'The child has a fever! What's wrong, Jancsi? We're only going across the river to Buda! It's not the end of the world!'

A dear, wrinkled face watched me, and repeated, 'It's not the end of the world!'

But it is too the end of the world!

Just like now. An old man setting out. Crawling out from his lair. Perhaps he should have done this earlier. (But when, I ask you? When?) Perhaps never.

But the chorus had been loud around me. The chorus of friends that night at the Pálmais.

'You've got to get away sometime!'

'Don't you see? It's absurd, the way you live!'

'And it wouldn't hurt your writing . . . take it from me!'

'You'll see, there are flea markets in London, too!'

'Cinemas in Berlin!'

'Streets in Warsaw!'

'Cemeteries in Prague!'

'Those little boîtes in Paris!'

'You've got to spend time in a Viennese coffee house!'

'Don't forget the museums!'

'Museums? No, that's not János's milieu! I can't see our János in museums or churches!'

Laughter.

'How do you know what his milieu is?'

They laughed and drank and raised their wineglasses in my direction. A toast to the great world traveller!

A woman suddenly popped the question:

'And what about America?'

'At a first go? No, better not. Let our János stay in Europe for now!'

'For now!' I, too, raised my wineglass. But I didn't drink. I just took in its crimson glow.

Zsuzsi touched my arm. Then, in a very quiet voice:

'What do you say we give it a try?'

And here I was in my pyjamas, wandering about without turning on any lights.

In the hall I grazed the sleeve of a coat hanging on the rack. For some sense of *security*. But what kind of *security*? Hugging that coat I may have nodded off.

A woman's barely audible voice from a distance. As if in the middle of a long harangue.

'. . . and you know, when I'm abroad I just can't help myself. I tell you I'm capable of fainting in the street. I must confess, London is my favourite place to faint.' (*Pause.*) 'I think I'm entitled to faint in London!'

Silence.

Suddenly I exploded:

'Well, I am not entitled to faint in London! Not entitled to faint anywhere! Not even right here on Klauzál Square!'

I was shaking with fury. Meanwhile, I was freezing. I practically wrapped myself in the coat that hung on the hook.

I fell silent, only my mouth was trembling now. I emerged from that coat. Why was I shouting in the hall in the middle of the night?

Why was the light on in the kitchen? I haven't been out there. Or have I? Did I drink a glass of water?

Where else have I been?

The light came on in the staircase. I heard the sound of the lift. That must be Dr Kaufman. Where did they summon her in the middle of the night? Usually, I run into her in the evenings, when she comes home. That tired, loyal face of hers. This evening, I won't be running into her. Or any of the other neighbours: Miklós Atlasz or Feri Csorba. This evening, I'll be running into a totally different crowd.

Faces of strangers in a crowded train station.

What are the faces of travellers like, lugging their suitcases toward the train? As they occupy their seats in the compartment? As they wave goodbye from the window? What is the conductor's face like?

The face of a border guard? A Customs officer?

It's as if I'm already hurled into the midst of that mad stampede.

Somewhere we shall embark on a sea voyage. In a port somewhere. Our suitcases will be transferred to a boat, along with ourselves.

What will Zsuzsi's face be like, as she turns to me?

And my face, first glimpsing the sea?

What is the sea like?!

A quick, unexpected punch. I feel dazed. That's it. A knockout.

I was lying on the sofa. I was not aware of pulling the blanket over me.

What is the ocean like?!

Dark and vast.

The whole world belonged to it once. It covered everything, was sovereign ruler. Gradually, it receded, with immeasurable hauteur. *Please show yourselves! Come forth, let's see you! You . . . who think yourselves mountains, better yet, peaks! Let's see what you look like.*

That's how it must have happened.

But what is the ocean like, *now*?! Right *now*! This hour! This very minute! Still the only truly vast power. Even if some day it will be all gone. Stormy or calm, it makes no difference. *The sea knows about me.* Knows every move I make. The way I toss and turn on this sofa. And pull at my blanket. And wallop the pillow. And suddenly get up and set out for the other room.

I got up. I set out for the other room. Oh, by now I knew my way around those suitcases!

No matter what, we've got to talk this over! Zsuzsi . . . please understand . . . this is absurd! Impossible! No way I can travel! I've been sick all night. A sudden attack . . . don't know what it is. It could happen to anyone. You should still go . . . that goes without saying. But you can't take an invalid along with you. No one would expect you to do that. As for my ticket, we won't demand our money back. No, we won't make any claims!

I was rehearsing something along those lines.

Then I was sitting on the edge of her bed. I gazed at Zsuzsi's face. That unsuspecting, otherworldly smile. Her shoulder twitched, as if she'd sensed a shadow falling over her.

That smile will be gone in an instant. The moment she looks up and glimpses that shadow, and must hear the same thing over and over: 'You've got to understand! You've got to understand!'

But she's had to understand so many things already. Give up her favourite outings, concerts, evenings at the theatre, birthday parties . . . Until nothing was left. Only the rules. The rules of this worn-out old man, who rises early in the morning. Stumbles over to his desk. Sits down by those flimsy scraps of paper. Then his tea has to be served. His tea and his toast. He takes a sip of tea. Then a bite of buttered toast. With an impatient gesture, he shoves the tray aside and begins his scratchy scribbling.

And yet, that night at the Pálmais I did get carried away. Who knows? Maybe I had a glass or two too many. But no! The enthusiasm was real enough. But it vanished soon ... evaporated.

Perhaps if there were no borders, and those inane passport controls ... Well, how would it be then? *You would still be stuck lugging around a forever frightened, half-crazed clown!*

I leant closer and closer until my face nearly touched hers.

What else lay in store for that face?

I slithered off the bed and crept into a corner. There I squatted, knees drawn up. I heard a sound from the bed. A thin, childlike voice. Then silence. No other sound followed. I waited a little longer, then noiselessly stole away.

Again, I was among the suitcases.

They seemed to be expecting me. They were helpless, just about desperate. Shirts with sleeves flung wide apart dangled from one. Another one shut itself up completely. They must have had a row of some kind. What caused the falling out? Was it the trip? Whether it was worth going? They'd hardly ever left the house before.

Arguments and counter-arguments were mustered. Insults flung. Old wounds and injuries torn open.

They suddenly fell silent. Discouraged, they wilted away. But as I entered the room ... Well, yes, some glimmer of hope animated them for a moment. What did they expect? That I would resolve their dispute? They pinned their hopes on me? Me, of all people?

I could hear my voice, a coward's voice:

'We'll go on a trip . . . yes, of course . . . why not?'

But I'd still like to take one last look around the staircase in our building . . . The staircase, the courtyard and the basement! Those ramshackle, dilapidated sofas, bent coat hangers, rusty buckets, superannuated sewing machines down there. Left behind at the last clean-up. So far, they have lucked out. But one of these days they'll be out on the pavement. The trash collector will come and then . . .

Suddenly those faces flared up again. Jittery, guttering candle flames. They interlaced, encircled me, winking and grinning.

'Portobello market in London!'

'Streets in Warsaw!'

'Cinemas in Berlin!'

'Cemeteries in Prague!'

'You've got to see them! You've got to see them!'

The faces disappeared. I waited for a while, to see if they'd reappear.

I clicked on the table lamp, and took the picture album, *Greetings from Old Budapest*, off the shelf.

I plunged into the turn-of-the-century city.

I saw the first tramcar setting out on Gyár Street. It was a pretty slow start. I tagged along for a while.

I looked at a view of Bécsi Street from Szervita Square. Gizella Square as seen from Harmincad Street.

St Roch's Hospital and the Folk Theatre.

I soaked in the warm pool at Császár Baths. I climbed out of the pool, only to lie down by the poolside, stretching my legs out on the steps. In the vast greyish-white colonnade baked bodies, loose swimming trunks, crossed arms, conversations.

'PHARMACY – PERFUMES'

I lingered in front of Gyula Eisner's pharmacy, The Two Lions. Should I go in? Shouldn't I buy something?

Or enter Mano Fanto's tobacco shop instead?

I greeted the King of Siam in front of the Parliament building. There he stood with his entourage on the steps of the Parliament, a somewhat baby-faced monarch wearing a top hat.

Should I sit down among the bowler-hatted regulars in the coffee house under the arcades of Drechsler Palace? I really wouldn't want to disturb them. Let them chat on and peruse their papers.

Or maybe stop in at the Cafe Japan? At the artists' table? I wouldn't dare to approach their august company!

I think I'd rather be with the writers and journalists at the Home Club. Yes, it looks more inviting. The way they all sit in the garden, playing cards, wrapped in cigar smoke.

Girls! Girls on ice skates! Gracefully gliding in the rink, arms straight out, as if they were going to fly away. They cling to each other, then let go. Behind them, the austere edifice of the high school. One of the girls raced in my direction, waved at me and laughed. Then whirled around suddenly and disappeared among her companions.

I stood in front of the Opera House.

Then in front of Jókai's statue.

I shut the album, turned off the lamp, and sat there motionless.

I stood up, perhaps to go somewhere. Instead, I remained there, clinging to the table's edge.

The darkness undulated around me. The room expanded, grew infinitely spacious. Now it was no longer a room, but a field lost in fog, tiny lights twinkling in the distance.

I smiled a dreamy smile.

'Horsie . . . where are you now?'

THE MORNING OF THE JOURNEY (1989)

Grey dusk lifting from the room. A thin strip of bright light sundered the grey murk—taunting rather than encouraging. And me in my pyjamas, surrounded by scattered suitcases. I must have spent the night here. Maybe I should stow myself away in one of those suitcases.

The first beep of the alarm clock still reverberated in the air. Then it sounded as if several clocks started chirping all at once.

In a long flowery nightgown, Zsuzsi scurried back and forth, lugging packages. She asked in passing:

'When did you last see a barber?'

I ran my fingers through my hair.

'My barber died.'

'So now you're not going . . .'

'I've been going to him for thirty years.'

'How long do you intend to mourn him?'

I stared out at the little park. It was unlikely that someone would turn up among the trees now. In the distance, drawn shutters, shabby shop signs.

'You could use a shave.'

'That I could, yes.'

I couldn't drag myself away from the window. All those rusty shutters! This was the morning of rusty shutters. Well, maybe not. Maybe this wasn't the morning of rusty shutters. This was a morning of quite another kind.

A soft, clear voice came from down there:

'Béla, Béla! Will you ever come back? . . . and when will that be?'

No answer.

I mumbled, half-asleep, in a stupor:

I look for her high,

I look for her low,

but Shanghai Lil's always on the go!

Behind me, hard, sharp clicks. The suitcases being locked.

'You could give me a hand.'

I reached out and groped in the air. But somehow I fell short of the suitcases.

Zsuzsi laughed.

'The way you move! It's like slow motion. You know what? Why don't you go and shave instead. Go on, pinch yourself a couple of times, daddy-o.'

Daddy-o in the bathroom. Studying his face. That temporary face. Soon to vanish from the mirror. Still . . . ! Those few gestures, lathering the face . . . they are still familiar. Also the way he rinses the blade, and then his face. He lets water into the tub. Climbs in, extremely cautiously. Later he reaches for a towel. Slow, protracted movements. But still, they are his own!

A door slammed somewhere.

Thumping of feet, racing down the stairs.

Voices in the staircase.

Voices.

'Are the repairmen coming today?'

'They're never coming!'

Another door slammed.

I ran to my room. In a tizzy I scribbled on a piece of paper:
The small pillow is a dead baby.
Simi's drinking beer.
Mumbles, shambles, turns on lights.
Richie chats through the whole class period,
Richie chats nonstop with his neighbour.
A horse standing in the room
on Christmas Eve.

I might be able to use these somewhere. In a story, or whatever . . .
Zsuzsi's calling:
'What's up? You fall asleep?!'

Facing each other over the breakfast table.

Tea, bread and butter, jam. Pretty much as always. Since time immemorial.

I dunked my face into a cloud of steaming tea. I did not feel like looking up.

All at once I could hear my own voice:

' . . . we lay stock still in our bunks. Nobody was asleep. Every-one waiting for the moment when she entered the dorm.'

Zsuzsi put down her teacup.

'What are you mumbling about?'

'Aw, it's nothing!'

'Who were you all waiting for? Who was supposed to enter? What's this all about?'

That touch of despair in her voice. Here comes the monologue! Another rap! Again she asked:

'What's this all about?'

'Key sentences. I must unravel Sister Anni out of these.'

'Why must you unravel Sister Anni?'

'It's a story . . . a story of sorts.'

Silence.

Followed by an alarming flurry of details.

'A Lake Balaton resort. Summer camp for children. We were bunked in barracks, in groups of ten. Under the care of the Sisters.'

'Sisters? That sounds really posh.'

'Well, they were very posh in their white smocks. Teachers or student teachers . . . I can't remember now. One thing I know: only one of them mattered. Sister Anni. Even our swim period was worthless unless she was the one who took us down to the beach.'

'So you fell for her?'

'We all did. Even Fellner, who was always sounding off about how women no longer interested him. 'Man, I'm way past that stuff!' But Sister Anni had such a radiance!'

'Radiance! Not bad!'

'The way she walked ahead of us in that blinding white smock! Out of the blue, she would reach behind her, grab someone by the scruff of the neck and pull him by her side. That's how they'd walk for a while. Almost hugging. Then abruptly she would let you go.'

'Did she let you, too, go like that?'

'No, she never grabbed hold of me. Not even once.'

'And that broke your heart?'

I swirled the tea in my cup.

'And yet . . . one night just before lights out, I was lying in bed with my eyes closed. Well, half-closed. So I could see her entering, all too well. My arms were flung wide apart. A soldier, fallen in battle. One who hadn't turned tail. My face . . . well, it changed somehow. Became more noble.'

'More noble?'

'Yes! A face you had to notice. You couldn't just walk away from it.'

'And Sister Anni?'

'She stopped by my nightstand.'

'Ooh, by your nightstand!'

'And she leafed through my copy of *The Nabob*. Now why are you looking at me like that? *The Nabob*, by Daudet. She even picked it up for a moment. She picked it up and held it in her hand.'

'And then?'

'Lights out. And she disappeared.'

I stopped.

Zsuzsi was also silent. She reached across the table and touched my hand.

'But now she knew that you read things like that. Daudet, *The Nabob*.'

'Well, yes, Daudet.' I drank a few gulps. 'So I'm in the middle of this lousy story. Sister Anni. I really shouldn't be travelling now. It would be highly irresponsible of me.'

Zsuzsi regarded me as she would some rare specimen. One that appeared harmless, for now. *For the time being!*

'We'll go to a coffee house in Vienna.'

'But Vienna is only the first stop!'

'Not even. Vienna is almost like home turf for you.'

'Why is Vienna like home turf for me?'

'That's where you got those vests. That literary grant-in-aid.'

'But not in Vienna. *From* Vienna! Yes, from Vienna! That's where they came from!'

'But why vests, of all things?'

Yellow sunlight flooded the walls, wickedly gloating sunlight.

'Still in pyjamas?' A giggle. 'You intend to travel in pyjamas?'

'Maybe I don't intend to travel at all.'

'Are you going to start that again?'

I stood up without saying anything. A deep despair took hold of me. Again? What did she mean, *again*? Did we have a fight during the night? Did I create a scene, and demand to be excused from this trip? Not at all! I gave in!

This whole idea started with our dear friends. Oh, those intrepid travellers! Globetrotters! Who sprint through museums. Nor do they neglect cathedrals. They infiltrate everywhere.

But I'm willing to bet they never even glance at an arcaded doorway or linger in some old courtyard. They never stop to pause on the pavement. Keep moving, no rubbernecking, please!

But they keep chanting the same old dirge, 'You must travel'. I must see the world. Maybe there's something else besides our local flea market!

Bravo! Touché. But let me insert one name here. Faulkner. Not a bad name, as names go. Well, Faulkner never left the South, and he managed to write some pretty decent novels. All right, granted, our local flea market is not quite the Deep South, but still . . .

I leant closer to Zsuzsi.

'And after Vienna, what?'

'Never mind.'

'What next, after Vienna?!'

Zsuzsi was gone. Her voice came from a distance:

'Get dressed! Just get dressed!'

I stood in front of a closet door, and screamed.

'I know London is the final destination! But until we get there . . . ? How many cities? How many countries?'

I tore open the door.

The astonishment of shirts, trousers and jackets, upon my bursting in.

I grasped a brown jacket by the shoulder, as if I wanted to lay my head on it. Should I wear this one? It looked quite serviceable. And that's what really matters. I'm looking for a stalwart, loyal friend. Someone I've known for a long time, someone who's known me for a long time. In any case, it should have capacious pockets, and . . .

With a petulant gesture I shoved it aside and walked away. I rushed out into the hall.

'Zsuzsi! Zsuzsi!'

Her head popped out from behind the kitchen door.

'What is it? What happened?'

'Would you kindly tell me at last where are we staying in London?'

'I must have told you at least five times.'

'No, you never told me.'

'You know, some day you'll be the death of me.'

'The death of you! Because of this?!'

She didn't answer. She pulled the door shut.

I was left standing in the hall. Suitcases lined in parade formation in front of the large mirror. Oh, they have talked it over among themselves. They've made up their minds.

I was unable to move.

I rapped on the door, gently. Then more and more violently. I rattled the doorknob. Hopeless. The door did not open.

'You know what? I'll go down to the park, and lie down on a bench. You can tear me away if you feel like it! If that's what you feel like!'

No answer.

I let go of the doorknob. And stared at the door in a foggy daze.

I pronounced a name:

'Wellington.'

Christopher Plummer played the part in the film. He played Wellington. Plummer. Did I pronounce it right? Plummer. Right, Zsuzsi? Plummer, Plummer!

The suitcases patiently endured the shouting. It did not surprise them at all, nor did my sudden silence.

I squatted in front of them, and spoke in a very low voice, like someone telling a secret:

'They were crazy about Galántai. Galántai, that horse-face. They were simply wild about him. Sister Judy, Sister Sári. And well, yes, Sister Anni, too! No denying: she, too, cast her vote for Galántai. Galántai, the best-looking guy in the whole camp. Such a hunk. Already a real man. Clark Gable-type. Galántai and Clark Gable! All right, forget it. But they held a vote, the Sisters did. For Top Boy. And Galántai took the palm. Pilczer was also in the running. Pilczer, and possibly Szalay. As for me . . . no way. My name never even came up.'

I stood and massaged my lower back.

Then I trudged back into my room.

I reached up on a shelf for a shirt, and my hand remained frozen in mid-air. Was it certain that Faulkner never went anywhere? Where the hell did I get my information?

I picked out a shirt. Flung the pyjamas in the air. The trousers landed on a nearby chair. The top flew off.

I brushed the brown jacket aside. As if I'd lost my confidence in it. So which one could I still trust? Maybe this rather threadbare greyish one. It has seen better days. But it was the kind you could always count on. A pal. A dear old pal.

I found a fifty in its breast pocket. How about that, we're quite flush, aren't we? Any letters, or messages? No, there was nothing else.

I flung it over my arm. We were going for a walk. Suddenly I started to hum:

My dear, if you want a honeymoon,
allow me to join you soon.
Allow me a little show and tell,
Oh, you'll love our honeymoon hotel!

All around, the barren summer wasteland of the parquet floor. The carpets rolled up on the top shelf of the closet. Like defeated political dignitaries. Ousted statesmen.

A door slammed outside. Steps. Zsuzsi's steps, approaching, then receding. But it all seemed to be coming from another flat. And not the neighbouring one, either. From somewhere way off. But here she was now, in front of my door! Maybe I could still talk to her! But about what, for god's sake?

I paused for a moment and leant close to the jacket.

'When Sister Anni took us for a swim in the lake, we never had to sing those marching songs. She never made us sing, or march in time.'

Lincézényi-Nagy and I visited her once. Dropped in on her. Or did we only plan to? Did we only plan to visit her?

I never dreamt about Sister Anni.

How long did I stand there? How long until I at last heard her voice?

'Coffee's ready!'

The aroma of fresh coffee filled the flat.

I found Zsuzsi in the kitchen, busy with coffee cups. She poured coffee. With an otherworldly calm. Meanwhile she looked me over.

'Are you planning to tour the provinces?'

'What do you mean by that?'

'I think you look just right for the role of a seedy father . . .' And she went on, before I had a chance to put in a word. 'You couldn't find anything more unattractive?'

'It has three secret pockets.'

'And what do you intend to put in those secret pockets? I bet they're just rips in the lining.'

She held out a cup of coffee for me. Meanwhile she eyed me rather warily. *Keeping an eye on me.* One never knew what I might do . . . Bolt? Disappear? Vanish into thin air?

But all I did was ask her:

'Couldn't we sit down?'

'No, we don't have time.'

So we had our coffee, standing up.

On the shelves, white containers. On the containers, in tiny golden letters:

SUGAR

CONFECTIONER'S SUGAR

FLOUR

SALT

Zsuzsi put down her cup. I was hugging mine, fingers wrapped tight around it. And I began in a strange, drawling voice:

'We were strolling on the tree-lined avenue . . . Grandpa's hands clasped behind his back. Occasionally he'd stop in front of the fenced-in garden of some villa. Look up at the treetops and the sky. And I, full of self-importance, pulled a little blue wagon. Grandpa had just bought it for me! The shopkeeper wanted to sell us a bus. A bus with a driver, a conductor and a load of passengers. A lady with broad-brimmed hat and parasol, a gentleman wearing a bowler, a white-bearded little old man, a brightly smiling boy, a girl with pigtails . . . That would have cost a pretty penny. For us, the empty wagon was just fine. Grandpa from time to time asked to borrow it. He wheedled until I'd let him pull it for a while. Suddenly he stopped. He practically froze in his tracks. His jaw sagged and began to tremble. He stood like that for a while. That apologetic look in his eyes. Then he staggered over to a bench and slumped down on it. I cried out, "Grandpa!"'

My shout echoed in the empty kitchen.

'Grandpa!'

I was alone.

Zsuzsi was gone.

Only the two coffee cups left on the counter. And the containers on the shelves.

The door wide open. The whole flat full of open doors. A windstorm sweeping the rooms.

The impatient burst of a car horn from below.

The taxi! Our taxi was here!

Still no sign of her.

I could hear the hum of the lift. That morose, menacing hum.

It brought Zsuzsi.

Along with a squat, red-faced man by her side. The two of them grasped the suitcases and dragged them toward the lift.

Zsuzsi ignored me as I stood there by the open doors. Only after their third trip did she speak.

'Don't forget to lock the door!'

I nodded.

'Yes . . . of course.'

But I still had not moved.

AT THE TRAIN STATION (1989)

'You've got a suntan.'

'Really? Where do you think I got it? In the compartment?'

Zsuzsi studied my face attentively.

And I asked once again:

'Would you care to tell where I got my tan? On the train? In our compartment?'

As if she hadn't heard. Still scrutinizing my face. And smiling, quite amazed. What happened? Did travelling change my face? Did I assume another visage? A travel face?

We were standing next to the train. Suitcases around us. They had got off earlier. Left the train earlier. Left us behind as well. They formed their own little set. They're getting ready to go somewhere. Perhaps they'd been invited to an international conference. With an invitation to speak.

Otherwise our train had glided smoothly enough into the station. With a touch of disdain. Wanting to get rid of passengers, the sooner the better.

'So what about my face?'

But she had already turned from me.

'I have to find a luggage cart.'

'A what?'

And Zsuzsi was gone.

Waves of arriving passengers around me. As if we'd wished to be free of each other. A lean woman stopped in front of me. She scrutinized me. Does she too think I'm tanned? Or just the contrary? But why does she pick just me to stare at in this chaos? A group of young people with backpacks. A lady with a cinnamon complexion wrapped in a dark lilac cloak. Childlike curious Japanese. There's plenty to see here! So why pick me?

'Why are you circling like that?' Zsuzsi showed up with a four-wheel cart. Trundling it around with ease. Meanwhile that peculiar look again. 'You're going in circles and talking to yourself.'

'Ah, the luggage cart . . .'

There is something touchingly neat about it. The way it waits here, ready and humble. Always ready to serve. Loaded with suitcases. That are now even more haughty, if possible. Well, yes, this is how they arrive at international conferences. Can't tell what questions may arise at a certain meeting. One thing for sure, they won't flop.

We rolled into the waiting hall. The endless field of black and white squares. Zsuzsi executed a semi-circle with her cart. Pulled up by a bench. Without letting go of the cart's shoulder, she nodded at the bench.

'Wait for me here.'

'You're going?' I stared at the suitcases. 'Where?'

'I'll find a hotel.' A moment's silence. 'Going out on the town.'

A rather confident voice. Zsuzsi knows where she's going. She's so at home everywhere. Oh yes! She knows this town. The streets, the squares, perhaps even the hotels. When could she have been here? When?

I tried ambling along her side. Gently severe, she pushed me back.

'You just stay here with them.'

Of course, the suitcases! I can't just leave them here.

Zsuzsi's hand on my arm.

'You don't have to take it so hard. We'll meet again.'

This sounded a bit uncertain.

In any case, Zsuzsi was gone. She's doing the town. And me with the suitcases. This is the only certainty. The company of suitcases.

They're still on the luggage cart. But so hesitant and uncomprehending. What's going on here? How much longer do we have to wait? We have invitations. An international conference of considerable importance. We might already be late for it. The opening remarks are over, and we're still at the train station!

I waltzed around them. No, they weren't about to trust me. Never did. Not at packing, getting on and getting off. They simply ignored me. And here they were compelled to have me along!

Hordes marched across the waiting hall. Gaping as if in a museum.

A man with black beard angrily looking around. Looking for a woman tired of long ago. Maybe his wife. One thing is sure: he wasn't too eager to find her.

Slightly steamed-up milky glass of a door. Shadows wavering behind it. Whoosh of waterfall.

I withdrew by the suitcases' side. Tried to give them a smile. And then a woman's voice:

'Sie sind so müde!'

A tall, greying woman's anxious gaze. How long has she been watching me? Sparkling white blouse, black apron. Pointing at the bench. Motioning for me to sit down. A kind landlady. She clearly came from behind that glass door. From those shadows. From the waterfall. The hall. The benches of the hall . . . it all belongs to her. The Madame of the place.

She said something else slowly, word by word. I kept nodding, grinning comatosely. Somebody stood next to her. A man with a white sailcloth cap. They leant close to each other. Spoke barely audibly. Meanwhile, they kept looking back at me.

The waterfall was louder and louder. Everything was lost in that whoosh.

How long did I stand like that?

Suddenly it was just the suitcases standing in front of me, sarcastic. What's up old boy? Nodded off again?

The faithful friend . . . we were trusted to!

That luggage cart! It disappeared!

Disappeared? Someone took it away. After removing the suitcases. No need to ask why! No! In this crowd, you can't go around opening suitcases! And why not? Haven't you heard of station thieves?

I was kneeling in front of the suitcases. My hands ran over the locks. Which one could have been opened?

I was unable to open a single one. The locks and straps refused to open for me.

I tugged and pushed the suitcases.

Suddenly stood up. *Towered over them.*

Just what did you have in mind? What kind of inspection should I hold? Fine, all right. Someone took the cart. After all, one can't just move in here and settle down. Occupy a cart for hours! With all this traffic here . . . This is a station! A metropolitan train station! Why must you start suspecting people right away? Robbery indeed!

Prams rolled past me. Among them a grey-haired man with a student's face. From time to time, he snagged a baby carriage. Gave it a push forward, then back. He patted a woman's face.

'Uncle Ziggy!'

But of course! Ziggy Kun, Father's old friend. Look at him! Over eighty and he still sets out on a trip like this! It's nothing for him!

I rushed after him.

'Uncle Ziggy!'

He turns toward me with cheerful wonder. Repeating in a strange foreign accent:

'Zigga . . .'

And now the entire hall is echoing with:

'Zigga! Zigga!'

Sudden silence. The prams are gone. He too . . . Uncle Ziggy.

And a cup of tea has arrived. Behind the tea, the Madame. With a worried look, offering me the cup. Slightly embarrassed. As if she'd planned the whole thing differently. Who knows? Maybe she'd planned to invite me. So I wouldn't have to drink my tea on this bench. Instead, inside, on a white tablecloth. But some-one has prevented that.

Clearly, a little room could be found. A tiny, sparklingly clean little room. Two doors a few steps away. One has a black bowler hat. A woman's hat with feathers on the other.

The Madame did not look back after she took the empty cup.

Zsuzsi had looked back at me. The glance of a worried mother. Why did she look like a worried mother?

I must change my shirt. This one got all sweaty during the train ride. But where can I change my shirt here? In the waiting hall? In this insane throng? Yes, indeed, right here in this throng. No one will notice. One or two moves and you're done.

The washroom of the toilet!

That's right, why shouldn't I go in? I could even wash, at least to the waist. Wash, change shirt. The Madame would not object.

She would not protest. Except that first I must open a suitcase. It seems I already tried that. The result was failure. Utter and complete. But I'm not giving up. Let's try again. Calm and methodical. You can't just assault a suitcase. You must find its knack. Yep, you must.

Shirts in that brown suitcase. Carefully folded and placed on top. Shirts are always placed on top.

Always on top!

Always on top!

That's what I crooned by that brown suitcase. As I leant over, seeking friendly assistance. Poked at the lock. Hopeless. But of course! It needs a key to open. But where's the key? It should be sticking out of that lock. Except it isn't.

'Zsuzsi!'

What do I want from Zsuzsi now?

She's off somewhere on the shores of a hotel.

Men in dark suit behind the desk. Bending over ledgers, reaching for the phone. Turning toward an arriving guest. Toward a guest arriving or one leaving. Never toward Zsuzsi.

Meanwhile, I started shuffling the suitcase around. Tugging and pulling at locks and straps. Turning the suitcase over. An ominous rattling inside. Knives? Spoons? Some other silverware? Let it go! Let it all go!

I stood up in a dazed vertigo.

A man with a full beard stood in front of me. Panting a bit, as if he'd been running. Smiling, rather embarrassed. Clearly, he wanted to ask me something. He just looked at me for some time. His smile wilted and faded. Then he turned on his heels and departed.

What was it that he saw in my face? What did he notice? What made him lose heart like that? Was it my face? This weary, eroded face?

'You've got a suntan,' Zsuzsi said when we got off the train.

Zsuzsi went off. To look for a hotel. But those desk clerks in their dark suits will never give her the key. Like some awful game. The key passing from hand to hand but never hers.

And me here with the suitcases. They look so incredibly worn out. They no longer wanted to travel on. As if they'd received some terrible news in the meantime. The organizers of the congress have rescinded their invitation. Without giving any reason. And there was no appeal.

A luggage cart strayed their way. But they didn't even notice it.

A thin man leant over the suitcases.

'Don't you remember me?'

I regard his brick-red visage.

'No, I can't say I do.'

A shadow of a smile crossed his face. Somehow this made me nervous.

'I have a poor memory for faces. You better tell me your name.'

'No I won't.'

'Did I write bad things about you?'

'I should say!' He fell silent for a moment. 'But that's not what matters.'

Fresh troops of travellers marched by. The ebb and flow of the throng. My eyes were stinging. A nasty stinging that brought tears.

'Say, do you happen to have any eye drops with you? Viscosa, or whatever . . .'

'Viscosa? What do you want Viscosa for?'

'I thought a few drops . . . You see my eyes . . . never mind. So tell me, what is the matter?'

He leant closer to me. It must have been a grievance bottled up for a long time. Perhaps from the old neighbourhood: Népszinház Street, or Sándor Square . . .

'Well, what is it?'

'You should have kept Klari Kosztola out of that novella or whatever!'

'Klári Kosztola!? Who is this Klári Kosztola?'

'Couldn't you think of some other name? Kati? Or Gizi? Oh no! You had to pick on Klári!'

'But believe me, I . . .'

'It was a despicable thing to do! ' He glared at me. Then suddenly turned his back on me. He fell in with a passing group. He was lost in the throng.

A madman. A bullying maniac. No matter, he's gone.

A bit of Hungary!

And I almost burst into tears. Such a treacherous assault, out of the blue! That was all I needed! Blowing my nose like a trumpet . . . Here on a bench in a train station abroad.

Next came a sharp, staccato coughing attack.

A prolonged howling. As if a dog from the outskirts of town had got loose in here. Why can't it stay still? This can only lead to trouble . . .

Could it be Zsuzsi was given a key at last?

She is ascending in the lift with key in hand. She marches down the length of a corridor. Opens a door. Without looking around in the room she marches to the window. She pulls down the shades. And throws herself on the sofa. And lies there motionless in the dark.

A shadow behind the glass door. The Madame. She is watching me. As I sit here by the side of my suitcases. Perhaps next thing she'll be out here. Or is she waiting for me to go in there? Why not? Perhaps that's what she is waiting for.

I can count on her. She'll take care of me. After all, she'd brought me tea . . . And assured a place for me on this bench.

Sie sind so müde . . .

So müde . . . She pronounced that with particular tenderness. So tenderly and dolefully, drawing out that *ü* in *müde* . . .

That's how it began.

But what began like that?

Some deeper sympathy. Let's call it that. You can feel that sort of thing. She won't throw me out if I go in there. She understands my situation. I have no choice, really. I can't stay here sitting on this bench forever. It would seem suspicious. I might get asked for my ID.

But that's all right. I have my papers. My passport . . . but where the hell did I put it! I pat down my pockets. With more and more urgency. Yanking out all sorts of tissue papers. Tissue papers raining from my pockets.

The Madame will take me under her wings. Now her husband, that's another matter. Why, he might even be glad if I was taken away. He'd already prevented me from drinking my tea in there. Maybe he isn't even her husband. Then my chances are even worse. But no! Madame must have the last word! She did yield to him about the tea. But now she has to feel that I . . .

They'll take me in. *They must take me in!* Even if not exactly as a member of the family, but somehow they'll tolerate me.

They'll offer me a bowl of soup. Perhaps they don't even like soup. Cheese is their favourite staple. I'm not particularly crazy about cheese. Except for smoked cheese, possibly . . . No matter. That's not what's at stake here, for now. One thing's sure: I won't take advantage of their trust in me. I know the rules. And in case I were get into an intimate relationship with Madame ... But no. That would be too risky. A fatal mistake. I better just lie low. Offer to do minor services. Good God! What kind of minor services?

Ho ho!

Let's not forget, I am not entirely without resources. I have shirts, nightshirts, pyjamas, nightgowns, robes, shoes, not to mention the rest. A wide selection, yessir.

I can start selling this off. A clearance sale.

And once the business gets going ... With just a little patience ...

Two open suitcases on the pavement of the waiting hall. Robes, shirts, blouses, pyjamas, slips, camisoles, socks, stockings, shoes.

A small crowd around the suitcases, browsing in silence. At times exchanging a look, a shrug of the shoulder, an elbow giving a nudge. They don't even notice me standing next to the suitcases. An elderly woman wearing glasses grabbing a pink camisole. Waving it around as if wanting to fly away with it. Dropping it back in disappointment.

The others still motionless.

One gentleman picks up my bathrobe. Holds it up, turns it around. Then tosses it back disdainfully.

Athletic shirts raised, then thrown back down. The vests fare no better.

Stockings waving in the air. Stockings and neckties.

Someone picked up a grey box, as if doing a great favour.

Perhaps only in order to put an end to this humiliating scene. And he sets out heading for the exit. And I, after him.

'That's my shaving kit!'

He does not turn around.

'Please sir . . . I shave every morning! I shave daily!'

Now he stops. Slowly turns about. With utmost reverence he hands me the box. Places it in my hands.

Voices whispering in the colonnade:

'He shaves every day!'

The whispering stops.

The woman with the glasses steps up to me. She touches my arm.

'You better start now! You can't put it off!'

What should I start now? What is it that cannot be put off? Could she mean shaving? The act of shaving?

I did not look at the woman. Did not turn to look at her.

'Excuse me . . . but I have no shaving cream! No shaving cream or soap. And anyway . . . You just can't ask me to . . . '

I clutched the box to my chest. And mumbled apologetically:

'Sometimes I skip a day or two . . . '

I hunkered on the bench. Did not look up. And now I was clutching emptiness. The box nowhere. It must have slipped out of my grasp . . . who knows!

Profound silence around me. As if everyone had gone from the waiting hall.

And then a piercingly clear voice:

'Well, that wasn't easy to do!'

Zsuzsi stood by the bench. Her face somewhat drawn, but her glance triumphant.

I just looked at her. Her face, her hair, her shoulder. And then my voice came so wan and hollow, a dust-rag being shaken out:

'You found a place?'

'A cosy little hotel! Room has a view of the courtyard, with an old tree down there . . . '

Slowly I got on my feet. One hand grasping the back of the bench.

I turned toward the glass door. Seemed like raindrops were gliding down the glass. A fine pearlescent mizzling rain. Thin black outlines of figures behind. Women and men, coming and going. Disappearing and reappearing.

A tall, grey-haired lady showed up, with her hand slipped under her apron. A strange, mysterious smile on her face.

From somewhere in the distance I could hear Zsuzsi's voice:

'Now what are you staring at? Can you tell me?'

POSTCARD FROM LONDON (1989)

What kind of garden was this? How did I get here? Around me, yellowish grass. Unbelievably stunted blades of grass. Pitiful flowerbeds. And a shadow bowing and scraping among them. The shadow of an emaciated old woman toting a watering can with dreadful weariness. More like utter exhaustion, in fact. Any moment she might keel over. Remain there motionless. Slowly sinking into the soil.

She turned around. Puffy face, small eyes slyly scrutinizing me. Maybe she'd spare me a sprinkling from her can.

'I hope you slept well here at our place ...' A pause, then somewhat suspiciously: 'And your wife?'

I motioned toward a window.

'Still up there.'

She nodded.

'Of course! Let her sleep some more.'

'I think she's up by now.'

But the old woman was gone.

I stood in the middle of the flowerbeds. As if rooted there. She might come back. Just as suddenly as she had disappeared. For she was not yet done with this garden. She'd hardly watered these flowerbeds. Mrs Verebes knows her duty. That's right! Her duty. The cultivation of misery. Of stuntedness.

I nearly shouted:

You call this a lawn! An English lawn! But this was my lot. What I got to look at.

That's right! Where was that brilliant, verdant English lawn?! I'd even heard a joke about it. The English lawn and the American tourist.

The tourist stops by a country house, sees the gardener mowing the lawn. Tell me, what's your secret, to get this lawn so lush and emerald-green? Well sir, no secret to it at all. You just keep mowing and watering. For three hundred years.

That's a good one. Really good!

But at least that American got to see a lawn! A broad, velvety expanse of grass.

Well, I am no American tourist, that's for sure. I get to see old Mrs Verebes' yellow grass in old Mrs Verebes' garden.

I was overcome by some desperate hope. Perhaps it would still see a glimmer of green . . . after all, we're in England, not at the flea market in Budapest!

I stumbled around between the flowerbeds. Tried to pick a blade of grass, but it slipped out of my hand. It recoiled, offended. It took a sarcastic bow.

I straightened up, as if to gather strength. Lay waste to this garden. Mess up the flowerbeds. The ones Mrs Verebes has been watering for three hundred years. Mowing and watering, these three hundred years . . . Mowing and watering . . .

I looked up.

Zsuzsi's face in our window. A dim smudge behind the murky windowpane. I waved. She did not wave back. Her face, her leaden face receded.

She's the one who'd sent me down here. Go outside! Do me a favour and please go!

I stammered some sort of dumb excuse. I'd been unable to sleep! Believe me, that's all! But she didn't even hear me.

Just kept eyeing me, with an unflinching resentment. Just kept repeating: 'Go outside! Go on!'

Zsuzsi's face disappeared from the window. What could she be doing up there? Trying to tidy up the room? Or just staring into the void? Perhaps she'll never come downstairs again. And I'll never go back up there. From here on, it would be just this garden for me. Maybe it's better this way. After what went on last night!

That impossibly narrow bed. Blankets all twisted and tangled. Mine slid to the floor. I tried to grab it. The bed creaked. Zsuzsi moaned, but did not wake up. After a moment her peaceful snuffling resumed.

When did I wake up? Maybe I never fell asleep. In any event, the bedsheet vanished from under me. It did not slip to the floor. It simply vanished.

Once upon a time someone might have still stretched out on this bed. Old Mr Verebes, perhaps.

But what do I care about old Mr Verebes!

I stared into the dark. Trying to orient myself. As one who sizes up the situation. What situation? There was no situation here to speak of.

A sink the size of a spittoon by the window. Some kind of fluid dripping from the tap. Tears dripping nonstop from a diseased eye.

In a corner, an enormous brown wardrobe. A brown wardrobe shut tight. The lock leering, askew. The key nowhere. 'I'll find it,' promised old Mrs Verebes with a dismissive wave of the hand. How many lodgers must have witnessed that gesture, how many heard that voice! And if that wardrobe were to open, the doors parting with a creak? Inside, a dark netherworld. Shelves and hangers, long gone.

Our clothes lay scattered, thrown all over the chairs, hanging limp. They'll never be the same again.

I leant forward into the darkness.

'I'm going home.'

I drew back, suddenly terrified. Withdrew into my cocoon. The wisest thing to do, for the time being. But my blanket abandoned me. It slithered over to Zsuzsi's shoulder. I yanked it back. Its burn-holes had black edges. The former occupant must have been a heavy smoker.

Who could have been my predecessor, anyway? Who could have sojourned here at old Mrs Verebes'? What kind of characters? One thing for sure, though. They did not spend much time in this room. All day they walked the streets. Wheeling and dealing. Then fell into bed, dead tired. Only to re-join battle on the morrow. Zsuzsi received the address from a film-industry type. A director. No, it was a gaffer. A gaffer? What's a gaffer?

I huddled with knees drawn up.

Tomorrow I'm going home. No way I'm staying here.

I'll talk it over with Zsuzsi. She'll have to understand.

Really not that much to pack. It's no big deal. Slap a few things into a suitcase, and done. Which suitcase would come with me on the road? On the road of shame? For the others would, after all, stay on in London. And they'd never let this one live it down. They'd patronize this renegade forever. Oh yes! The London bunch would!

I leant over Zsuzsi, as so many times before. I had looked at her face for whole nights at a time. Her breathing was barely audible. Was she dreaming? She never spoke about her dreams.

I'll wait. I won't wake her yet.

Impatience drummed inside me.

Was this how I must wait for the dawn? Cowering in bed, hugging my knees?

Slowly, I slid out of bed and pulled on my slippers.

I cast another glance at Zsuzsi, and scurried out of the room.

The stunned silence of the staircase. The steeply rising steps. The silence of closed doors.

What does this character in pyjamas want? Where's he going? What's on his mind?

From the depths downstairs came a sound of coughing. Stubborn, choking coughs. The stuff of crime novels. Practically shook the whole building. Who could it be? An elderly tenant, a bedridden invalid. Never leaves his room. Yet he knows everything going on. He's aware of the slightest noise. A door closing, a creaking on the stairs. Nothing escapes him.

I should drink a cup of tea. A cold cup of tea.

But where was the kitchen? Where indeed? It should be here on the ground floor. But of course! That's where Zsuzsi prepared our breakfast. Tea, butter, jam. Just like home. Except for somebody asleep on the ironing board. That's right, he's sleeping there right now. He'd make a racket if I woke him up. But he won't make a racket, because I can't find the kitchen. It is lost in the dark.

I stood around for a while. Then started to climb the stairs rising into endless distance. Did I intend to visit someone? Perhaps Mrs Verebes, of all people?

A slip of paper stuck on a doorknob. Somehow I was able to read it in the dark.

I am in the parlour.

A message from one Hungarian to another.

But where was that parlour? Old Mrs Verebes' parlour? And was someone still sitting there? A man? Or a woman? Makes no difference. Sitting there in a chair, snoozing. Or more likely, sunk in the sleep of oblivion. It had to be the most comfortable room in the house. May even have an easy chair or two, who knows. Perhaps more than one person seeking shelter there. A haven of sorts .

I took the slip of paper from the doorknob, and flung it into the dark.

My English father! Perhaps he was camping out there.

Good Lord! I once had an English father! I inherited him from some Lutheran organization after the war . . . I can't quite recall . . .

Hilary Fox.

Yes, that was his name. Sent me packages. Food and clothing. And letters and photos, naturally. A pudgy man, with a reassuring, old-fashioned smile. A decent man, a small-town physician. I, too, sent a photo, featuring a somewhat less reassuring smile. The letters were translated by one of Father's friends. Baron Manó Sennyei. Who was working as a translator at the time. He also wrote the replies, in my name.

Hilary Fox even sent a picture of his daughter.

Hilary Fox.

Vanished. Sank away. Or rather, it was I who vanished.

Those years. Those notorious Fifties. Years of mud-grey terror.

At a corner table of the coffee house, Manó announced:

'No more letters, my young friend. This is not a good time for correspondence. We must say goodbye to dear Hilary Fox. Hilary Fox is over.'

Hilary Fox wrote a few more times. He sent a few more pairs of trousers. Then he gave up.

My English father! My English father!

One slipper dropped from my foot. Slalomed all the way down the stairs. Should I look for it? Go hunting for it? It was hopeless in the dark. Might as well kick off the other one too. But it was practically welded to my foot. It insisted on staying.

So I limped upstairs rather off-balance, holding on to the banister.

On high a door opened. Just a crack.

The opening revealed a man with a prickly white beard. His gaze mistrustful, furtive. Nurturing some ancestral chip on his shoulder. Just aching to feel insulted.

A familiar face. Maybe we'd never met, but the face was still familiar. I might have seen his photo somewhere. *His portrait.*

But of course! Right next to Lajos Kossuth. In a hall crammed full of people. Perhaps the House of Representatives. Surrounded by a crowd. Some even jumped up on their seats, waving their hats. Kossuth's hand on the shoulder of this man with the prickly beard. As if to introduce him. As if to ask for a vote of confidence. At any rate, this man had played a role alongside Kossuth. And not just any role. He was a minister . . . yes, the prime minister.

Bertalan Szemere!

His eyes flashed, taking my measure with unspeakable scorn.

'What are you snooping around for, young man?'

He leant closer to me. I could just about feel his breath. His steely eyes practically pierced me. After a moment, the door closed.

Bertalan Szemere vanished.

Doubtless, he was still there behind that door. Waiting, watchful. Who knows, I might ring his doorbell. And then he wouldn't be able to get rid of me so easily. But why all this fear? After all, he craved to hear news. More than anything, he craved news from Hungary.

A girl with red hair wearing a sweat suit ran past me down the stairs. She gave me a silent laugh. She ran out the front door, into the dark. To run and run on the street. A dawn jogger on familiar streets.

I turned back to go downstairs. One of my slippers still with me. The other has escaped. But no! There it was, waiting at the foot of the stairs.

I stood in front of our door.

Who would greet me inside? The sink? The blankets? Or Zsuzsi herself? Maybe she was awake already? Somehow sensing the silence around her?

No, not at all! She was still asleep. Again I leant over her. I could not postpone it any longer. Had to get it over with. The sooner the better . . . the sooner the better!

'Zsuzsi!'

She looked up. The way a light suddenly turns on. She was looking at me, still somewhere in dreamland. Instantly closing her eyes. Unwilling to acknowledge the face leaning over her. Unwilling to acknowledge anyone or anything. But she could feel that face hanging over her.

'Believe me, I didn't mean to wake you!'

'You didn't mean to.'

She still didn't look at me. Her face hardened.

' . . . and it's a lot easier than you would imagine! Think of it as mailing a package.'

'What package?' (In a tormented, headachy voice.)

'Well, not exactly a post-office package, but something like that.' My attempt at laughter sounded rather pathetic.

Zsuzsi gave me a sidelong glance.

'Why are your hands on your knees?'

'What's that?'

'You are bending over the bed. With your hands on your knees.'

I squatted down by her side.

'And what if I'm bending over? What if I'm doing push-ups? Is that what's most important now?'

She pressed her lips together. Maybe she'd never speak again. Won't answer me ever. Or hear what I say. No question. No answer. Still, barely audibly:

'What's most important?'

The darkness was slowly dissolving. A murky gloom filled the room.

I put my hand in the empty washbasin. Drew my fingers across the thin, dark cracks. For a moment my elbow was into the basin.

'I told you, it's no big deal. We devote a morning to it, and it's done.'

'We devote, we devote.' (A moment's silence.) 'Devote a morning to what?'

'We go to a travel bureau. We buy a ticket.' (Insinuating voice.) 'One ticket. Train . . . boat . . . or better still, plane. Yes, the plane would be best. Then I wouldn't have to transfer.'

'And you'd feel right at home on it. When was the last time you were on an aeroplane?'

'A few years ago . . . quite a few years ago. When I flew to Szombathely. To give a talk about films, old films.'

Zsuzsi raised herself on her elbows.

'So you'd go by plane . . . '

'Or by train, if that's the only way. I can put up with one or two transfers.'

'Oh, of course.' Suddenly, she turned to face me. 'And what about me?! How much am I supposed to put up with?!'

I leant against the windowsill. And in a very unconvincing voice:

'I don't understand you . . . I really don't.'

'Really?! Really?!' She chanted, in a mocking tone. Then eyed me in silence.

'You . . . you are right at home in London. I've noticed it, on the very first day. I don't know how it is but I've never seen you feeling so at home.' I faltered.

She nodded encouragingly. Go on! What else was there to hear? What else did she have to find out now?!

'You can even speak English. Where did you learn to speak English? Me, I can't even manage German. Not one godforsaken sentence. I tried many times. It's hopeless.' (*Silence.*)

'Believe me, you'll be much happier without me. I just keep doing one dumb thing after another. The other day in that cathedral . . . you know, where all the poets, writers and scientists have their monuments . . . Ben Jonson, Burns, Wordsworth, Keats and the rest . . . Westminster! Yes, that's where it was! And it's not even a cathedral! Abbey, of course!' (*Pathetic chuckle.*) 'Did I say cathedral? Anyway, Westminster Abbey! The way those tourists barged in! And their guide with his umbrella stabbing the air! Charge! And they march right through those funeral monuments, squawking and giggling. Well, I flew into such a rage . . . I had to run outside. Believe me, I didn't want to create a scene!'

Not a word from Zsuzsi. Frozen face. Frozen eyes.

Silence.

And me, suddenly sounding like an anxious uncle.

'And you, too, must get away from this place. I can't let you stay at Mrs Verebes'.'

There was a glint in her eye. Like when you throw a pebble in a still pond. A glint that comes and goes.

'I bet that she gave us the crummiest room. And were you aware that there's a parlour? That's right! A parlour! Mrs Verebes never said a word about it. She looks down her nose at us. That's just great! That tops it all! That woman condescends to us! So you've got to move out of here! I can't let you stay in this dump! Maybe find a modest little hotel, at least there . . . We can certainly afford that much.'

A pair of trousers flew at my face. A pair of trousers and a jacket. A shirt fluttered across the room. And a shout:

'Go away! Please, go away!'

Her voice choked up. Only her panting could be heard. And then her desperate shouts again:

'Go away! Go wherever you want . . . just leave, please leave!'

A rake! A rusty rickety rake, lying there, flung across a flowerbed. I approached it slowly, cautiously. Yet with a certain severity. As if I were about to rouse some old, drunken tramp. *All right, that's enough now! Get up! Off you go!*

But this thing would never get up again. No, it would never get it together again. Get up and go? You've got to be kidding.

I bent down for a closer look.

Gaptooth was too mild a term. Barely one or two teeth left. Making it even more alarming, if that was possible. No, this was no tramp. An ancient hired hand, rather. Laboured hard until the last gasp. But that must have been a long time ago, ages ago. When he just keeled over. Never to rise again. And nobody raised it. Nothing remarkable in that. Probably old Mrs Verebes left it here. Or possibly old Mr Verebes.

If I'd offered to help it would not have accepted. Oh no! Thank you very much. It's no use. This is how things are from now on.

I leant forward to stare at it.

Ah, the tales you could tell! You'd have a lot to say about old Mr and Mrs Verebes. About former tenants. Transients as well as residents. They probably weren't too crazy about this garden. Of course, old Mrs Verebes always kept it in order. But that order never made this garden flourish. That order proved to be its death. The garden's demise. And yours, as well.

What can you tell about old Mr Verebes? Were you friends? I have a hunch he liked to spend time with you down here. But only when Mrs Verebes was not around. Did he detest Mrs Verebes? Or was he past hatred? When did he die? When was he buried? And where?

Now just wait a minute!

Could it be that old Mr Verebes is laid to rest somewhere here? Was he interred here? Yes, why not? No need to make such a big fuss about that sort of thing. It would have been the simplest solution. There probably weren't many at the funeral. The obsequies. If you could call it that. Old Mrs Verebes, and one or two tenants.

Could there be others resting here as well? Hungarians ... and perhaps not only Hungarians. In unmarked graves.

I lifted the rake. Lifted it and replaced it carefully, as if adjusting a pillow under it.

On top of a red double-decker bus, with Zsuzsi. Weaving along, slightly dizzy, in a maze of streets.

This bus had showed up for me. From somewhere afar—from my childhood. It visited me, recognized me, and picked me up.

'You know, Father and I would always ride on the top of the bus. I would run up ahead, up to the top, and ...'

I fell silent.

Staring at the streets. At buildings, squares, parks, cinemas and film posters. At this strange cavalcade along the route of the red bus.

AN AFTERNOON SLEEPER (1992)

With Zsuzsi by the River

As in a fairy tale, the boats floated by slowly in the soft, white light. It was a light barely broken by the river's glimmer. Fresh, young laughter rose from the boats, and occasional shouts from one boat to another. Gentle bubbling laughter. Then silence. The young ones . . . they'll always be in those boats. Disappearing around the bend.

'This is their river. The river of youth.'

'The Cam.' Zsuzsi touched my arm. 'The River Cam in Cambridge.'

'I'd never heard of it before.'

'That doesn't mean you have to hate it . . . or any of the other things here.'

'Not at all! You'll introduce me to all of these cathedrals, museums, and, of course, rivers.'

Zsuzsi's clear voice:

'So this is the River Cam.'

At a Restaurant with Zsuzsi

I was smoothing out the tablecloth near my lap, slowly, humbly. I had to stall for time. This was most important. Yes, but time for what? To be able to look someone in the eye? Faces appeared on knife blades, gliding up and down. They rose and sank. Another flash or two, and they vanished.

A knife lay in front of me. But of course. The table was set, all so cosy. Plates, cutlery. I picked up the knife slowly, and saw my face, a frail blur on the blade.

Zsuzsi by my side, studying the menu. Or was she watching me?

Could that be Mother sitting by my side? Smiling nervously, biting her lips. Ready to say something critical.

Sit up straight! Don't sit so crooked! Where are your hands? Why are they under the table again?

Mother dreaded my movements. That I might suddenly snatch away the tablecloth, together with plates and glasses. 'Like your father! Just like your father!'

Whereas Zsuzsi dreads my smile. A certain smile of mine.

Zsuzsi is wary. And with good cause! This ageing, difficult child is capable of anything. Unpredictable tantrums, and . . .

My arm is up on the table top, suddenly lying exposed there.

Zsuzsi stares, almost mesmerized.

'You're so thin!'

'I was always like this.'

'No, not this thin. You must exercise.'

'Right here? You think so?'

Zsuzsi ignored that.

'I'll take you to the Lukács pool. You must start swimming again.'

Slowly, unobtrusively, I withdrew my arm. Once more it was lost somewhere down below. Perhaps it would turn up at another table. In front of that young couple or that dignified old gentleman. I just hope it won't create a scene.

Suddenly the News Reel came on inside my head.

'Oxford-Cambridge!'

Zsuzsi's eyes lit up like a little girl's. Ah, at last here comes something exciting.

'Every year the two universities' crews compete in the traditional boat race.'

Zsuzsi was all attention now. But the reporter's voice faded. Then resumed, timid, faltering.

'Recently . . . Oxford has claimed the larger share of victories.'

'Where did you see it? Which cinema? The one with two projection rooms, what was it called?'

'Bodográf.'

(*Silence.*) Then a sudden burst of anger.

'But it's not called that any more! Now it's the Coalminer! How can you name a cinema the Coalminer?! Coalminer!'

A few heads turned my way. What was this desperate shouting?

A woman wearing a white apron stood in front of me. A few greying strands in her black hair. A kindly, compassionate face. The smile of a nurse. Yes, she would exempt me from gym class. From gym and swimming. It's enough if I take long walks. Say, after lunch, and maybe before bedtime at night. But nothing too strenuous! All in moderation.

Her face was endless patience. She waited. For a word, for a smile. In any case, for our order. Except she was looking at the wrong person.

Her eyes glided away from me, and turned to Zsuzsi.

A few quiet, intimate sentences. As if they'd known each other for a long time. Meanwhile Zsuzsi laid her hand on my wrist. Don't worry, I won't order anything fatty, anything that . . .

The waitress kept nodding, and gave me a sidelong glance. Smiling and nodding, she floated away on the wings of that smile.

'I ordered some red wine as well.' Zsuzsi released my wrist. 'Some dry red wine.'

I repeated after her.

'Dry red wine.'

A face leant across the table. A thick, solid beard. Solemn, almost sorrowful eyes. Giving me a prolonged, pensive look.

I rose halfway.

'Tatu!'

He gently pushed me back down, keeping his eyes on me. Then in a barely audible voice:

'This time you may return my greeting.'

I gestured awkwardly.

'Sit down, please join us.'

He did not sit down. He did not join us.

Zsuzsi's voice came from somewhere far off:

'What happened?'

Tatu turned toward her. He shook his head, embarrassed.

'Nothing, really . . . Nothing at all.'

'But you two were friends.'

'Yes, we walked in Károlyi Gardens many a time.'

'Yes, Károlyi Gardens!' I tried to smile. 'We strolled and listened to the band. The Budapest Philharmonic, directed by Dezső Bor.'

'And you didn't return my greeting.'

'You're saying that János didn't return your greeting?'

Tatu drew back.

'But that was later . . . much later. By then the music stopped. But let's drop it . . . Please, forgive me, the whole thing is so silly.'

'Did you two have a fight?'

'No, not at all! But I don't mean to bother you . . . I'm such an idiot. Please excuse me, ma'am . . . And you too!'

'Tatu! Please don't leave!'

But he was already winding his way among the tables. He stopped once, to wave. Then he was gone.

Zsuzsi's voice, near despair.

'You didn't return his greeting?'

'I don't know now.'

'You know very well.'

'It was such a long time ago. One afternoon in the winter of 1944. There he was standing in front of me on the street, next to an overturned tramcar.'

'And you didn't recognize him?'

' I did recognize him! Why wouldn't I have recognized him?!'

'Why are you shouting?'

'No . . . no, I'm not shouting.'

Yes indeed. Why should I be shouting? I can tell this in a calm voice.

The way Tatu stood in front of me on that ravaged, snowy street. Clutching a package to his chest. A package wrapped so meticulously it was scary. An aeroplane circled above us. Meandering, lost.

Tatu acting so strangely, almost unfriendly. Practically rigid with tension. As if he'd run into an Arrow-Cross patrol. His mouth moved, without a sound. As if he'd lost his voice long before. The package slid aside for an instant. That yellow star! That grimy, yellow star, spattered with slush or something. He shifted the package back in place, clutching it tight. His glance becoming even more antagonistic. As if he couldn't be sure I'd let him pass. Then he and his package were gone.

'Maybe he wanted to ask you a favour.'

'He didn't want anything from me. That plane kept making those sad circles. Then suddenly it was gone too. Lost in that filthy sky.'

'The sky is never filthy.'

'It was, back then.'

'And who else did you fail to greet in those days?'

'Oh there were people I said hello to! And visited, and delivered packages to. And sat next to, on the tram . . . yes, in the back of the car, among the yellow stars!'

I faltered.

What a pathetic spiel. What a shameful, lame rap.

I fell silent.

'Magda Friedmann said hello before I did. When we bumped into each other on the street . . . in April, 1944. Her beautiful, clear eyes clouded over. There was terror behind that haze. She said hello. She said hello before I did. I'd never felt so ashamed.'

'Did you see her again?'

'Never. And I never saw the others either. Girls from the old neighbourhood . . . Rosie Král, Vera Rottmann, Itza Pajor . . . They all disappeared. And so did our neighbourhood, Kálmán Tisza Square! While I slept in the afternoons!'

'What do you mean by that?'

What indeed. What could an afternoon sleeper mean by anything?

Once more I was fiddling with the tablecloth.

'They set fire to the barn with Pista Wahrhaftig inside.'

'What are you saying?'

'They locked him and his companions into a barn, and then . . .'

'Enough, please . . . stop.'

I stared off into space.

'The dead of another era . . . inconvenient, untimely . . .'

'What're you mumbling now?'

'Oh, nothing. It's just that my dead are, by now . . .'

'What about your dead?'

'Nothing . . . nothing . . .'

A slim-necked wine bottle appeared in the air. It descended in the company of plates and wineglasses. For a moment it wavered, as if it did not trust me, but at last it landed on the table.

Of course, it was the white-aproned waitress. All of this was her doing. By now she didn't waste any time on me. She negotiated with Zsuzsi in a soft undertone. Still, it was about me, yes indeed. The entire lunch was composed, starting with the consommé, to get me back on my feet again, make me my old self. She had discussed it with the kitchen staff. *You know, he's so depressed, he just stares off into space. Poor thing's nothing but skin and bones . . . and that frightened smile on his face! No, it's not from the war—I don't think he ever served in the army. No, it's some other thing . . . I can't put it into words . . . But the young lady is something else, she's made of different stuff!*

Leaving our table she gave me a smile. *Go ahead, don't let it get cold!*

'Please, take it easy.' Zsuzsi leant over my plate. 'Don't wolf your food. There's no need to rush.'

I sank into my soup, pervaded by a kind of timeless serenity. A weird, unknown sensation. No, there was no need to hurry, here. Or, for that matter, ever again. No need to hurry, ever again!

'Burnett used to come here.'

'Who's that?'

'Burnett. Author of *The Secret Garden*. This used to be the gathering place for writers of children's books.'

'Did they ever have readings?'

'Never! Nor did they ever discuss their works. They talked about cigars, wine, and of course, women.'

'A charming bunch!'

Sunlight flooded the room, a warm, golden brown light. It glanced off the wine bottle. I said something else about Burnett and the others. That they admitted only the best writers into their circle. The real stuff.

I poured. We clinked glasses.

I thought I heard music. A gentle, pure sound that permeated everything. I could see those boats again, floating downstream in that improbable white light.

Something burst out of me. A cry? A sob?

'A mistake! It was all a mistake!'

Zsuzsi took my hand.

'What's wrong?'

I faltered, all choked up.

'Don't you see? This is where I should have lived my life . . . here in this restaurant by the river . . . '

She gazed at me and held my hand. 'Yes, of course . . . still . . . ' She fell silent, her eyes resting on me.

I spoke through my tears with a kind of furious insistence.

'No reason to feel ashamed of this.'

'No, of course not.'

'If we're not ashamed to laugh, why should we be ashamed to cry . . . ' I ran out of breath. I could only gasp the name.

'Milán Füst!'

'Milán Füst?'

'He said that.' Suddenly my voice cleared and regained its strength. 'If we're not ashamed to laugh, why should we be ashamed to cry? Why indeed?'

The shadow of a smile crossed Zsuzsi's face. The shadow of a tired smile.

Around me, stillness. And distant whispers.

The white-aproned waitress materialized, heading my way. She was almost at our table. Kindness and firmness personified. She knew what this was all about. She knew what needed to be done. She'd find a room for us. She'd talk it over with Zsuzsi. After all, they understood each other so well. Suddenly she stopped short. A hesitant, forbearing smile on her face.

I downed another glass of wine, and sawed at my cutlet. Meanwhile I rattled on, senselessly, helter-skelter.

'We'll take long walks, go boating, sip our coffee . . . yes! . . . oh yes!'

Was this the place to tell about it? Right now? Right here? In this English restaurant?

About how I stood there in that editorial office. In front of the man with glasses who wore the green shirt of the Arrow-Cross Party. He crossed his arms and scrutinized me. With the eyes of an entomologist. He had collared me on the street, as I was loitering around the editorial offices. He suddenly linked arms with me.

'Well, well, my young friend?'

'Uh, I was only . . .'

'Why don't you tell me about it upstairs.'

He herded me ahead of him in the narrow corridor, then stopped me abruptly.

'Wait a minute. You must have been up here before, you seem to know your way around . . .'

'Yes, I've been here once or twice.'

'Well, well!'

'But that was . . .'

' . . . during the former regime.' A curt, mocking laugh. 'A little while back.' He tenderly pushed me into a room. 'Perhaps in this very room.'

I shook my head. No, not here! A desk with a few newspapers and proof sheets. A chair that seemed lost and out of place.

This man with the glasses . . . A thin, bony face. A face you'd see in a cafe. He could be working for one of the moderate papers, *Pesti Hírlap*, or *Ujság* . . . What was he doing wearing the green shirt of the Arrow-Cross? What was he doing here?

And these walls! These bare walls!

'What are you looking for, young man? What did you expect to see? A picture of Hitler? Or Szálasi?'

Then in a sharp, cold voice:

'Have you brought something? Are you looking for someone?'

'The editor. Mr Hajós.'

'Ah, you mean Hoarse Hajós!'

'Beg your pardon?'

'You wouldn't know about this. You see, there's Hoarse Hajós, Dummy Tarnai, Studs Barabás.' He stopped. Then, in an official tone: 'What is your business with Mr Hajós?'

'I want to withdraw my *Watermelon*.'

'What's that you want to withdraw?'

'*Watermelon*. That's the title of my story.' A moment's pause. 'I left it here a month ago.'

He nodded, smiling.

'Oh, but of course! I should've known. A writer . . . a young writer . . . Stories . . . poems . . .'

'I've never written a poem.'

'C'mon! Everyone starts with poems.'

'No, not me.'

He seemed to find this annoying.

'Well, anyhow! So you left *Watermelon* with Mr Hajós. There's a small problem, however.' Again that scrutinizing gaze. 'He's no longer an editor at this paper. *He's resigned from the staff of this periodical.*' A mocking smile. 'Hoarse Hajós is no longer with us.'

A glum, morose silence.

'When did he leave?'

He leant across the desk. His face stiffened.

'Now you look like a pretty smart fellow. A deceptively dumb face, but you're no dummy. So I think you might have already guessed when. Right after that particular change of regime. It was a bit surprising, I grant you. But in fact it was not that unexpected.'

He laughed soundlessly.

'*Machtergreifung*. The takeover of power, if that makes more sense to you.'

He drew back, paced the room, took a look out of the window.

'I trust you don't expect me to hunt up your *Watermelon* right now?'

Abruptly he turned to face me.

'What was that you said? . . . You want it back?'

'Yes. I would like my story back.'

'And why is that?' He slowly paced along the desk, swaying his head morosely. 'Tell me. Have you ever published anything?'

'Two stories. *Buddies*, and . . .'

He waved me off impatiently.

'I'm sure it was Hoarse Hajós who accepted them. But never mind.' (*Pause*.) 'And why do you want your story back now?'

A mudslide of panic overcame me. Why on earth did I have to loiter in this neighbourhood? What business did I have here?! I should have known very well that . . .

'It needs more work. I'm still working on it.'

'Really! You don't say.'

I kept quiet. No need for further explanations.

He kept leaning closer and closer.

'You'd like to polish up the manuscript. Maybe you'll rewrite the whole thing. Give it another go. And then you'll bring it back . . . Right?!' (*Silence.*) 'You wouldn't dream of taking it to another paper. Or am I wrong? Could I be mistaken?'

Suddenly he turned away. As if he'd gotten tired of the whole scene. Tired of me, mostly. He simply forgot about me.

I stood there deflated.

That's when I noticed the pictures. The pictures leaning against the wall, stacked against each other with their backs to the wall. Waiting to be taken away. Perhaps to a deep cellar, perhaps somewhere else. Whose portraits were they? King Charles IV? Count Gyula Andrássy? The former editor, whose name had disappeared from the masthead?

I took a step toward them. The floor creaked.

I slipped out of the room.

A newspaper spread open on the kitchen table. This is one paper I'm not going to take into the living room. Perhaps it will simply vanish from the kitchen table. No, it won't. It will never vanish. It will stay spread open here forever. Someone had slipped it into the mailbox, along with one word on a piece of paper.

Congratulations!

Paper in hand, I stood in the dark, early morning hall.

Someone is watching me. Standing behind me, watching every move I make. The way I open the paper in the hall. And close it. And open it again. *Watermelon.* That's what it says under the black line. In the feuilleton section, under the line. Unter dem Strich.

Why am I saying this aloud? *Watermelon.* Underneath it a name, my name.

Then I was in the kitchen. I tossed the newspaper on the table.

I looked at it from far off, flattening myself against the wall.

I lay down on the green grass of an endless meadow. Suddenly I sat up, as if I'd been reprimanded.

Near me, a flock of shorn sheep. And another flock, in full fleece. Putting their heads together in meek simplicity, infinite wisdom.

Near them, a cheerful, sun-tanned man. Old friend of the flock. Its guardian shepherd. The iron crook in his hands. One intimate swoop, and he's snagged a lamb by the neck. The next moment he's already shearing it with a clipper. One piercing burst of the machine, and the lamb is shorn. The good shepherd grabs another one. One after another . . . one after another.

The good shepherd has no regard for the sheep. Not for the sheep nor for the meadow. The good shepherd is simply that gesture itself. That single, ancient gesture.

Now the flock stands shorn of all earthly vanity, shorn bald.

The shepherd's crook has no more work to do, neither does the clipper. But that strange whirring still hangs in the air. It fills all of this space.

Zsuzsi is coming across the meadow, carrying a package. She casts a glance at the sheep. Then a somewhat amazed glance at me, as if she'd stumbled on a clump of potatoes.

'Why are you sitting here? What are you waiting for?'

I stretch out my hand toward her.

'Help me up!'

On a Walk with Zsuzsi

'Those umbrellas! You've got to see those Japanese umbrellas!'

'What kind of umbrellas?'

'I told you, Japanese umbrellas! Japanese rice-paper umbrellas.'

'Rice paper . . .'

'You'll help me pick one out.'

'Me? You want me to . . . ?'

Zsuzsi nodded and laughed.

With an unconscious gesture, I reached into my pocket.

A scrap of paper! An unbelievably crumpled scrap! On it, a jumble of barely legible scrawls.

Mrs Fodor in a bathing suit.

Kabos grilling meat

The old lady refusing to touch the furniture

The glasses clinking inside the cupboards

The ladder tilting

The sun setting

the wind remains

Whoever hides these in my pocket?

And at home in my drawer

in my wallet

among my letters

and among my shirts in the dresser.

And look! Even here! Now, even here!

Uh-oh. A crossed-out line.

I know this line!

I know this line quite well!

I've known this line for a long time. From *Festive Breakfast*.

Yes, it was in that story of mine. Except that it dropped out of there. I deleted it, and inserted it into *The Weeping Trees*. An old Gypsy woman looks up at the sky and says, 'The rain's creeping up on us.' An old Gypsy woman looks up at the sky and says nothing. In my story *In the Shadow of the Grandstands*, an old football fan watches the sky, the billowing clouds. 'The rain's creeping up on us.' No, he doesn't say anything, either. He just looks up at the sky.

That line stays crossed out.

Crossed-out line

Dropped line

No place for it.

At a Clothes Shop with Zsuzsi

The cold glare inside the booth. Four mirrors around me, four mirrors and four faces. On one side, a sharp diplomat's face. Not exactly glowing with confidence. And that deep, dark shadow under the eyes. This diplomat is about to be relieved of his duties. Something is not quite right about him. His services are no longer needed. He's being recalled. And God only knows what will await him back home . . .

Facing me is a sly old greybeard. Winking. A dirty old man. Never did a stroke of work in his life. He chased little girls instead.

A superannuated actor. Face fallen apart. Eyes glazed. Forget about ever getting another part. Not even as an extra.

A haggard, leaden face. A night waiter. Not exactly seedy, but somehow unreliable. He has no steady customers. A very few strays, at the most.

The door of the booth opens.

A heather-green jacket appears. Behind it, Zsuzsi and the silver-haired salesman.

'Try this one!'

The salesman steps up to me. Gently, expertly he eases the jacket on me. And takes it off right away.

'No, no, we're off the mark here. Out of the question. Not even if the gentleman insisted!'

The two of them eyeing me, nodding repeatedly.

Then I'm alone again.

Zsuzsi's voice from out there. As if she were apologizing for me. I bet she's explaining about my left shoulder. 'You see my husband's left shoulder slants a little lower.'

But madam, not to worry! A slanting left shoulder ... A *slightly* rounded left shoulder ...

Ah well! The two of them go forth to pull out one jacket after another. An endless ramble, accompanied by an intimate little chat.

Meanwhile I shuffle around in here. I emit a few alarmed snickers. I don't look into the mirror. I don't dare. Maybe I should start exercising ... working out, swimming.

But how long must I wait in this cell?

Any moment the door might open, jackets flying all over the place. Jackets soaring, hovering, burying me.

Then again, they might've forgotten all about me. Who knows!

Zsuzsi's had enough of her old man. He and his rounded left shoulder. And the salesman's had enough of his shop. So they decided to go out for an ice cream.

I hug my old jacket, fingering its sleeve.

It hangs on the hook, the lining turned inside out, rather rumpled. But what an air of superiority! *Please, no tears now, maestro! I know my place. It's quite all right. After all, when in England, one buys an English tweed jacket. Period!*

I sat down on a small round stool. Who knows? Maybe I'll be sitting here forever guarding my old Budapest jacket.

'What are you doing, cowering in here?'

I looked up from under my old jacket.

'Mother!'

There she stood in front of me. Who knows how long she'd been there, smiling that strange little-girl smile of hers. She suddenly leant toward me.

'Don't worry, she'll be right back.'

'Of course she'll be back. Why wouldn't she?'

The smile vanished as she straightened up.

'In her place, I'm not sure if I'd come back.'

'That's sweet of you, mother.'

She eyed herself in the mirror, adjusted her hat. Seemed to have forgotten about me. She laughed into the mirror.

'You could offer me something to eat!'

'But Mother! . . .'

'All right, all right, don't panic.'

'You were going to say something. That in Zsuzsi's place you'd . . .'

She spun around once, then stood still.

'Zsuzsi used to love to go dancing.' (*Silence.*) 'She was a very good dancer.'

'How do you know that?'

'My dear boy, you and your foolish questions!' (*Silence.*) 'The point is these days she doesn't dance much any more.'

'Well, certainly not with me.'

'Certainly not with you!'

'But Father never danced, either! He looked down on that sort of thing. He despised dancing.'

'Despised, my foot! On the contrary, your father was a marvellous dancer. But you wouldn't know about that.'

'But perhaps I . . .'

'Oh, forget it!' (*A superior, worldly wave of the hand.*) 'Tell me, do you at least take her out every once in a while, somewhere nice . . .'

'No I don't! I never take her anyplace *nice!*'

She shook her head, but gently, indulgently somehow. Her hand moved toward me in a caressing gesture, but stopped short.

'Oh, don't get so excited, little Lord Runciman!'

'Little Lord Runciman?'

'Don't you remember? For a while I used to call you that. Little Lord Runciman.'

She spun and whirled among the mirrors.

'How are you, my dear Lord Runciman? How did you sleep? Did you wake up on the right side of the bed? Because that's very important! And how does your Lordship propose to spend the day? Will you be riding out, sir? Alone? Or in some lady's company?'

She disappeared in those mirrors. Only her laughter echoed.

Lord Runciman! Little Lord Runciman!

Then there was silence again.

I would have liked to ask her a thing or two.

Mother, do you remember those hansom cabs? And those brawling drivers? Their cab stand was under our window. We watched from behind the curtains. They used to hit each other with their whips. You told me not to watch. 'You mustn't, my little Jancsi!' But I wouldn't budge. So you shoved me into my room. I plopped down on the bed. You leant over me, and pummelled me down as if I were a pillow. You were yelling. What were you yelling? Suddenly you kissed me. You yanked me up. And again, there we stood by the window. You put your arm around my shoulder and drew the curtain aside.

('You didn't get a letter from them either?'

'A letter? Not even a postcard.'

'Zsuzsi writes two-page letters even when she's away for a weekend in Leányfalu. But János never writes.'

'He's such a wet blanket. And always acting so superior. But really! What makes him so cocksure?'

'I hear he received some kind of an award. Pro Urbe, or something like that.'

'But isn't he Jewish?'

'Pardon me, but I couldn't care less.' [Silence.] 'But I think he is Jewish. Pro Urbe . . . !')

The slashed seat of a leather banquette in a cafe. I lean over it. Maybe we could have a little chat. But no, it doesn't feel like talking. What's more, it hates to be looked at. *I appreciate your interest! Now please move along!*

A deep gouge in the wall of a cinema. Practically a cavern. Looks like knife work. This wall's been knifed. I stick my finger in the hole, move it around. I try to penetrate deeper. Am I looking for someone?

I'm watching the river. The merry company of punters. The trees with their branches bending over the water.

The Cam . . . the River Cam!

The river of youth. But even an old man may sit down by its banks.

In London at Mrs Verebes'

A fine, clear morning. Zsuzsi and I might take a walk later. For the time being I was standing around in the hall. That girl, the way she sat there on the patio chair . . . Head thrown back, eyes closed. As if we were actually in a garden, sunning herself.

In fact she was sunning herself in the cross-draught between the opened kitchen and bathroom windows. What was this? Some kind of fresh-air cure? And why was I still standing behind her? Why hadn't I fled long ago? Draughty places wreak havoc with my head. Draughts are the death of me.

But I couldn't drag myself away.

The girl with the red hair! We kept bumping into each other in various parts of the rooming house. She always smiled at me. And my smile always came too late. By that time she was always gone. The English girl. And now there she sat in the draught. What a crazy idea! Whatever made her think of this? When she could be out walking. And not unescorted, either.

But she didn't feel like going out. Did someone disappoint her? Cheat on her? Treat her badly? Still, she must have a girlfriend or two. Someone to take her out, maybe introduce her to a boy, to a nice kid. Could it be she doesn't even have a girlfriend?

Suddenly she turned around, and smiled. Again, only for an instant. Her smile vanished, but she didn't turn away. She kept looking at me.

Cold sunlight from the kitchen. And from the bathroom . . . I think I'm going to close the bathroom door.

I made a move toward the door. She jumped up and grabbed my hand. She shook her head with a kind of excruciating stubbornness. All at once she let go of me. Her face grew long, seemed to have aged. As if she were terribly exhausted.

She must be insane. The girl is insane. Quiet, harmless . . . Maybe not all that harmless. Who knows! Any minute she might be at my throat. A tussle in front of the bathroom. No, thanks!

This house belonged to her. She inherited it from her parents. Mrs Verebes was merely some sort of housekeeper. Nah! Mrs

Verebes had seized the reins a long time ago. Dispossessed the girl. It was child's play. The girl should be grateful she's still on the premises. Old Mr Verebes might have had a few kind words for her. Perhaps he even took her for walks occasionally. Or to the cinema. But Mrs Verebes would create such scenes! 'Listen to me, you old imbecile, think you can . . .'

What was this girl's name? What did they call her? How did they address her?

When was the last time that name was heard?

I kept stubbornly repeating to myself:

What's her name? What's her name?!

Suddenly it was on my tongue.

Madge!

Julie!

Mary!

Names. English girls' names from the films at the Roxy.

Susanne!

Norma!

Kate!

Jean!

The girl wheeled around toward me, on her chair. She held one armrest with both hands.

There I stood, bent over her.

Go away! Please go away, anywhere!

She just kept looking at me.

Then her eyes lost their intensity. Slowly, almost without stirring, she turned away, on her chair. She'd had enough of me. Enough of this strange character shouting in an alien tongue. But I can't just leave her here. I'm going to yank her out of that chair . . . take her away . . . drag her off!

Zsuzsi's voice came from the depths:

'Jancsi!'

Mother's voice from the depths:

'Jancsi!'

Open suitcases in the room. Bags and satchels. The door of the wardrobe open. Drawers pulled out.

Packing: a trial run!

Zsuzsi looked inside a suitcase. Was it trustworthy? Could we still depend on it? A quick, effortless, yet thorough inspection. My hand followed hers, over suitcases, bags, drawers. Just like a helpless auxiliary cop.

My hand lingered in one drawer. I contemplated those thin, dusty fingers. Suddenly it burst out of me.

'That wasn't the real Churchill yet at Gallipoli! The assault on Gallipoli was an unfortunate move . . . a disaster.'

Zsuzsi's curt laugh.

Slowly, in instalments, I withdrew my hand from the drawer.

Pyjamas flew into the suitcase. Pyjamas, sweaters, towels. The suitcase swallowed everything.

'Let's lock it. Press down the top.'

Zsuzsi and I faced each other across the suitcase.

I attempted to press down. I gave it a try.

The locks clicked. I heard Zsuzsi's voice over the clicks.

'So, I married an afternoon sleeper.'

'Beg your pardon?'

'That's what you said at the restaurant . . . back in Cambridge.' (*Silence.*) 'Everyone disappears around you . . . those girls . . . your friends . . . the park, the street . . . and you sleep on.'

She knelt behind the suitcase, and looked away into the distance.

'How can anyone be the wife of an afternoon sleeper?'

Suddenly she rose.

'Listen! Don't you want to visit someone?'

'Who should I visit?'

'Maybe one of your friends.'

'Here . . . in London?'

'Why not? Perhaps someone who came here . . . after 1956.' (*Silence*.) 'Isn't there anyone?'

'Oh, Tóni Balla, and Gyuricza, and maybe Sitzu Blum . . . Nah, forget it!'

'Wouldn't they like to see you?'

'Well, I think they'd say hello to me.'

(*Silence*.)

'Could it be you slept through 1956 as well?'

She caressed my face. Her eyes lit up for a moment. The guttering flame in an oil lamp.

'You didn't, did you? Tell me you didn't!'

The thud of running feet echoed in the building. The hard click-clack of bootheels on the stairs.

The long, piercing ring of the doorbell. Doors slamming.

But no voices.

I retreated into the bathroom, and lathered my face. I shaved. I dragged the razor across my face with impossibly slow, drawn-out movements.

Ah well. At least I'd be clean-shaven. For the last time . . . That's right, perhaps for the last time.

They might be banging on my door any minute. Or else they'll simply kick it down. A soldier in a fur hat will burst in, and holler at me. And drag me away from here. Won't even have to drag me. I'll go as I am, face all lathered up. Dried shaving cream crinkling on my face.

A woman's voice from an upper floor.

'I told you to stay down there!'

Who did she tell? Her husband? Her son?

They were slamming rifle butts against the stairway steps. Against the lift's cage. How idiotic. Why slam a rifle against the lift? An alien noise. The building's full of alien noises.

They say the Russians like children. But I'm not a child. They say the Russians like old people. But I'm not old enough yet.

The ceiling light is blinking. Blinking, but stays lit. I'll turn it off, when the time comes.

I was scraping my chin with the razor. Then under my nose. The soapy water dripped languidly from the brush. I lathered some more. I scraped some more. Lifeless gestures.

Suddenly I turned away from the mirror, from my face.

How long did it take me to go from the bathroom to the hall? And how long did I stand out there?

I was waiting for a noise of some kind. For those thudding footsteps. The doorbell ringing. The door slamming. The shouts.

But there was nothing. The building was submerged in silence.

I can't wait any longer. This is an impossible situation. I must find out what's going on. I've got to take a look. Take a peek.

I flattened myself against the glass pane of the hall door. Tight against the glass. A shadow left behind by a long-gone tenant. And again I waited.

Suddenly I ripped the window open.

A snub-nosed boy came running down the stairs. A huge fur hat with a red star. Grey coat, shoulder straps, belt and rifle. That heavy, ponderous army coat almost crushed him.

Seemed like he'd crash into me. Go right through me.

But he didn't even notice me. He didn't see anything. His face hovered in a mist. He was steaming. He didn't even know where he was, or where he was rushing. Onward, down, down . . . Into the void.

I was a face covered with soap suds, stuck in the grillwork of the front door window.

The keys!

Where did these come from? What pocket? From the torn lining? With a ghastly, netherworldly clatter they had slithered down my trouser leg into limbo. My fingers reached in, slipped down after them, ripping the lining some more. But they lost their way in the labyrinth of torn passages.

The malicious clinking of those keys.

What a depraved bunch. They'll never surface again.

But suddenly there they dangled from my fingertips, all together on a ring. They dangled swinging there with such insolence! Shedding crumbs and lint and shreds of lining. The keys themselves were incredibly sticky.

Were these really my keys? This squat little one with the square head! And this blackened little guttersnipe! That's right! Guttersnipe! There's no other word for it.

Who are they? What kind of rabble is this?

Zsuzsi looked on at this whole production.

'You mean to tell me you carried them with you? In your pocket? All the way . . . throughout this trip?!'

At Home

Everything is in place.

Well, yes, everything's back in place again. The suitcases from the trip have returned to their nook on the upper shelf. The ones left at home had to make room for them. Nothing strange about that. They asked only one thing of the globetrotters. No travel reports, please. Spare us those travel reports. Just forget about them, OK?

Same thing with the jackets.

The stay-at-homes slid over on that dangerously creaking rod. And the great travellers moved in. You can't say they had an air of arrogance, but still . . . The stories they could tell . . . Yes, they had a tale or two to tell. But in this present atmosphere? After this kind of reception?

The telephone rang with alarming petulance. As if its attempts had been frustrated for weeks. By the time I got there it stopped ringing. It sat there in ominous silence.

'I'll go get the mail.'

'Oh, it can wait.'

'But my opening remarks might be in the *Nation*.'

'What opening remarks?'

'Mácsai's exhibition. Perhaps you'll recall?'

'Oh yes. When you and the maestro stood in front of that ancient yellow-stucco building. Like two evicted tenants.'

'The interior balconies all around us.'

'I don't think anyone's painted as many walkaround balconies as Mácsai.'

'The balconies as the world's stage.'

'You're waxing philosophical.'

'Anything can happen on those balconies.'

'Oh balconies, shmalconies!'

We sat at the dinner table. Tea, butter, cheese, salami, slices of bread in a basket.

A pleasantly lethargic, silent moment.

Zsuzsi was pouring tea, when the door opened without a sound.

The white-aproned waitress peered into the room. She cast one quick glance at the table. A smile lit her face. Maybe she had something to say. Deliver an invitation to her restaurant. Made out in our name, valid forever.

She withdrew. The door closed behind her.

I leant across the table.

'They dined at the same table.'

'Who did?'

'Professors and students. You know, at that college in Cambridge. Perhaps the professors sat at one end of the table. Perhaps their food was served separately.'

'That's possible.'

'But still, they ate at the same table.'

I said no more. Then, in a fit of rage:

'Well, I never sat at the same dinner table with Professor Pázmán at Barcsay! Or with the others, Illés Edvi, Volenszky, and Samu Magyar!'

'So, why would you want to have dinner with them?'

'Are you kidding? It would make me puke!'

'Well, then?'

'I don't know . . .'

I had to smile. I could feel that smile flooding my face.

'I put on a black academic gown. Oh yes . . . that's right! And the others, too . . . Race across the courtyard wearing them. Sikuta, Ambrus, Strém, Ábrahám . . . Ring, ring goes the bell. Dinnertime! Dinner's served! The table's already laid in the gym. Illés

Edvi at the head of the table. Tomorrow it will be Samu Magyar's turn, then Professor Kondói-Kiss.

'Aha! Who do I see at the head of the table now, if it isn't Profesor Hajba! Past-master of slaps and ear-twisting! Not to mention his other tricks! He never runs out of ideas . . . oh, his brain's teeming with them.

'But no sir! Professor Hajba, you're not allowed to sit at the head of the table! Understand? You're simply not allowed, and that's that!

'Ambrus and Nánási, in their black gowns, step up on either side, each grabs an arm, take him out and bounce him. Just like that.'

I nodded, deeply satisfied.

Then I was walking around the table holding a bologna sandwich.

'You know that old man wanted to talk to us.'

'What old man?'

'The one who sat in the library in that black leather armchair. Surrounded by enormous shelves loaded with leather-bound tomes. The dust of centuries, but it wasn't depressing at all. It was time itself. And it seemed like no one had ever leafed through these volumes. They were all ancient, but he was the oldest of them all. He sat there dangling his long, emaciated arms. His face and hair had a yellowish cast. But his eyes shining like a squirrel's.'

'When have you seen a squirrel's eyes shine?'

'What I mean is, he had that same eager curiosity. But why do you ask?'

'Oh, never mind. So tell me, why did you bring up this old man?'

'He must have been a professor. A scientist, or perhaps a writer. Makes no difference. Now he's just an old man, waiting for someone to sit down by his side, and strike up a conversation. Yes, he might have written a novel once upon a time, perhaps just a single novel. But now all he wants to do is chat.'

'And he goes home at night?'

I pulled up a chair, and sat down by Zsuzsi's side. I looked at her face for a long time.

'Home? Where is home?'

Slowly, I got to my feet, still looking at Zsuzsi. Then, clearly articulating each syllable:

'A tiny window high up there. Above the bookshelves. And someone was peeping behind it.'

'You were dreaming.'

'No, not at all! I remember quite clearly. That eye nearly filled up the window. Beyond it, a narrow strip of sky. The eye seemed to recede from time to time. One could wait for it to disappear. But no . . . it watched steadfastly. And somehow it was so familiar.' (*Silence.*) 'Perhaps it was my father.'

'Would you like another cup of tea?'

'Yes. Thank you.'

I set out holding my cup of tea. Once again around the table.

I wandered off to distant regions, toward doors and corridors. A lonesome tourist, long ago left behind by his group. They vanished from his side. Scattered. They would no longer recognize each other if they happened to meet again.

I stopped abruptly.

That wall at the college! That memorial wall. For dead students. Those who died at the front . . . at various fronts. But now they were together again, on this wall. Not all of them were English. There were Swedes, Norwegians, Danes, Italians. And one Hungarian! Yes, there was one Hungarian among them.

What was his name?

I don't know. I don't remember. I should have made a note then and there. But I just stood in front of that memorial. A Hungarian student at Cambridge. A poet.

I ought to remember his name! After all, I recall reading a few of his poems in *Nyugat*, in an old, old issue. That old issue of *Nyugat* had a yellow cover. Or was it green? Kind of greyish-green?

And I think I've even read one of his essays. A philosophical essay, of sorts.

Babits, too, had a fondness for this poet. Mihály Babits, poet, critic, editor of Nyugat. He had nourished hopes for this young man and kept track of him. Perhaps he even wrote about him. Yes, that's quite possible. He had, in fact, published the young poet's verses in *Nyugat*. Under the poems, in elegant italics, was the poet's name. But what was that name?

No! I'm not going to telephone anyone. I'm not going to ask anyone. The name will pop up, suddenly, unexpectedly. After all, it's impossible that . . .

'Who are you talking to?'

I turned toward Zsuzsi.

'Lion's heads on the doorknobs.'

'What lion's heads? And what doorknobs?'

'On the cast-iron gates of that college.'

'Weren't they paws? Lion's paws?'

I nodded obediently. 'But of course! Paws!' And kept repeating that. As if the teacher had told me to write it in a ruled notebook, one hundred times.

Paws!

Paws!

Paws!

Paws!

Unexpectedly, I smiled.

'And in the yard, the students were rehearsing a play! A school play!'

I was so happy to say that phrase.

A school play!

I moved closer to Zsuzsi.

'Did you know I always wanted to play the part of Trigorin?'

'What? You wanted to be an actor?'

'No, not at all! I just wanted that one role . . . Trigorin, the novelist in *The Seagull*. The way he's always scribbling notes, and chasing after women. Just imagine, Aladár Fáy had played Trigorin in a cherry-red vest! My God! Trigorin, as bon vivant!'

'So you wouldn't play him in a cherry-red vest?'

'Or in a yellow one! Or a green one!'

'Then how would you play him?'

'A threadbare vest . . . not exactly fraying, but slightly thread-bare . . . Down-at-the-heel shoes . . . And yes! I almost forgot . . . his hat . . .'

'What kind of hat?'

'Quite weathered.' (*Silence.*) 'You know, he's a successful writer, this Trigorin, his works are even published abroad, and he's quite talented . . . Except of course he's no Turgenev!'

'Yes . . . tell me more . . .'

But I ran out of words.

I shook my head, almost choking with irritation.

'Ah, let's drop it! This is absurd! It's madness! Let's drop the whole thing!'

FURNITURE (EXCERPT, 1981)

He was standing in the room. The room at night. He'd crawled out of bed half-asleep. He threw on the terrycloth robe and slipped out of the bedroom, noiselessly drawing the door shut behind him. And suddenly he was in the dining room.

The furniture paid him no attention. They were aware of him, but simply ignored him. Let him just stand there in the doorway.

Moonlight shone through the curtain. The room was immersed in silence and in that strange white light.

The stillness of furniture. The way the chairs surrounded the dining table. Perhaps they'd just finished discussing something. They had a meeting. The dining table had some news to impart. The chairs passed it on to the cupboard. The cupboard to the large chest of drawers and to the small chest of drawers. They conferred in whispers. But it all stopped when he appeared.

Deep silence. The huffiness of the table. And the chairs. Here he is! He had the nerve to show his face!

The man kept twisting the belt of his robe. He pulled it tight and then loosened it. He was waiting for a sound. A creak. He eyed the chairs, tilted slightly forward, leaning on the table. Slowly, almost without moving, tumbling over the table.

They know, of course they know by now!

He began walking around the table. Touched the back of a chair. As if trying to explain. Or make excuses. Listen here! Who knows when we'll ever get to it . . . you might be here for months . . . half a year even. And believe me, it wasn't my idea!

They paid no attention to him. Ignored him completely, as he moved around them. What a ridiculous character! Trying to lay the blame on someone else!

He paced around them. Stroked a shoulder here and there. With an unexpected gesture he pulled out one of the chairs. He sat down stiffly, and stayed still. Well, then! Let's talk about it!

But they hadn't the least inclination for anything of the sort.

Next, he leant forward. He slid his palm along the table top.

'The truth of the matter is . . . '

'The truth of the matter! Let's hear it!'

' . . . we should have sold you a long time ago!'

There! He said it!

He remained like that, leaning forward. His let his eyes take in the company. The members of the club.

They didn't say anything. Perhaps waiting for more to come. Go ahead! Let's have it all! We are nothing but rickety junk! We don't belong in this flat! In this *better kind* of a flat!

The man wrapped himself in his robe. For a moment he turned the neighbouring chair to face him. Then pushed it back. Cast another glance at the chairs. As if he had meant to sit down for a moment in every one of them, out of some misguided sense of tact.

A shadow swung back and forth on the curtain. It swung forward, and dove into the dark.

He heard the sound of breathing. Deep, even breathing. Then a low, mocking laughter. And a barely audible voice.

'No, you're not coming with me! I don't need to be escorted anywhere!'

Who could that be? A little girl? What little girl?

The man waited, listening. But the voice said no more. That girl could be standing behind his back. As well as the others, who'd come to occupy the room at night.

Come to occupy?

That's ridiculous. It has always been theirs.

Meanwhile a man's voice. Somewhat plaintive and reproachful, as if it had been speaking for a long time. 'But I'd always accompanied you to Aunt Gizi's! Ever since you've been going there for violin lessons. I introduced you to Aunt Gizi.' A pause. 'And let's not forget it was I who talked you into it. You would never have thought of it yourself, to play the violin! Tell me, isn't that true?!'

Followed by frantic whispering.

Silence. Expectant silence. And again, that mocking laughter. As if that girl was lying on the bed. Turning from one side to the other. Lying on her stomach. Patting down her pillow. Stifling her laugh in the pillow. You'll never again escort me anywhere!

Voices floated across the room.

As if several were speaking simultaneously. Reviling somebody.

The man raised himself halfway. They were scolding Father! For having squandered everything. (Squandered . . . my God!) He could never be trusted with anything. And he always left his things lying around.

A woman's voice. 'You left everything lying around! Tossed all over the place! You left your tea cup on the table! The salami skins!'

The man was standing now. He grasped the back of a chair. Who was that voice? It had no resemblance to Mother's voice. Who was it then? What woman? How did she get here? And Father . . . will he tell her off? Strike back?

But Father said not a word.

Another woman's voice, choking up. 'Why can't you stay with me? Why must you always go out?'

Silence descended on the room. The infinite sadness of the night. Broken by a man's voice.

'Your memories are too deeply rooted in the past.'

'The past! The things you say!'

Again, the rest in whispers.

Who is this woman? Who is this man? And the others? Sitting around this table?

There he stood, clutching that chair. His hand ran down the back of the chair and slid off. He could feel the chair give a sigh of relief. It relaxed. The resentment of the furniture. Their hostility and resentment.

He left the room.

He turned around at the door, as if to say something, just something in farewell.

'That will be unnecessary, sir! Utterly unnecessary!'

The instant he pulled the door shut, they started in.

'What a hypocrite!'

'What did he want here, anyway?'

'Are we supposed to feel sorry for him?'

'He wants us to feel sorry for him. That takes the cake!'

Annoyed, grumpy creaking.

Silence. The silence of the furniture.

In a Small Shop

A blue set of furniture in the lifeless light of the display window. Table and easy chairs by the window. Behind them the sluggish cupboard, the miniscule book stand. A sofa lost in the gloom.

At times a passer-by stops. Stares at the ensemble. Shudders and scampers away. Plunges into the street.

No one visits this shop. The manager himself has disappeared. Or perhaps he's taken cover somewhere behind a blue kitchen cabinet. Dares not move. Perhaps the furniture has attacked him.

These morose, dusty pieces. In an unguarded moment, they might crash through the plate glass and leave this scene behind, full of slivers of glass, split upholstery, broken legs. Just to get away from here. Why indeed should they stay?

There are no customers for the blue ensemble. Nobody wants to sit in those easy chairs. Nobody opens that cupboard. And who would take out the wineglasses from that liquor cabinet? Whoever would pour from that bottle?!

Or maybe not? A merry little company will show up? They seat themselves at the table. Pull out the easy chairs. The ladies sit down on the arm of the easy chair and kick out their legs. They pour from the bottle! Raise their glasses high. Clink glasses.

What are you saying!

That glass is not glass. That wineglass is no wineglass.

And that book? With the blue binding, on that shelf? Is it a novel? A romance? A travel book? Where will it take the reader, to what distant lands? And who is the author? The author of the blue volume? Whose only work this is. His one and only work, in an edition of a single copy. To be found here at this shop. Among the pieces of furniture. But no one enters to pick it up from the shelf and leaf through it. And anyway! This book has no pages. Nothing between those blue covers.

Yet who knows! Perhaps a long time ago . . . when they placed this book here . . . Perhaps back then there might have been something behind the title page. Other pages. Printed pages. But they have vanished. Turned into thin air. Just like the book's title. The author's name. The author has no name.

At night the man appears to whom this shop has been entrusted. He creeps forth from behind the kitchen furniture. He sits down in the easy chair. He bows his head and rubs his bald pate with slow movements. Then stares at the street.

A blue set of furniture in the shop window. Table, easy chairs, cupboard, book stand, sofa. They have no visitors. No one looks them up. Nor do they expect anyone.

In a Fancy Furniture Shop

They are strangers. Don't know each other. Don't want to know each other.

The double sofa bed practically takes over the entire shop. Cupboards along the wall, built-in shelves. Solid, brown easy chairs. Light brown squares on a dark-brown ground. Floor lamps. A magazine rack made of wrought iron.

Walkways among the furnishings. With strollers speaking in soft voices. Not a loud word spoken. One balding man is coughing. He turns away alarmed, pressing a handkerchief to his mouth. A young couple standing in front of a coffee table, in pious contemplation. The young man whispers in the girl's ear. She blushes. Are you serious? We're really buying this? He nods. Of course, we'll have to wait a bit. She nods as well. Wait . . . yes, we'll wait . . .

A woman clinging to her husband's arm.

'It was sold! They promised to hold that sideboard for us, and . . .'

She chokes up, leaning close to him. 'Speak to them! Say something to them!'

The man hangs his head. Slowly he frees his arm from his wife's clutches. He sets out toward the glass-walled office cubicle.

The manager wearing a brown smock sits behind the glass. She is scribbling something in the light of a small table lamp. Could be she is scribing runic signs on a sheet of paper. She looks up. Her face is severe and forbidding.

The man stops in front of her cubicle. He ventures an alarmed smile. He leans closer, then pulls back his head. He withdraws along the side of the cubicle and beats a hasty retreat, in the direction of the bookcases.

His wife looks on in numb disbelief. Stands there some time, petrified. Then takes off after him, through the furniture.

A golden tawny afternoon. An afternoon for five o'clock tea. Maybe waitresses will come carrying trays. Serving coffee, whipped cream and cake. A dear old man with white hair and sun-browned face will sit down in an easy chair and launch into story-telling. Children and adults settling in a circle around him. We want a story, Uncle Oscar!

The shop manager appears on the scene. Will she ask someone to leave? Perhaps that young couple. They have been here an awful long time! No, this is not a cafe, nor is this Margit Island. You can understand that . . .

But she does not ask anyone to leave. She merely looks around. Surveys the scene.

A veritable crowd assembles around the double sofa bed. The rest of the furniture is relegated to the background. The built-in shelves, the easy chairs, tables, coffee tables and marble-topped tables with candelabras.

A woman is sprawled on the sofa bed. Her hair is loose, her eyes are shut. A smile spreads over her face. Slowly she begins to roll. She rolls smiling, with her eyes shut.

The empty field of the sofa bed.

Sales girls in brown smocks scurry across the hall. As if they'd intended to body-search someone, without creating a scene.

They stand around hugging the wall, with an air of watchful wariness.

Strollers stroll about.

Groups form, and break up, only to recombine. Acquaintances greet each other.

The shop manager is back in her cubicle. She's having her coffee. In front of her stands a tall, grey-haired lady, busily explaining something. The manager sips her coffee with a pensive expression.

The husband is fleeing from one easy chair to another, then dives behind a couch. He's ready to crawl away, but the wife is on his trail.

'So that's where you're trying to hide?!'

Tormented whimpering from behind the couch.

A man with a yellow moustache is examining the books on a shelf. *Sándor Dallos: With a Gold Brush. István Fekete: Chee.*

The yellow moustache leans closer.

Babayevsky: Knight of the Golden Star.

The coffee cup is empty in front of the shop manager.

The grey-haired lady is still remonstrating. She lowers herself to her knees in front of the shop manager. Down on her knees, she clasps her hands together.

'I must have that table at any cost!'

The shop manager steps over her body.

'I might have to give you a good hiding, Mrs Fonyo! My God, the things you ask of me!'

But she is already past her. She confronts the yellow moustache.

'Excuse me, this is not a lending library!'

And she removes the Babayevsky from his hands, takes him by the arm and escorts him outside.

The crowd parts in front of her on her way back her cell.

The pleasantly narcotic lull of the late afternoon.

Suddenly silence descends and it gets dark.

The strollers are gone. As are the shop manager and her sales girls.

The light goes on in the display window. Inside, the cold indifference of the furniture left behind.

In a Yard

The easy chairs were burning in the yard. Easy chairs deprived of their arms and legs, tossed on the pyre. Their backs bent back, toppling into the flames.

A wiry, wrinkled woman with a crooked fire iron was poking the kindling under them. At times she practically leant into the flames. Then she pulled back and stood up straight. She was wearing a beat-up leather vest and unwieldy mud-flecked boots. She glanced back toward the ramshackle house with its haphazard roof. Maybe the others too would come outside. Tables, cupboards, kitchen cabinets. Stagger out to throw themselves into the flames.

She poked at the back of one of the easy chairs. Burn, baby, burn, that's right, keep burning! She must have been getting ready for this for a long time. For the punishment of the easy chairs. The day had arrived at last. She dragged them out of the room. From their old places, their wonted quietude. Of course, that was no easy task. The hatchet had to have its play.

Recalling all of this made her chortle.

Little arms all chopped off,
Little legs all chopped off!

Just like a nursery rhyme.

In any case, that fine little hatchet did its job. And she lugged all those little arms and legs out here. Followed at last by the bare trunks. Earlier she had built the pile for the bonfire. It just needed to be lit. Then toss on the chopped-up easy chairs. After that, nothing to do but watch.

She started yelling. As if seized by a sudden attack of rage.

'I've had enough of you! The whole lot of you!'

She ran out of breath.

Several people were now standing around her. They came from the hillside. From nearby houses and gardens. Neighbours, acquaintances, strangers. They looked on as she circled the flames in her leather vest and boots.

A man wearing a sweat suit inquired: 'What are you doing, Etus?'

'What do you think I'm doing? You can see very well!' She wiped her forehead with the back of her hand. 'I've already ordered new chairs. I went to town last week . . . shopped around a bit.'

The others stood as if speechless with astonishment.

'Why? I'm not allowed to go to town? I'm not supposed to buy new easy chairs?'

'But of course, my dear Etus.' (An older woman's voice.) 'Why shouldn't you?'

'I bought some modern furniture. But I made sure it is comfortable.' She poked at the bonfire. 'Had enough of these. No one can make me keep them forever . . .'

'You are right, Etus.' The elder woman stepped closer. 'Why don't you come inside, I'll make a pot of strong coffee, we can chat a bit.'

The other just shook her head, 'No, no! The delivery men could be here any minute.'

'The delivery men?'

'They promised the easy chairs would be delivered today. They said they'd be prompt and quick about it.' Her eyes passed from one face to another. Possibly she expected to hear a voice. A comment.

She was surrounded by expressionless faces.

She stood in the middle of the circle, as in some strange game. As if she were supposed to guess something about these faces. About their silence. She circled around in her worn vest and boots. She anchored down in front of a man.

'You, Professor! You saw me going down to the bus station.'

'I'm not a professor.'

'Not a professor?'

'He's the professor.' Pointing at another man. 'Biologist.'

Confused, she looked from one face to another. Really, it was like some party game. Where you had to guess something about someone. She had made a mistake. Blundered. She lost her way among these faces. Should she give up? Give up this whole hopeless . . .

These faces . . . so cold. As if suddenly the entire company had been replaced by others.

She hung her head. Mumbled something about the shop where she placed her order. 'They were very polite . . . and courteous. The manager himself helped to choose the easy chairs. The shop manager. Wrote down my name and address.'

'Well, then the delivery men should be here soon.'

'Of course they'll be here soon!' (Irritated voice.) 'Today! I cannot leave here! You must understand!' (A hesitant smile.) 'I am unable to accept any invitations. I must stay here.'

'You know best, Etus.'

She looked down from the hilltop toward the highway. Cars raced by. Buses and motorcycles. She looked on for a while, then, in a worried tone: 'They'll be able to drive a truck up here, no? Because the road is pretty poor. And it rained yesterday. And the day before. And this slippery, muddy road . . .'

'Oh, they'd be able to drive up here. From the direction of the resort hotel.'

'The resort hotel?' With deepest amazement. What resort hotel? When was it built? Who are the people at that resort hotel? Her lower jaw tensed. Slowly it began to grind humbly yet ferociously. As if she had just realized something. They are cheating! They always think of something, and they're always cheating! Like now with this resort hotel!

The smoke was floating up. The smoke of easy chairs burnt at the stake.

The upholstered backs had already been consumed. Only the springs could be seen.

'The great lords! They lounged about inside, all comfy and cosy. By what right? That's what I'd like to know. I thought of selling them. It had occurred to me. But who'd buy these?'

'Maybe a parish priest would, Etus.'

'A parish priest?'

'A parish priest in a vicarage.'

'A vicarage!' She chortled. 'But I don't know any parish priests. Where am I supposed to dig up a parish priest?'

The smoke was gradually dispersing. The neighbours, too, were dispersing. They disappeared from the yard.

She was still chuckling as she bent over the soot and cinders.

'Parish priest indeed!'

It was conceivable that she might dance around the hilltop. But she remained standing there motionless.

For an instant she turned toward the house. The door was ajar. Behind that door, the plundered rooms.

She turned her head away.

This hilltop. This was all that remained in front of her. And the collapsed pyre. Dark ashes, blackened cinders. Springs and nails among the ashes. What did not burn. What survived.

The bare skeletons of easy chairs.

In the Bay

Chairs swimming in the waters of the bay. Drenched wrecks. One already missing its back spinning about idly. Another carried an impossibly blackened cushion. It might have been a sofa cushion once upon a time, casually tossed on the chair. To make the seat more comfortable. Somehow it had managed to stick to that chair. But whoever had been sitting on it must have just tumbled into the water. He must have fallen asleep. Never noticed as he slid into the bay.

He won't ever wake up. Just keep on slumbering tranquilly down below.

That cushion will eventually follow him down. After the cushion, the chair. So that he will drift about in the deep, keeping his old, accustomed place, his head tilted to one side, his mouth slightly open.

Anyway, he was never the favourite of the group. Because he would always nod off so quickly. It was enough for him to eat a little, and drink a bit. He never told any jokes. He never laughed when someone told a joke. Occasionally he flirted with the landlady. He would have liked to pinch the landlady's chubby daughter. Pat the taut butt of the landlady's kitchen maid. And the landlady herself. Oh my goodness! . . . So he ate a little, and drank a bit. Pensively stared. And dropped off to sleep. He was not the centre of attention in the group.

Yet now he is surrounded by the others. The company. The card-players with cards in hand. The drinking buddies holding wineglasses. Women with their hair falling forward, gracefully offering little plates. That down-home feeling. That cosy atmosphere that needs cultivation. Women in nightgowns, women in evening gowns.

Naughty little brats gliding by the sleeping man. Winking at each other they give a tug to his nose, his ear.

A girl seats herself on his lap. One of those truly depraved girls. Her nimble fingers dripping with water begin to unbutton his pants. Buttoning and unbuttoning. She stops halfway. She slips off and vanishes somewhere among half-open clamshells and algae.

And he is left there with his pants half-unbuttoned. A smile floating across his face. An underwater smile.

He spins about and revolves once or twice on his own axis. With his knees drawn up, as if he were still seated on a chair. On that old chair of yore. A tremor passes over his face. Bubbles issue from his mouth. That's how his face leaves him, via tiny little bubbles.

Chairs swimming in the waters of the bay. Chairs, chair legs, arm rests, chair backs. Swimming and floating, or barely stirring.

On the Street

There they stood on the pavement's edge, near the thick trunk of an old tree. A little brown coffee table and the chair. So thin as to be nearly translucent in the autumn sunshine. An elderly couple behind whom the doors have closed. They ended up on the street. But they still know how to act. No beggars, they.

Someone had removed the table's drawer. Lifted it. Took it away. Now the table stood there, robbed. But if possible even haughtier. Go ahead, help yourself! As long as we still have anything worth taking away! As long as . . .

The thin chair, as if trying to be reassuring. Forget it, old man! It's not worth bothering about!

Why should they bother about them? The passers-by. The gawkers. Who stop for a moment to stare. A boy knocked once on the table top, then was gone. A man who needed a shave kept tapping on it for a long time. He simply couldn't leave off. Tap-tap-tapping. Perhaps some musical composition. The monotonous, gloomy music of the street.

A girl sat down on the chair. Dangled her legs. Then jumped up and ran away laughing.

An old gent in black seized by an attack of coughing. It came on suddenly, as he was standing around. Gasping for breath he clutched the back of the chair. Practically collapsed on top of it. The chair bore it stoically. Then the old man staggered away. Looked back for an instant, a rather reproachful look. As if the chair had caused it all.

There were some who picked up the chair. Held it up for a moment. Then put it down.

. . . some who stuck a hand where the drawer had been. Groped around in the empty air. As if searching for an important document. Or a letter.

. . . and some who merely stared.

'A pair of oldsters!'

They did not try to explain. They did not rail against anyone. *It was so-and-so's fault that we got here, he's the one we can thank for this!* No, they did not revile anyone and they did not complain.

No use crying over spilt milk.

They stood outside near that tree in the autumn sunshine. Worn and thin and translucent. And somehow profoundly superior.

In the Room

Once again in the room at night. Among the furnishings of the dining room. As if he had received a message. That they were waiting for him in this room. Someone needed to speak with him. Anyway, he got up and set off toward the dining room. Actually this was what he'd been waiting for. He had not been sleeping. Maybe a half hour, an hour at most. Doors opened and closed. Now he was standing in the dining room. Waiting for a voice. Once again, waiting for a voice. For someone to talk to him.

The chairs around the table. Close by the table. One of them slid back slightly. As if offering him a seat. He started toward it but did not sit. Somehow he could sense that dark mockery. Well, what's wrong? Take a seat, if you dare. Lean back! Dangle your feet! Why not?

Unnecessarily, he touched the chair's back.

He began his promenade in the room.

Stopped by a window. Stared out into the dark. The moon had disappeared. The futile glow of a few streetlights. A man trudging along the empty street. Glanced up here for a moment.

He noticed me. Saw my face. My cowardly face. He knows, too, why I'm standing around here. He's stopped down below and keeps looking up here. He does not move. Who could that be? Do I know him from somewhere? A writer of sorts? An old editor? Perhaps he's already been up here before. Sat in this very room. Drank an espresso. We chatted. He stood up, walked past the vitrine. All those photographs! Who is this man with the pipe in the garden? Your grandfather? And this woman with the shawl around her neck? He walked past the vitrine. Past the large chest of drawers. All this antique furniture! You rarely see these nowadays! In any case, that fellow's been here once before. He never came back. And here he comes now, perhaps on his way from some night club. He remembered this building. This room. This furniture. These massive, antique pieces.

The man in the street has disappeared.

He's coming up here. He's ringing the super's doorbell, and is coming up. Possibly slightly tipsy, but the super will bring him up in the lift. He will ring the doorbell. I won't turn on the light if I let him in. I won't turn on the light in this room either. We'll sit in the dark and chat. Or stay silent.

He turned away from the window.

They sit around the table, listening. Not even a chance word from them. They're watching him as he paces around the table. They bend over the table top as if passing cards to each other. But only to keep an eye on him meanwhile.

Not a peep out of them. No whispers, no titters. Silence reigns over the entire nocturnal company.

The door of the tall cabinet opened. Just a crack, as if pushed outward by a fingertip. Soft coughing sounds from inside. And a small creak, as if someone turned over to the other side. After lying on one side for a long time. That's the least he's entitled to do!

He sat on a chair between the vitrine and the wall. That puny little chair managed to put up with him here in the corner. And he just watched as that cabinet door . . .

Someone's hand will now appear there. And start to wave in the dark.

Another creak. And a barely audible voice.

'I really don't mean to disturb you, sonny, but I am going to crawl out of here at last, if you don't mind!'

And he wedged in his corner.

While that quiet, clear voice continues:

'I gave you enough time to pull yourself together, perhaps you've even finished your piece for the theatre by now. Tell me, why do you have to write drama? Because formerly you never . . . Fine, fine, I'm not saying that . . . but still! Dramatic works! You might have read me something from your play! And anyway, you might have dropped in to see me! You know I always keep a bit of wine or some cognac around. (*Sly chuckles.*) Yes, I've kept a few bottles in reserve. (*Slight pause.*) Well, time to crawl out of this . . . What are you staring at? Give me a hand! Just hold on to my arm! Just the arm! Well, sonny?'

A Wardrobe

'They found him inside that wardrobe. Hanging in there, strung up, like an overcoat. He had meant it as a joke, an ultimate, cruel joke. He would have had to leave the hotel the next day. Did I say leave? He was being thrown out! Evicted! He had not been able to pay the rent for a long time, with no hopes of . . . Oh, by then he'd been sacked from every newspaper in the land. He'd worn out his welcome everywhere. It must have had something to do with his manner. His character. If anyone told him anything, he would just keep staring and nodding. It was simply infuriating. Enough to make you fighting mad.

'He looked down at everyone. He was condescending.

'Once he crossed swords with an undersecretary at the foreign ministry. Somehow he got away with that. As I say it was mostly his character . . . it was something about his character.

'As I recall there was nothing else in that hotel wardrobe. No shirts or jackets.

'He was the only thing hanging in there.

'The cleaning woman found him in the morning. Perhaps something seemed off to her. That slightly open door of the wardrobe. She looked inside. She took a peek. And there he was hung up carefully.

'Imagine the expression on that woman's face! Did she keel over? I doubt it. They are used to seeing so many things. They're tough. Just like the wardrobes. The wardrobes at the hotel. At least in the outlying districts, in the vicinity of train stations.

'But it's possible that there was an old pair of down at the heel shoes or a worn-out overcoat in that wardrobe. Anyway, there he was, hanging from that brown rod. The Editor.'

In the Basement

An empty window frame leaning against the wall.

The dead grey screen of a cashiered TV set.

A chandelier in the depths of the cellar. A blinded, exiled chandelier.

Detail from a Room

Why were the drawers all pulled out? The drawers of that puny little brown nightstand?

Was the man looking for a letter? A letter addressed to him? Or maybe a letter he wrote to someone but did not send? And suddenly one morning that woman came to mind again. That letter. He leapt out of bed and attacked the nightstand. Beginning with the top drawer. Slips of paper, bills, an ancient commuter pass, prescriptions. And of course there were letters! Except for the one he was looking for. Not in the top, middle or bottom drawer. Photographs with incredibly age-worn faces, coffee-stained business cards, theatre programmes, invitations, torn calendar pages, nail scissors, Band-Aids, a crumpled handkerchief, a rock-hard lemon, empty spectacle case—all there, except for that letter! The goddamn letter was nowhere.

He reached in under the bottom drawer. As if there were another drawer there. Except he couldn't find it. His fingers groped empty air.

He pushed back the drawers. Only to yank them out again. Practically tore them out. Again and again he found the handkerchief in his hand. And that ancient lemon. The season's tickets, the notices, the tax bills.

But where was that letter! . . . If he mailed it now, things could still turn out all right. Olga would reply in a few days. A week, at the most. And they'd meet again. Take a walk on the island, or anywhere. But he must find that letter!

He stood up for a moment. Ran his fingers over his unshaven face. He might try to write it again . . .No, a letter like that could not be written twice . . . 'My Dear Olga!' No, it was out of the question.

Once again, he flung himself at the drawers. He dug up all three. Then he started shoving the nightstand. Dragged it out to the middle of the room. Shook it by the shoulder.

The top drawer suddenly fell out. He did not bother to pick it up. He eyed it with something akin to satisfaction as it lay there by his feet. Go on! Who's next? Let's see the next one!

He was suddenly exhausted.

The drawers on the floor among all that trash. A regular garbage dump. He bent down as if intending to pick up the mess. Or maybe climb in and join the pile himself.

He jumped up and raced out of the room.

The nightstand lay there, ransacked.

In the Attic

They threw it out.

Two of them grabbed it, one on each side. Grabbed it by the arms, took it up to the attic. They stopped at times to catch their breath. And to take a look at the old thing. That bent back! The mouldy green upholstery in tatters. One arm half-broken. They looked at each other. *Wouldn't you like to sit down on it? Won't you have a seat? Go ahead!* And they guffawed. Then picked it up again and carried it off.

Possibly it left the flat on its own. This doddering ancient old man. When they started to give it very strange looks. When they started making comments of a certain kind. How long do we have to look at this thing? This is a flat, not a junkyard! So one night it simply left. Stumbled off, headed for the stairs.

It knew where it belonged.

In the attic. Yes, yes, up there among the lumber.

Now that broken arm was in its lap. This way it was even haughtier and more distinguished. Even in this ruined state it stood out among its companions.

Oh, those companions!

Not that it wanted to complain, not a word of complaint, but still!

Suitcases, held together by blackened twine. Baskets falling apart, stuffed with yellowed newspapers and magazines. An ancient jacket, carefully folded on top of a basket. Boxes with lids askew. A snaggle-toothed rake. How did it get here? Suitcases, baskets, worn clothes, fine, all right. But a rake?

Enough to make you fighting mad.

Well, no matter. It must be endured. Just as all else must be endured.

But some day they'll realize, downstairs, what they have lost. When they really want to lie down and stretch out for once. But really stretch! The way you are never able to do on one of these fashionable, dainty little pieces of crap. Yes, they'll remember then!

Let's not kid ourselves, they won't be sending a delegation. No, no. It will never again return to that flat. Because then they'd have to admit that they've made a big mistake. And they haven't the gumption to do that. What a bunch of cowards! So we can't count on anything like that. It's not in the cards.

No, they will sneak up here one by one. Cautiously, furtively. And then sit down in the armchair! They'll have that broken arm repaired. A minor operation. Won't cost a fortune. Nothing to be scared of. And then they can really stretch out!

Whenever someone disappears from the flat below, the rest wink at each other. We know where he's gone. We know where he's hiding!

We'll just have to wait a while.

A Picture

Lying on the steps of the staircase. A small watercolour. It might have slipped out of the back of the armchair when that old thing was ejected from the flat and carried up to the attic. And no one bent down to pick it up. Or if they did, it was just to give it a glance. A fleeting glance. A picture, a little picture.

A forest scene. The setting sun's light painting the leaves a golden brown. And the little stream. Also the stag by the stream. Looking back toward the trees. Waiting for his mate. Come! Come! Nothing to be afraid of!

A forest scene at twilight.

Down in the lower left corner, a name signed in tiny letters. The name of the water-colourist. Adolf Hitler.

The Deceased

They got along quite well with each other. The furniture and the deceased. He lay sprawled on the floor of the room opening on the garden. Face resting on the carpet so peacefully, as one who'd at last found a haven. A bright red and white watering can next to his outstretched arm. He must have been on his way to the garden early in the morning. But he collapsed and the water splashed on the flowers of the carpet.

The furniture stood around him. The dining table covered with green tablecloth, the high-backed, rather touchy chairs, the tobacco-brown cupboard.

From the direction of the kitchen came the scent of toast.

Through the open door, the wet glint of the sun in the garden. The transparent blue of the sky. Tranquillity itself.

Then a door will slam,

thudding footfalls,

a scream,

shouts,

sobs,

a woman throwing herself on the deceased, crazily shaking him by the shoulder,

telephone ringing,

the room filling with various figures,

the siren of an ambulance,

and they keep shaking and tugging the deceased.

The Hall of Easy Chairs

He entered a hall, and saw easy chairs. Red, blue, green, yellow and grey easy chairs.

Perhaps they were having a convention. Gathered here from many rooms for a conference. The conference had been interrupted. Not on his account, not at all! They must have had a disagreement. Followed by hurt feelings. But the assembly did not disperse. They remained together in this silence. A few formed separate groups. And a few just by their lonesome selves. Some even turned their backs to the rest and stared out the window.

A black writing desk in the corner. Just as solitary and lost as the man in the doorway.

He stepped further into the hall. He dared to venture inside. To walk among the easy chairs.

They turned to look after him, with a profound disapproval. What's this? Why is he promenading here? He smiled awkwardly, as if in greeting. He nodded at an easy chair. Please, don't let me interrupt! As you were! Resume the stream of your conversation.

What an idiot!

The grey easy chair by the window slowly turned in his direction. It had been staring at the street, at the park. That café in the park. But now it turned toward the man.

What should we resume? What stream are you talking about?

A yellow easy chair's arm gave him a mocking nudge. *You say you didn't mean to interrupt? That's really sweet of you! Why don't you sit down?*

Subdued snickering.

But really now! Won't you sit down?

They shoved and poked him.

He was perched on the edge of the desk. He forgot how he'd ended up there. But suddenly he jumped up and there he was. With legs pulled up and knees pressed together.

Two allies. He and the desk.

The desk was imagining the worst. *Why is his palm all over me? Get off me!*

The easy chairs around the desk. Suddenly roused from their eternal boredom. They came to. As if about to perpetrate some ominous prank. They would certainly take care of this fellow. They wouldn't let him get off easily. *Tell us a story! Talk to us! Let's keep the stream of conversation flowing.*

He drew his feet under him. Sliding his legs sideways. He leant to the side, quite gracefully. Posing for a sculptor.

The easy chairs spread out comfortably. Self-important and puffed up. Club members.

No hope whatever, of breaking through this ring! Perhaps if someone else entered. But whoever would come in here? He himself had accidentally . . .

'It was an accident!'

The cruel mirth of the easy chairs. *What's he hollering about? No need to holler. And why all the excuses? He's here, and so what!*

He was up on all fours now on the desktop. The next moment he might throw himself into an easy chair. Might as well be done with it . . . the sooner the better!

His hand set out. With sneaky, tiny movements it slid forth on the desktop. A letter-opener . . . if only I came across one! I'd let them have it! They would reconsider matters. Or if I could phone somebody. But no telephone, and no . . . What kind of desk is this?!

I am what I am! I was just fine here in the corner! Got me in a fine pickle, I'll say!

The easy chairs were nudging each other.

Well, well! Those two are having a nice chat! As if we weren't even here! Totally ignoring us! Maybe you could spare a word or two for us, my dear sir! Are you married, or a bachelor? Flirting around with a different dame each day?

Again that quiet snickering.

He dangled his legs, then pulled them up again. He spun about. Why not? After all, that's the sort of thing they expect. An inane sideshow. Should I take off my jacket? My vest? What else should I take off?

He turned his back on them. Defiantly stared off toward the corner. Then turned back. He found he was still faced with them.

They are waiting for something. But what?!

He sat hunched over on the edge of the desktop. Shut his eyes. As if determined to cast himself down among them. One quick move and . . .

The man was standing in the doorway. Red, blue, green, yellow and grey easy chairs. A few of them in small groups. A few, alone by themselves. One grey easy chair, its back turned on the entire company. Just staring out the window.

THE TOBACCONIST (EXCERPT, 1979)

The man standing in the doorway of the restaurant wore the broad-shouldered, long-sleeved black coat of a tram conductor. Possibly a sacked conductor. Must have done something. They fired him straight off the tram. He trotted the distance of many city blocks wearing that coat.

He pressed close to the doorpost. Cast a cautious glance in the direction of the coatroom attendant. She might call out any moment. You must check that overcoat!

But no . . . She was engrossed in a crossword puzzle.

The headwaiter, wearing a pince-nez, approached. 'I'll take four Lotto tickets!'

The man in the conductor's coat did not move.

The headwaiter stood looking at him for a moment. Then turned back toward the inside of the restaurant. Whispered something to one of the waiters. Now both of them were looking at the man.

They'll send me away. They'll come over and send me away.

But those two seemed to have forgotten about him. The headwaiter strolled among the tables with his hands clasped behind his back. The other waiter abruptly picked up a plate.

So I can go inside! Go inside, take a seat, place an order. I have enough on me . . . Perhaps I still have enough left.

He eyed the tables. The empty tables. Artificial flowers in a skinny little vase. Leftovers on plates. Cigarette ashes scattered over the tablecloth.

Slowly he moved forward.

Perhaps intending to inspect each and every table. The guests he ignored. Possibly they even irked him a little. Why were they sitting around in here?! It was time to get going! Finish your lunch and move on!

Those tables. Those empty tables.

Abandoned beer bottles. Glasses with foam stuck on the edge. Espresso cups. Remnants of melted sugar on the bottom.

He examined all of this one by one. He paused by an ashtray. Pushed it over slightly. Maybe looking for something on the table. A slip of paper. A message scrawled on a slip of paper.

'Are you looking for someone?' The head waiter now stood next to him.

He just stared at the tabletop. At the smudges on the table-cloth.

'Who are you looking for?'

At last he opened his mouth to speak. 'He's not here.'

Again, silence. He and the headwaiter stood by the table. A few waiters also appeared. He slowly lowered his body. Drawing circles. Hesitant, vague circles.

'Well then, perhaps . . .'

The ring of waiters drew closer.

His raised his eyes from the tablecloth. His glance lit up. The way a puddle of water glistens.

That cigarette box on the neighbouring table!

Cigar stubs, cigarette butts, broken toothpicks. And a dark-crimson cigarette box on the ashtray.

He was over there instantly.

The waiters just looked on. A vulture descending on that table. Two claws clutching the table's edge. Grabbing that box. Turning it around, examining it.

A dark-crimson cigarette box with a five-branched golden crown. Two lions supported the crown. They stood rampant on their toes, curling tails ending in pompoms raised high.

His fingers slipped into the box. Double compartments! He pulled a cigarette out of the inner one. A broken, forgotten cigarette. He carefully placed it next to the ashtray, and pocketed the box. He strolled past the line of waiters. Stopped by the coat check. As if he wanted to show off his find.

The coatroom attendant peered up from her crossword puzzle. Stunned amazement. Who was this man in that coat? That's how he came in? Sneaked inside wearing that?

But he was already out in the street. He took out the box. Blew way the tobacco filaments. Cleaned it off using his fingertip. He eyed the five-branched crown. And those two lions! Dignified and yet still so funny. With their styled, frizzy manes. Tails curling up, with their pompoms. Some barber must have given them a sadistic cut. Made them practically bald. He must have been stopped at the last moment. You've taken off quite enough . . . But those two lions would never recover from the shock.

He crossed the stream of cars and buses at the intersection. Fingers palpating that box in his pocket. As if afraid it could disappear any moment.

From the other side of the street he looked back at the restaurant. That gigantic door of glass. A crowd of waiters might come pouring outside. The headwaiter with his pince-nez, followed by the rest. The woman from the coat room. Milling about in exasperation. Where did that guy go?

They'd leap into pursuit. The chase would be on.

Perhaps that was just what he was waiting for on the other side of the street. With the box in his pocket.

He turned into a side street leading to the park.

Proceeded on a walkway in the park.

Sat down on a bench near the playground.

Girls were playing hide and seek among the trees. Girls rode high-flying swings. Boarding school girls wearing blue aprons and red stockings. There was only one girl running around in a yellow cardigan. The Exception. Her long black hair blazing as she dragged a girlfriend by the wrist over to a tree. Then another friend to a nearby tree.

The man took out the box. He placed it by his side on the bench. Meanwhile keeping his eyes on the girl. On the Exception.

By now she was flying high on a swing. She had forgotten all about the other two girls.

The man put the box in his lap. He ran a finger over one of the lions. Down along the mane and up the curling tail, stopping at the pompom. His finger pressed down on it. Perhaps to prevent the lion from letting go of the crown. From taking off and abandoning his companion.

The Exception threw her head back and closed her eyes. Her full lips moved barely perceptibly. Maybe she was speaking to someone as she flew through the air.

The other two down there by the trees. One of them started giggling. With her neck pulled in, she ran over to the other one. Whispered something in her ear. And quickly ran back to her place.

The man put the box back on the bench.

Suddenly the Exception was standing in front of him. Shook her dark mane. In a somehow disapproving way.

The other two followed, keeping their distance. Timid yet insolent.

The man reached for the box.

'No need to stick it under my nose!' The Exception hopped on the bench. Picked up the box. Inspected the crown and the lions holding the crown.

The man crossed his legs. Slightly miffed, he turned aside. *She's not interested in the lions. Not the least bit.*

The two girls approached clutching each other's arms. Their sandals creaked on the gravel. They halted when the Exception looked up.

She ignored them. Put the box down on the bench. She swung her legs nonchalantly. Did not deign to notice the man turning toward her. She leant forward with her head and shoulders hunched. Picked up the box once more. Gave it a flick with the tip of her nail.

'I already have this kind!'

'With the double compartment?!'

'A dozen! Already have a dozen!'

'But this has lions!'

The Exception no longer heard this. She'd leapt up and raced away. Casually sweeping the other two along with her. Screeching and laughing they let themselves be dragged off.

The man moved aside on the bench. As if he'd never seen that box. Known nothing about it. He stared in the direction where the Exception had run off.

Abruptly he stood up. He walked around the bench and set off for somewhere.

The box with its lions stayed behind.

A CROSSING (1983)

Zelk: What's this? A new story?
Me: Will you take a look at it?
Zelk: If you can recite the forward line of MTK.
Me: Braun, Molnár, Orth, Opata, Jeny.
Zelk: What was the name of MTK's English coach?
Me: Jimmy Hogan.
Zelk: And who was his favourite? Gyuri Orth?
Me: You think I'd fall for that? It was Csibi Braun!
Zelk: Let's see that story.

The sea opened up before him, and gave way. The waves rose high. It seemed they might crash over his head. But they withdrew without a sound, and parted. The way was clear.

And he simply marched in, that otherworldly smile on his face, a bottle in his hand. His reddish-brown beard unkempt, the faded raincoat buttoned all the way up to his chin. No jacket, and no shirt under the coat. His trousers hung loose, sketchy and uncertain. But he was unperturbed. He held his bottle high. Not to show off, no, not at all! The label had long ago soaked away from that bottle. Just as everything had worn off him as well. He marched on, not the least bit hurried. Rather leisurely, in fact. The waves were no longer threatening. The sea could be trusted.

Still, such a passage should not be rushed. Someone had commanded the sea. Ordered it to calm down. A lord. The lord of the seas. Who had favoured him with friendship. Such friendship must not be abused.

He sensed he was being followed. They were following in his footsteps. They had flocked behind him and set out in his wake. They were giggling. They were whispering. But he did not turn his head. Did not look back. He had no desire to see them. The parasites. The freeloaders. The lord had opened the way for him, and him alone.

He moved the bottle in front of his eyes. It might contain a few more swallows. Just a few more swigs. And if they think he'll offer them a drink . . . No way! If he treats anyone, it would be none other than . . .

He raised the bottle. Held it up high. A hand will soon wave at him from up above. Thanks, old man!

The sky darkened. Not quite an angry sky, but still . . .

He hid the bottle inside his coat. Held it close to his chest. Blinked repentantly. Sorry, didn't mean to offend! Please believe me!

Onward, onward, with head downcast. There was no need for this. I've irritated him, angered him against me.

But no, the lord was not angry. Maybe clouded over for a moment. But he did not lash the sea into a fury. Keep going, old man! Go on your way!

And he went on his way.

Just as the others. No doubt they too halted for a moment. They got scared. But then they saw it was nothing serious . . .

Here they come after me! What do they want? Reach the other shore? What other shore? That's right, what shore?

Scrawny trees in the wet sand. As if they had just risen from the deep. The depths of the sea. And the sea had withdrawn. Leaving them behind.

The old man stood in front of them. He clutched the bottle closer to himself. His one and only friend. The only one he could still count on. He blinked mistrustfully. He saw benches behind the trees. He must reach one of those. And sit down, lie down on it. But it wasn't that simple. He felt dizzy. Perhaps it was the air. The sharp, merciless sunlight. He staggered and headed for a bench. One hand grabbed a tree, which almost snapped, frightened and surprised.

He slowly slid to the ground alongside the tree. The bottle now between his feet. Fine. Who said he had to reach that bench?

He sat there, gaping.

Grey buildings. Gates, windows, balconies. Tiny black dots and thin lines. The park came to life. Men and women emerged from the buildings and shops.

Well, well! The others must have already arrived here! And moved right in, made themselves comfortable. Nice move. Clever move. Little while ago they were still behind me on the road. No one had tried to cut in front of me! Who would have imagined such a thing! And now, just take a look! They got here ahead of me somehow!

They were standing around him now. Men, women and children. One woman in a blue smock, from the video-rental shop on the corner, bent down to him.

'Oh my God!'

'What is it?'

'Look at him! Just take a look! How could they let him out like this?! Whoever it was, he ought to be prosecuted . . .'

'Who should be prosecuted?'

'Whoever let him out on the street like that!'

'What do you mean, let him out? They shoved him out!'

'All the more reason!'

'Why? Would you have kept him?'

'Oh, that smell!'

'Smell? You call that a smell? He stinks! He reeks!'

'Someone should take that bottle away from him!'

'And what good would that do?'

The old man down by that tree! He's looking at me! Since when?

On a balcony, high up. A woman sitting on a tiny stool. Had been sunning herself. Suddenly she leant forward, bending over the railing.

That old man down by that tree! He's been looking at me! For how long now? He's blinking . . . winking at me. Yes, he's actually winking at me. Next thing, he'll start waving. Does he know me from somewhere? Impossible! Or could it be?

Yes indeed. The old man was nodding in a familiar way. No, he did not wave. But why, indeed, should he wave? Now he shut his eyes. But only to look up here again.

Up on the balcony the woman drew back. She flattened herself against the wall. *He came to see me. Came for a visit. But he can barely move! He can't even stand up! But wait! He'll spring to his feet in a second!*

She stopped thinking, and pressed herself against the wall.

Down below, the woman in the blue smock spoke.

'We should telephone.'

'Who do you want to call?'

'Who? An ambulance . . . Shouldn't we call for an ambulance?'

'We-e-ell . . .'

A police car cruised by the park.

'That cop should have stopped!'

'But why?'

'Why! Why! Must you always be quibbling?!'

'What do you mean I'm always quibbling?'

Then he stood up. He raised himself. As if he'd had enough of all this foolery. Enough of this drivel! Grabbing the bottle by the neck he lurched toward a bench. With tottering steps, his beard a sea of mud, his face twitching.

'He made it!'

'After that first step I could have sworn that . . .'

'Some first step!'

He lay on the bench with eyes wide open. People bent over him.

'Those eyes! That childlike, clear countenance!'

'Sure, sure, childlike and clear!'

'Yes, he has a childlike countenance!'

'C'mon, this one's past having a countenance!'

'Please don't say that!'

Another moment and the storm would break out. But no, the talking stopped, as if someone had suddenly reprimanded them. Now they just stared at the old man on the bench. At his bottle, lying on the ground. At the ball rolling past it.

A boy reached for the bottle. The hand dangling from the bench grasped the boy's wrist. A barely felt but nonetheless firm grip. It let go as soon as the boy released the bottle. The boy drew back, rubbing his wrist.

'Did he hurt you?'

The boy shook his head, no, no. But he kept rubbing his wrist. Meanwhile frowning at the bottle.

The woman on the balcony kept her eyes on the old man. *He's lying on a bench down there. On a nearby bench. On the nearest possible bench. Next thing he'll be up here, at my place. Sprawled on the sofa. Leg dangling, or pulled up. I'll have to spread a newspaper under him. But why on earth did I look down there?! Why must I always be gawking?! If I had only stayed close to the wall, sunning myself . . . Makes no difference. He would have come up here anyway.*

An ambulance pulled up near the park. Two men in white coats got out. They approached at a slow, leisurely pace.

'Who called?'

'I did.' The woman pointed at the video shop. 'From there.'

The men turned in that direction. Maybe they'd rent some videos. Watch a film. Why not?

The old man sat up and reached for the bottle under the bench. After all, maybe he should offer a drink to his guests! But the way those two stationed themselves in front of him! Not moving an inch, hands in pockets.

The driver also got out of the ambulance. He stretched in the sunlight. A few limbering movements.

The woman's face up on the balcony brightened. *At last they'll take him away now! Put him in that ambulance and haul him away!*

The two men stepped closer to the old man. Perhaps they'd lift him by the arms. One of the two almost placed his hand on the man's shoulder.

The hand hovered in mid-air.

The ambulance men looked at each other. They turned away from the old man and headed back to their vehicle.

The woman in the blue smock sprang in front of them. She practically threw herself at them.

'You can't just leave him here!'

'Why not?'

They gently pushed her out of the way. And said, walking away:

'No hospital would admit him.'

'Admit him?' (*As if scared of the word.*)

'They won't admit him. The state he's in.'

And just before the ambulance door closed:

'There aren't any hospital beds! Anywhere . . . not a one . . .'

The driver left off his limbering gymnastics. Got in the ambulance and started the engine.

The ambulance drove off.

Everyone stood there. As in the wake of a vanished apparition.

They left him here. Wouldn't take him away. So that now . . .

She retreated from the balcony, back to her room. Pacing with arms folded. Halted by the sofa. Patted down the cushions.

His head will be lying here. His sweat-drenched head. As he sprawls over the sofa. But perhaps he won't lie down right away. He'll wander around in the room. Peer into the mirror. When was the last time he did that? Has he ever seen his face? Is he seeing it for the first time? He keeps blinking. His fingers massaging under his eyes. Raking through his beard. That matted, tangled beard. He sits down at the table. His head nods forward. Crashes to the table. He falls asleep. His hat rolls away. I'll have to find it. Where do I put it? Where can you hang such a hat? On my coat rack? It will hang on my coat rack?

A boy and a girl running toward the bench. Were they here for the old man? Pick him up and take him away?

Reaching the bench, they separated and ran on opposite sides of it. Without a glance at the old man. Didn't even see him. They just ran past him, with their innocent laughter as their fingers touched in mid-air.

The old man sank against the back of the bench. Reached into a pocket as if to pull out something. A letter, or some sort of message. He tilted, then collapsed over the bench. His hat fell and rolled away. It reeled, teetered. Came to a hesitant halt. A hat as hard as tin, resting upside down.

The woman in the blue smock picked it up. She seemed rather surprised by this gesture. She stood holding the hat, then stepped slowly, almost ceremoniously toward the bench. She held the hat high, as if it were some dreadful relic. She stopped, and held it above the man.

'Put it on him already!'

'His forehead should be rinsed off first. It's all bloody . . .'

'Ah, it's nothing! Just a scratch, the blood's dried.'

Standing there as if she'd never rid herself of that hat: 'Still, it should be washed off .'

She placed the hat on the man's chest. Deposited it there.

Maybe he's no longer on that bench. They took him away, carried him off. Perhaps the ambulance came back for him. Or whatever! If I go out on the balcony now, and look down . . .

She went out on the balcony but did not look down.

Then her glance slowly travelled below. Her terrified glance. Took in the trees in the park. Her eyes rested on each individual branch. Then the building on the other side of the square. An open window. A freshly fluffed pillow on the windowsill. A duvet folded flat.

And the bench!

All at once it was in front of her: the bench in the park. And that group gathered around the old man. What were they looking for in his pockets?

What do they want from him?

Hands rummaging through that filthy trench coat. A moment earlier they'd been afraid to touch it. Now they were practically rifling through it.

'Is there an ID! He must have some identification on him!'

'Carry an ID.? Someone like this?'

'A personal ID . . . Name . . . address . . .'

'You trying to be funny?! He's homeless! And nameless!'

'Everyone has a name!'

'What makes you think that?'

She sank down on the other end of the bench. 'He must have come here to find his daughter. He's looking for his daughter.'

'Why does it have to be a daughter?'

'He's been living with his son until now. But now the son's had enough of him.'

'I can see his point.'

'There's got to be some address, a piece of paper.'

'We searched his pockets. See for yourself. It's no use.'

The old man sat up again. He was looking at the woman. The others slowly backed away. Leaving the two of them on that bench like a rather peculiar married couple.

A sparrow landed between them. She turned her head left and right. First looking at one, then at the other. And flew off. My blessings upon you!

'Please . . .' The woman began. 'Could you tell me . . .'

She faltered.

That bearded head! It was even larger now. It had expanded frightfully. And it was steaming . . . The way it was steaming! And his trench coat slid open. The things that peek out from there!

The man seemed to have become aware of something. With a sly little half-smile he pulled the coat together. He slid his feet off the bench. Now he was sitting up quite properly.

'As I was saying, if you could only . . .'

Something was happening. Finally something was happening. And as if she were reading from an old novel: *Matters were coming to a head.*

The old man stood up. He rose. He grabbed a hold of the two lapels of his coat. Childishly clowning.

The woman stood up too. She wanted to ask him to sit down. Sit back down, for God's sake! But she could not utter a word. The others too just looked on as the old man slowly doddered around the bench. Leaning on its back rest. Sliding his hand along it. Himself following that hand.

The bench was left behind.

But he still held his hand like that in the air. He reached the next bench.

Onward, onward.

From one bench to the next. Each bench passed him on to the next one.

The woman by his side. In case he fell. But he doesn't fall. He staggers and stumbles along, holding on to benches. Or to thin air. But he's not going to fall. I can leave him alone now. I can let him go on his way. Well then? What am I still doing here?

What does she want from him? How far is she going to accompany him? Will she take him home? Is she going to take care of him? She's trudging by his side like an abandoned wife.

An abandoned wife. Who does not create a scene. Does not go into hysterics. She remains silent. But she will not be parted from him.

Someone shouted at her:

'Gizike!'

She stopped. But did not turn back yet. She kept her eyes on that slowly receding figure.

He'll be back. He's leaving now, but he'll be back. After a few days. Or possibly tomorrow. Once again he'll sit on that bench. Sit, lie down, stretch out. And blink looking at this balcony, winking slyly. Then struggle to his feet. Take a few tottering steps, stumble across the entrance, climb the stairs. He'll trip a few times but will arrive on the third floor. Won't ring the doorbell, he doesn't know doorbells, but will simply fall against the door, or stand swaying in front of the glass panel of the door.

He has left everything behind. Everyone fell away in his wake. Even the woman who had accompanied him for so long. And trees, benches.

Only the air now. That undulation translucent, bright. Then suddenly surging pale and cold.

He stopped for a moment. Then he dove into the undulating air.

A bottle lying under a park bench. A blackened bottle without a label. Some dark liquid still sloshing inside.

THE VETERAN (1992)

The doorbell woke him. Shattered the afternoon dream. That sweet, peaceful afternoon dream. He lay back on the sofa, pelted by that ringing. He did not get up. No, not yet! He clutched the sofa's edge. Let them ring. Keep on ringing! Maybe they'd leave.

But they did not leave. It must have been a group assault on that doorbell.

Giddy and dazed, János Zsámboky staggered out to open the door.

And they came pouring in, simply swept him aside. A troop of boys and girls. One of the boys threw himself on the sofa. Two girls grabbed his feet and yanked him off.

'We're here visiting veterans!'

'Beg your pardon?!'

'We're collecting veterans. You know, those old-time activists in the Movement . . .'

'Why aren't you collecting stamps or matchbooks or pebbles?'

'Excuse me?'

'You heard me. Stamps, matchbooks, pebbles.'

'But this is the class project we were assigned.'

That voice! Where did that dry, official tone come from? He scanned the faces. As if irked, riffling through a book.

They, in turn, eyed him like some prehistoric fossil. Any second they might step right up to him and touch him with cautious curiosity. Would it remain in one piece? Or fall apart?

A girl's voice from a far corner:

'We challenged Cukor Street High.'

'Why would you challenge Cukor Street?' He found himself feeling somehow sorry for that charming old street. That defenceless old street.

'To compete. To see which school can collect more . . .'

'. . . veterans! All right, I get it. A school competition. And who was it who sent you here?'

'Mrs Zsóka.'

'Your homeroom teacher?'

'Yes, our homeroom teacher.'

'But she didn't come along.'

They looked at each other and shrugged.

'No, she didn't.'

'Well, give my regards to Mrs Zsóka. Make sure you do that. And what else did she tell you?'

Silence.

Then a voice, as if reading from a slip of paper:

'János Zsámboky, 25 Mező Street, Flat 4-B. A long-time veteran of the Movement.'

A stranger's name, a stranger's address.

That's right. It all sounded so alien, this name and this address. But why not! Why couldn't János Zsámboky have participated in the Spanish Civil War? In the battles by the River Ebro. A losing cause, but there, by the Ebro, we'd still pushed them back. (Them . . . ? But who was 'them'?)

'The impatience of palms.'

'What about it?'

One of the boys was poking at the scraps of paper on the desk. He pointed to one.

'Here! It says right here, The impatience of palms. Why are the palms impatient?'

He brushed the boy off the desk.

'Leave that alone!'

Embarrassed titters.

'I was only looking at these . . .' And the boy pointed at the small slips of paper. 'Are you a writer, too?'

'Mrs Zsóka forgot to tell you?'

'No, she only told us that . . .'

'. . . I threw bombs . . . hid out in the hills . . . led my squad on raids . . . ?'

He ran out of breath. His eyes ran over the visitors. That chubby kid sprawled in the armchair! Just about ready to light up a cigar! He irately spun the boy out of the chair.

'Perhaps you might yield this seat?'

'Let Mr Zsámboky sit down!'

'No, not Mr Zsámboky! This girl right here!'

And he flung a skinny little girl into the chair. She promptly disappeared. Sank right in.

Zsámboky was still yelling at the boy.

'No one's ever taught you that?'

He fell silent. What am I shouting for? What am I trying to prove?

Unexpectedly, he sat down on the carpet. Cross-legged in the middle of the carpet.

'And how many veterans have you found so far?'

'Two. But one of them was dead.'

'Then he doesn't count.'

'Yes he does. His wife said that . . .'

'You mean his widow.'

'Oh yeah. Anyway, his widow said that she helped him in the struggle, together they'd smuggled parts out of . . . out of some factory. Important machine parts.'

'Well, I'm afraid I can't boast of anything like that.'

'Did you ever hand out illegal fliers?'

'I didn't hand out fliers. I didn't hand out anything. And if you really want to know, I never provided a hideout for anyone, and no one ever had to hide me.'

Meanwhile his eyes took them in.

Legs dangling from the sofa. Knees pressed together. A boy's palm slid under a girl's bottom. And refused to budge. Found a home there. Two girls switched sweaters. One was nibbling on a cookie. Her neighbour complained: 'Hunyadkurty, you're getting crumbs all over!'

Maybe I should offer them something. OK, OK, but what? Grape juice, cola, tonic . . . See what's on hand. But wait a minute. Am I insane? Serve them refreshments? These little whippersnappers, who just burst in on me like that?

Veteran-collectors?

Trash collectors! That's right! Little brown-nose trash collectors!

I am going over to the neighbour's. Crash on their sofa. Get my quota of afternoon sleep. Sleep this whole thing off.

In the kitchen he moved about as hesitantly as if he had stumbled into a strange flat.

A half-empty wine bottle on the table.

DEBRŐI LINDENLEAF

Semi-dry

Empty bottles on the kitchen floor. Rather seedy-looking bottles.

But no sign of soft drinks. No grape, no cola, no tonic.

What now? Should I take in this half-bottle of Debrői? Is this what I should *serve* them?

He hovered, bewildered.

General Franco had unleashed the civil war. He and another general. The two of them were always mentioned in tandem, at least in the beginning. What the hell was the other one's name? They'd brought in the troops from Morocco. Those notoriously murderous . . .

Squeezing an old cork in his hand, he re-entered the room.

One of the boys sat on his desk, smoking a cigarette. Blowing pensive smoke rings.

'Mr Zsámboky, didn't you keep a diary? About, you know, *those* times?'

'Diary? What diary?' He tossed the cork away. 'What diary and what times?'

Meanwhile his eyes strayed to that girl. Poker face and dark blonde hair. Wearing a pink outfit. Maybe not exactly pink, more like . . . At any rate, well turned out. Bored stiff by all of this. Can't imagine what she's doing here.

Zsámboky stared at her. Stared in amazement. Feeling the kind of thrill he felt when he picked up his first woman at a cinema.

'And your father?'

The girl didn't even seem to hear him. Slowly, as if in agonizing pain, her head turned in his direction.

'What about your father? I mean, what does he do?'

Her look was distant, uncomprehending. Then she gave a barely perceptible shake of her head. She's leaving. She's going to stand up and leave. But no. Unexpectedly, she spoke.

'He's a hairdresser.'

'A barber.' The mocking voice of a boy. 'Is he still on the juice?'

The girl smiled at him. And in tender, honeyed tones:

'Fuck off, Tihanyi!'

'But my dear girl!'

For Zsámboky, that first woman and the cinema vanished, everything blanked out. He stretched out on the rug. Someone leant over him.

'Mr Zsámboky! What are those books in the corner? . . .'

He pulled himself up halfway.

'One of my novels. Just published abroad.'

He said it like that, ceremoniously. Published abroad.

A small group formed in front of the books. As if they had never seen each other before. Just happened to bump into each other here.

A boy turned around.

'Mr Zsámboky, you've been published abroad?'

'It's no big deal.'

'These are Cyrillic letters.'

'Then it must be . . .'

'Bulgarian. One of my novels in Bulgarian.'

They surrounded Zsámboky. They ogled him as if he had dropped in their midst from one of the bookshelves.

Steps in the hall. Hesitant footfalls. Someone went out. Looking for the toilet? I'm not going to volunteer. No sir. Let him look. Keep looking! Keep looking! For the veteran's bathroom!

He lay flat on his belly, his fingers tracing, caressing, brushing the patterns of the rug.

'How many push-ups can you do, Mr Zsámboky?'

Suppressed giggles.

Then a voice:

'Kalocsai, behave yourself.'

'You behave yourself!'

Zsámboky sat up, wrapping his arms around his knees.

'I'm not doing my workouts.'

A girl, looking him over: 'You're so skinny! Real skinny!'

'Yes, I'll make a good-looking corpse.'

'C'mon, Mr Zsámboky!'

Mr Zsámboky was already standing at the window, staring at the park below. Good-looking corpse . . . What did I mean by that? Trying to spook them? Frighten them? Well, if that's what I intended, I wasn't too successful.

'There used to be vendors' stalls here once upon a time.'

'Stalls? Where?'

The girl in the checked shirt moved back slightly.

'Sorry, was I in the way?'

'No, no, not at all. Oh yes, the stalls . . . Vendors' stalls. The park used to be called Vendors' Park.'

'My dad calls it Teleki.'

'Yes, of course. Teleki Park. But the old-timers called it Vendors' Park.'

Now it was just the two of them by the window.

The girl with the checked shirt and János Zsámboky. His eyes rested on that bright and lovely face. A restful stop.

'And what could you buy there?'

'Anything. A full range of ladies' and men's fashions. That goes without saying. Books and records, old theatre and film magazines, bathtubs, basins, heirloom beds and antique chandeliers! But that's nothing. Miss! You in the market for an aeroplane?'

'An aeroplane?'

'You said it! Nowadays better families all have an airplane. It doesn't have to be quite the latest model . . . And where else would you find it, if not at Vendors' Park!'

'An aeroplane! An aeroplane?'

She was silent. Her finger touched Zsámboky's arm.

'And the stalls? What happened to the stalls?'

'They disappeared. Along with the vendors.'

'But why?'

'Why . . . ? Why indeed . . . ?'

They stood by the window, looking down at the park. The empty park.

'Time you got off Mr Zsámboky's back!'

A bony-faced boy pushed the girl aside. He eyed Zsámboky for a moment. Then the question popped out.

'Were you in one of those camps?'

'Camps? What kind of camps?'

'I mean, in a . . . '

'Prison camp? Concentration camp?'

Silence. From somewhere in the distant past, he could hear that pinched, shuddering voice: 'Where is that you want to take me? What kind of camp? Is there some camp left for me?! Let's hear it! What can I look forward to?!'

The boy gravitated toward the door.

'We better get going. We really didn't mean to bother you.'

'No bother at all! Why don't you stay a while! Let's talk some more . . . let's talk!'

But they were already on the way out.

Zsámboky right behind them.

'Wait! We didn't even say goodbye!'

Not a sound. They left without a goodbye, without looking back, even. They galloped down the stairs. The stairwell echoed their thudding footfalls. Then it seemed they'd all at once halted at the bottom of the stairway.

And from way down there, a voice:

'Did you know Lenin?'

Zsámboky regarded the desolate, worn steps. Convulsively clutching the handrail, he leant over.

'No, I didn't know Lenin.'

THE DAY OF GLORY (1992)

Little Balla! I'll take them over to see little Balla. A seedy figure, living in a courtyard on the outskirts of town. He predates the building itself. No one else knows the neighbourhood like him. I just tap him on the shoulder, and he'll start spilling the beans. The Germans will love little Balla.

West German TV!

A 'TV special' about Budapest neighbourhoods. They must consult me, of all people. There they sat yesterday at Gerbeaud's, a lady and a gentleman. Herr Werner and Frau Werner. Here to scout locations. Accompanied by an interpreter. A rather surly, doughy-faced lad. Strange. I've known other faces of that type who weren't so morose. He introduced me to the Werners.

'Herr Zsámboky!'

He was clearly no fan of my writings. In fact, he would have rather sat with almost anyone else at the same table. Well, buddy, you'll just have to put up with me. Of course, he had to say a few words about my stories. Just a few words.

'*Ach so!*' The German gentleman smiled.

The lady nodded and may even have said something.

The interpreter interpreted . . .

'The lady says she has heard of you.'

'She has? Maybe she's even read one of my . . .'

The Germans put their heads together and consulted in a low voice. They flashed encouraging looks in my direction.

But the interpreter did not provide a translation for my benefit.

So, today, they are coming for a visit. At 11 a.m.

It's ten of. I have ten more minutes.

I can offer them coffee. I have coffee, wine and liqueurs.

On the table, long-stemmed, rather murky-looking glasses. Maybe if I polished them a bit . . . No, they would still remain murky.

The doorbell.

The German gentleman and the interpreter stand at the door.

'And the lady?'

Herr Werner made a gesture. As if the lady had vanished from his side, this very moment.

The bored voice of the interpreter.

'She had to go see a doctor . . . unexpectedly.'

The interpreter's hat sported a long, greyish-white feather. His face, if possible, was even more morose than yesterday.

Suddenly German words welled up within me, rather tottering German words. '*Ich bedauere ehr.*'

Faint surprise on Herr Werner's face.

'Herr Zsámboky!'

'Bravo, Maestro!'

'Oh, it's nothing. Please have a seat.'

Herr Werner sank into the easy chair. The interpreter on the sofa, his hat by his side. The feather quivered, less assertive now.

I poured red wine, and raised my glass.

'May I . . .'

My glass circled in the air, alone. It did not find any company.

Herr Werner seemed stuck in the chair. He inspected his glass of wine somewhat warily, finding the glass rather dubious, and the wine, and possibly me as well. From the sofa, the interpreter waved his glass at me.

Ah well. So we won't clink glasses. But why's this fellow waving at me. I'm willing to bet he writes. Stories. Or long, deadly boring novels. Never published a line. And hates anyone who has . . .

'I think I'll go plug in the coffee.'

I ended up not plugging in the coffee.

That volume! My stories in German! Ten or fifteen years ago I'd had a volume published in German.

'Moment! Moment!'

My hands fluttered over the lower shelves. Jerky, nervous gestures, as I flung aside a few books. Suddenly that dark green, slender little volume was in my hand.

'If you'll allow me . . . *Wenn Sie gestatten . . .*'

'But you speak German quite well.' Meanwhile he kept blowing, gently blowing on that feather.

The German gentleman picked up the book, and handed it back almost immediately.

The interpreter barely gave it a passing glance.

'There's no need, Maestro! Spare us the book signing.'

'But . . .'

'You already gave a book yesterday.'

'Yesterday?'

'That's right, at Gerbeaud's.'

I stood with that book in my hand. And the two of them grinning at me.

'Well, then . . .' I awkwardly raised the bottle.

Herr Werner pointed at his glass. It was full.

But the interpreter's head bobbed up and down. 'Hit me again, Maestro!' He sipped pensively. 'I think I read one of your stories at the barbershop. When I was a kid. In *Tolnai's Magazine*. Before the war, the barber had a subscription.'

'Good for you.'

'I seem to recall a title . . . was it "Autumn Twilight"?'

'I don't recall ever writing a story called "Autumn Twilight".'

A glum silence descended on the room.

I fired a name at them. Like a pistol shot.

'Fritz Kortner!'

Herr Werner raised his head. He repeated, barely audibly:

'Fritz Kortner?'

I lobbed up some other names.

'Albert Bassermann!

Heinrich George!

Oscar Homolka!'

Pause.

'The ones who first taught me what film-acting was all about . . . In *Dreyfus* . . . in the film *Dreyfus*. Up till then, only the story interested me. But when I saw *Dreyfus* at the Phőnix Theatre, I realized there was something else to the films. Namely, acting!'

Again, I sounded the roll-call, with added info.

'Fritz Kortner as Dreyfus!

Albert Bassermann as Colonel Piccard!

Heinrich George as Zola!

Oscar Homolka as Walsin Esterházy!

And Fritz Rasp . . . yes, I believe Fritz Rasp was in that film too.'

The German gentleman nodded, somewhat alarmed.

The interpreter suddenly put on his feathered hat. 'I believe it's about time we got rolling.'

Herr Werner took his time rising. Next moment he was at the window, looking out at the park.

And me, assuming the role of commentator, like marginalia in an ancient text.

'There used to be stalls down there. Stalls and vendors. Generations of vendors . . . And what if I told you that . . . '

Behind me, silence. The interpreter was not doing his job.

I turned around. The face under the feathered hat was stolid.

'Don't take it personally, Maestro, but we really ought to . . . '

I let my guests go ahead, and locked the door. I held on to the key. Felt as if I'd gotten stuck in the lock together with it. An icy wave of terror seized me. Good God! Where was I taking these two? What park? What street? What building? It felt as if I'd suddenly lost everything. My parks, my streets, the whole district.

But there was still little Balla! No need to panic. Little Balla would save the day.

An eternity passed while I extracted the key from the lock.

The corridor, bathed in an opaque greyness.

Herr Werner was reading the nameplates. He seemed to get a rise out of them.

'Pál Misley.

Imre Bragyova.

Béla Hadics.

Miklós Atlasz.'

He chuckled, repeating this name. 'Atlasz! Miklós Atlasz!'

Should I ring every doorbell? Invite every tenant out into the corridor? Introduce all of them to Herr Werner? So they could chat a while? Or just stand at attention for muster, in front of their doors?

Three strangers in the lift, pressed against each other.

After a few moments, the lift came to a stop. The door opened practically on its own.

Shadows and utility pipes accompanied our descent in the shaft. The pipes formed a network on the staircase walls. A network that cut into the walls. Shadows drifted around them.

A voice welled up from these shadows.

'*Die Marmorbilder stehen und sehen mich an / Mein armes Kind was hat man dir getan?*'

Where did this couplet come from? I could never learn anything by heart. I was notoriously poor at memorizing anything. So where did it come from?

Herr Werner applauded.

'*Ja! Ja! Goethe!*'

'Herr Werner is charmed!'

Silence.

The interpreter leant toward me.

'So when did you forget your German?'

'What's that?'

'I mean, when did you manage to unlearn it?'

'Now listen here . . .'

'Cool it, Maestro! By now, it really makes no difference.'

'I've got nothing to hide.'

'Naturally . . . nothing . . .'

'So what the hell do you mean?'

'It was silly of me. Let's drop it.'

It was as if they had arrived late and missed the funeral. They stood in the middle of that courtyard, hesitant and sort of hapless. The whole thing was meaningless now. The funeral must have been earlier, at dawn, or shortly thereafter.

The courtyard had been swept hopelessly clean. The building itself receded into the distant background. The galleries running around the courtyard, here and there a door, a window. It all seemed to have just emerged from the misty autumn air.

The tip of my shoe touched a pebble. If only they hadn't swept this courtyard so meticulously clean! Now it really wasn't much of a sight for foreign TV.

Someone cleaned up this place today. Perhaps God Himself. He must have been tremendously bored, and devoted this day to courtyards in our district. Yes, He chose today to clean up the courtyards.

Ah, here's something got left behind!

A shoe lying in the grass. Humble and unobtrusive. Who knows how long it has been lying there! Although it's possible it showed up only a moment ago.

In any case, I walked over to take a look. I motioned to my guests. Gentlemen, come a little closer, please!

Herr Werner shot the interpreter a somewhat hesitant glance. The latter took off his hat, then put it back on.

A worn-out, ancient shoe. Its mate gone, the shoelace worn to a frazzle. I squeezed its side, I tapped its toe-cap.

'Patent-leather. Evening wear. Theatre, opera, soirées.'

'How touching. Maybe you'll put it in a story someday.'

'I don't like touching stories. As for what I write about . . .'

'. . . I know, I know, that's nobody's business but yours, Maestro!'

I started shouting:

'Little Balla!'

And hurried off, across the patch of grass, past the galleries.

A voice behind me:

'Maestro, you're not running away?! You're giving up too soon!'

I stopped, and turned to face him.

'I'm not running away! And no one's giving up!'

'Oh, I'm sure you'll come up with something for Herr Werner.'

'I'm glad you have confidence in me.'

By then Werner caught up with us.

The interpreter smiled.

'Eine kleine überraschung von Herrn Zsámboky.'

'Ach ja! Eine kleine überraschung!'

The back courtyard was an impossibly tiny space, apparently awaiting the scrap collector. Tumbledown chairs leaning against each other, slashed mattresses, cracked toilet bowls and sinks, crushed boxes, broken tiles, cups, ancient, dilapidated suitcases with fraying labels, an open crate containing books, magazines, socks and a beret. Postcards piled in a washbasin: a white-bearded man in a black jacket laid out on a bier, the smiling face of a danseuse, a man in a borsalino in front of a poster, a skinny, tired general flanked by two women at a train station. Creases, creases everywhere . . .

In the far corner of the courtyard, a tiny hovel. A mere heap of plaster fallen from the building proper.

I attempted to negotiate the rubble.

'Hey Balla! Little Balla, come on out!'

Nobody came out.

Behind me, I heard a crash, and clatter. As if a stack of dishes had toppled, crockery crashing. I heard curses muttered in German. And half-suppressed giggles.

'Gotta hand it to you, you're giving the old man quite a work-out!'

Without looking back, I kept shouting.

'Hey Balla! We're waiting for you! A whole troupe here!'

Now even the German gentleman joined in.

'Bállá! Bállá!'

We shouted, rattled, stumbled about in unison.

A cold, sharp voice floated from somewhere upstairs:

'What do you want with Balla? He died years ago.'

We trudged off in silence. A single sentence echoed in my head.

I have sampled every human delight.

Thomas Mann! Of course, he was one for sampling! Thomas Mann had sampled every delight . . . every human delight.

A sublime sentence. A sublime sentence by a lofty spirit.

As for me, what have I sampled?

'Maestro, pray tell, where are you taking us now?'

A forgotten wooden house among the buildings of brick and stone. Its peaked gables and balconies lay low, behind a dark-brown fence.

But what was this?

A bird-feeder?

For old flea-market vendors flying in through the window. To circle a few times around the lamp before flying out into the open.

This old house is oblivious of its neighbourhood. And its neighbours. It has refused to recognize anything or anyone besides itself. This was quite natural. It really was nothing to boast about. But this house was far from boastful. I have walked past it for years, for decades, several times a day. Yet I had never stopped in front of its fence. I never even noticed it. Although it might have been waiting for me. But no, not at all. This house had no expectations. And here I was, suddenly showing up with these two strangers! Who were now engaged in conversation. Yes, they were discussing something, just the two of them. The quiet, sardonic chortle of the German gentleman. And the interpreter, as if trying to get him to simmer down. Then slowly turning my way.

'But, Maestro . . . we'd like to hear a few words about this house. Can you tell us a little bit about it?'

'It got lost and ended up here.'

'Can you expand on that?'

I shrugged.

'Do you always shrug things off?'

And before I could say anything:

'You all have that shrug and wave of the hand.'

'And what do you mean by "you all"?'

Without bothering to reply, he eyed me with a kind of profound loathing.

The gate, as if impelled by a sort of deceitful courtesy, opened before us.

We did not enter right away. It all seemed a bit suspicious. Any moment a voice might call out. A morose voice. Sight-seeing, eh? This way, gentlemen, step right up! Do come in!

We paused for a moment.

Then we entered.

Herr Werner suddenly chortled.

'*Der Hausherr!*'

Yes indeed. The landlord received us. An ancient chair with a crooked back.

Herr Werner lit a cigar. The cigar smoke, somewhat out of place, drifted about.

Questions were fired. First in German, then in Hungarian. Questions, just like an official questionnaire.

'Does anyone live in this house?

A single family?

Several families?

Is it an old-age home?

A shelter?

Awaiting demolition?

Condemned?'

A moment's pause.

Then once more:

'Anyone still live in this house?'

'I'll go find out.'

I caressed the back of the chair. Then I set out toward the stairs.

'*Aber Herr Zsámboky!*'

'What're you doing? Are you crazy? Those stairs are about to collapse!'

As I took the first step, the stairs gave a surprised creak. Not at all plaintive—more like a subdued note of triumph. Well now, what have we here! Seems like someone still has faith in us!

Slowly I ascended to the top. I grasped the handrail of the gallery, and looked down. I cast a bold glance into the abyss.

'*Bravo, Herr Zsámboky!*'

'Good job, Maestro!'

In defiance I leant on the handrail. It groaned as someone roused from deep sleep, in a stunningly brusque manner.

I pulled back. Give the old thing a chance to calm down. But it didn't. The whole contraption quaked in a veritable paroxysm of rage.

A doorknob slipped into my hand. Unexpectedly, as if it had just sprouted from the wall. One turn, and I was in a dark room.

No, it was more like a chamber. A council chamber, judging by that oblong table. But what about the chairs? Where have the chairs gone? And the occupants of the chairs?

A champagne bottle in a dim corner.

Who drank champagne here?

A solitary man?

A party. Or, more likely, a couple. Someone picked up a girl and brought her here. Maybe it was Agi Suszter from Lővőlde Square.

The long table of the council chamber.

I put my fist on that big table. It rested there.

The presiding officer hereby opens the meeting. The president of the Council of Market Vendors.

Decisions were made at this table. Judgements rendered. Paying due attention to all aggravating and mitigating circumstances. Permits issued and revoked. Some banned forever from Vendors' Square. Votes cast by a show of hands. Heated debates before the vote. Insults. Vendors at each other's throats. A tangle of hands flailing in air. Council members crashing onto the table. Only one person remaining calm. The president. But gentlemen! You're acting in an undignified manner! Gentle-menn ...!

A creak in the doorway.

Followed by a voice.

'Why are you banging on that table?'

We stand in front of a jaundiced yellow building. The roof is reddish. That, too, seems part of the symptoms.

'This is where the Party-Wagon used to pull up.'

Herr Werner shook his head, not understanding.

The interpreter: *Herr Zsámboky erzählt . . .*

And on and on with his spiel.

Herr Werner's eyes lit up. His laughter exploded.

What is Herr Werner cackling about? What on earth could the interpreter be translating? Is he cracking jokes? Making up stories?

'Are you quite done?'

'But Maestro!'

But I was not about to be stopped.

'When the back door was opened, they practically had to scoop those girls out. Out of the paddy-wagon, in one big heap. Slaps and blows, whenever a girl screamed too loud, or tried to resist. They always had an audience. The windows and balconies filled up. Spectators came from distant streets. There was shouting and applause. Margó! Here comes Margó! And Teri Grósz! I bet they'll give 'er a haircut again! And the girls were pushed and shoved through the gate into the hospital courtyard.'

'Your little bunnies.'

'Are you trying to be funny?'

'You started it, with your Party-Wagon.'

'Yes, I may have, but now. . .'

'. . . we're done, I get it.' (*Pause.*) 'I hope you occasionally bumped into those girls under more pleasant circumstances.'

'No, I didn't.'

Why in the world did I bring them here? To this terminally gloomy chapel on the outskirts? To be enfolded, just for a passing moment, in the wavering glow of the saints on the walls, the creaking of these worn-out benches, the snuffling, wheezing, gasping cough of the old folks, with their bent backs kneeling in prayer?

But only for a moment.

And we are already back on the street. Herr Werner and the interpreter lead the way. And I behind them, lagging a bit. I could just take my leave. They wouldn't even notice. Why am I trotting in their wake?

Someone shouted after me.

'You could have said a prayer for your dear mother!'

The interpreter turned around.

'What was that about your mother?'

'Her memorial service . . . This is where it was held.'

'Wouldn't you like to . . .'

'No, don't bother, there's no need!'

'But why not? We can easily go back. Herr Werner will understand.'

He was just about to touch Herr Werner's arm. I stayed his hand.

'No, thanks. Not now . . . Perhaps some other time.'

A wind arose. A cutting, insidious wind. A thin yellow streak of light slithered along the walls, followed by shadows. Slanting shadows with shoulders hunched up. They chased each other and coalesced.

A girl slid down to the ground next to a wall. Strands of hair in her face. Suddenly she jerked her head up, and looked around. Like one who arrived here from a faraway, foreign place. With slow deliberation she pulled a shoe off her foot. Maintaining a queenly hauteur, she kept shaking nothing out of it.

I bent down to her.

'It's all right, Vera, it's all right.'

'Who's that, an old acquaintance?'

'Does it matter?'

'Will you introduce her to Herr Werner?'

'Sure, why not?'

We passed under an endless arcade of scaffolding. I peeked into a doorway. Just a quick look, on the go.

A trash bin. Its lid flipped up. A man dangled his naked arm from the bin, with the nonchalant elegance of one sitting in a theatre box.

I leant against a thick tree trunk in the park. Around me, broken twigs on a carpet of fallen leaves. The tree trunk itself full of stabs and wounds, the constant target of countless knife-throwing contests.

The interpreter sat on a bench jotting down notes, his feathered hat by his side. Was he writing a short story in that notebook? Or did he work in some altogether different genre? Who knows . . . Reports. Meticulous reports that include the minutest particulars. Or else only a sketch, the broadest outlines . . . Poor slob. The stuff he might report about me to the secret police wouldn't earn him a bowl of soup. Not even a bowl of warm soup. Reports of no interest about a person of no interest. After all, I had not even been deemed worthy of one lousy house search. After the 1956 revolution some of my friends were arrested. They questioned one of them, quite casually: 'And what about Zsámboky, what kind of stuff does he read?' 'Chekhov.' 'Really? Only Chekhov?' 'Well, Chekhov, and Krúdy.' The interrogating officer nodded listlessly. There were no further questions.

This fine fellow should be aware of that, yet he jots down his report as a matter of routine. You've got to stay in shape, always ready.

Or maybe he's merely doodling. He's bored and he's doodling. Sketching trees, houses, maybe me. No, not me. He's had enough of my face.

Herr Werner appeared on the path in the company of a tall redhead. They seemed as intimate as if they'd known each other for a while. He had his arm around her shoulder, like a mischievous uncle.

I peeled myself away from the tree trunk.

'Hédi! Hédi Rottmann!'

'I take it you know her well.' This, from the interpreter, as if he'd been standing by my side all that time. In attendance, like a good friend. 'After all, everyone knows each other in this park.'

'And yet I don't know Hédi at all.'

'But Maestro!'

'I tried to pick her up once, but she didn't respond.'

'Well, if she didn't respond . . .'

'Herr Werner can go to bed with her tonight.'

'No, not tonight.'

Silence.

Suddenly I burst out:

'Dürrenmatt grabbed the cab right in front of me.'

'Dürrenmatt? In front of you? And when was that, pray tell?'

'After the closing reception at the Writers' Conference.'

'Is that so! The closing reception!'

He harrumphed and shook his head. As if he considered the story highly unlikely. Then suddenly turned to me:

'And what about those stalls?'

'What stalls?'

'Upstairs, you started to say something about the stalls and the vendors.'

'What's there to say . . . They're all gone!'

He watched my face, as if it were a stage. But the performance was over. The show was finished. The players were gone, the sets were struck. The lazy and negligent crew had left a few props behind.

Herr Werner appeared, sporting a friendly, neutral smile. As if returning from an outing.

I looked at the derelict park.

'One day, a tank showed up here.'

The interpreter took a step backward.

'A tank? What kind of tank?'

He shot a worried look at Herr Werner. He did not translate. But there was no need to translate. That word filled the whole park.

Tank!

'Near the end of the war. It crossed the tram tracks, slowly. . .'

'. . . majestically.'

'No, not majestically at all. Frightened and lost, rather. Like one who'd lost his companions or ran away and now didn't know which way to turn. It spent the night alongside the stalls.'

'And fired off a few shots.'

'It fired a single shot, and even that was . . .'

'. . . go ahead, say it: so cowardly, so awkward.'

'. . . no, not cowardly or awkward. More like someone trying to legitimize himself.'

'Because they were afraid of this populace!'

'No . . . not of this populace.'

Again that look of dark loathing. Why all this hatred? For me, as well as for this *populace*. He said something to the German gentleman. Then he slowly turned in my direction.

'Herr Werner wants to congratulate you.'

'What for?'

'Your conduct.' (*Pause.*) 'Not shitting yourself.'

'But I did. Yes, I shit myself.'

'All right, so you shit yourself. Herr Werner wants to know if your house was hit.'

'No, we weren't hit. But they could have blown our building to smithereens out of sheer nervousness.'

'Nervousness?'

'Don't you see? They were so jittery in that tank, and when they're like that there's really no way of telling . . .'

I faltered. I didn't feel like continuing these inane explanations. But I still added one more thing.

'It spent the night here. By morning it was gone.'

'And did it come back?'

'Why should it have come back? It vanished. Wandered off.'

'But where?'

'God only knows! How should I know? Maybe it took off in the direction of the Tin Christ.'

'The Tin Christ!'

'A tavern on Mátyás Square. On the side there was a crucifix with a Tin Christ. It stopped there for a rest, then away it went . . . onward . . .' (*Pause.*) 'Maybe we'll meet again somewhere. Why not? Exchange a few words, if the occasion so demands.'

'If the occasion so demands.'

I walked around the tree. I touched its bark. I fondled it. A loose bit of bark stayed in my palm.

I heard voices. Indistinct whispers. Then someone touched my shoulder.

'Herr Werner will contact you. Right now, he's on a very tight schedule . . . You understand . . . '

He said something else that I didn't hear.

I kept looking at that wounded tree in the silent park.

A CORNER OF THE TABLE (1974)

I'd never really owned a decent fountain pen. Although I always coveted those serious, respect-inspiring pens. Thick as a torpedo. Or able to write in different colours.

Somehow these always managed to avoid me. Or didn't seem to stay with me very long. If by chance I found a 'better piece', soon she'd be gone. Abandoning me, just like that.

I can't help it, they don't feel at home among my scraps of paper. These meagre slips of paper, the playing field of my writing. The back of a letter written to me. My scraggly lines may meander into the body of the text. Telegrams are even better, lots of empty space on them.

But those serious pens detested that sort of thing.

So it was pencils, pencil stubs, old pens. Around me when I laid out my first strips of paper on the table. And razor blades, and caps for protecting pencil points. I whittled away at my pencils with those old blades. Practically whittled them away. While staring at my slips of paper. Waiting for something to happen. A sign from somewhere that I don't have to begin writing. That exemption was on the way.

But the release never arrived.

The dreadful moment when you must begin. Gave me the shivers and stomach cramps. That I'd never be able to begin and there was nothing to begin anyway. All this in the morning. Yes, mornings I was still able to muster strength.

At all events, pencil sharpening was part of the morning routine. And pencil-point protectors—I always laid those old pencil-point protectors out on the table.

As for that table . . .

You could hardly call it a desk. An enormous round table, round as a pond. Somewhere on the other shore sat my parents, at breakfast or lunch. Mostly they fought. Horrendous squalls passed over that table. Who knows when those fights first began. Maybe one morning long before I was born. Father once smashed a plate against the wall and stormed out. Or Mother rushed out of the room, slamming doors. Then suddenly there was silence. Father and Mother were finally gone. I was left alone with my slips of paper. A half an hour . . . or an hour, and I jump up from the table. Start circling around it. Bend over my paper slips. Cross out one thing and add another. Then I leave the room to shave. And race back with foam on my face to insert another word.

Then I rush off to another table.

The empty upper gallery of a cafe on the far side of town. Next to last table by the windows. Where I lay out my slips of paper. Once more, I begin the curious production that has no resemblance to writing. My lines look more like neuropathological squiggles. Notes, inserts, deletions—one big impenetrable mess!

'And I'm supposed to be able to read this?' asks the waitress, leaning forward. 'You know anyone who can read this?'

I say something in reply and the conversation is on.

She talks and talks. About her husband and his live-in parents who never leave them alone. I keep nodding and shrugging, and jot down a few words.

The waitress flies off only to have another take her place.

'You know that sculptor who's been coming here lately—what a sourpuss!'

She gives me the lowdown on the sculptor and the cafe's clientele. I keep nodding and jotting. The trays keep coming and going and I am deep into my manuscript.

'Are you listening at all?' a girl once asked me.' Do you ever listen to anybody?'

What could I say?

'These papers! Always these putrid slips of paper!'

But that isn't too bad, actually quite bearable. They still come and go, I hear their voices around me.

But when I dig up my typewriter from the back of the closet and place it on the table . . . Then I am really by myself alone. No running off to somewhere else. No trays flitting about me. The girls are all gone.

This is when I feel the desert boredom of everything I've written. Delete, delete! I work much like a film cutter in the cutting room. Throw out, cut all redundant parts! Cut the drivel!

A kind of rage possesses me . . . I feel like shredding and devouring these bits of paper. Certainly not many are left after I stop typing.

There's silence . . . the silence of exhaustion.

The typewriter remains on the table for a while. Surrounded by scattered manuscript.

Pencils, pencil stubs, old pens and a grumpy typewriter. The things around me.

A List of Sources

These writings originally appeared in the following volumes:

- *Mi az, öreg?* (Budapest: Magvető, 1972)

- *Fél hat felé* (Budapest: Magvető, 1974)

- *Tájak, az én tájaim* (Budapest: Magvető, 1981)

- *Átkelés* (Budapest: Magvető, 1983)

- *Önéletrajz* (Budapest: Magvető, 1989)

- *Huzatban* (Budapest: Magvető, 1992)

The pieces titled 'Furniture' and 'The Tobacconist' are excerpts from, respectively, the novella-length compositions ' A bútorok' and 'A trafik', in the volume *Tájak, az én tájaim.*